Chloe

charmz™

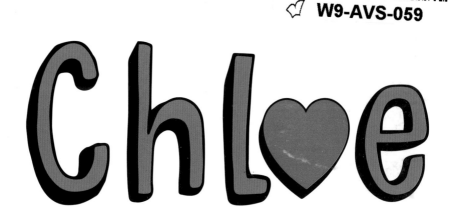

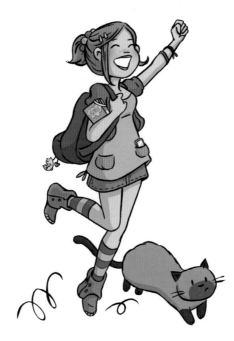

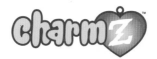

MORE GRAPHIC NOVELS FROM

STITCHED #1 "The First Day of the Rest of Her Life"

SWEETIES #1 "Cherry Skye"

Chl♥e

Story by Greg Tessier
Art by Amandine

NEW YORK

Thanks to you—you're not dreaming, no, no!—and to you over there, too—don't hide, don't be shy! And to you, too, of course, how could I forget you? In short, thanks to all those who were able to awaken my curiosity and who will certainly recognize themselves in these few lines.
—Greg

Thanks to my incredible support group (Drac, Sam, David, Yaooo and Tomatias!) Thank you to Mom and Dad, for your encouragement and advice! Thanks, too, to ZouZou for the first read-through along with Fleurette in the bedroom in Villeneuve! Thanks to Greg for having the idea for this awesome collaboration! And an especially big thanks to Pierre, the charming young man from the office next door, without whom this book would be very bland!
—Amandine

Mistinguette [CHLOE] volume 1 "En quête d'amour" © Jungle! 2011 and
Mistinguette [CHLOE] volume 2 "Baisers et coquillages" © Jungle! 2012
Jungle!, Miss Jungle! and the Jungle! logo are ® 2017 Steinkis Groupe
www.editions-jungle.com. All rights reserved.
Used under license.

English translation and all other material © 2017 by Charmz.

CHLOE #1
"The New Girl"

GREG TESSIER and AMANDINE – Story
AMANDINE – Art and color
AMANDINE – Cover
JOE JOHNSON – Translation
SASHA KIMIATEK – Production Coordinator
DAWN GUZZO – Diary page design
JEFF WHITMAN – Assistant Managing Editor
RACHEL GLUCKSTERN, GREG LOCKARD – Orginal Editors
MARIAH MCCOURT – Editor
JIM SALICRUP
Editor-in-Chief

Charmz is an imprint of Papercutz.

ISBN HC: 978-1-62991-772-6
ISBN PB: 978-1-62991-763-4

Printed in China
May 2017

Charmz books may be purchased for business or promotional use.
For information on bulk purchases please contact Macmillan
Corporate and Premium Sales Department at (800) 221-7945 x5442

Distributed by Macmillan
First Charmz Printing

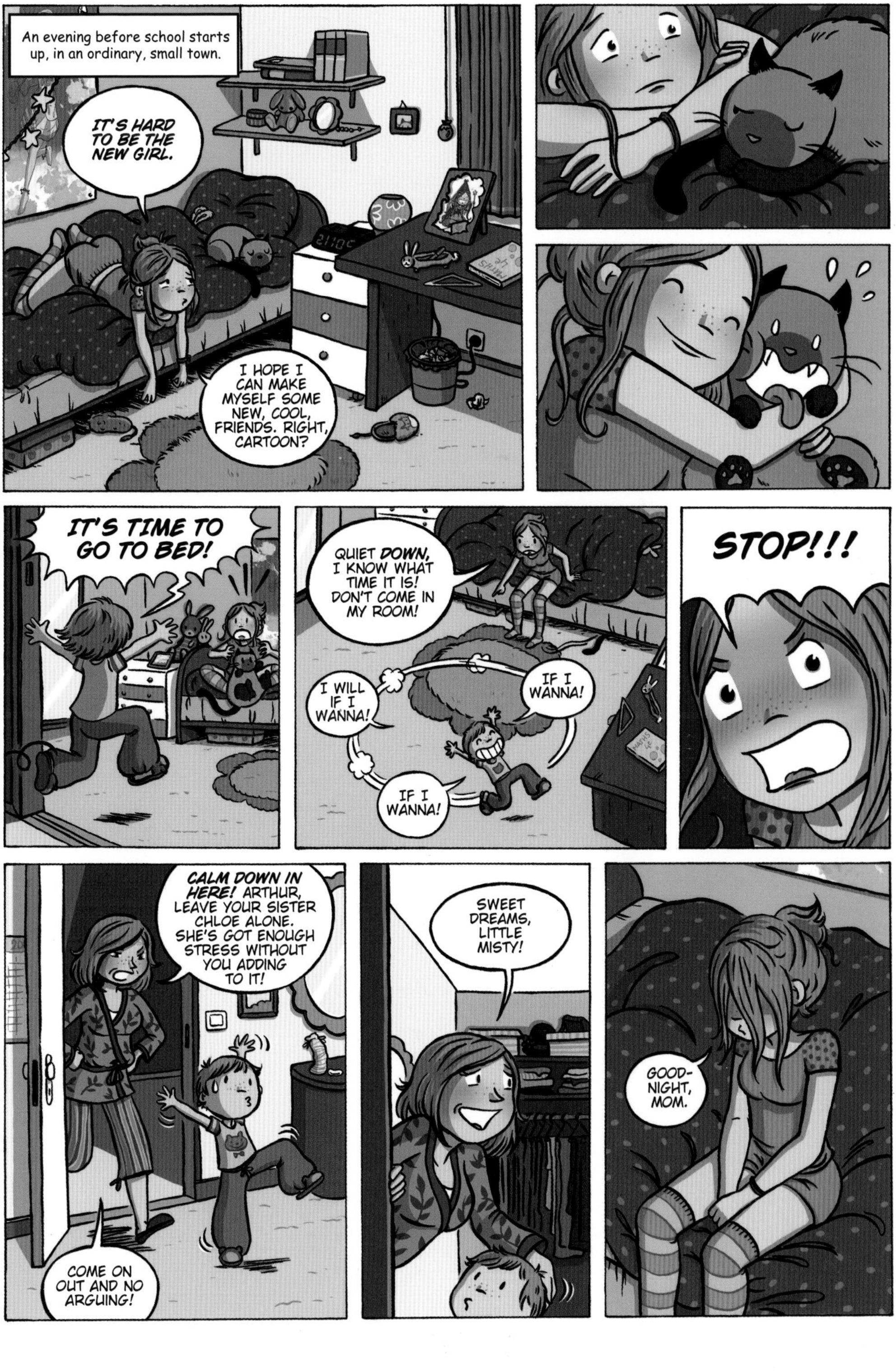
An evening before school starts up, in an ordinary, small town.
IT'S HARD TO BE THE NEW GIRL.
I HOPE I CAN MAKE MYSELF SOME NEW, COOL, FRIENDS. RIGHT, CARTOON?
IT'S TIME TO GO TO BED!
QUIET DOWN, I KNOW WHAT TIME IT IS! DON'T COME IN MY ROOM!
I WILL IF I WANNA!
IF I WANNA!
IF I WANNA!
STOP!!!
CALM DOWN IN HERE! ARTHUR, LEAVE YOUR SISTER CHLOE ALONE. SHE'S GOT ENOUGH STRESS WITHOUT YOU ADDING TO IT!
COME ON OUT AND NO ARGUING!
SWEET DREAMS, LITTLE MISTY!
GOOD-NIGHT, MOM.

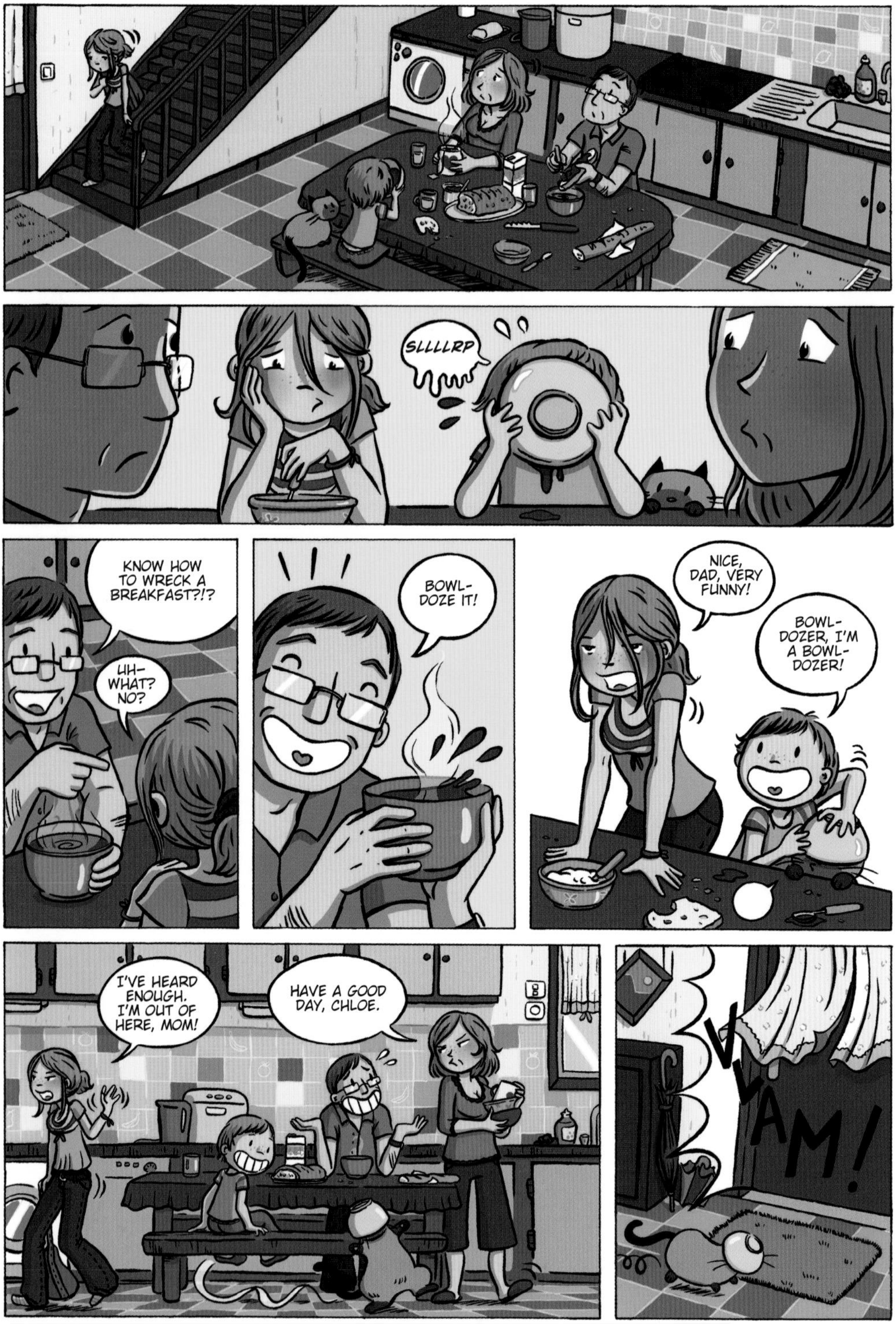

SLLLLRP
KNOW HOW TO WRECK A BREAKFAST?!?
UH- WHAT? NO?
BOWL- DOZE IT!
NICE, DAD, VERY FUNNY!
BOWL- DOZER, I'M A BOWL- DOZER!
I'VE HEARD ENOUGH. I'M OUT OF HERE, MOM!
HAVE A GOOD DAY, CHLOE.
VLAM!

1st Quarter

"Observation Mode"
engaged

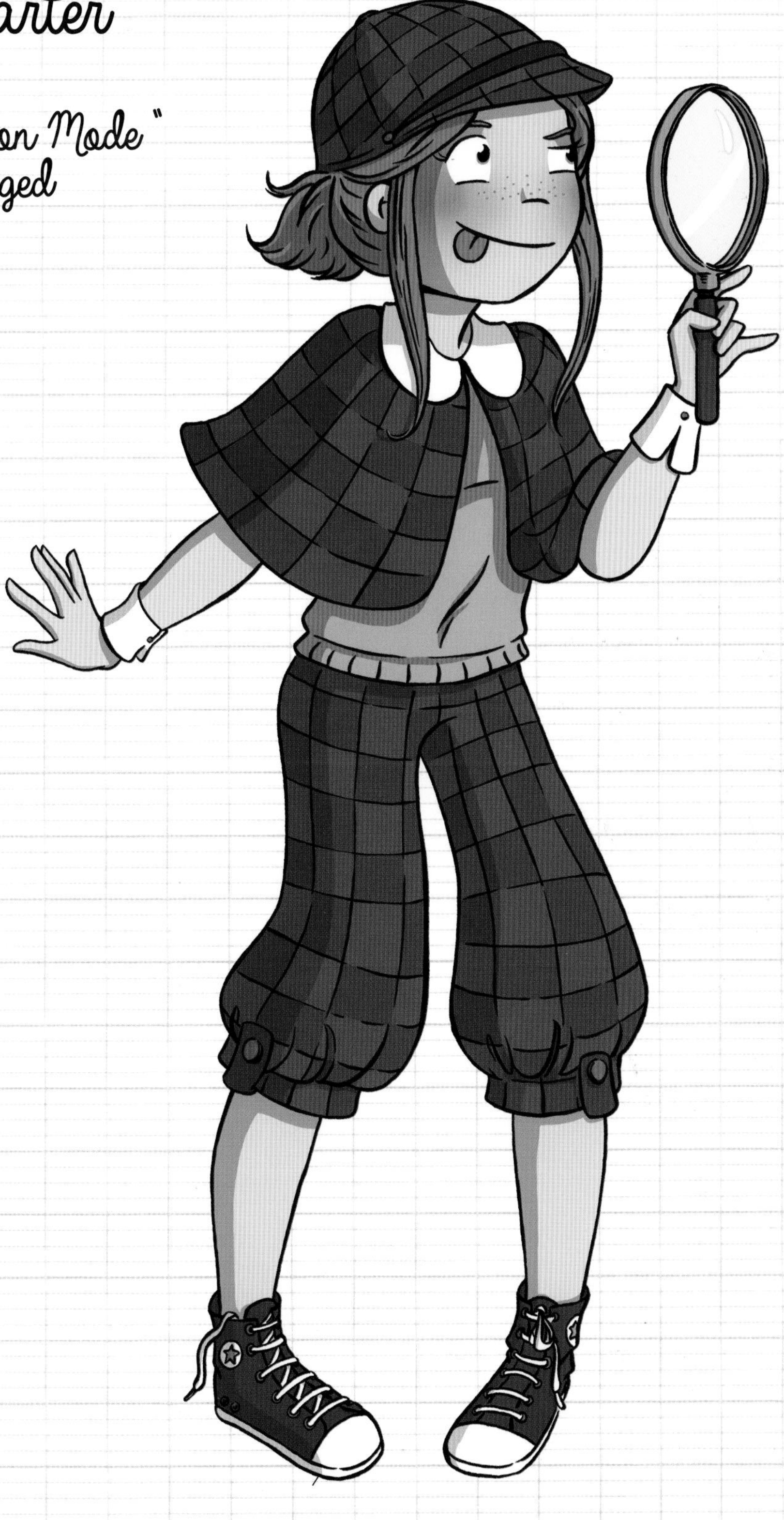

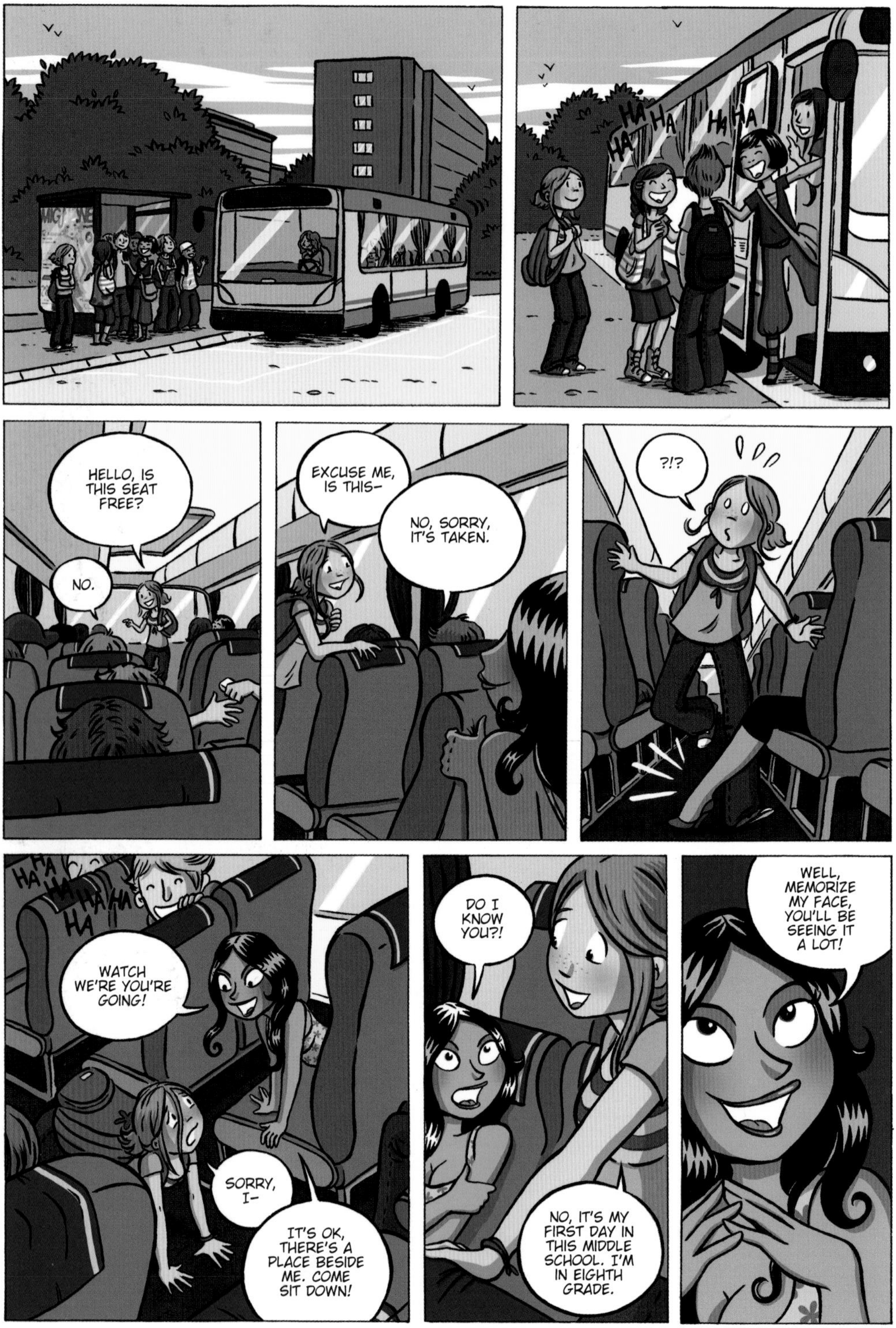
HA HA HA HA HA
HELLO, IS THIS SEAT FREE?
NO.
EXCUSE ME, IS THIS–
NO, SORRY, IT'S TAKEN.
?!?
HA HA HA HA HA HA
WATCH WE'RE YOU'RE GOING!
SORRY, I–
IT'S OK, THERE'S A PLACE BESIDE ME. COME SIT DOWN!
DO I KNOW YOU?!
NO, IT'S MY FIRST DAY IN THIS MIDDLE SCHOOL. I'M IN EIGHTH GRADE.
WELL, MEMORIZE MY FACE, YOU'LL BE SEEING IT A LOT!

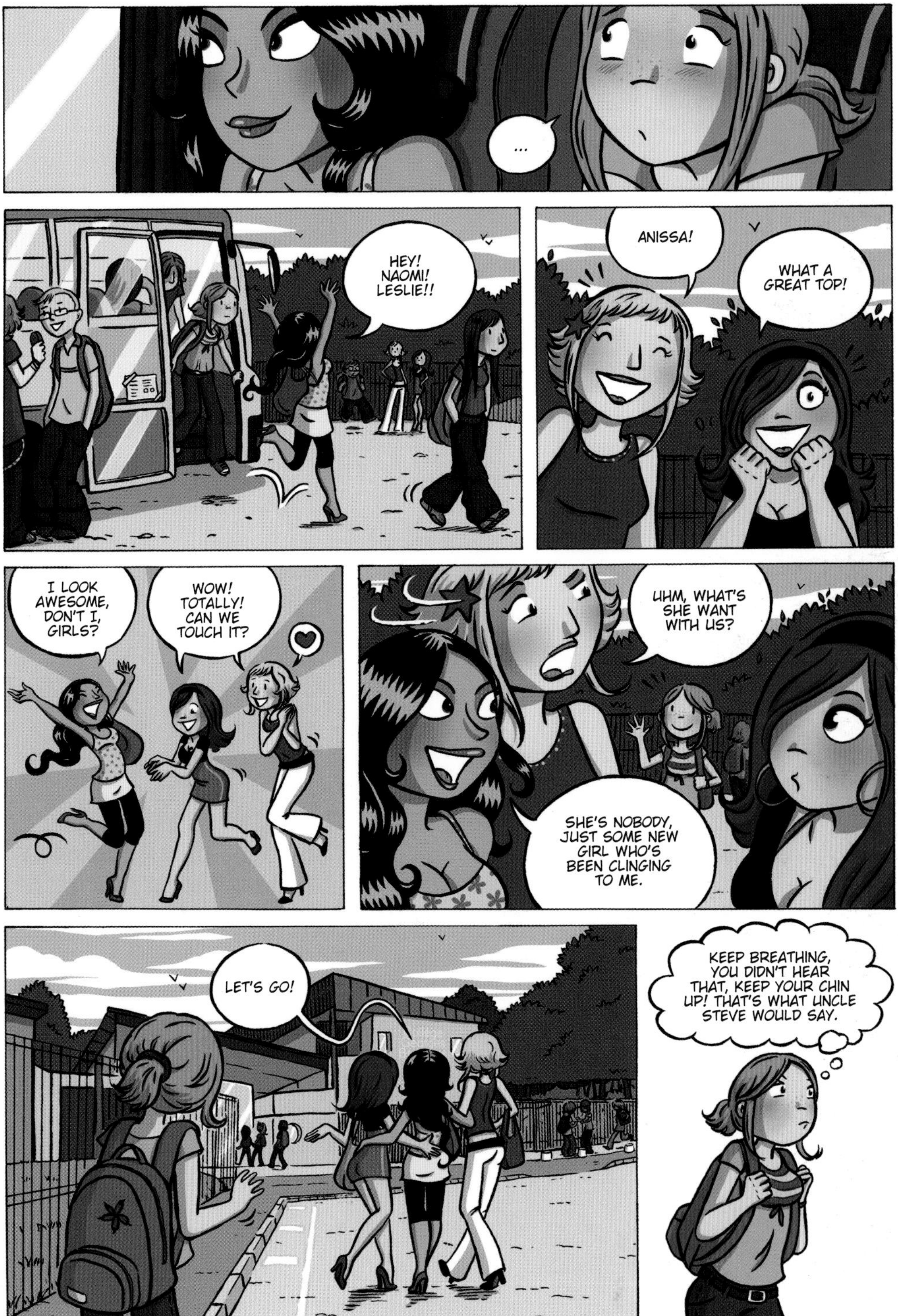
...
HEY! NAOMI! LESLIE!!
ANISSA!
WHAT A GREAT TOP!
I LOOK AWESOME, DON'T I, GIRLS?
WOW! TOTALLY! CAN WE TOUCH IT?
UHM, WHAT'S SHE WANT WITH US?
SHE'S NOBODY, JUST SOME NEW GIRL WHO'S BEEN CLINGING TO ME.
LET'S GO!
KEEP BREATHING, YOU DIDN'T HEAR THAT, KEEP YOUR CHIN UP! THAT'S WHAT UNCLE STEVE WOULD SAY.

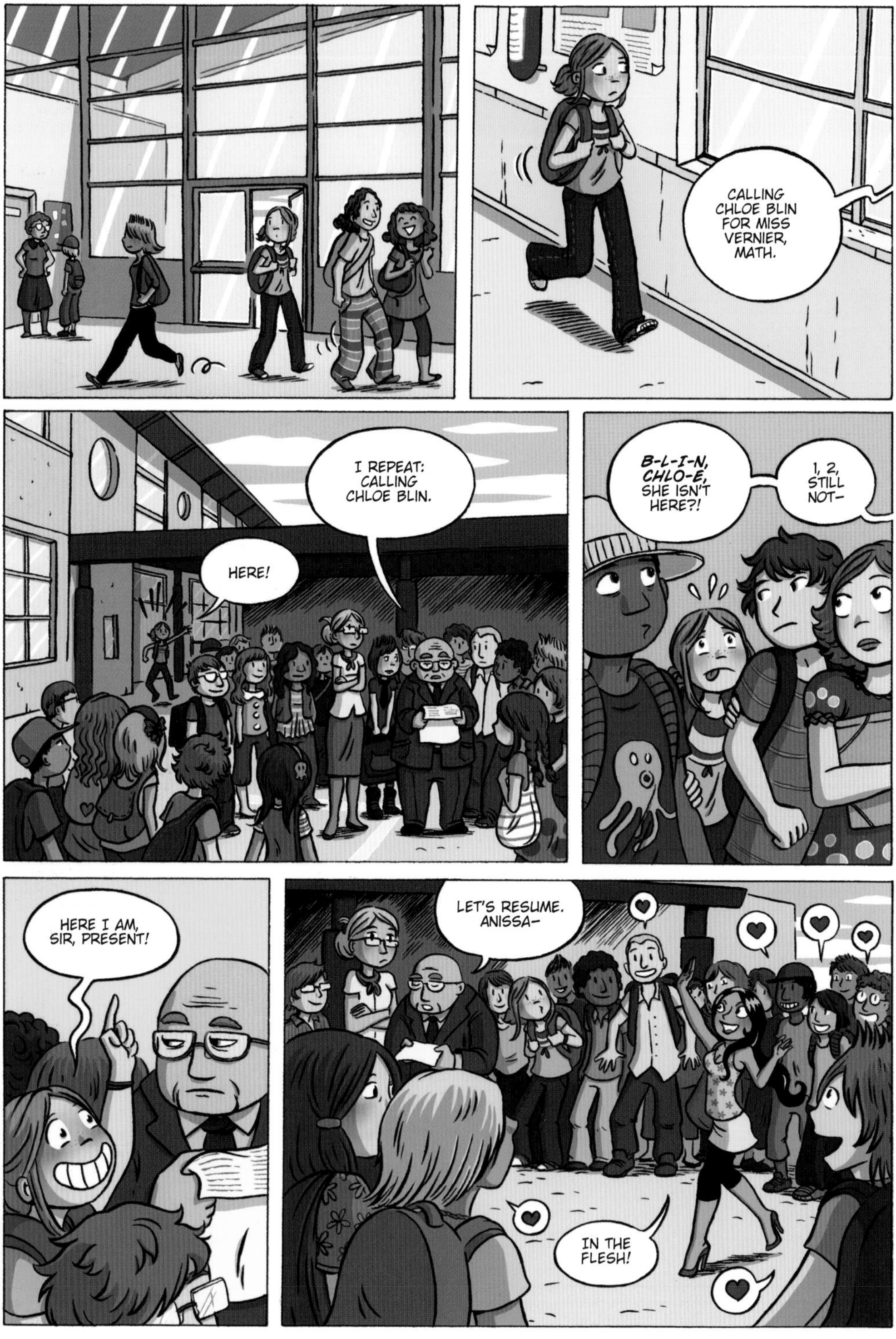
CALLING CHLOE BLIN FOR MISS VERNIER, MATH.
I REPEAT: CALLING CHLOE BLIN.
HERE!
B-L-I-N, CHLO-E, SHE ISN'T HERE?!
1, 2, STILL NOT-
HERE I AM, SIR, PRESENT!
LET'S RESUME. ANISSA-
IN THE FLESH!

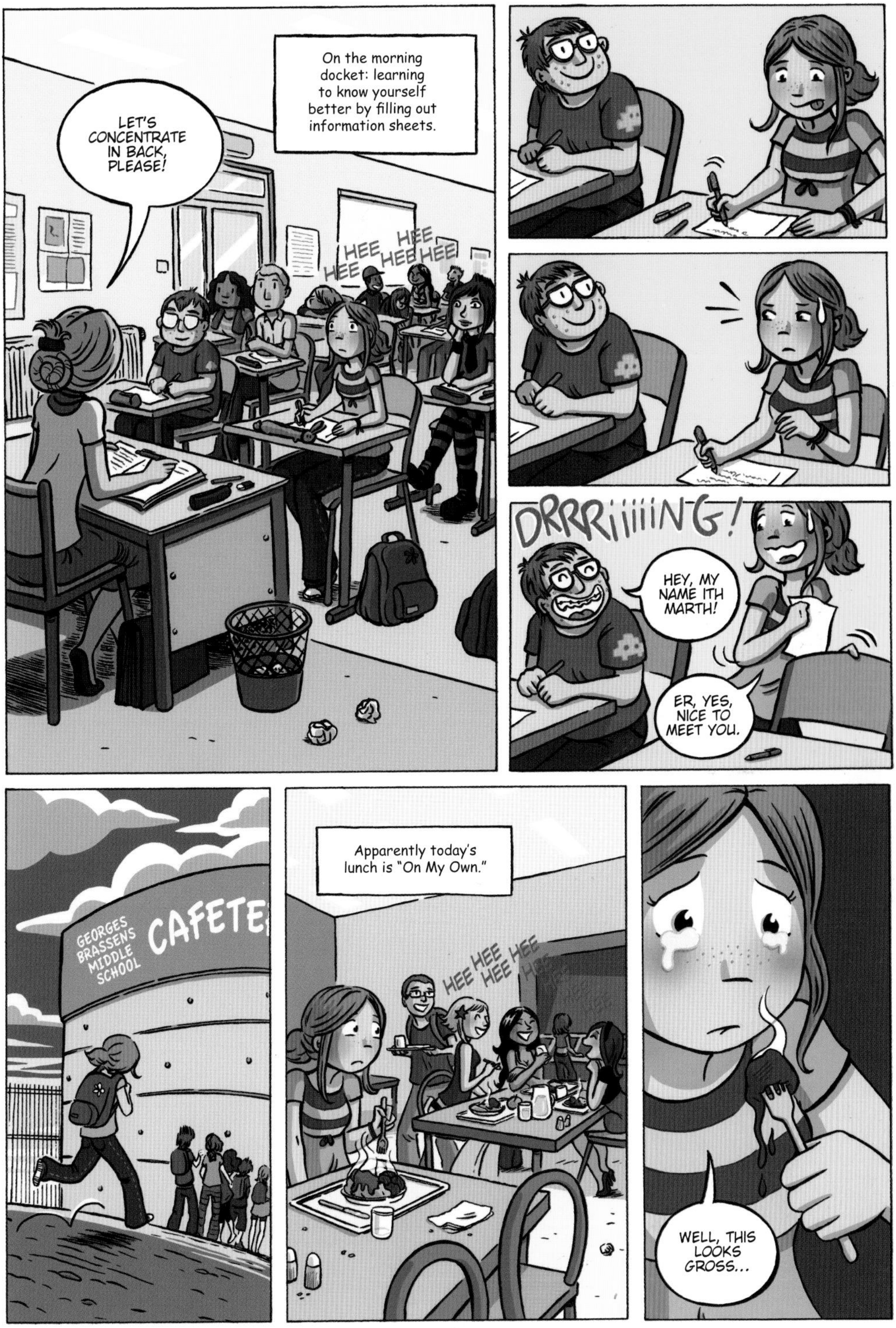
On the morning docket: learning to know yourself better by filling out information sheets.
LET'S CONCENTRATE IN BACK, PLEASE!
HEE HEE HEE HEE HEE
DRRRiiiiiNG!
HEY, MY NAME ITH MARTH!
ER, YES, NICE TO MEET YOU.
GEORGES BRASSENS MIDDLE SCHOOL
CAFETE
Apparently today's lunch is "On My Own."
HEE HEE HEE HEE HEE
WELL, THIS LOOKS GROSS...

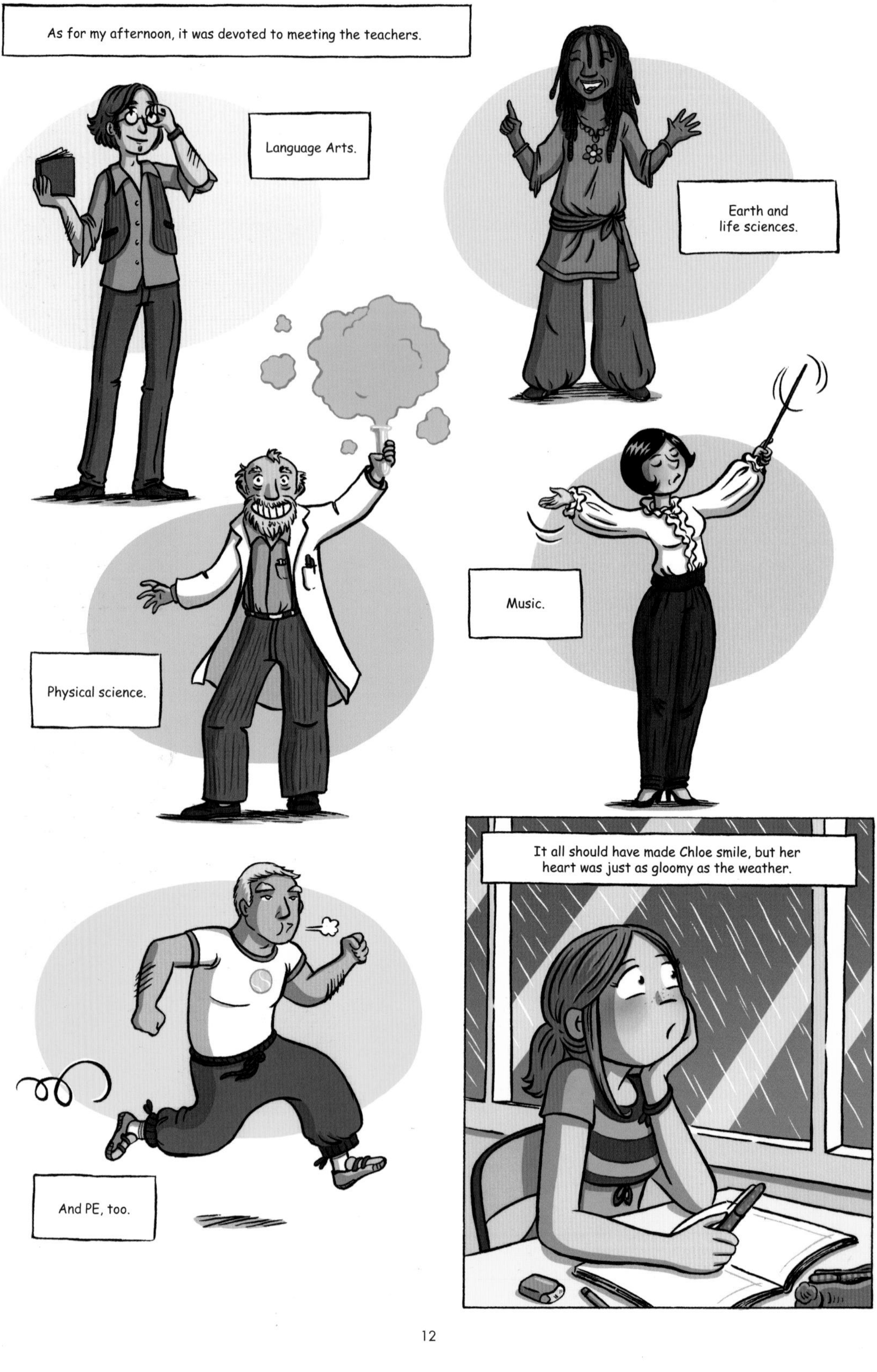
As for my afternoon, it was devoted to meeting the teachers.
Language Arts.
Earth and life sciences.
Physical science.
Music.
And PE, too.
It all should have made Chloe smile, but her heart was just as gloomy as the weather.

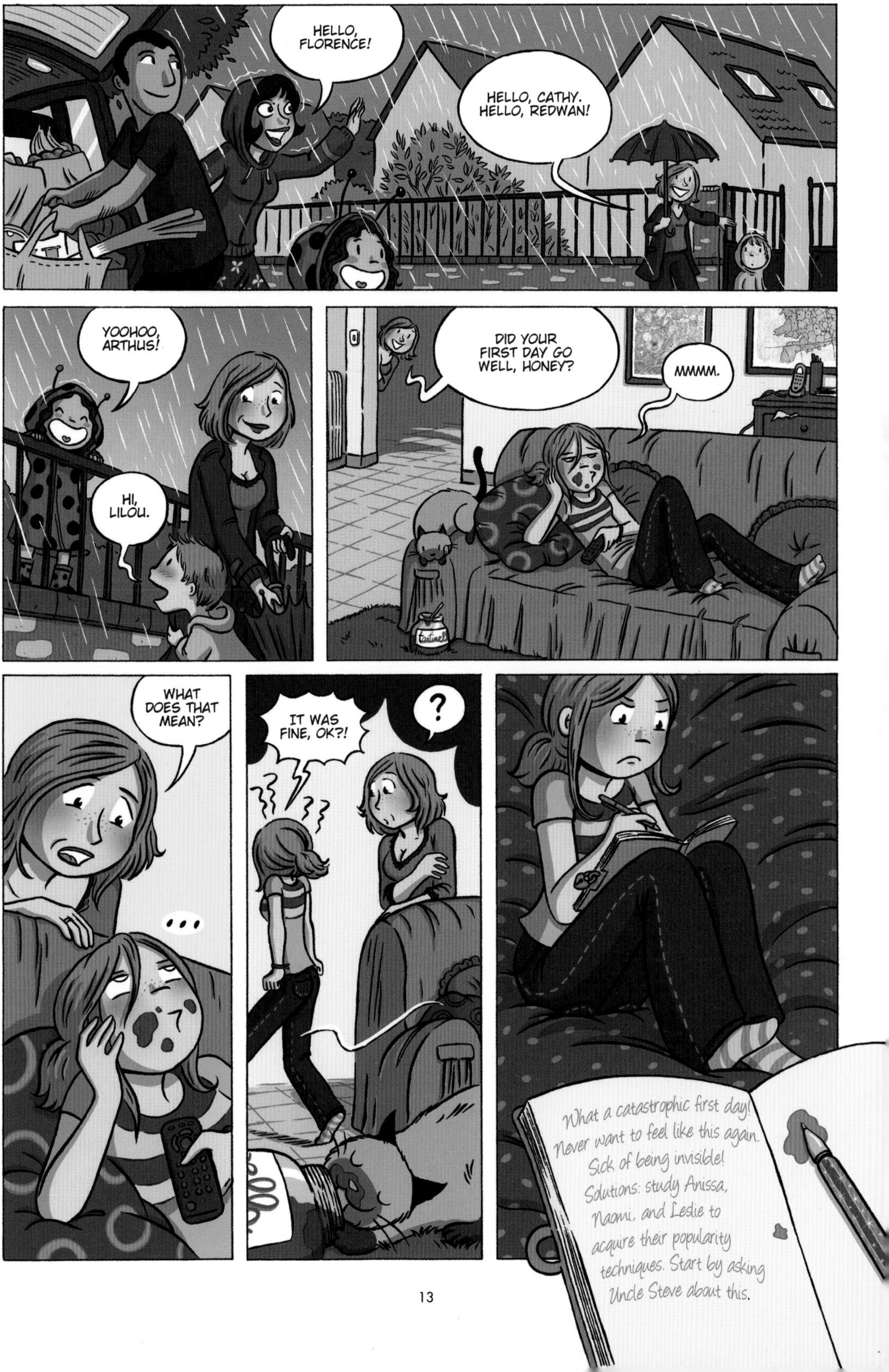

HELLO, FLORENCE!
HELLO, CATHY. HELLO, REDWAN!
YOOHOO, ARTHUS!
HI, LILOU.
DID YOUR FIRST DAY GO WELL, HONEY?
MMMM.
WHAT DOES THAT MEAN?
...
IT WAS FINE, OK?!
?
What a catastrophic first day! Never want to feel like this again. Sick of being invisible! Solutions: study Anissa, Naomi, and Leslie to acquire their popularity techniques. Start by asking Uncle Steve about this.

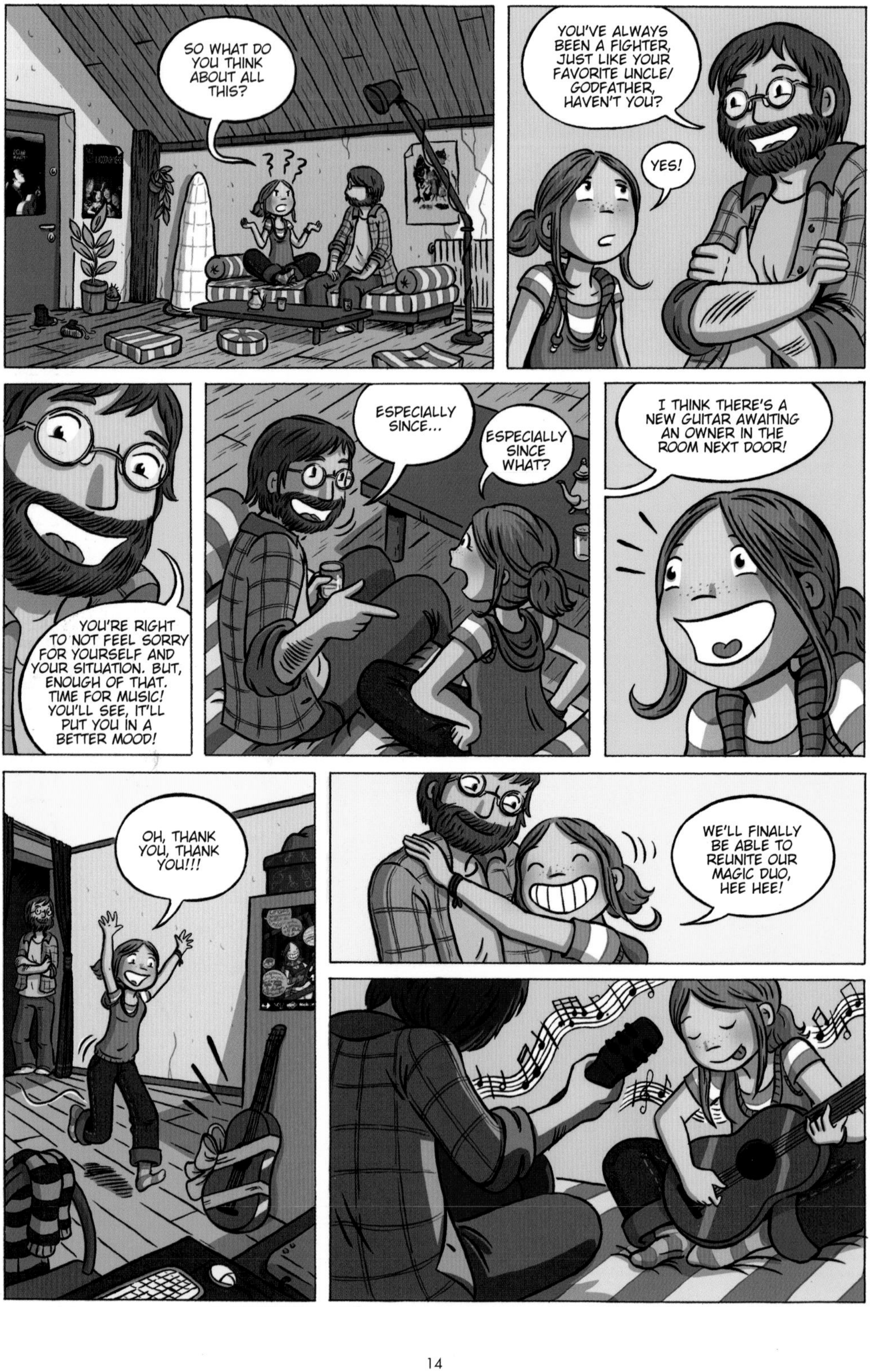
SO WHAT DO YOU THINK ABOUT ALL THIS?
YOU'VE ALWAYS BEEN A FIGHTER, JUST LIKE YOUR FAVORITE UNCLE/ GODFATHER, HAVEN'T YOU?
YES!
YOU'RE RIGHT TO NOT FEEL SORRY FOR YOURSELF AND YOUR SITUATION. BUT, ENOUGH OF THAT. TIME FOR MUSIC! YOU'LL SEE, IT'LL PUT YOU IN A BETTER MOOD!
ESPECIALLY SINCE...
ESPECIALLY SINCE WHAT?
I THINK THERE'S A NEW GUITAR AWAITING AN OWNER IN THE ROOM NEXT DOOR!
OH, THANK YOU, THANK YOU!!!
WE'LL FINALLY BE ABLE TO REUNITE OUR MAGIC DUO, HEE HEE!

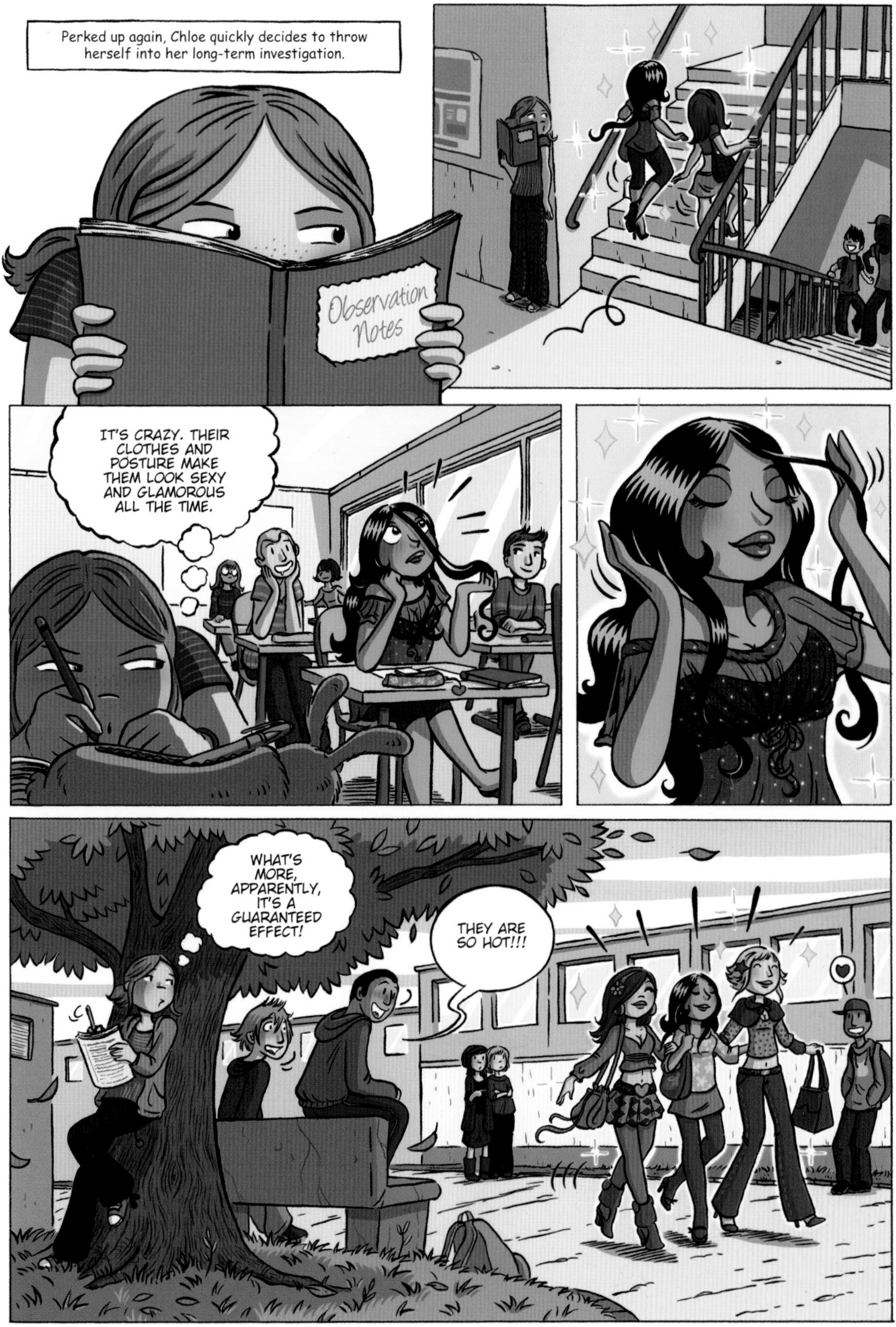
Perked up again, Chloe quickly decides to throw herself into her long-term investigation.
Observation Notes
IT'S CRAZY. THEIR CLOTHES AND POSTURE MAKE THEM LOOK SEXY AND GLAMOROUS ALL THE TIME.
WHAT'S MORE, APPARENTLY, IT'S A GUARANTEED EFFECT!
THEY ARE SO HOT!!!

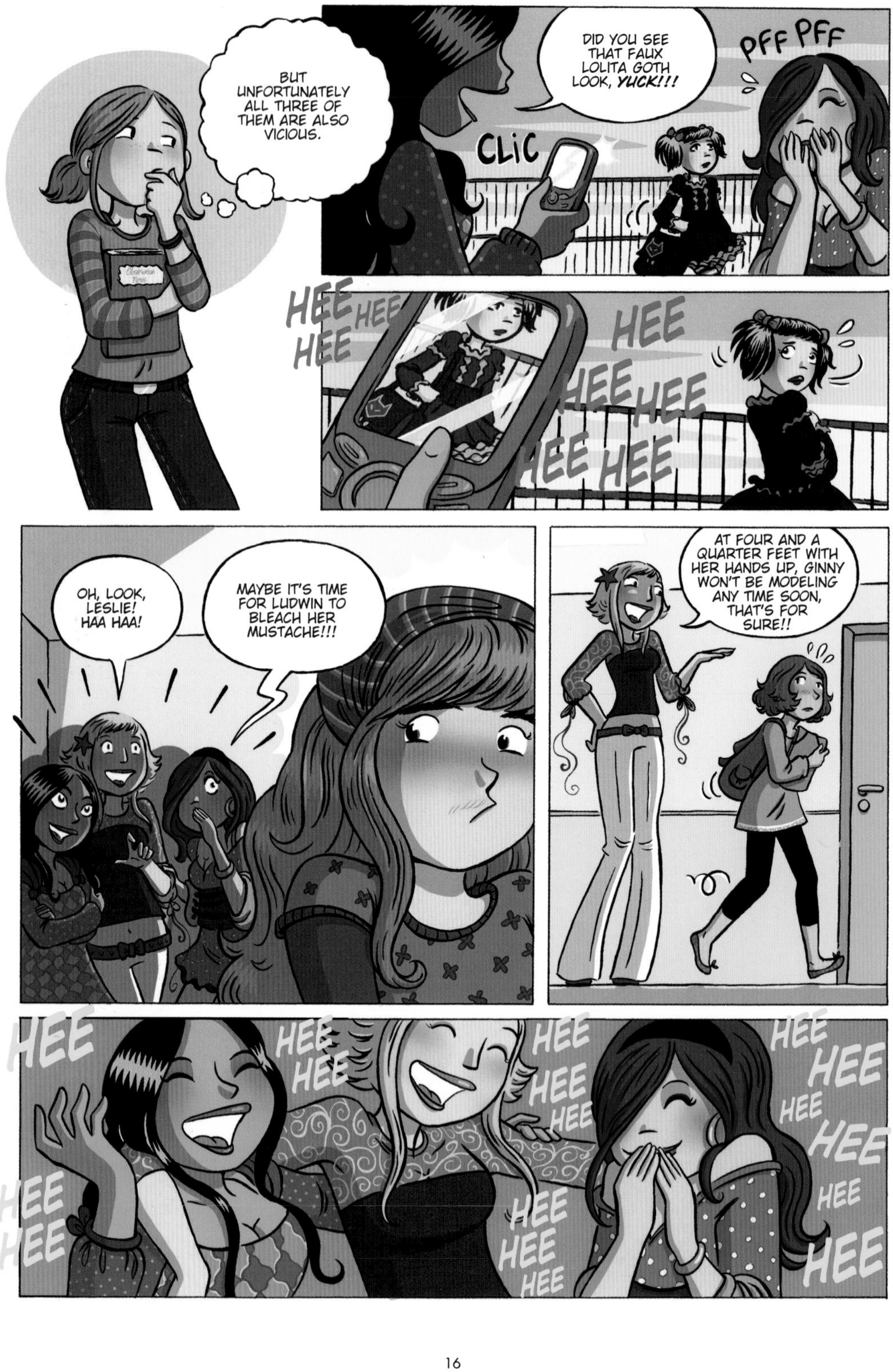
BUT UNFORTUNATELY ALL THREE OF THEM ARE ALSO VICIOUS.
DID YOU SEE THAT FAUX LOLITA GOTH LOOK, YUCK!!!
PFF PFF
CLIC
HEE HEE HEE
HEE HEE HEE HEE HEE
OH, LOOK, LESLIE! HAA HAA!
MAYBE IT'S TIME FOR LUDWIN TO BLEACH HER MUSTACHE!!!
AT FOUR AND A QUARTER FEET WITH HER HANDS UP, GINNY WON'T BE MODELING ANY TIME SOON, THAT'S FOR SURE!!
HEE HEE HEE HEE HEE HEE HEE HEE HEE HEE HEE HEE HEE HEE HEE HEE HEE HEE

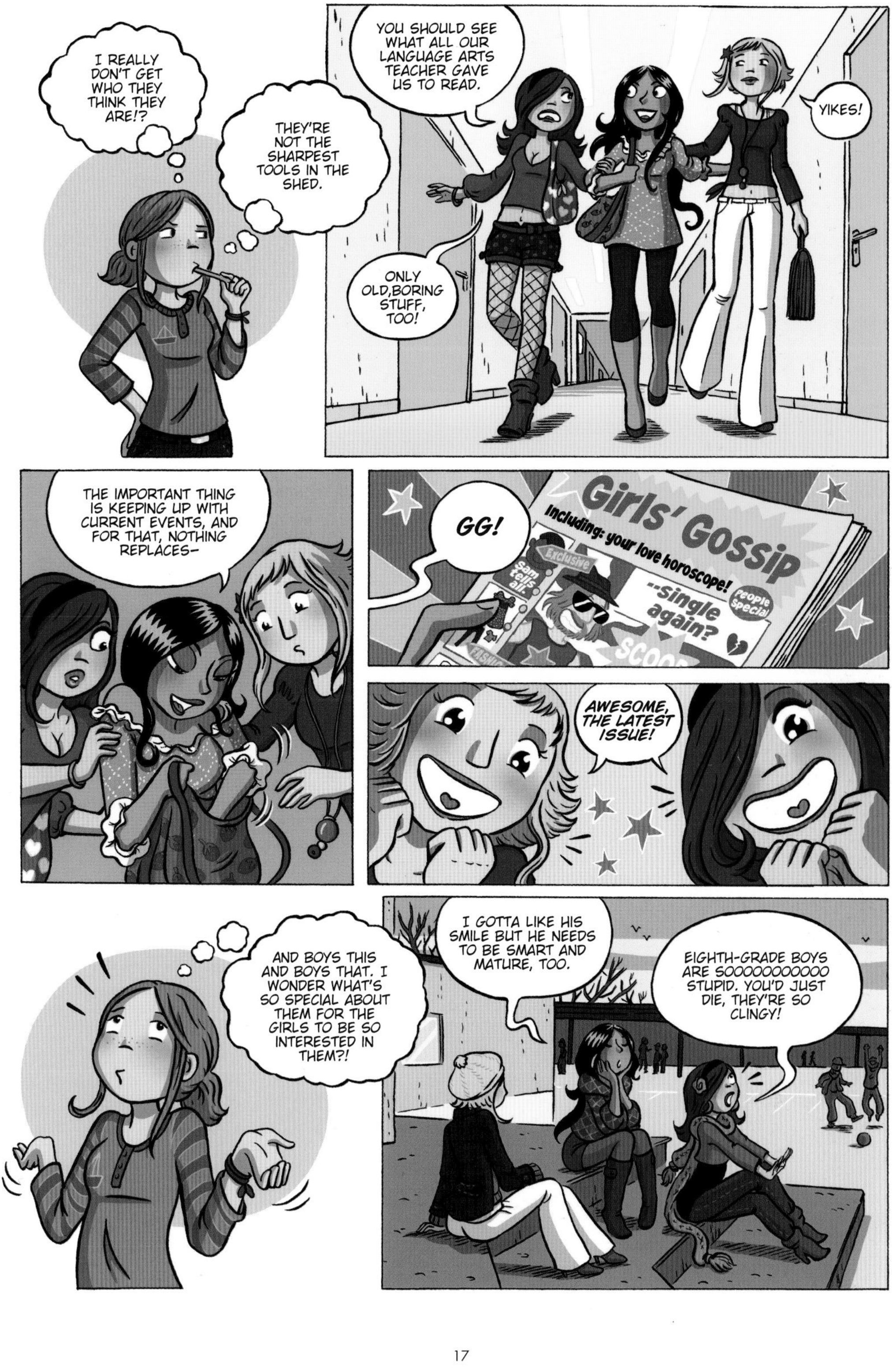
I REALLY DON'T GET WHO THEY THINK THEY ARE!?
THEY'RE NOT THE SHARPEST TOOLS IN THE SHED.
YOU SHOULD SEE WHAT ALL OUR LANGUAGE ARTS TEACHER GAVE US TO READ.
YIKES!
ONLY OLD,BORING STUFF, TOO!
THE IMPORTANT THING IS KEEPING UP WITH CURRENT EVENTS, AND FOR THAT, NOTHING REPLACES–
GG!
Girls' Gossip
Including: your love horoscope!
Exclusive
Sam tells all.
--single again?
People Special
AWESOME, THE LATEST ISSUE!
AND BOYS THIS AND BOYS THAT. I WONDER WHAT'S SO SPECIAL ABOUT THEM FOR THE GIRLS TO BE SO INTERESTED IN THEM?!
I GOTTA LIKE HIS SMILE BUT HE NEEDS TO BE SMART AND MATURE, TOO.
EIGHTH-GRADE BOYS ARE SOOOOOOOOOOO STUPID. YOU'D JUST DIE, THEY'RE SO CLINGY!

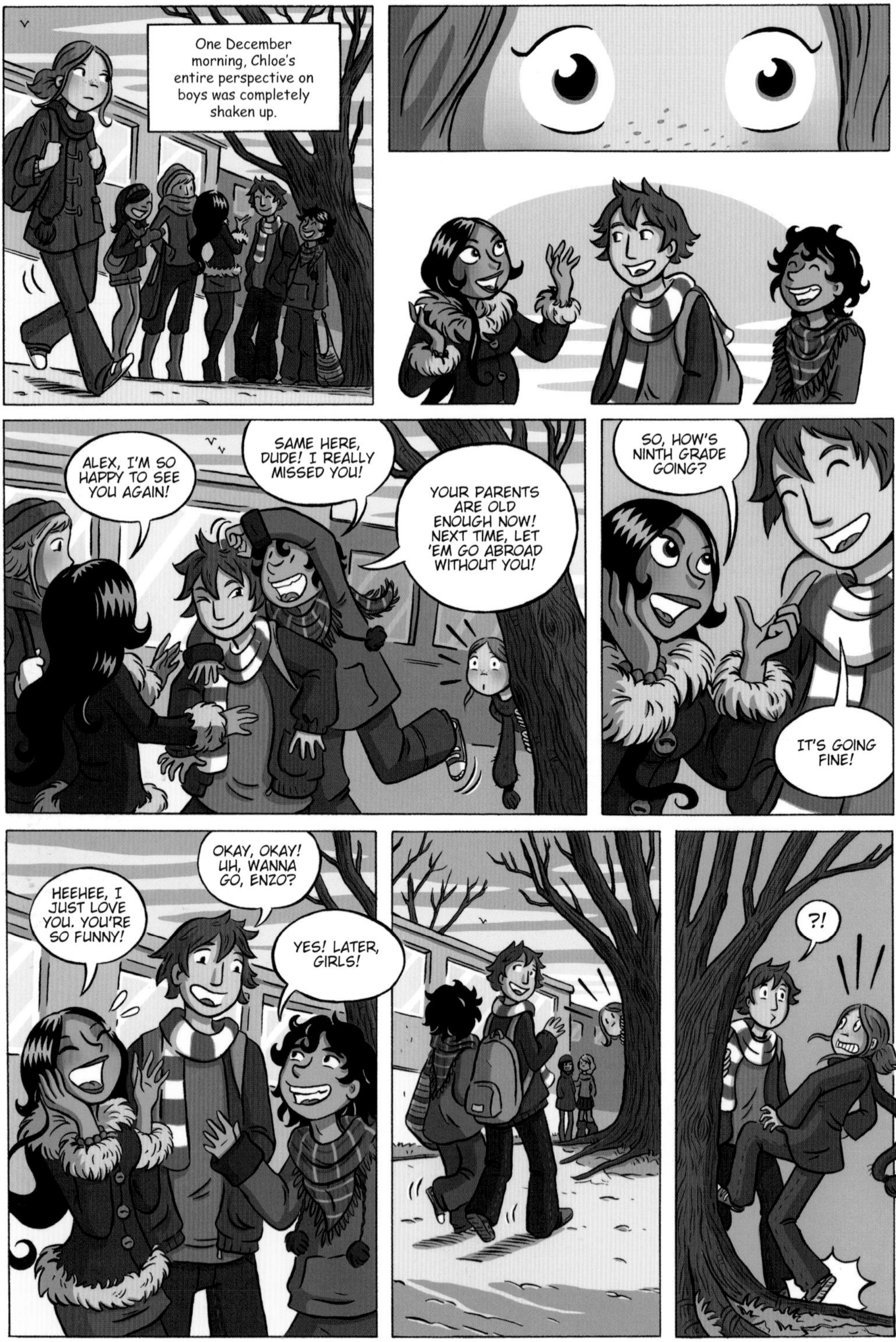
One December morning, Chloe's entire perspective on boys was completely shaken up.
ALEX, I'M SO HAPPY TO SEE YOU AGAIN!
SAME HERE, DUDE! I REALLY MISSED YOU!
YOUR PARENTS ARE OLD ENOUGH NOW! NEXT TIME, LET 'EM GO ABROAD WITHOUT YOU!
SO, HOW'S NINTH GRADE GOING?
IT'S GOING FINE!
HEEHEE, I JUST LOVE YOU. YOU'RE SO FUNNY!
OKAY, OKAY! UH, WANNA GO, ENZO?
YES! LATER, GIRLS!
?!

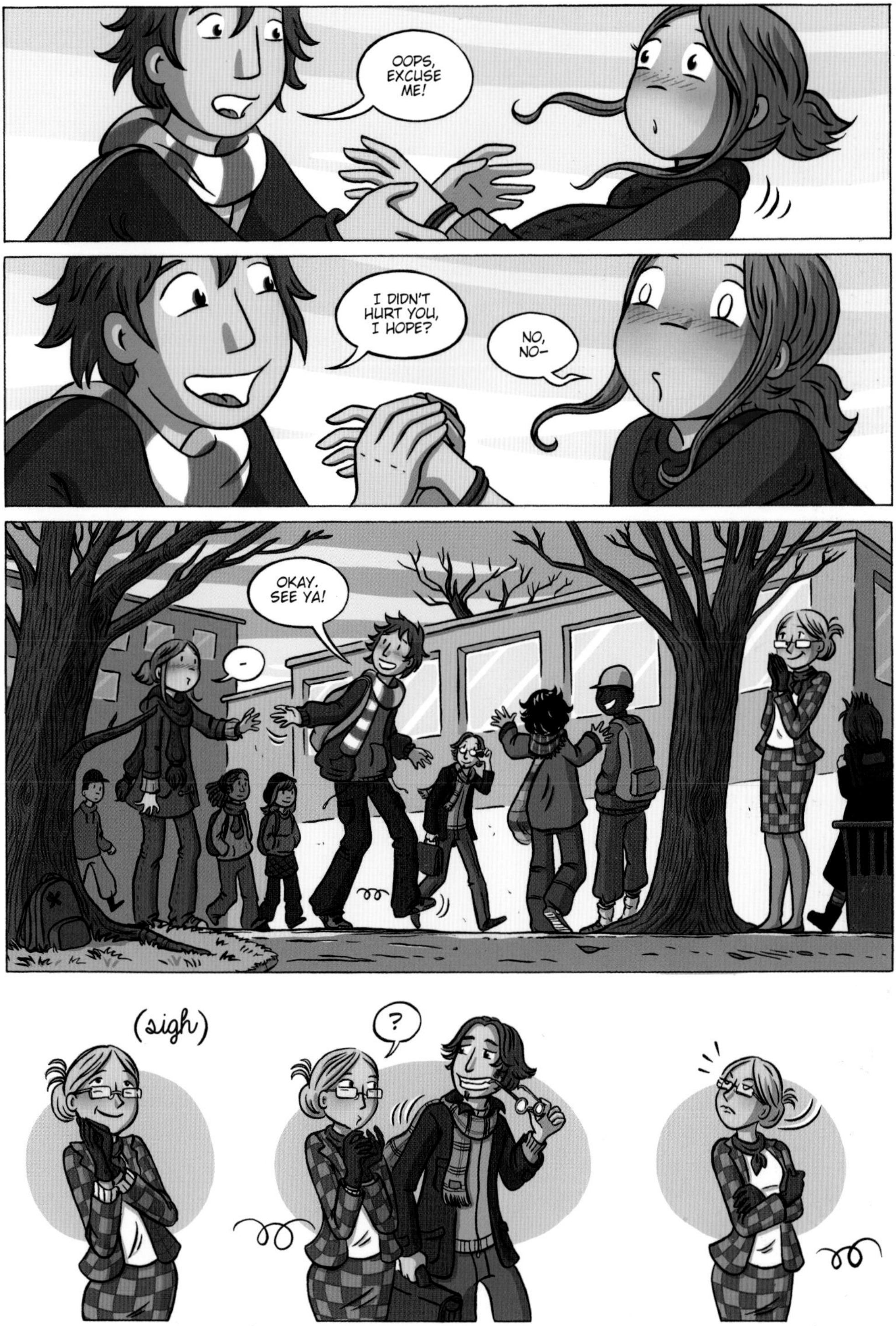
OOPS, EXCUSE ME!
I DIDN'T HURT YOU, I HOPE?
NO, NO-
-
OKAY. SEE YA!
(sigh)
?

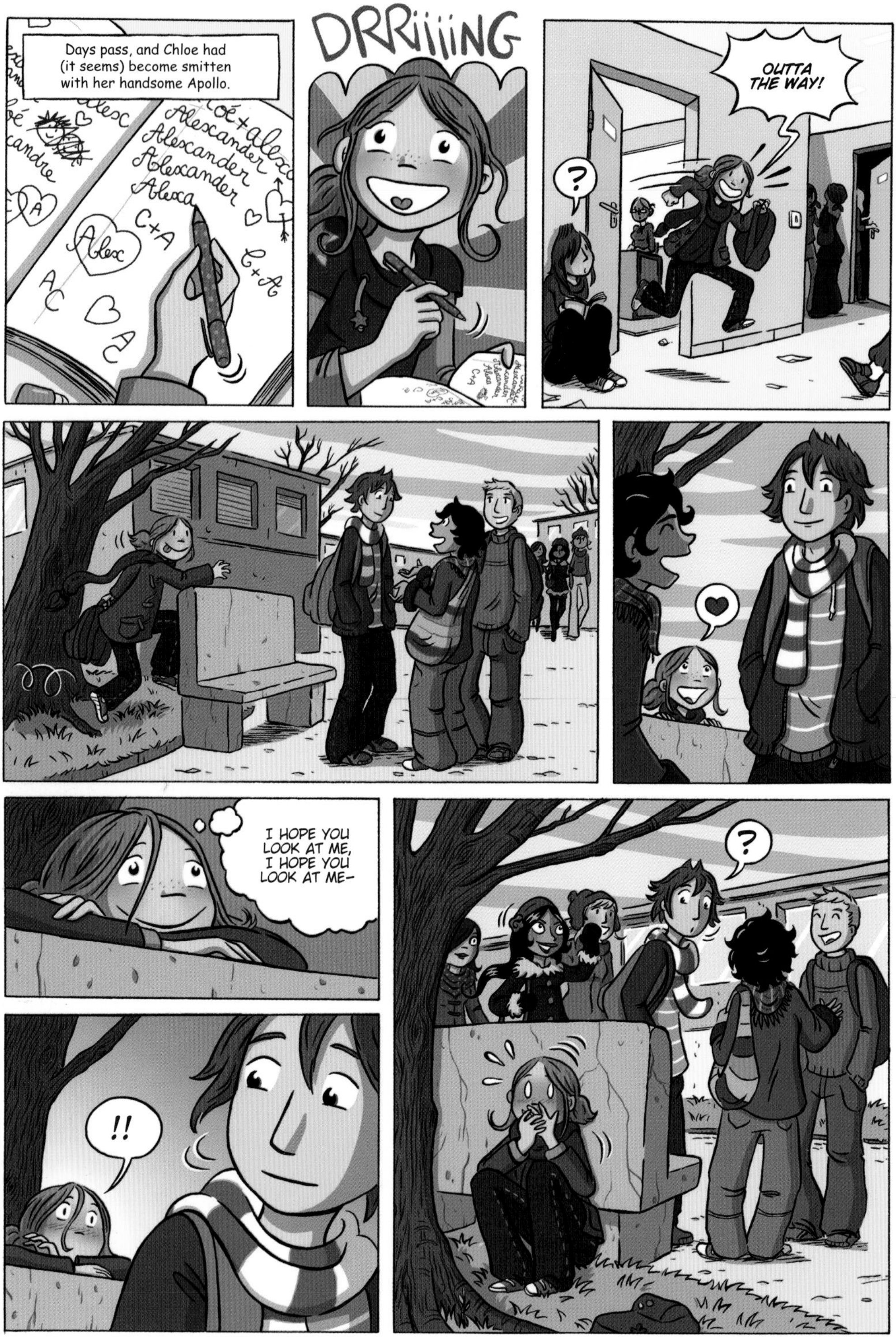

Days pass, and Chloe had (it seems) become smitten with her handsome Apollo.
DRRiiiiNG
?
OUTTA THE WAY!
I HOPE YOU LOOK AT ME, I HOPE YOU LOOK AT ME–
?
!!

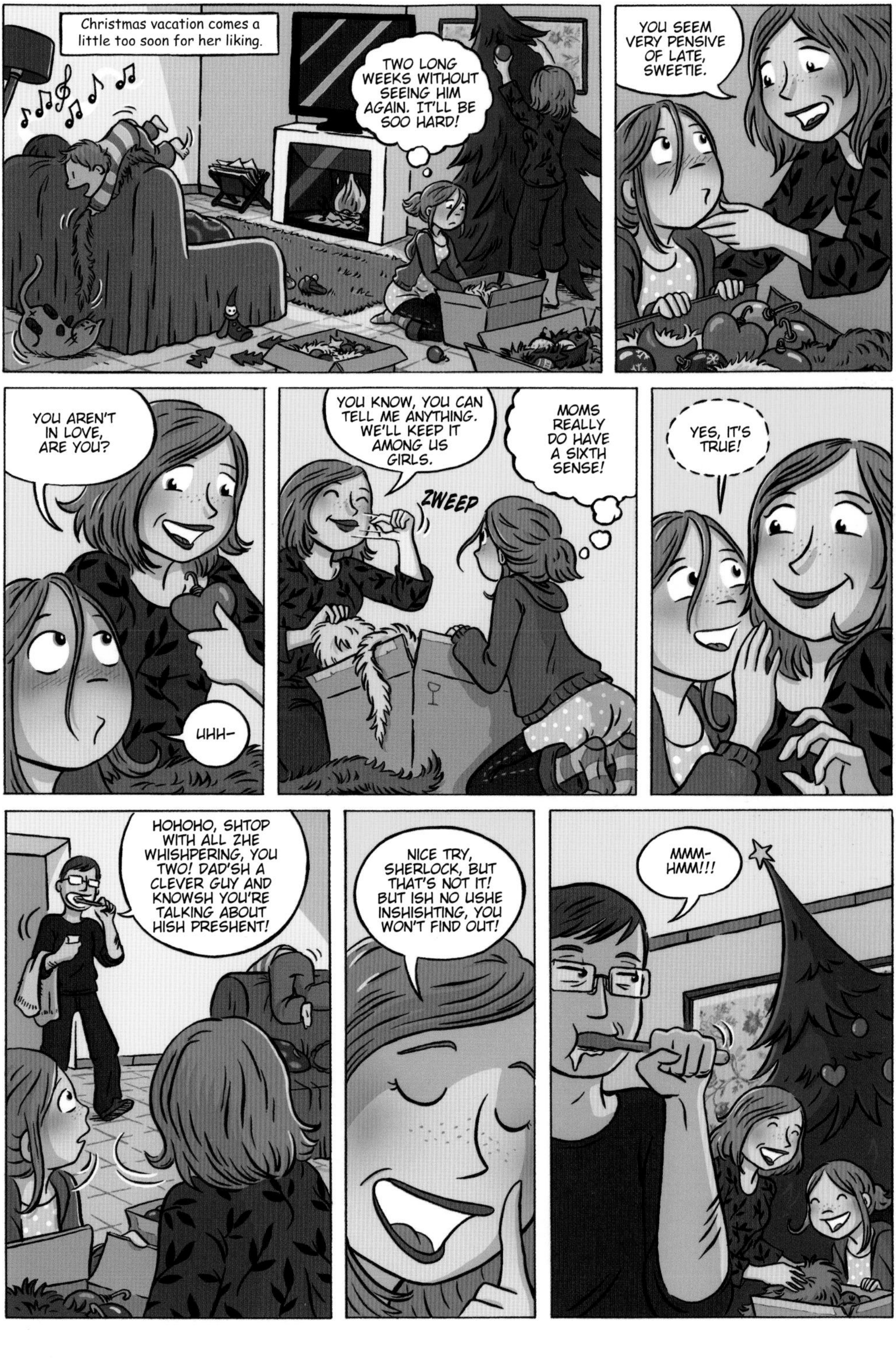
Christmas vacation comes a little too soon for her liking.
TWO LONG WEEKS WITHOUT SEEING HIM AGAIN. IT'LL BE SOO HARD!
YOU SEEM VERY PENSIVE OF LATE, SWEETIE.
YOU AREN'T IN LOVE, ARE YOU?
UHH-
YOU KNOW, YOU CAN TELL ME ANYTHING. WE'LL KEEP IT AMONG US GIRLS.
ZWEEP
MOMS REALLY DO HAVE A SIXTH SENSE!
YES, IT'S TRUE!
HOHOHO, SHTOP WITH ALL ZHE WHISHPERING, YOU TWO! DAD'SH A CLEVER GUY AND KNOWSH YOU'RE TALKING ABOUT HISH PRESHENT!
NICE TRY, SHERLOCK, BUT THAT'S NOT IT! BUT ISH NO USHE INSHISHTING, YOU WON'T FIND OUT!
MMM-HMM!!!

Report Card
1st Quarter

BLIN, Chloe or "Misty"
- Eighth Grade, Group C -

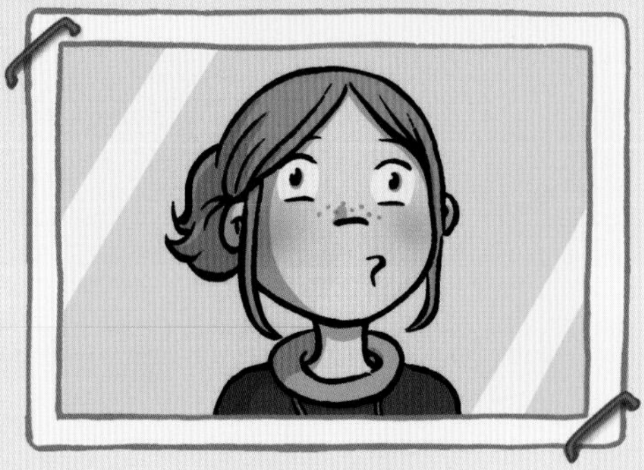

Subjects	Student Grade Averages	Suggestions for Improvement
Appearance	B	Average. A little originality would be welcome.
Self-confidence	D	Disastrous beginning. Annoying tendency to become withdrawn. You must forge ahead!
Observation Skills	A	Off to a very good start, but be careful about your inattentiveness.
Attractiveness	C-	Below average. Observing is fine, but the desire to be attractive mustn't be overlooked for all that.
Popularity	D	Mediocre. You build your own popularity!
Average for This Period	C	

General Comments:
Showed effort, certainly, but often Chloe lacks initiative. She often adopts a wait-and-see stance and lacks selfconfidence. The majority of readers advise her, from now on, to target her research. She will have to redouble her efforts in the 2nd Quarter.

Notification: this grade report is the original copy and must be preserved,

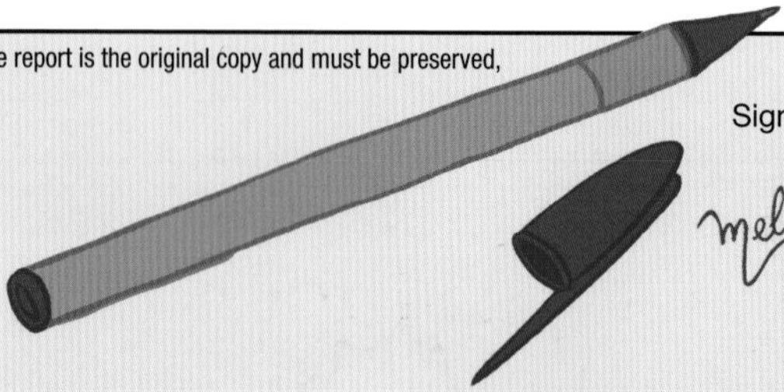

Signature of the home room teacher:

Melle Vernier

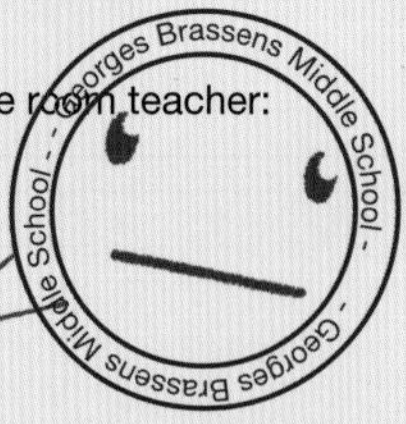
- Georges Brassens Middle School - Georges Brassens Middle School -

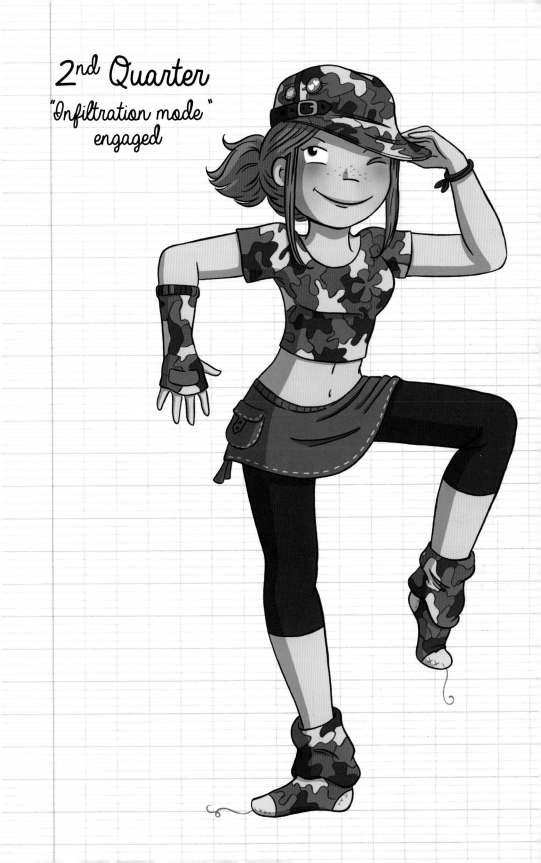

2nd Quarter

"Infiltration mode" engaged

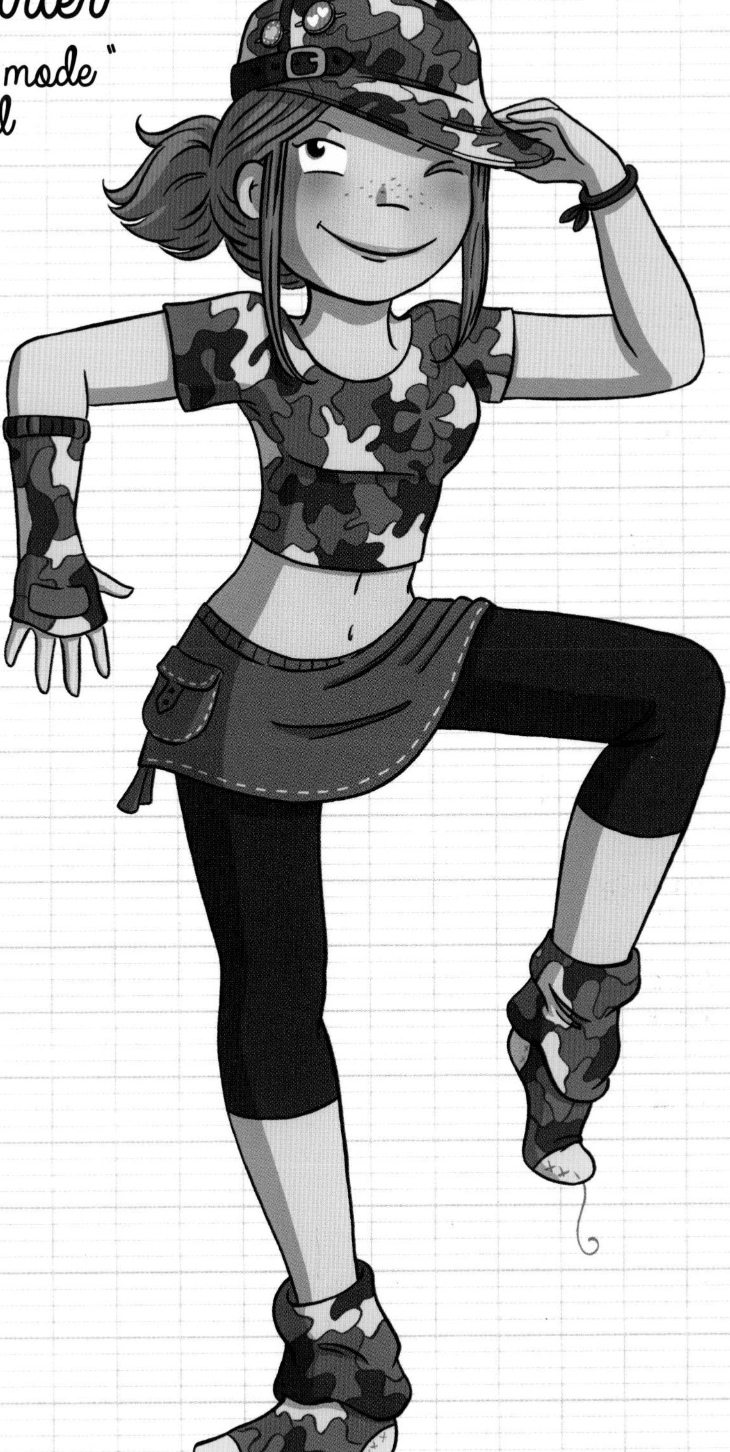

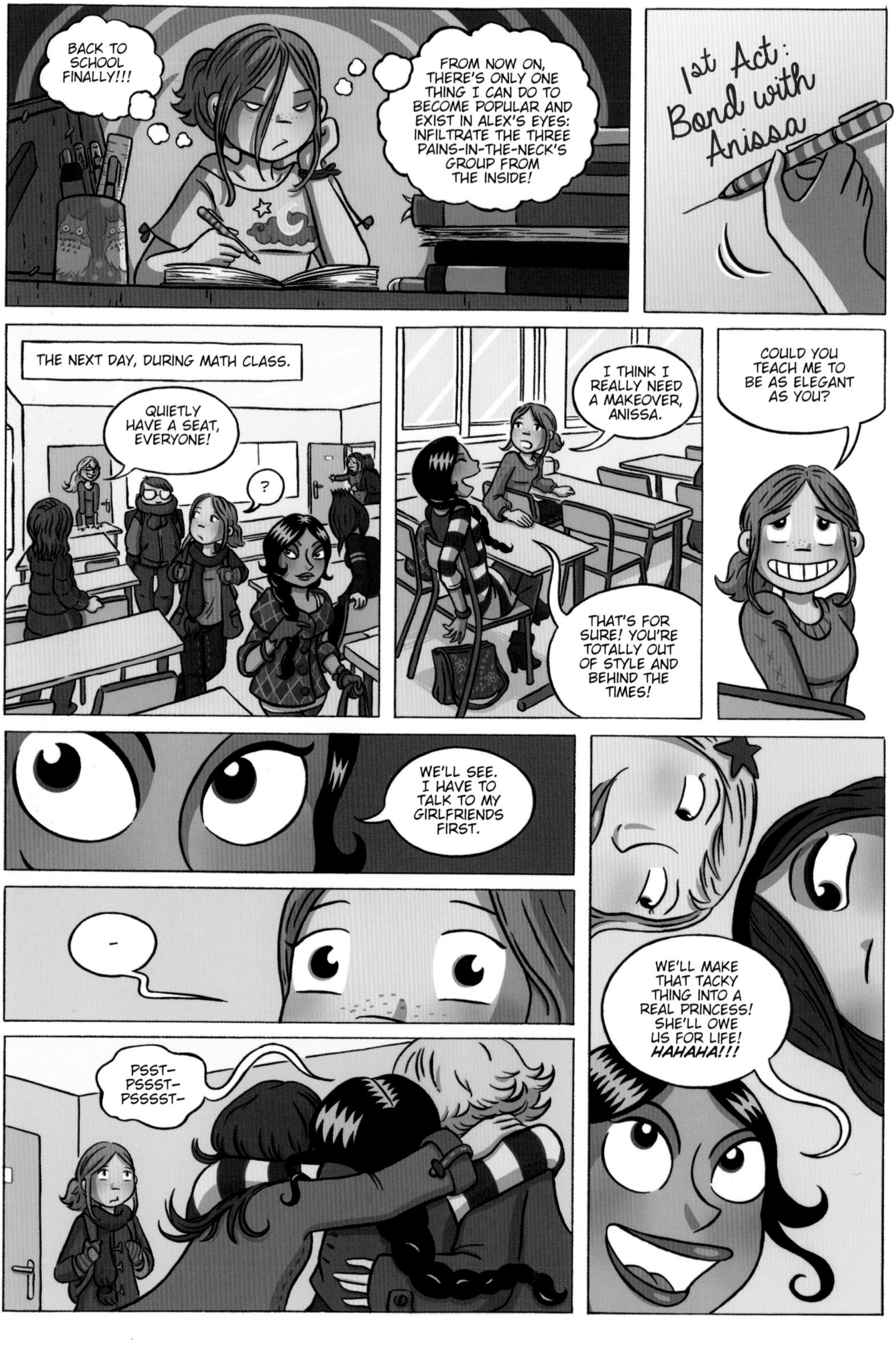
BACK TO SCHOOL FINALLY!!!
FROM NOW ON, THERE'S ONLY ONE THING I CAN DO TO BECOME POPULAR AND EXIST IN ALEX'S EYES: INFILTRATE THE THREE PAINS-IN-THE-NECK'S GROUP FROM THE INSIDE!
1st Act: Bond with Anissa
THE NEXT DAY, DURING MATH CLASS.
QUIETLY HAVE A SEAT, EVERYONE!
?
I THINK I REALLY NEED A MAKEOVER, ANISSA.
THAT'S FOR SURE! YOU'RE TOTALLY OUT OF STYLE AND BEHIND THE TIMES!
COULD YOU TEACH ME TO BE AS ELEGANT AS YOU?
WE'LL SEE. I HAVE TO TALK TO MY GIRLFRIENDS FIRST.
-
PSST- PSSST- PSSSST-
WE'LL MAKE THAT TACKY THING INTO A REAL PRINCESS! SHE'LL OWE US FOR LIFE! ***HAHAHA!!!***

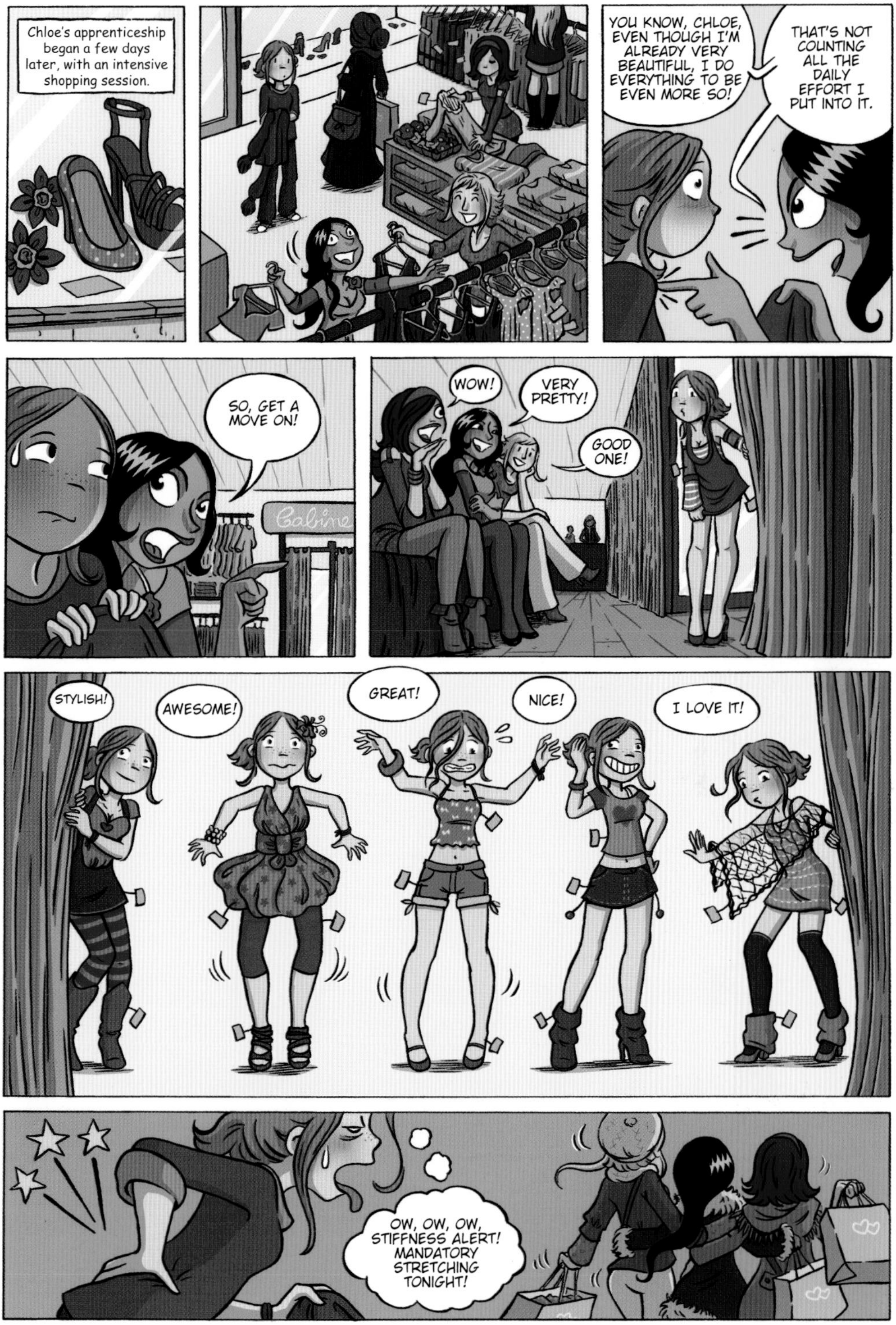

Chloe's apprenticeship began a few days later, with an intensive shopping session.
YOU KNOW, CHLOE, EVEN THOUGH I'M ALREADY VERY BEAUTIFUL, I DO EVERYTHING TO BE EVEN MORE SO!
THAT'S NOT COUNTING ALL THE DAILY EFFORT I PUT INTO IT.
SO, GET A MOVE ON!
Cabine
WOW!
VERY PRETTY!
GOOD ONE!
STYLISH!
AWESOME!
GREAT!
NICE!
I LOVE IT!
OW, OW, OW, STIFFNESS ALERT! MANDATORY STRETCHING TONIGHT!

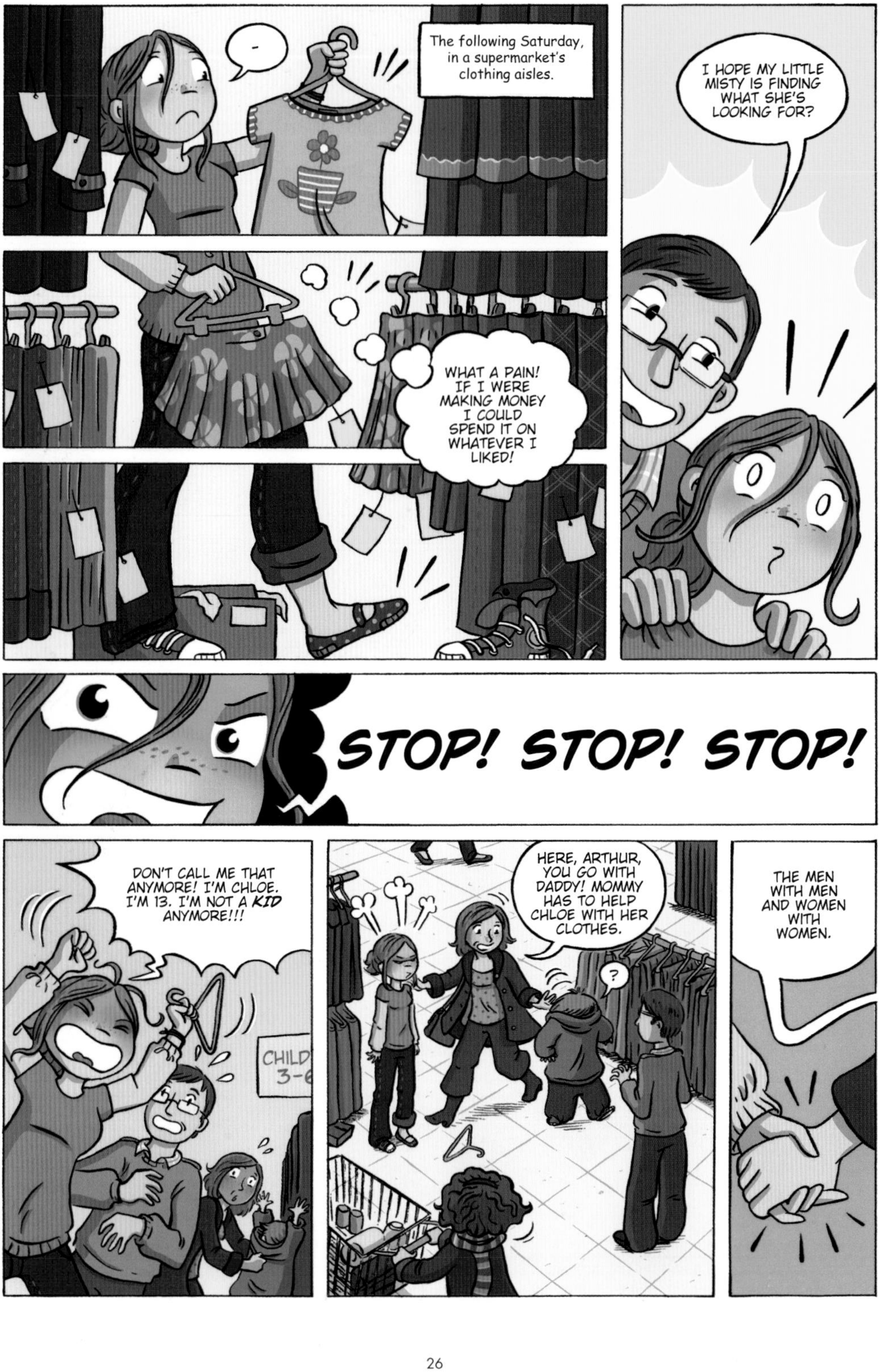
The following Saturday, in a supermarket's clothing aisles.
-
I HOPE MY LITTLE MISTY IS FINDING WHAT SHE'S LOOKING FOR?
WHAT A PAIN! IF I WERE MAKING MONEY I COULD SPEND IT ON WHATEVER I LIKED!
STOP! STOP! STOP!
DON'T CALL ME THAT ANYMORE! I'M CHLOE. I'M 13. I'M NOT A KID ANYMORE!!!
CHILD 3-6
HERE, ARTHUR, YOU GO WITH DADDY! MOMMY HAS TO HELP CHLOE WITH HER CLOTHES.
?
THE MEN WITH MEN AND WOMEN WITH WOMEN.

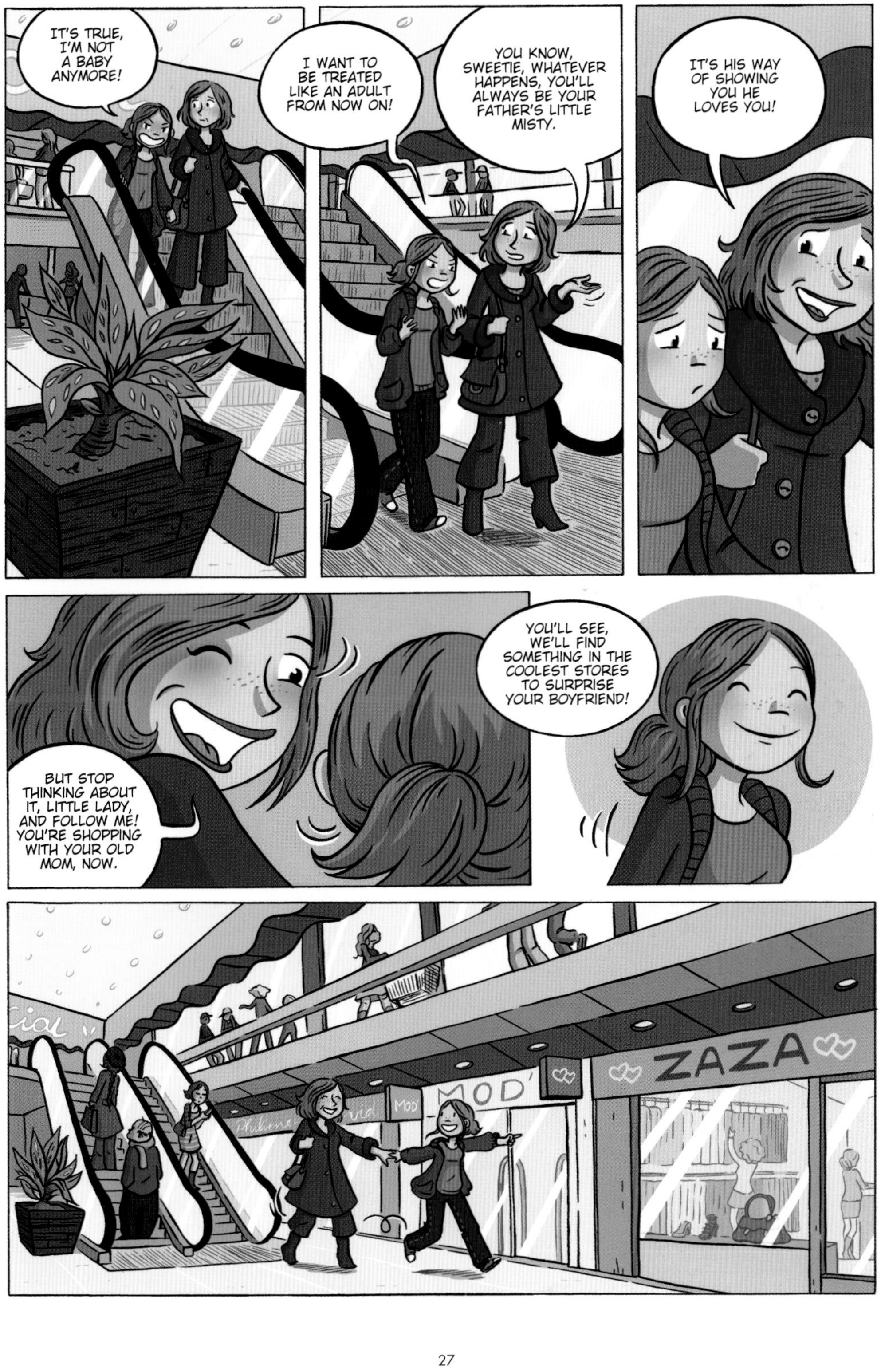
IT'S TRUE, I'M NOT A BABY ANYMORE!
I WANT TO BE TREATED LIKE AN ADULT FROM NOW ON!
YOU KNOW, SWEETIE, WHATEVER HAPPENS, YOU'LL ALWAYS BE YOUR FATHER'S LITTLE MISTY.
IT'S HIS WAY OF SHOWING YOU HE LOVES YOU!
BUT STOP THINKING ABOUT IT, LITTLE LADY, AND FOLLOW ME! YOU'RE SHOPPING WITH YOUR OLD MOM, NOW.
YOU'LL SEE, WE'LL FIND SOMETHING IN THE COOLEST STORES TO SURPRISE YOUR BOYFRIEND!
ZAZA
MOD'

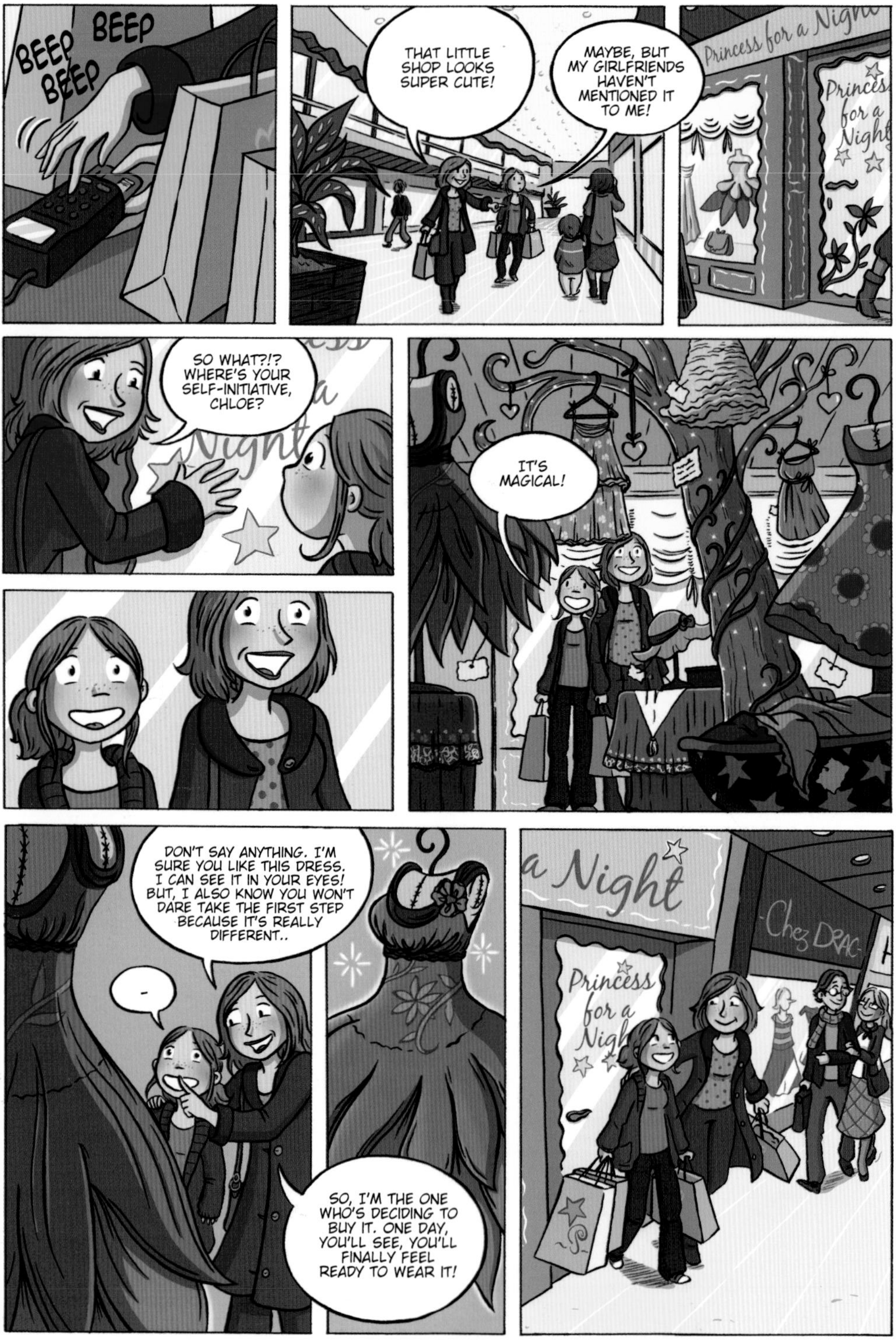
BEEP BEEP
BEEP BEEP
THAT LITTLE SHOP LOOKS SUPER CUTE!
MAYBE, BUT MY GIRLFRIENDS HAVEN'T MENTIONED IT TO ME!
Princess for a Night
Princess for a Night
SO WHAT?!? WHERE'S YOUR SELF-INITIATIVE, CHLOE?
IT'S MAGICAL!
DON'T SAY ANYTHING. I'M SURE YOU LIKE THIS DRESS. I CAN SEE IT IN YOUR EYES! BUT, I ALSO KNOW YOU WON'T DARE TAKE THE FIRST STEP BECAUSE IT'S REALLY DIFFERENT..
-
SO, I'M THE ONE WHO'S DECIDING TO BUY IT. ONE DAY, YOU'LL SEE, YOU'LL FINALLY FEEL READY TO WEAR IT!
a Night
Chez DRAC
Princess for a Night

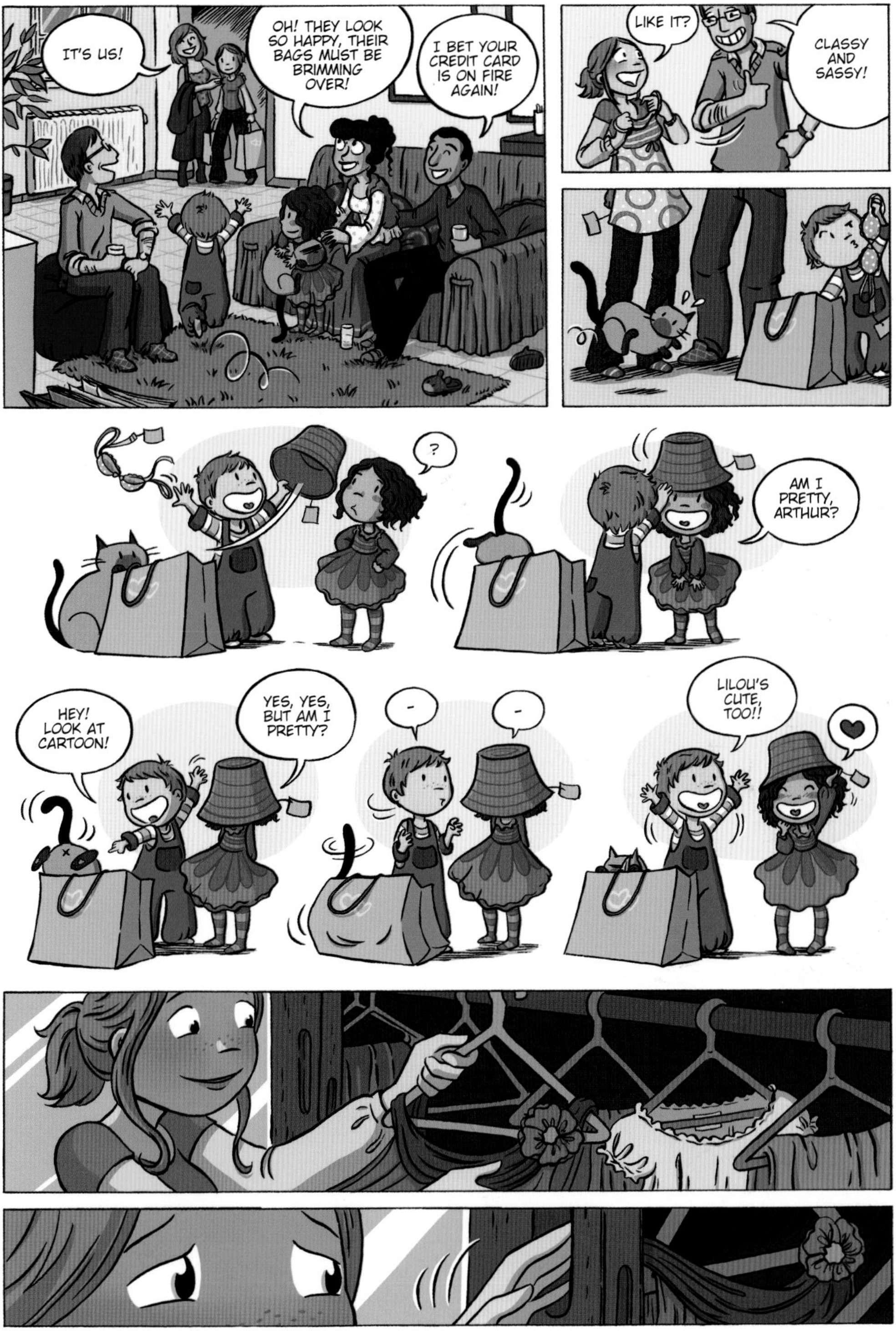
IT'S US!
OH! THEY LOOK SO HAPPY, THEIR BAGS MUST BE BRIMMING OVER!
I BET YOUR CREDIT CARD IS ON FIRE AGAIN!
LIKE IT?
CLASSY AND SASSY!
?
AM I PRETTY, ARTHUR?
HEY! LOOK AT CARTOON!
YES, YES, BUT AM I PRETTY?
-
-
LILOU'S CUTE, TOO!!

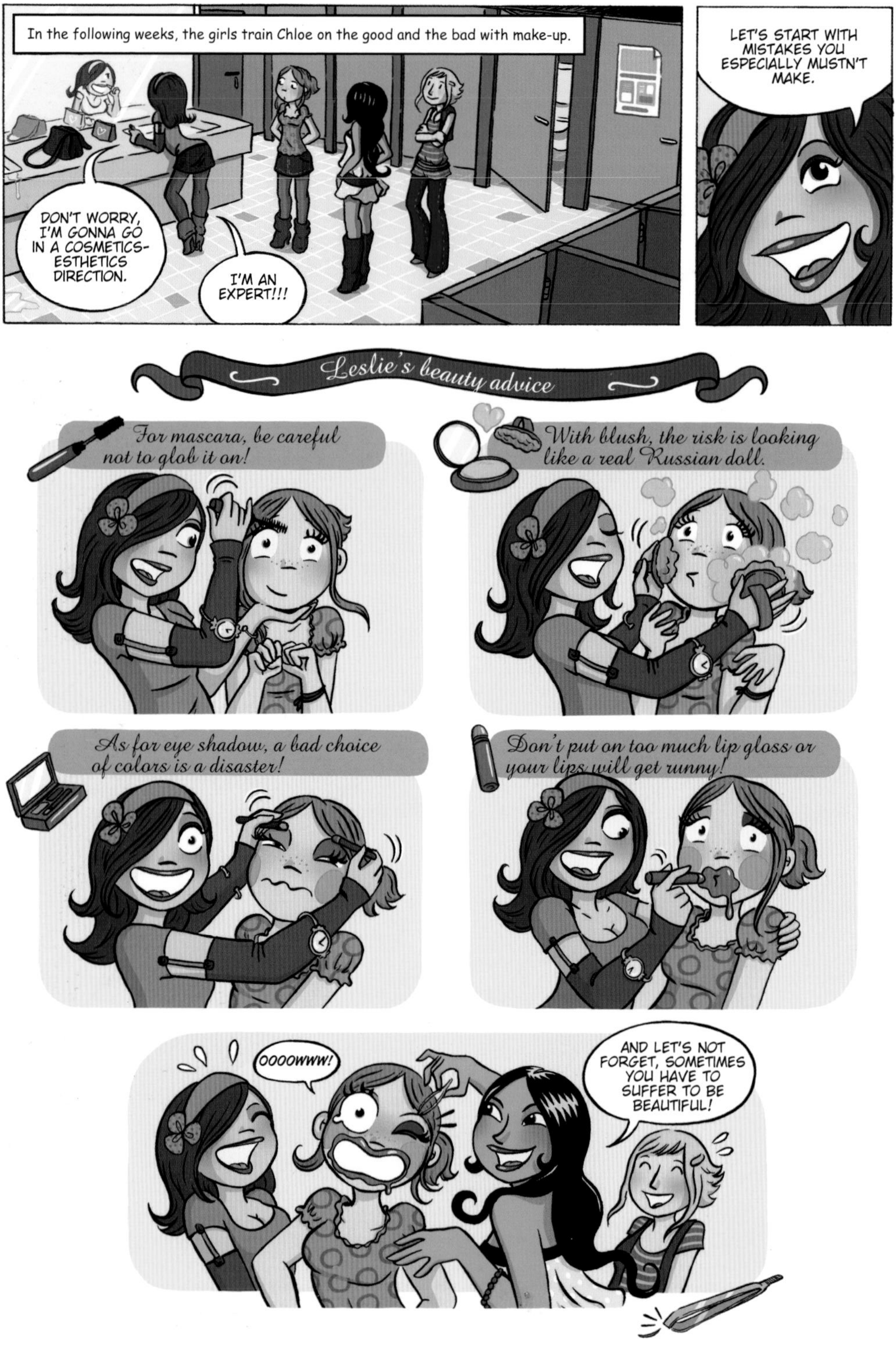
In the following weeks, the girls train Chloe on the good and the bad with make-up.
DON'T WORRY, I'M GONNA GO IN A COSMETICS-ESTHETICS DIRECTION.
I'M AN EXPERT!!!
LET'S START WITH MISTAKES YOU ESPECIALLY MUSTN'T MAKE.
Leslie's beauty advice
For mascara, be careful not to glob it on!
With blush, the risk is looking like a real Russian doll.
As for eye shadow, a bad choice of colors is a disaster!
Don't put on too much lip gloss or your lips will get runny!
OOOOWWW!
AND LET'S NOT FORGET, SOMETIMES YOU HAVE TO SUFFER TO BE BEAUTIFUL!

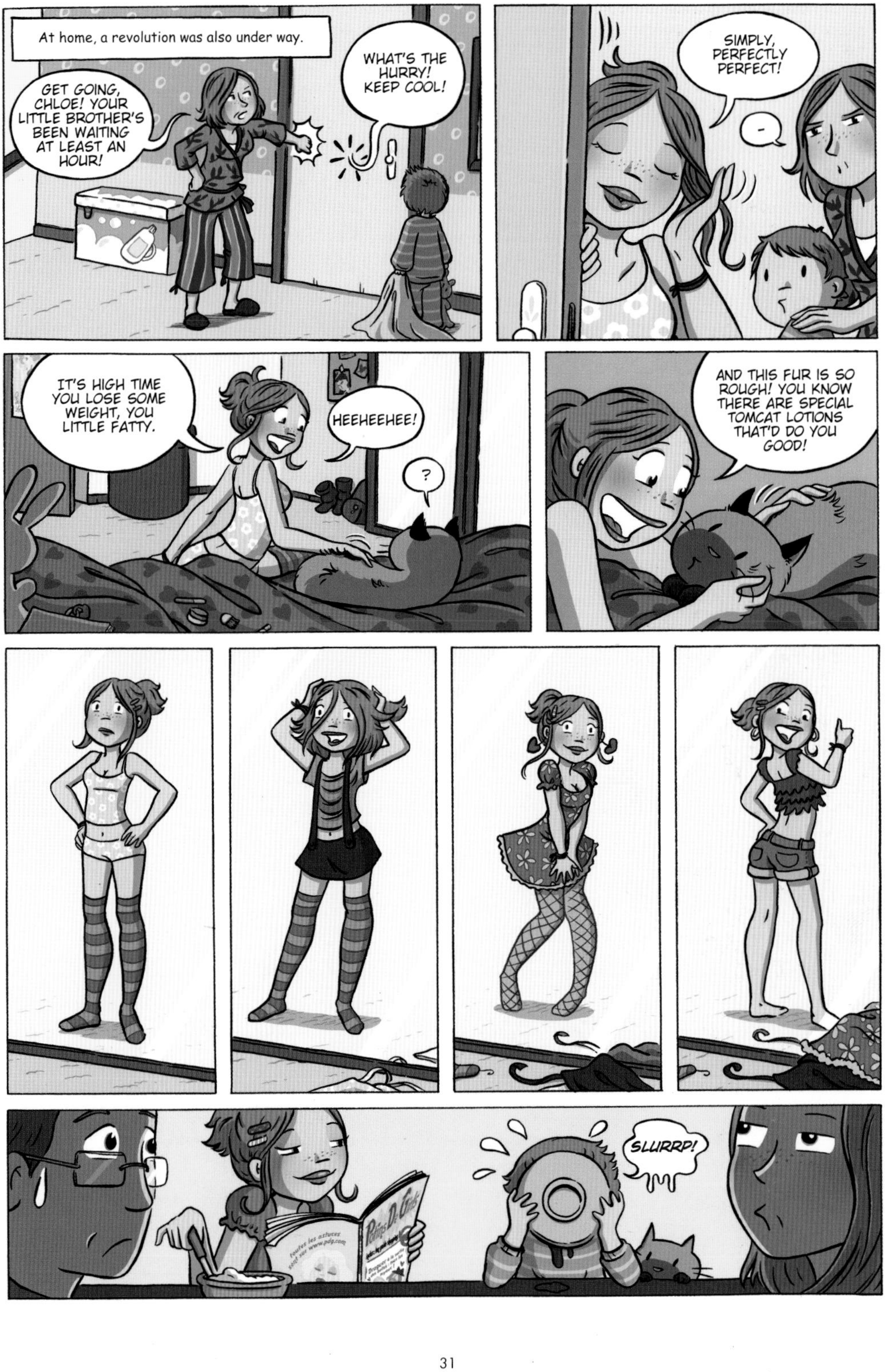
At home, a revolution was also under way.
GET GOING, CHLOE! YOUR LITTLE BROTHER'S BEEN WAITING AT LEAST AN HOUR!
WHAT'S THE HURRY! KEEP COOL!
SIMPLY, PERFECTLY PERFECT!
-
IT'S HIGH TIME YOU LOSE SOME WEIGHT, YOU LITTLE FATTY.
HEEHEEHEE!
?
AND THIS FUR IS SO ROUGH! YOU KNOW THERE ARE SPECIAL TOMCAT LOTIONS THAT'D DO YOU GOOD!
SLURRP!

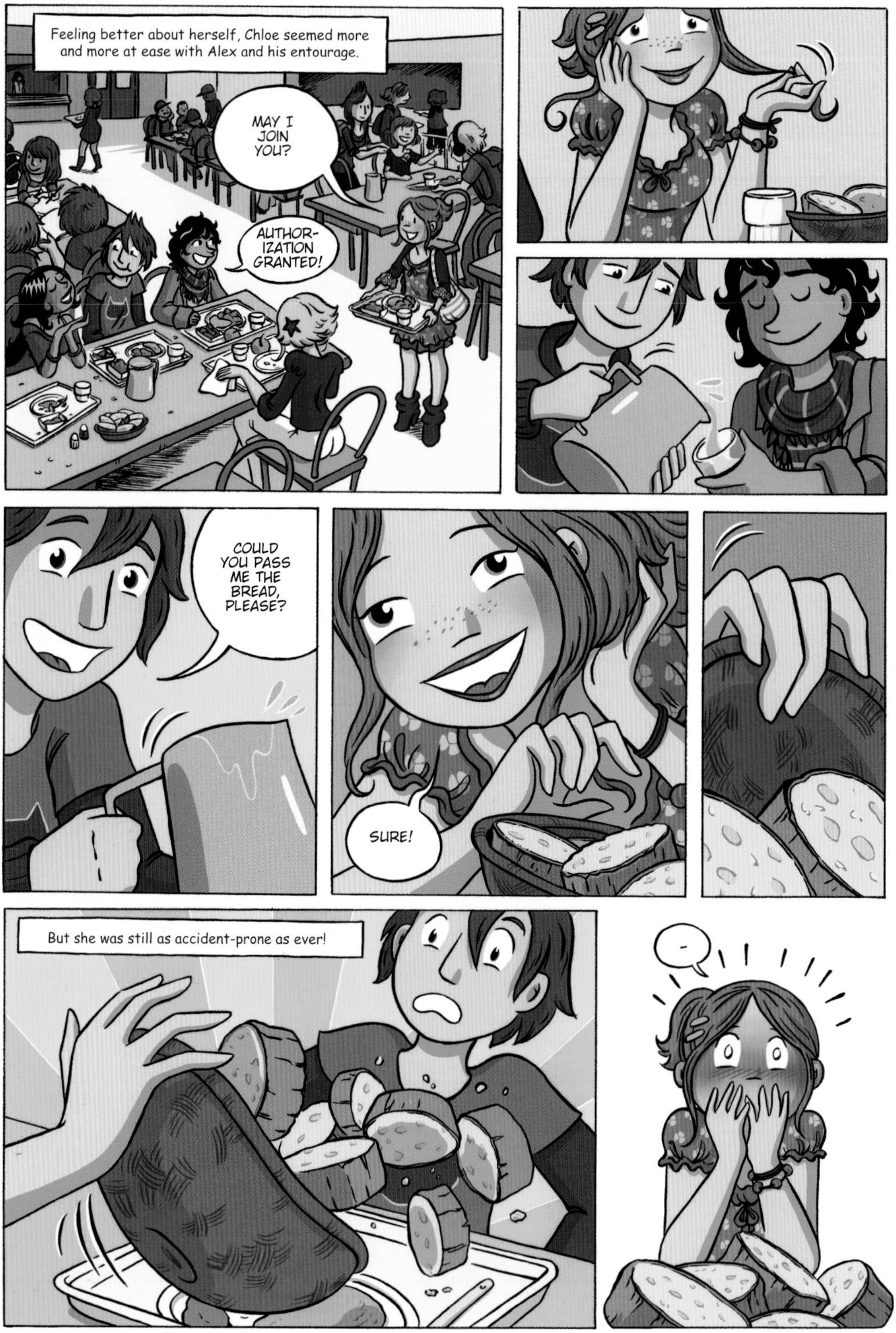
Feeling better about herself, Chloe seemed more and more at ease with Alex and his entourage.
MAY I JOIN YOU?
AUTHOR-IZATION GRANTED!
COULD YOU PASS ME THE BREAD, PLEASE?
SURE!
But she was still as accident-prone as ever!
-

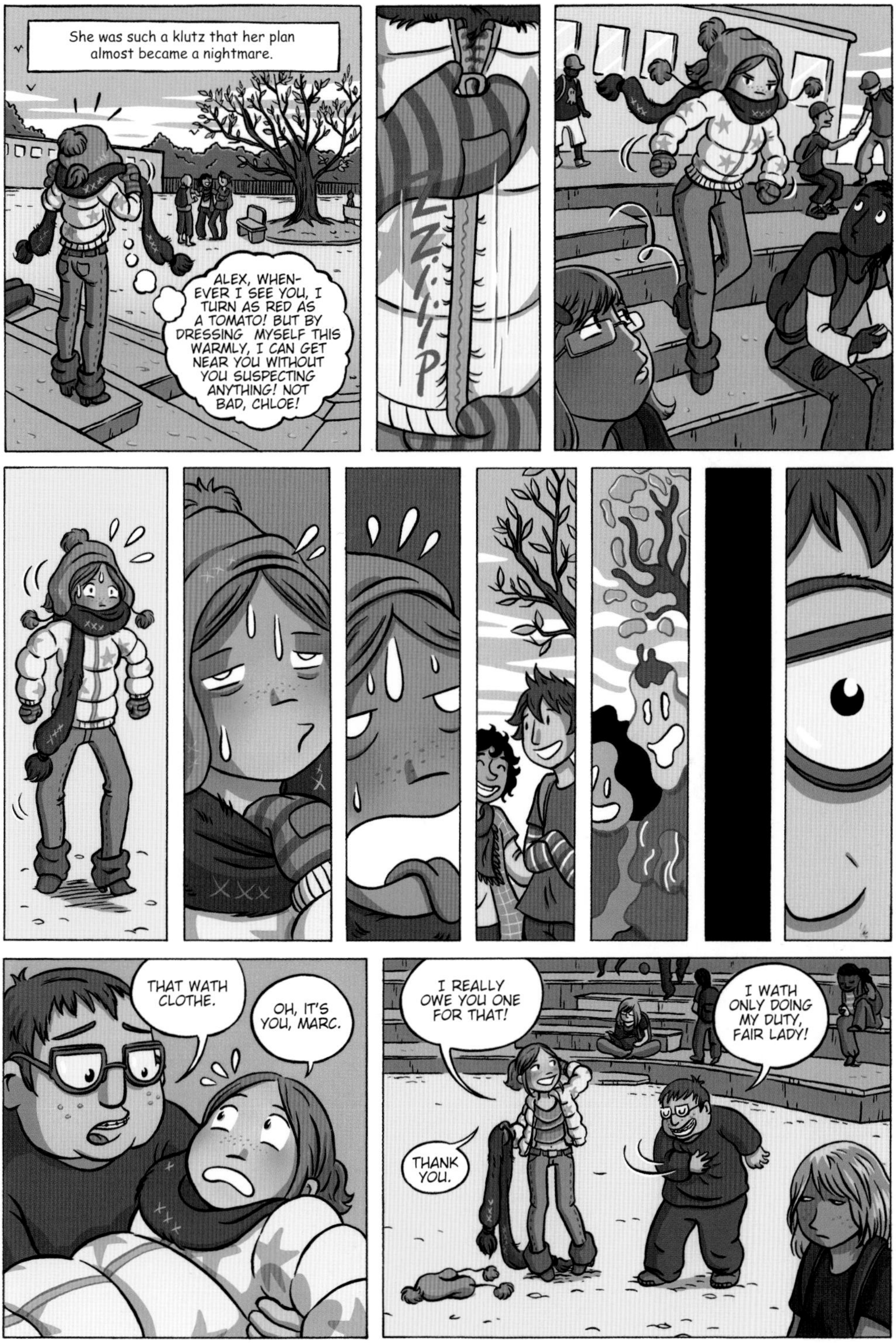
She was such a klutz that her plan almost became a nightmare.
ALEX, WHENEVER I SEE YOU, I TURN AS RED AS A TOMATO! BUT BY DRESSING MYSELF THIS WARMLY, I CAN GET NEAR YOU WITHOUT YOU SUSPECTING ANYTHING! NOT BAD, CHLOE!
ZZZIIIP
THAT WATH CLOTHE.
OH, IT'S YOU, MARC.
I REALLY OWE YOU ONE FOR THAT!
THANK YOU.
I WATH ONLY DOING MY DUTY, FAIR LADY!

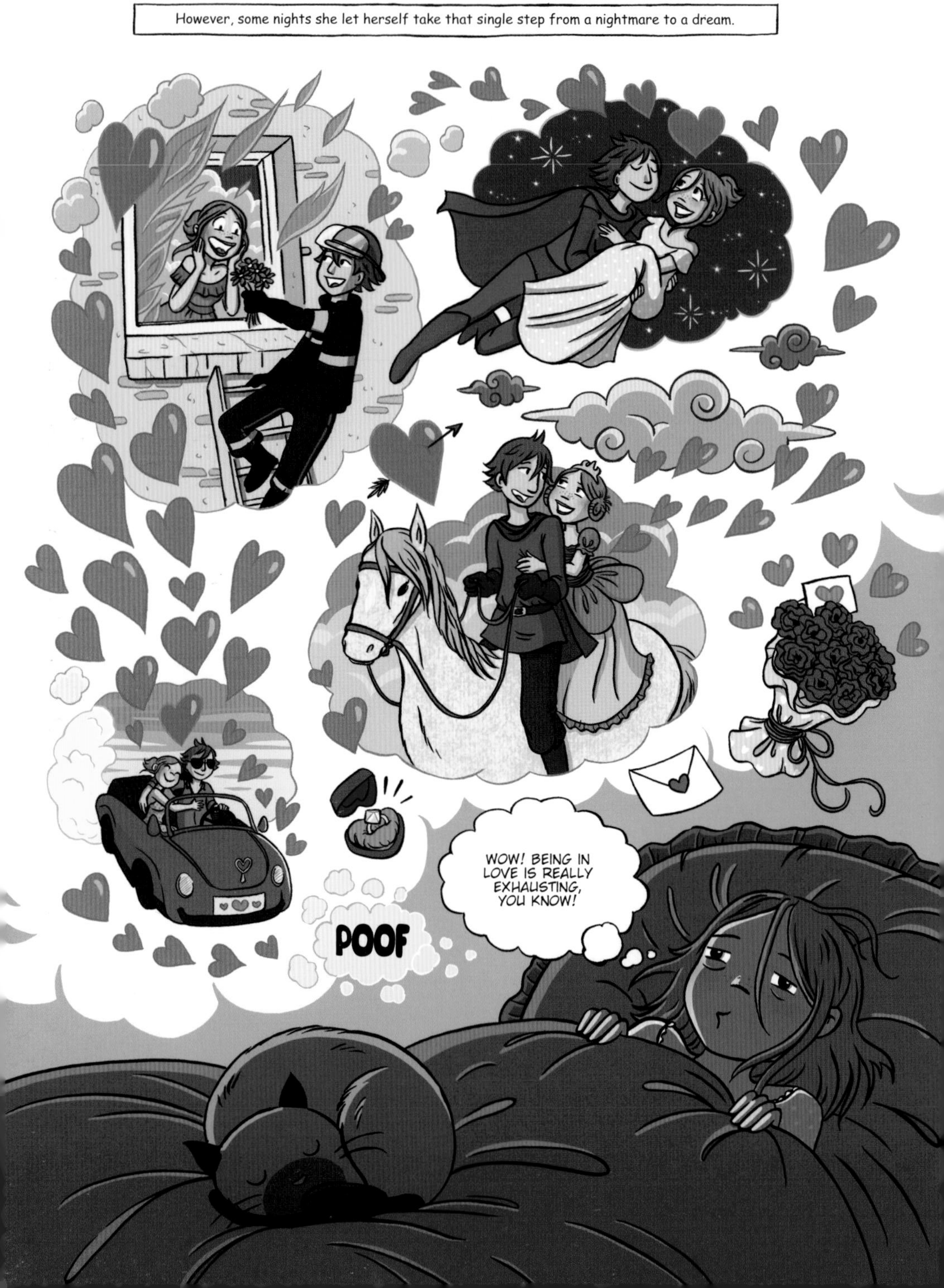
However, some nights she let herself take that single step from a nightmare to a dream.
WOW! BEING IN LOVE IS REALLY EXHAUSTING, YOU KNOW!
POOF

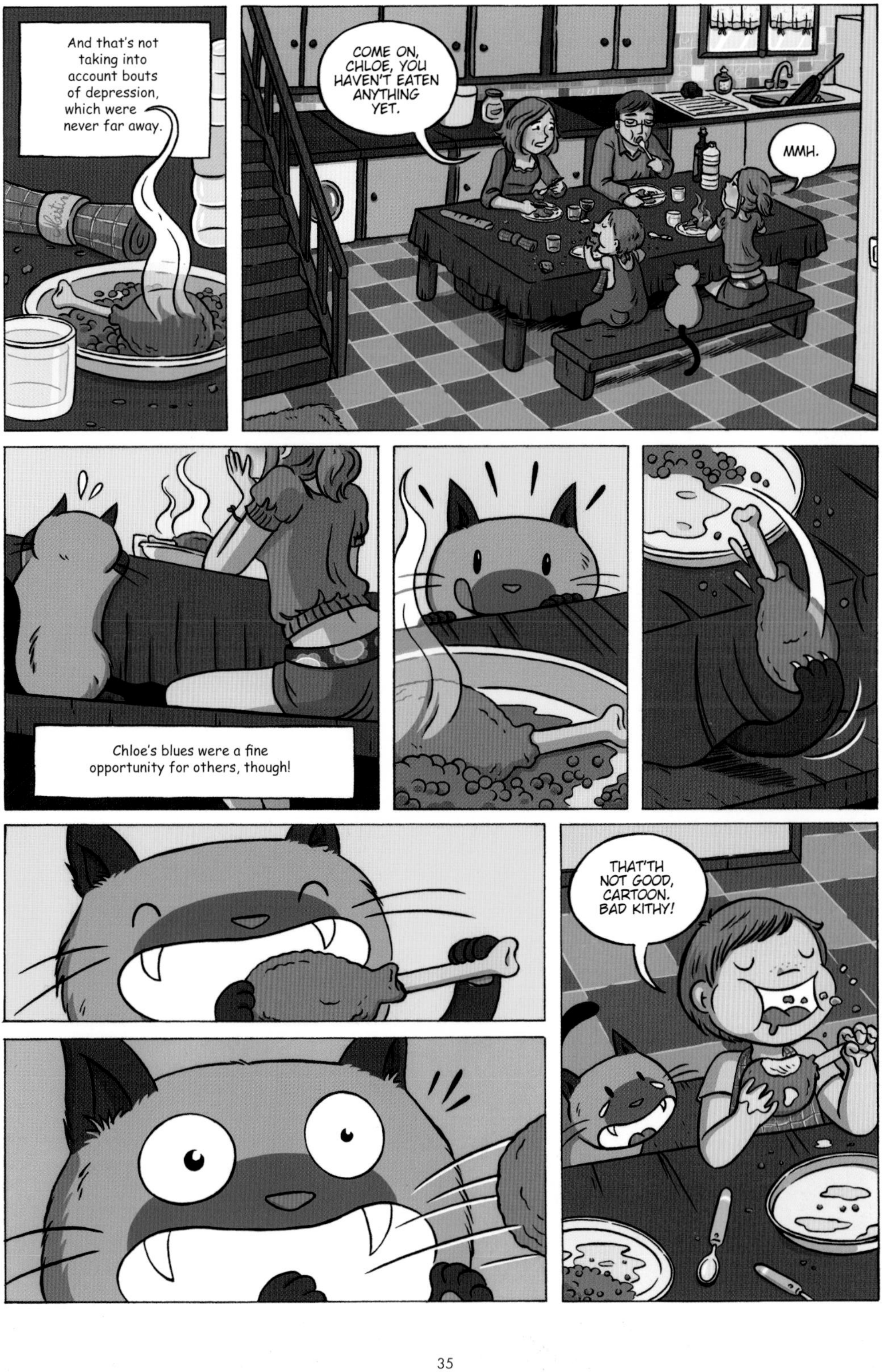
And that's not taking into account bouts of depression, which were never far away.
COME ON, CHLOE, YOU HAVEN'T EATEN ANYTHING YET.
MMH.
Chloe's blues were a fine opportunity for others, though!
THAT'TH NOT GOOD, CARTOON. BAD KITHY!

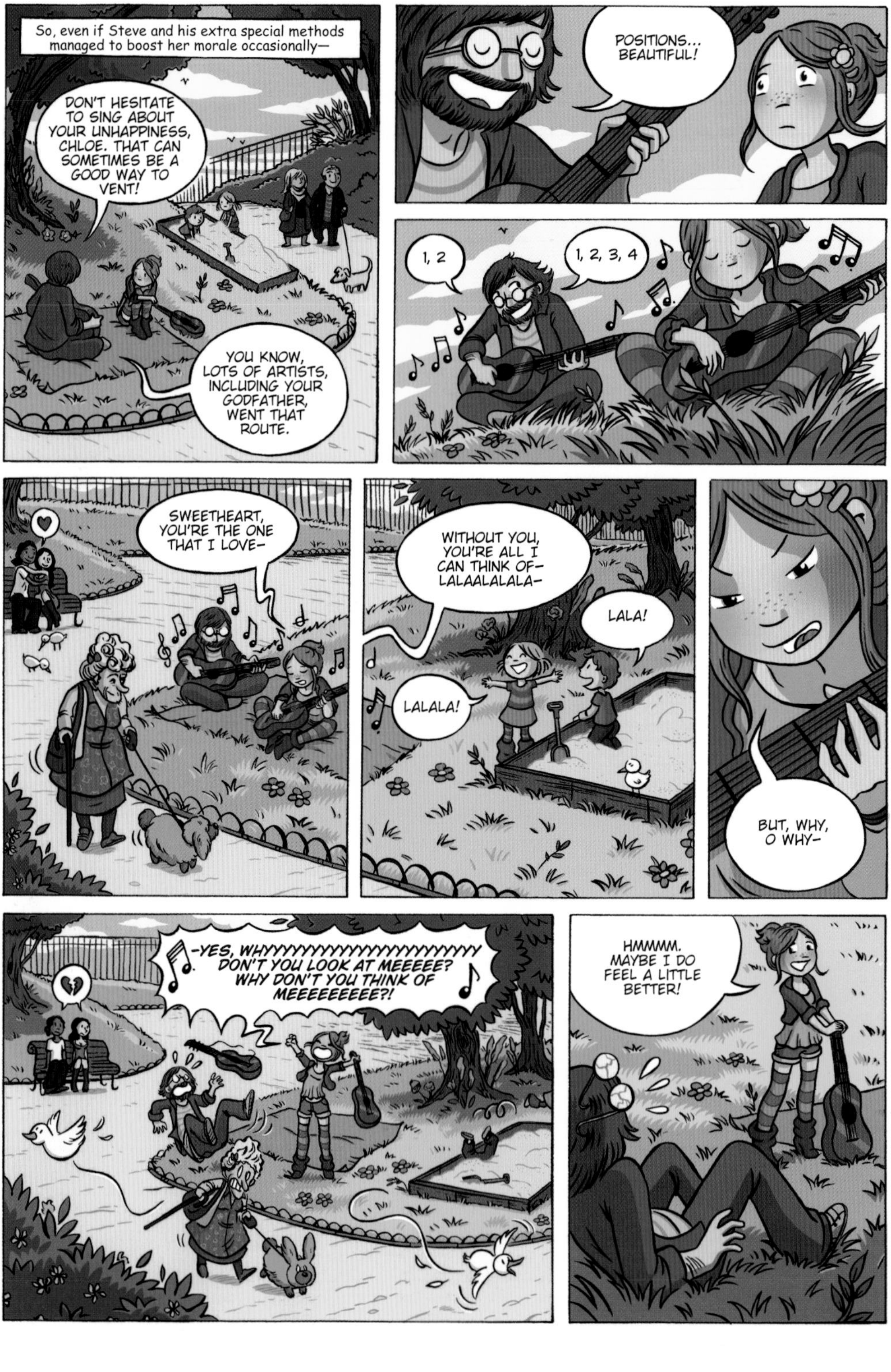
So, even if Steve and his extra special methods managed to boost her morale occasionally—
DON'T HESITATE TO SING ABOUT YOUR UNHAPPINESS, CHLOE. THAT CAN SOMETIMES BE A GOOD WAY TO VENT!
YOU KNOW, LOTS OF ARTISTS, INCLUDING YOUR GODFATHER, WENT THAT ROUTE.
POSITIONS... BEAUTIFUL!
1, 2
1, 2, 3, 4
SWEETHEART, YOU'RE THE ONE THAT I LOVE-
WITHOUT YOU, YOU'RE ALL I CAN THINK OF- LALAALALALA-
LALA!
LALALA!
BUT, WHY, O WHY-
-YES, WHYYYYYYYYYYYYYYYYYYYYYYYYY DON'T YOU LOOK AT MEEEEE? WHY DON'T YOU THINK OF MEEEEEEEEE?!
HMMMM. MAYBE I DO FEEL A LITTLE BETTER!

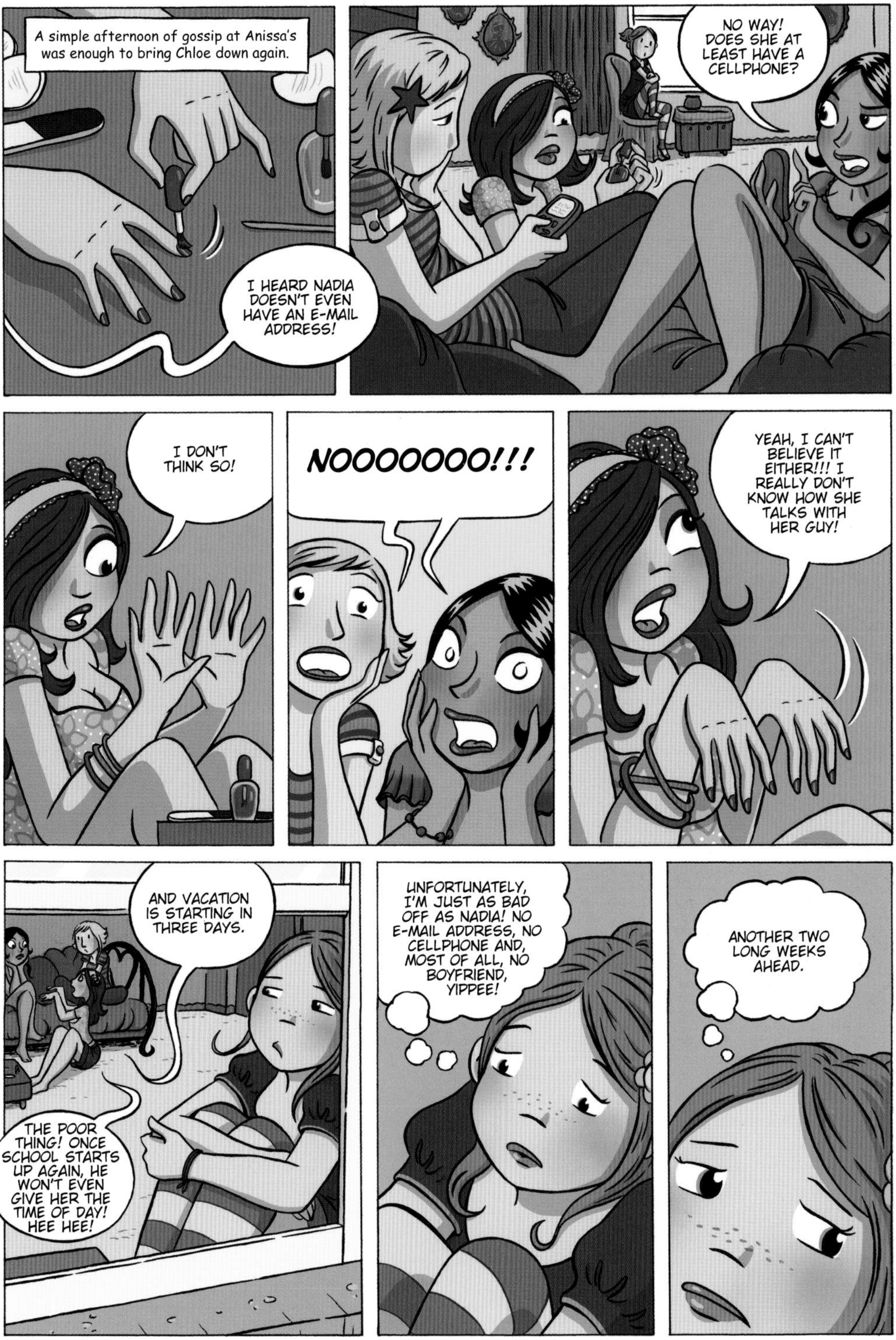
A simple afternoon of gossip at Anissa's was enough to bring Chloe down again.
I HEARD NADIA DOESN'T EVEN HAVE AN E-MAIL ADDRESS!
NO WAY! DOES SHE AT LEAST HAVE A CELLPHONE?
I DON'T THINK SO!
NOOOOOOO!!!
YEAH, I CAN'T BELIEVE IT EITHER!!! I REALLY DON'T KNOW HOW SHE TALKS WITH HER GUY!
AND VACATION IS STARTING IN THREE DAYS.
THE POOR THING! ONCE SCHOOL STARTS UP AGAIN, HE WON'T EVEN GIVE HER THE TIME OF DAY! HEE HEE!
UNFORTUNATELY, I'M JUST AS BAD OFF AS NADIA! NO E-MAIL ADDRESS, NO CELLPHONE AND, MOST OF ALL, NO BOYFRIEND, YIPPEE!
ANOTHER TWO LONG WEEKS AHEAD.

Report Card

2nd Quarter

BLIN, Chloe or "Misty"

- Eighth Grade, Group C -

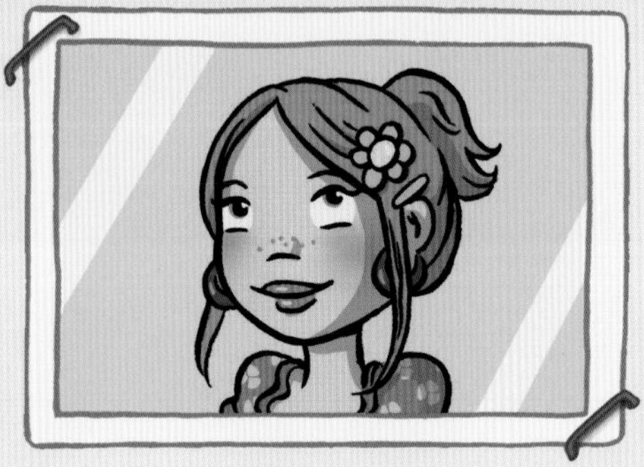

Subjects	Student Grade Averages	Suggestions for Improvement
Appearance	B	Truly invested. But be careful not to worry too much over it, or else you won't know which way to turn!
Self-confidence	C	Even with highs and lows in succession, good instances of taking the initiative are to be noted. Encouraging.
Observation Skills	A	Continued interest in the material. Good job.
Attractiveness	B	Doing better. Motivated to participate.
Popularity	C	Keep going, success is at the end of the road.
Average for This Period	B	

General Comments:

Chloe made notable progress this quarter. She's undeniably more comfortable with herself. Readers are aware of that and support her.

Notification: this grade report is the original copy and must be preserved,

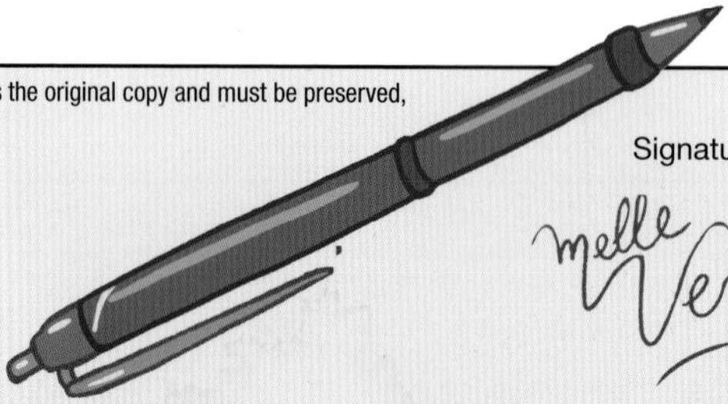

Signature of the home room teacher:

Melle Vernier

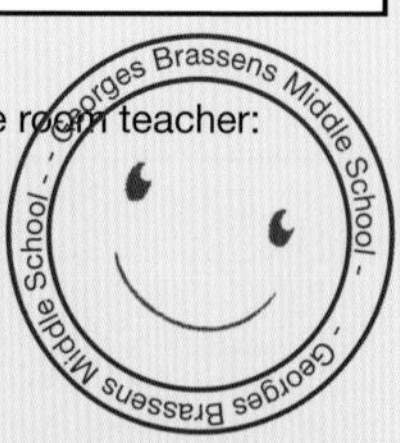
- Georges Brassens Middle School - Georges Brassens Middle School -

3rd Quarter
"Adventure mode"
engaged

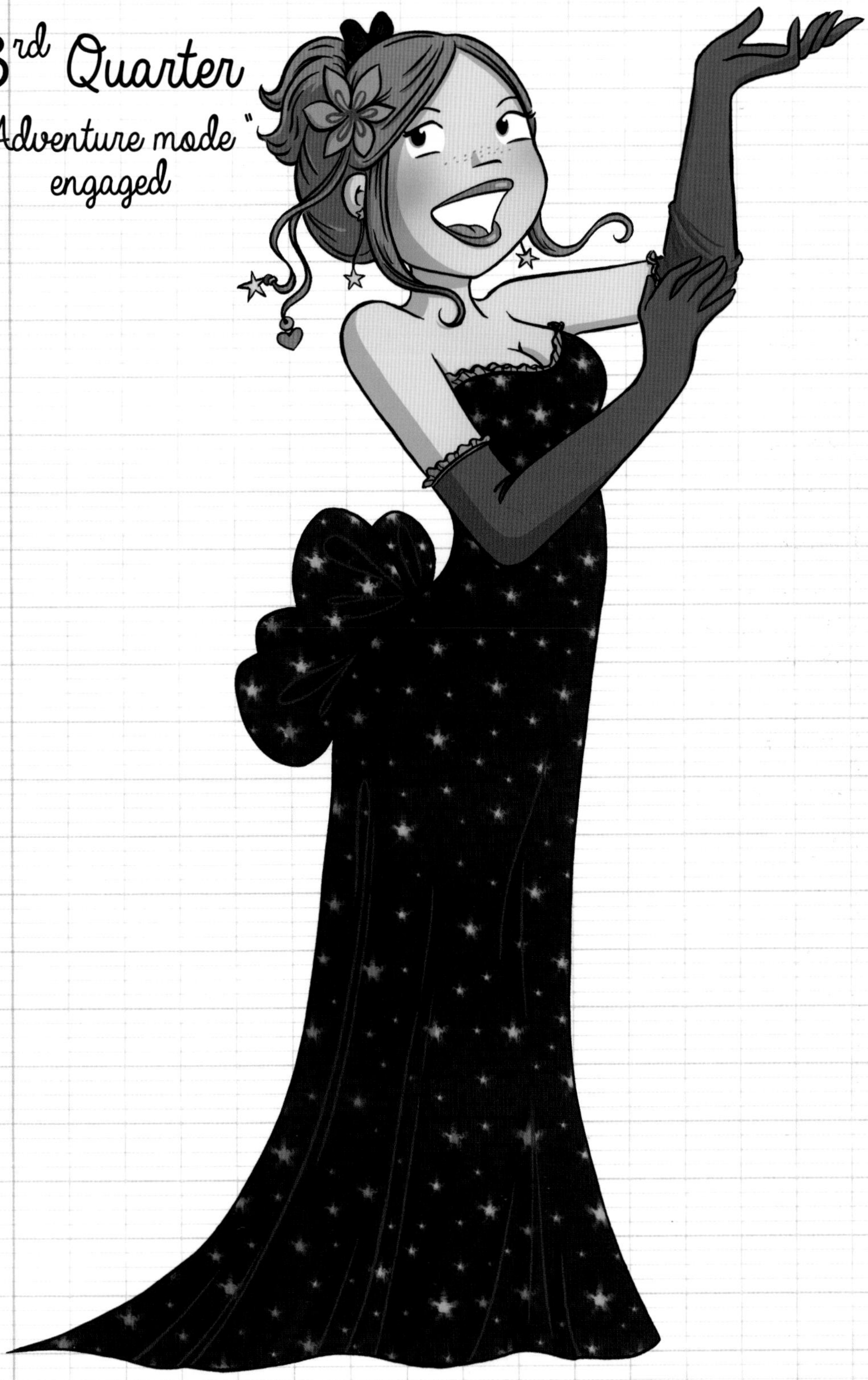

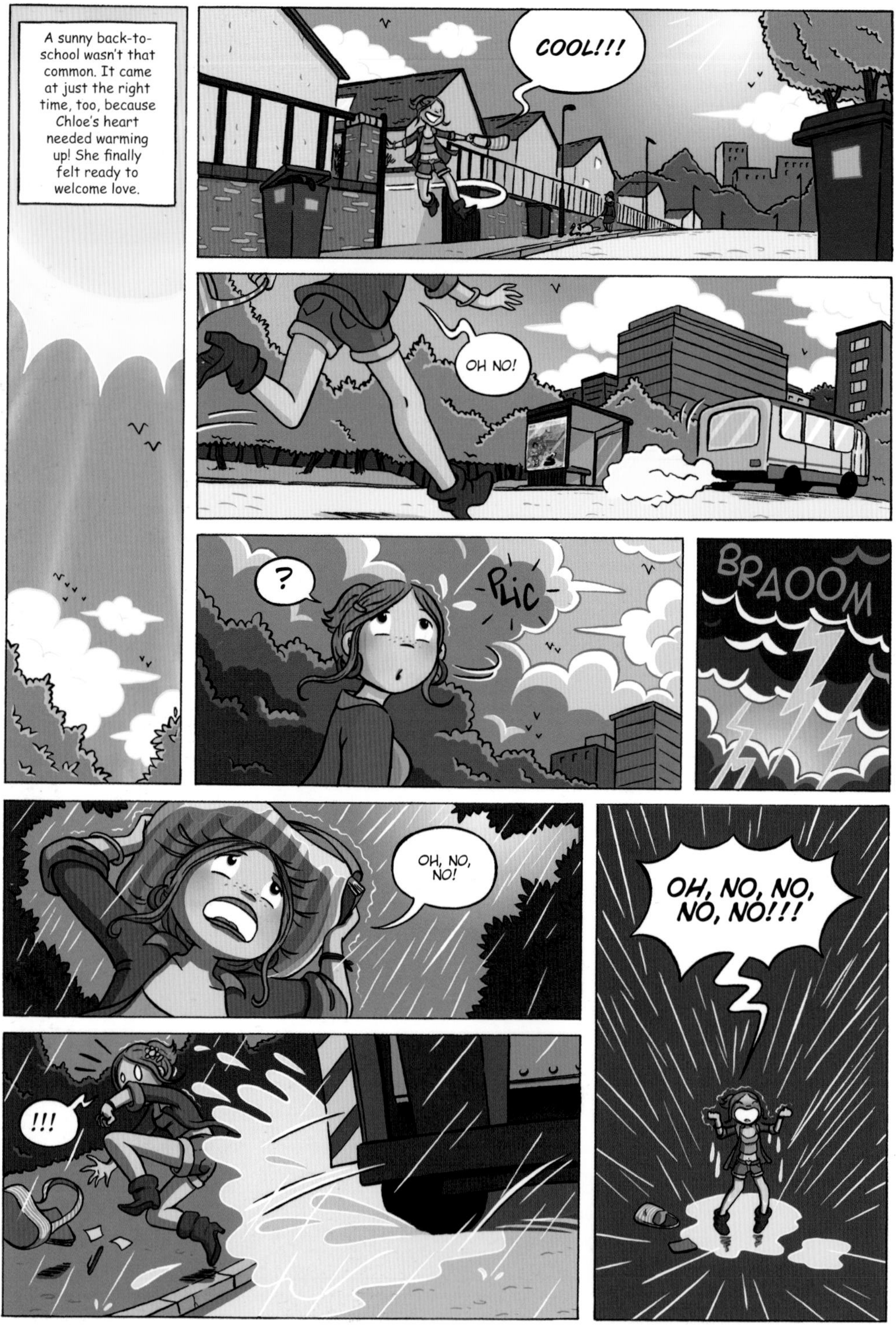
A sunny back-to-school wasn't that common. It came at just the right time, too, because Chloe's heart needed warming up! She finally felt ready to welcome love.
COOL!!!
OH NO!
?
PLIC
BRAOOM
OH, NO, NO!
OH, NO, NO, NO, NO!!!
!!!

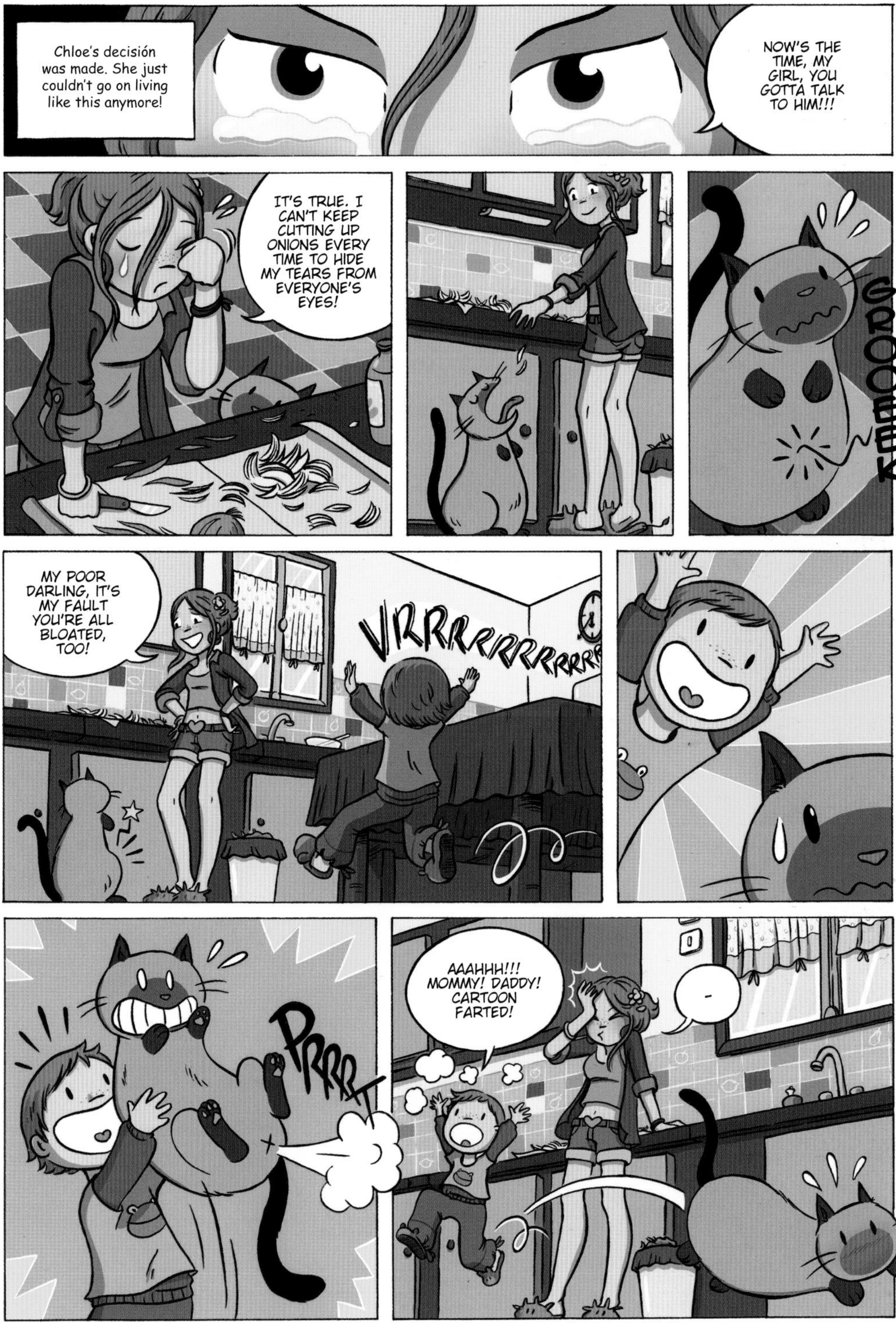
Chloe's decisión was made. She just couldn't go on living like this anymore!
NOW'S THE TIME, MY GIRL, YOU GOTTA TALK TO HIM!!!
IT'S TRUE. I CAN'T KEEP CUTTING UP ONIONS EVERY TIME TO HIDE MY TEARS FROM EVERYONE'S EYES!
GROOEEK
MY POOR DARLING, IT'S MY FAULT YOU'RE ALL BLOATED, TOO!
VRRRRRRRRRRRRR
PRRRT
AAAHHH!!! MOMMY! DADDY! CARTOON FARTED!
-

WARNING: DON'T EVER FEED CATS ***ONIONS,*** ITS TOXIC FOR CATS.

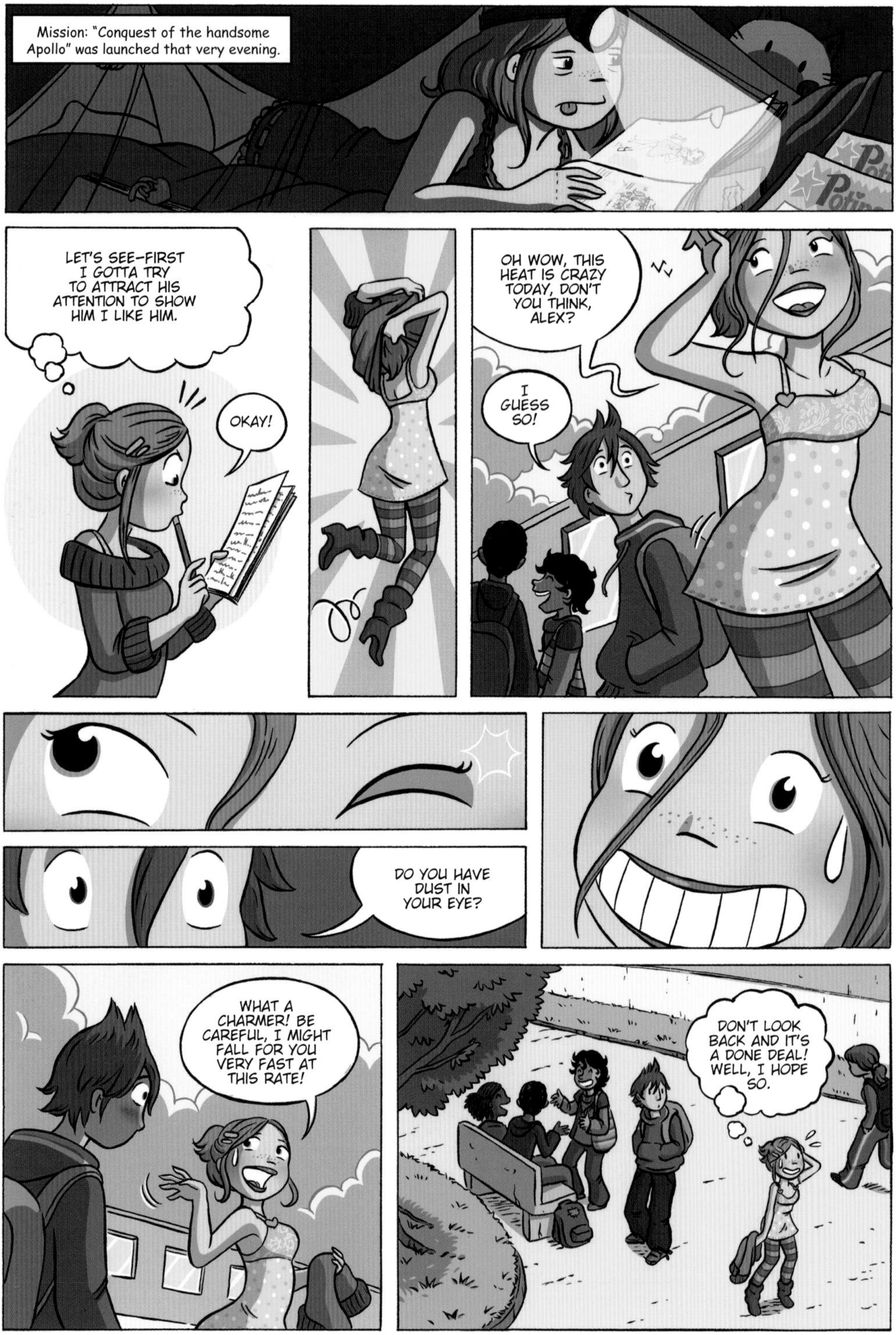

Mission: "Conquest of the handsome Apollo" was launched that very evening.
LET'S SEE-FIRST I GOTTA TRY TO ATTRACT HIS ATTENTION TO SHOW HIM I LIKE HIM.
OKAY!
OH WOW, THIS HEAT IS CRAZY TODAY, DON'T YOU THINK, ALEX?
I GUESS SO!
DO YOU HAVE DUST IN YOUR EYE?
WHAT A CHARMER! BE CAREFUL, I MIGHT FALL FOR YOU VERY FAST AT THIS RATE!
DON'T LOOK BACK AND IT'S A DONE DEAL! WELL, I HOPE SO.

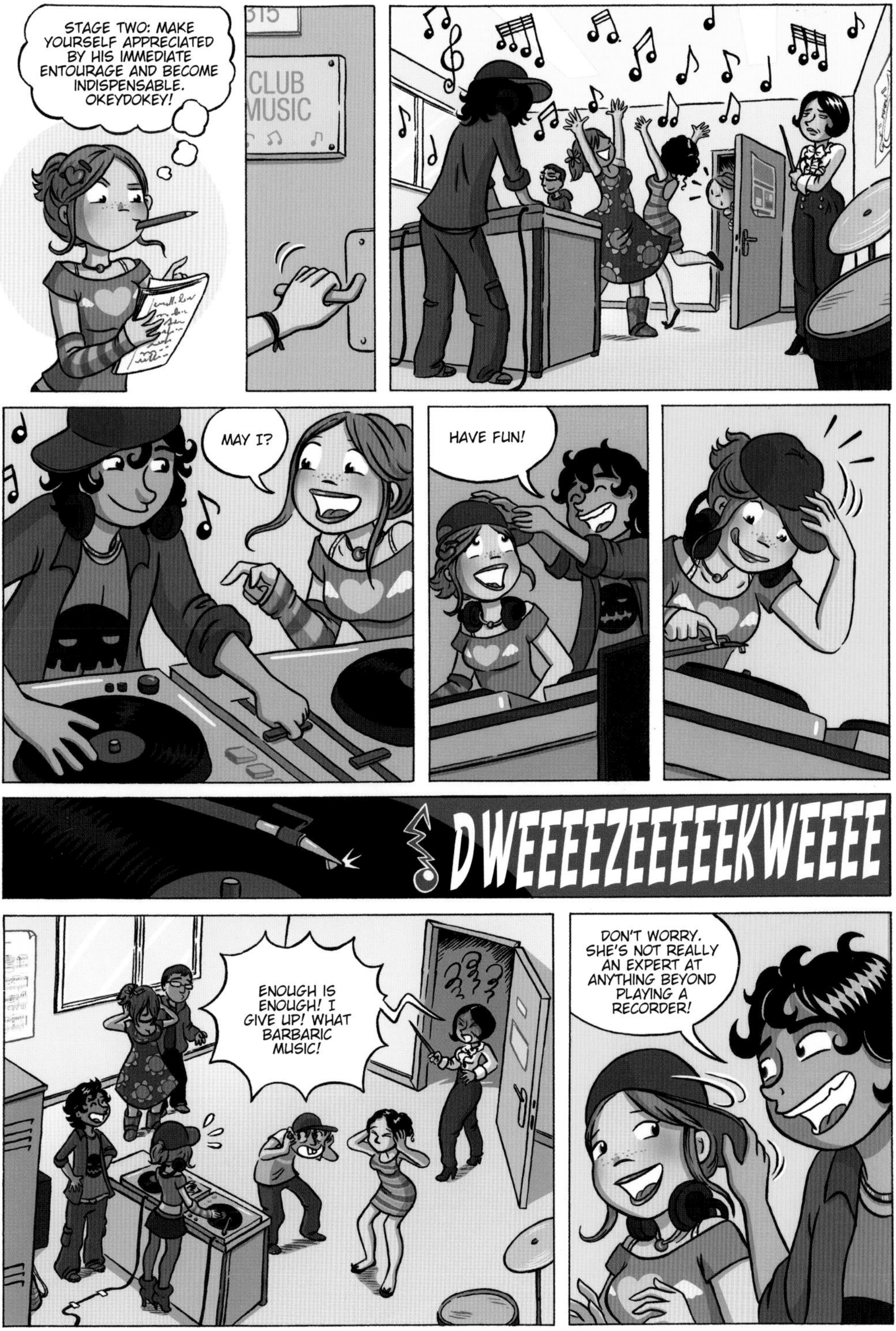

STAGE TWO: MAKE YOURSELF APPRECIATED BY HIS IMMEDIATE ENTOURAGE AND BECOME INDISPENSABLE. OKEYDOKEY!
315
CLUB MUSIC
MAY I?
HAVE FUN!
DWEEEZEEEEKWEEEE
ENOUGH IS ENOUGH! I GIVE UP! WHAT BARBARIC MUSIC!
DON'T WORRY. SHE'S NOT REALLY AN EXPERT AT ANYTHING BEYOND PLAYING A RECORDER!

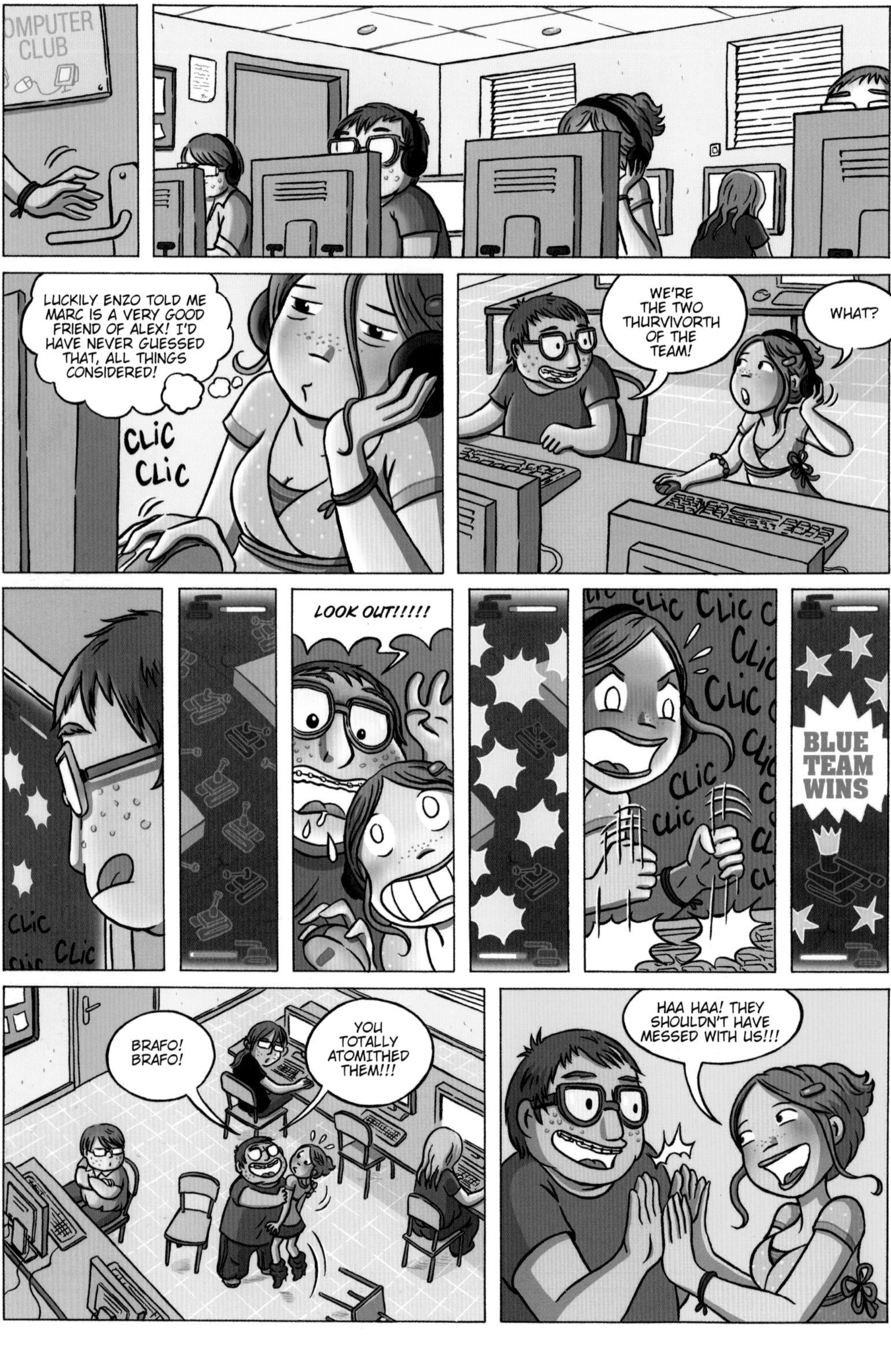
COMPUTER CLUB
LUCKILY ENZO TOLD ME MARC IS A VERY GOOD FRIEND OF ALEX! I'D HAVE NEVER GUESSED THAT, ALL THINGS CONSIDERED!
CLIC CLIC
WE'RE THE TWO THURVIVORTH OF THE TEAM!
WHAT?
CLIC CLIC
LOOK OUT!!!!!
CLIC CLIC CLIC CLIC CLIC CLIC CLIC CLIC
BLUE TEAM WINS
BRAFO! BRAFO!
YOU TOTALLY ATOMITHED THEM!!!
HAA HAA! THEY SHOULDN'T HAVE MESSED WITH US!!!

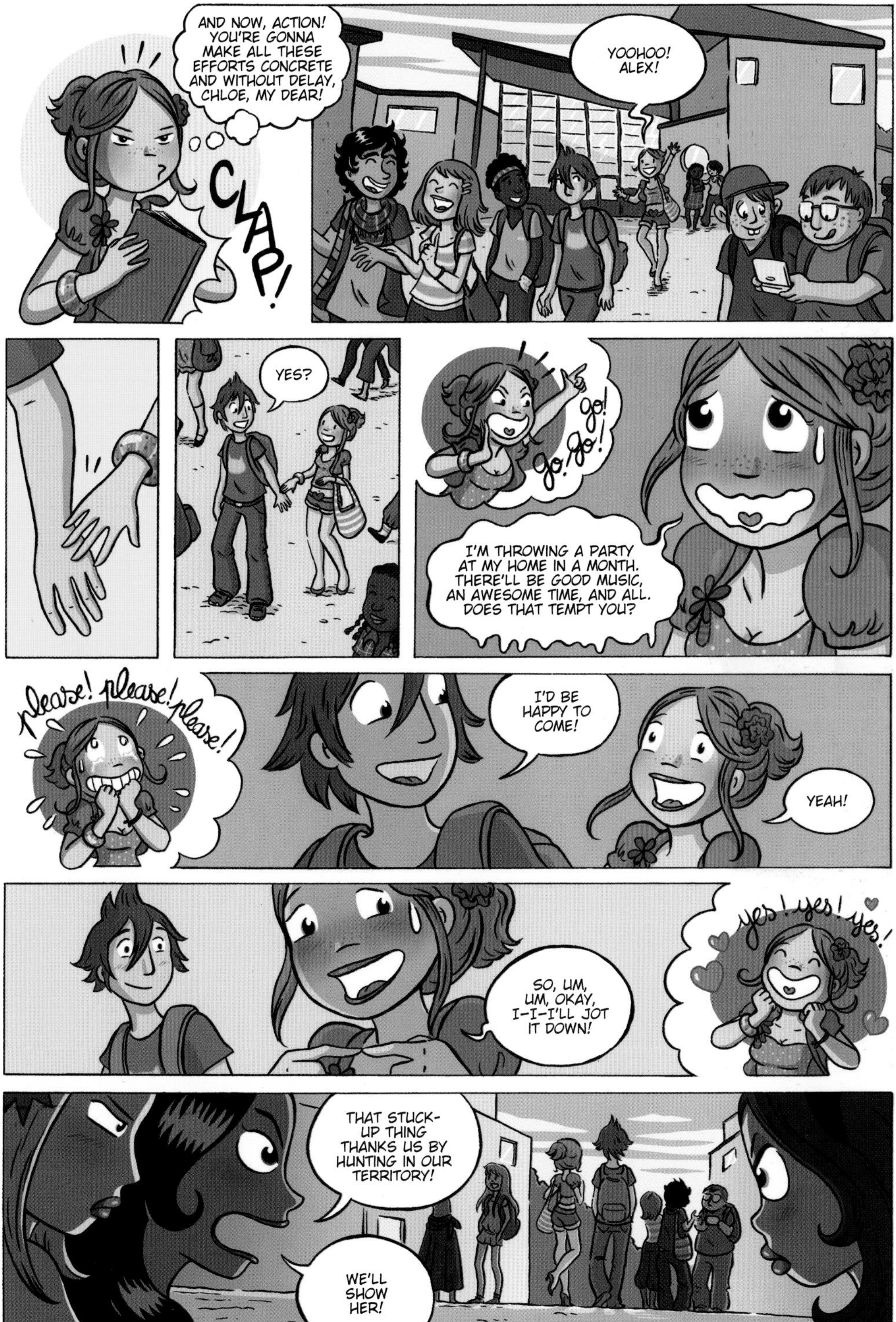
AND NOW, ACTION! YOU'RE GONNA MAKE ALL THESE EFFORTS CONCRETE AND WITHOUT DELAY, CHLOE, MY DEAR!
CLAP!
YOOHOO! ALEX!
YES?
GO! GO! GO!
I'M THROWING A PARTY AT MY HOME IN A MONTH. THERE'LL BE GOOD MUSIC, AN AWESOME TIME, AND ALL. DOES THAT TEMPT YOU?
please! please! please!
I'D BE HAPPY TO COME!
YEAH!
SO, UM, UM, OKAY, I-I-I'LL JOT IT DOWN!
yes! yes! yes!
THAT STUCK-UP THING THANKS US BY HUNTING IN OUR TERRITORY!
WE'LL SHOW HER!

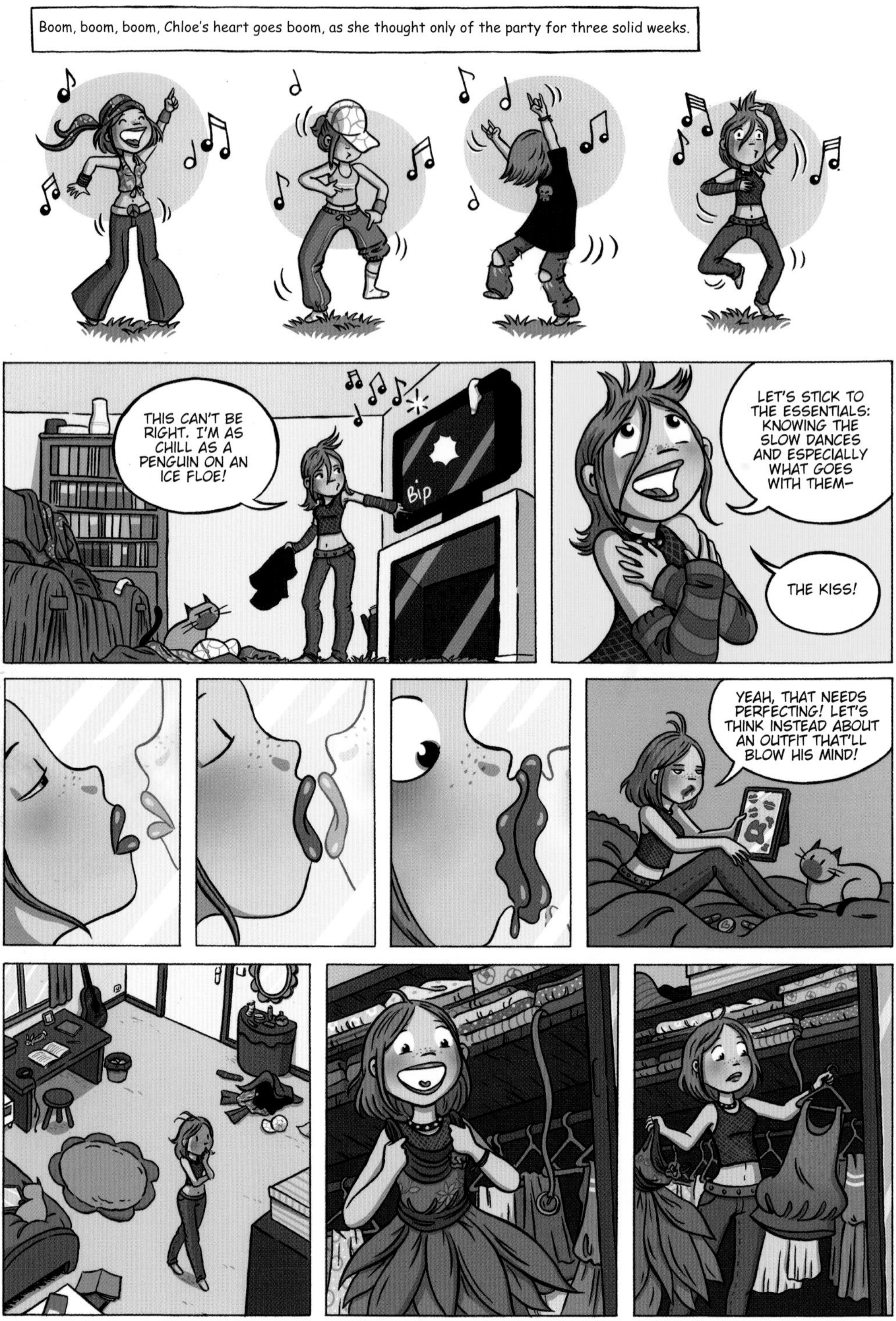
Boom, boom, boom, Chloe's heart goes boom, as she thought only of the party for three solid weeks.
THIS CAN'T BE RIGHT. I'M AS CHILL AS A PENGUIN ON AN ICE FLOE!
Bip
LET'S STICK TO THE ESSENTIALS: KNOWING THE SLOW DANCES AND ESPECIALLY WHAT GOES WITH THEM—
THE KISS!
YEAH, THAT NEEDS PERFECTING! LET'S THINK INSTEAD ABOUT AN OUTFIT THAT'LL BLOW HIS MIND!

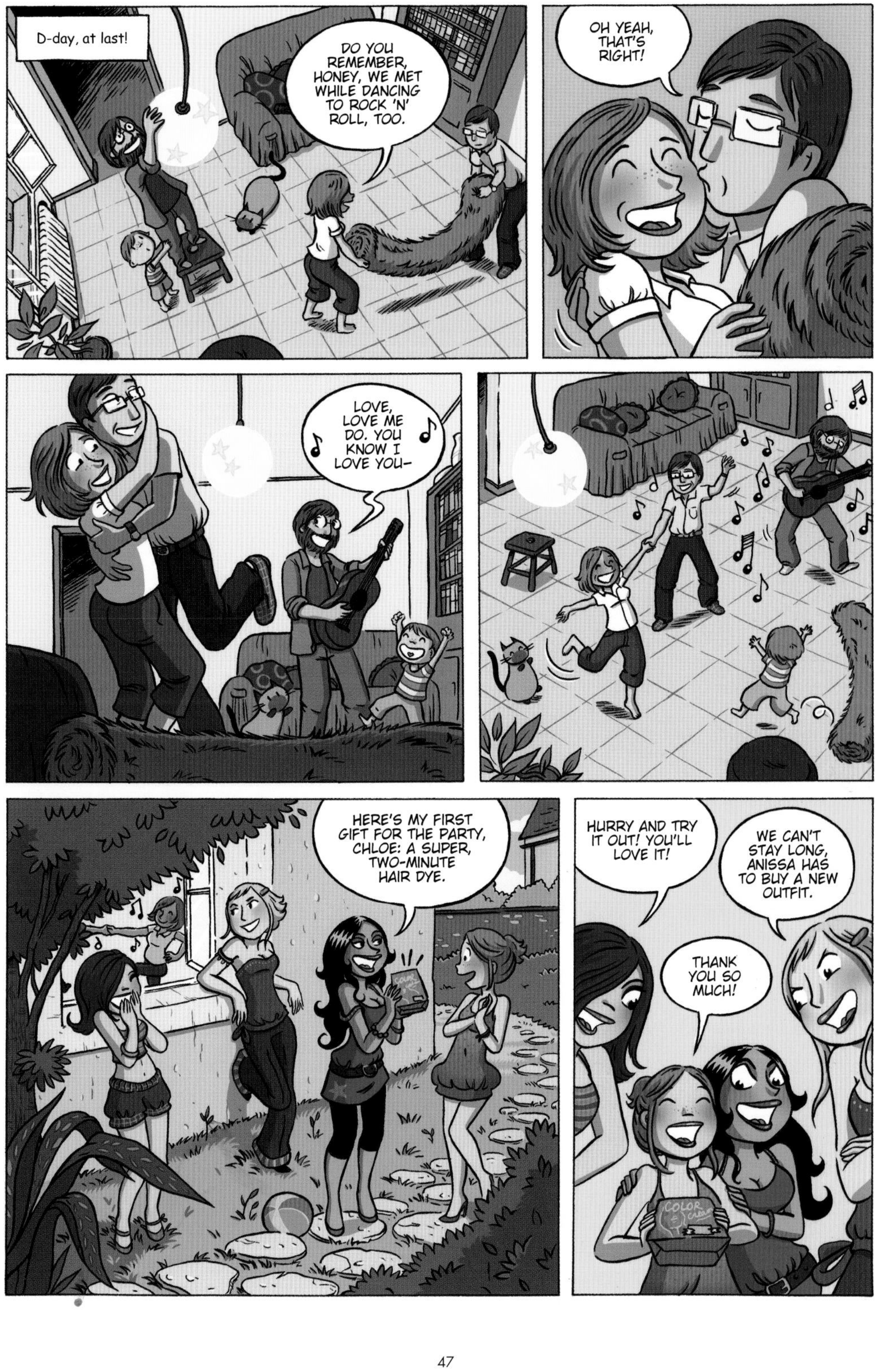
D-day, at last!
DO YOU REMEMBER, HONEY, WE MET WHILE DANCING TO ROCK 'N' ROLL, TOO.
OH YEAH, THAT'S RIGHT!
LOVE, LOVE ME DO. YOU KNOW I LOVE YOU–
HERE'S MY FIRST GIFT FOR THE PARTY, CHLOE: A SUPER, TWO-MINUTE HAIR DYE.
HURRY AND TRY IT OUT! YOU'LL LOVE IT!
WE CAN'T STAY LONG, ANISSA HAS TO BUY A NEW OUTFIT.
THANK YOU SO MUCH!

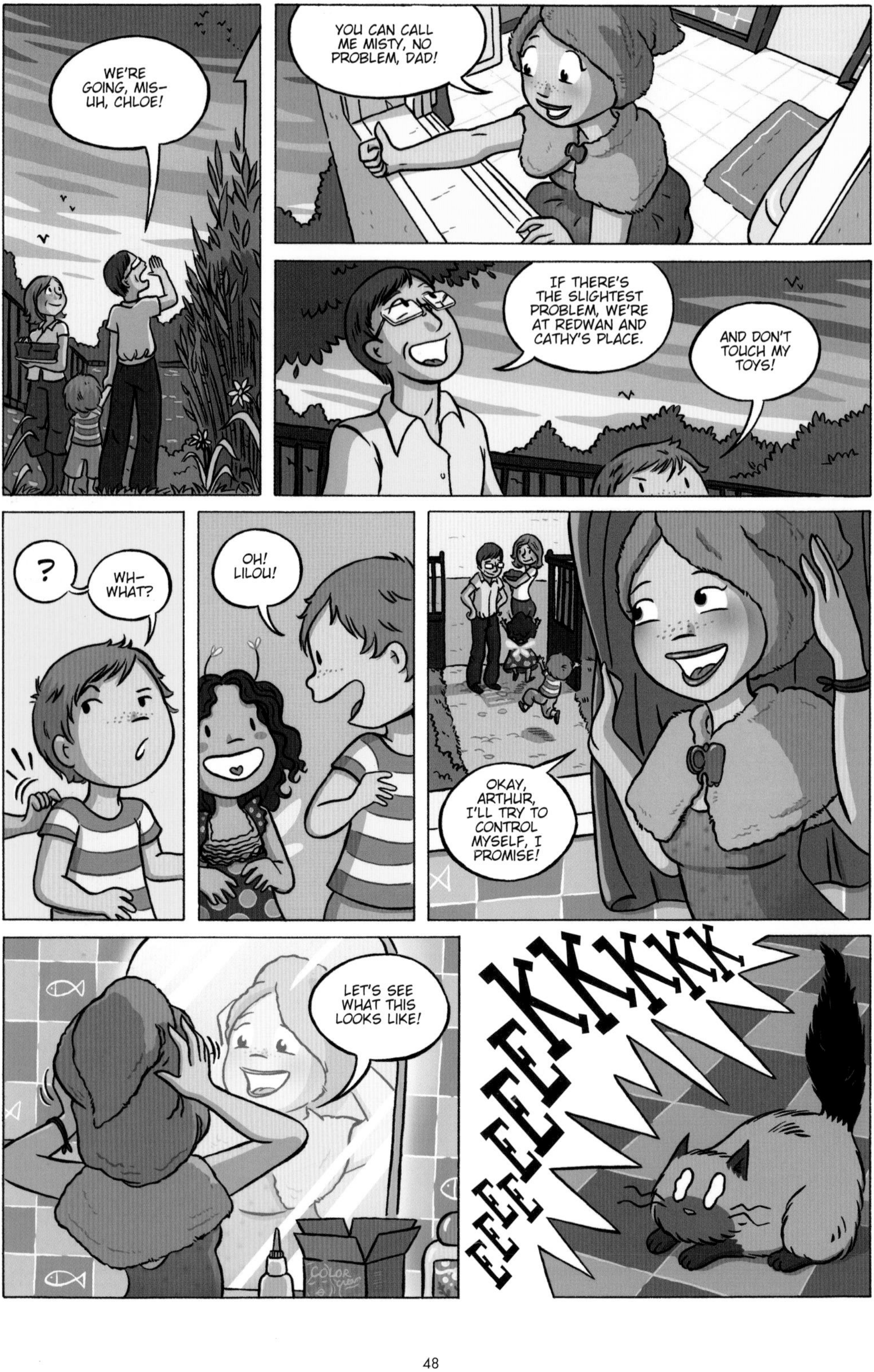
WE'RE GOING, MIS- UH, CHLOE!
YOU CAN CALL ME MISTY, NO PROBLEM, DAD!
IF THERE'S THE SLIGHTEST PROBLEM, WE'RE AT REDWAN AND CATHY'S PLACE.
AND DON'T TOUCH MY TOYS!
?
WH- WHAT?
OH! LILOU!
OKAY, ARTHUR, I'LL TRY TO CONTROL MYSELF, I PROMISE!
LET'S SEE WHAT THIS LOOKS LIKE!
EEEEEEEKKKKKK

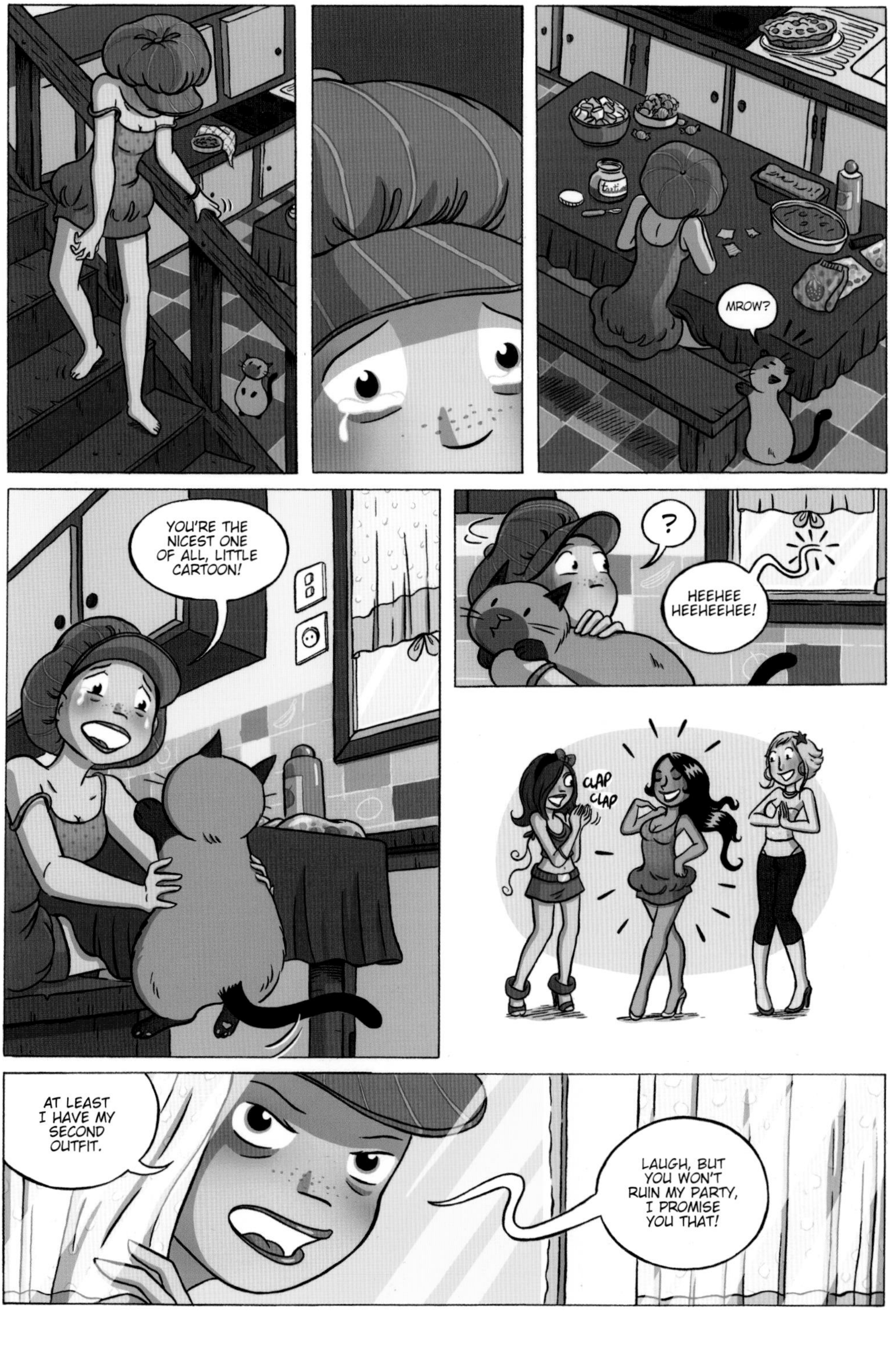
MROW?
YOU'RE THE NICEST ONE OF ALL, LITTLE CARTOON!
?
HEEHEE HEEHEEHEE!
CLAP CLAP
AT LEAST I HAVE MY SECOND OUTFIT.
LAUGH, BUT YOU WON'T RUIN MY PARTY, I PROMISE YOU THAT!

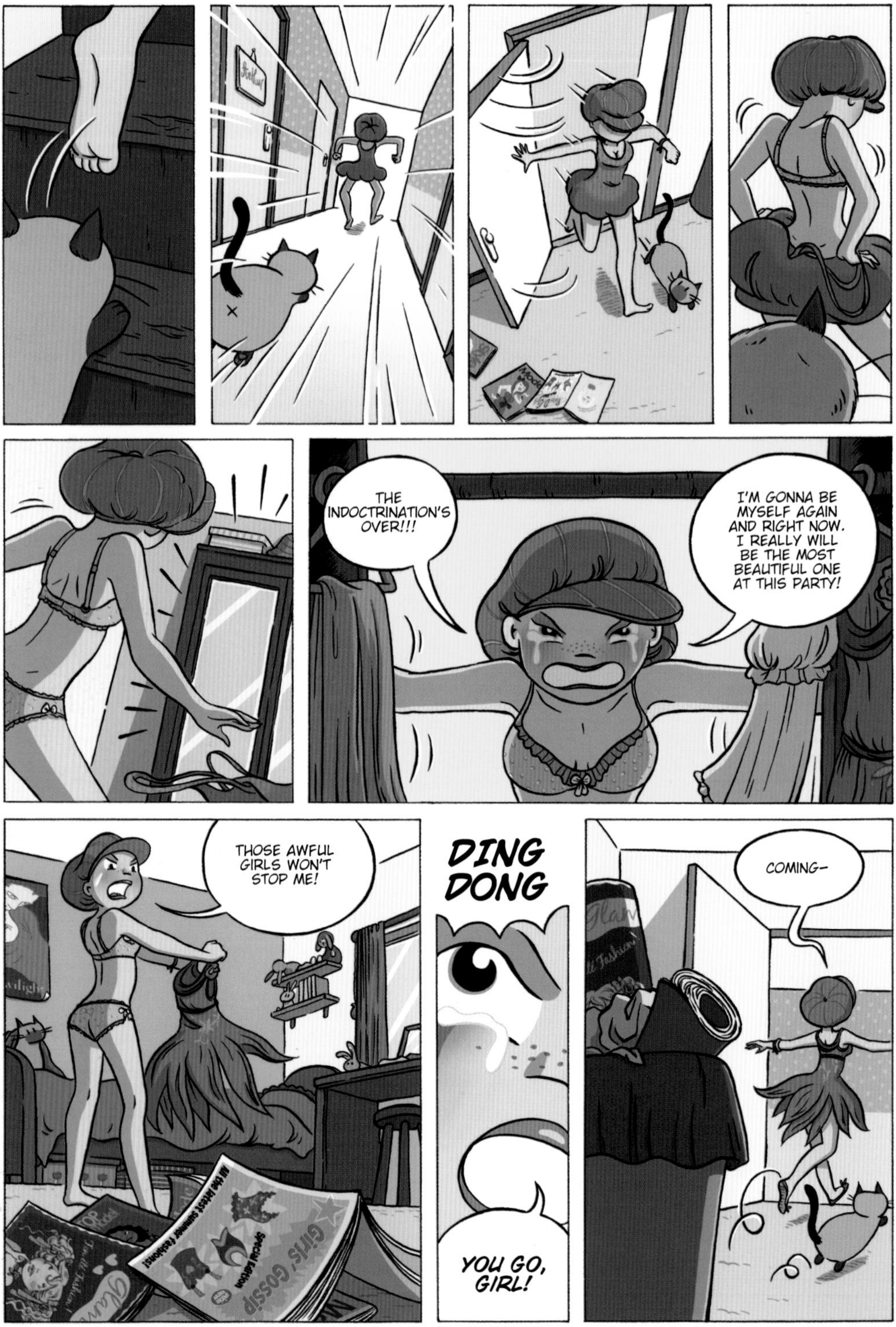
THE INDOCTRINATION'S OVER!!!
I'M GONNA BE MYSELF AGAIN AND RIGHT NOW. I REALLY WILL BE THE MOST BEAUTIFUL ONE AT THIS PARTY!
THOSE AWFUL GIRLS WON'T STOP ME!
All the latest summer fashions!
Special Edition
Girls' Gossip
DING DONG
YOU GO, GIRL!
COMING–

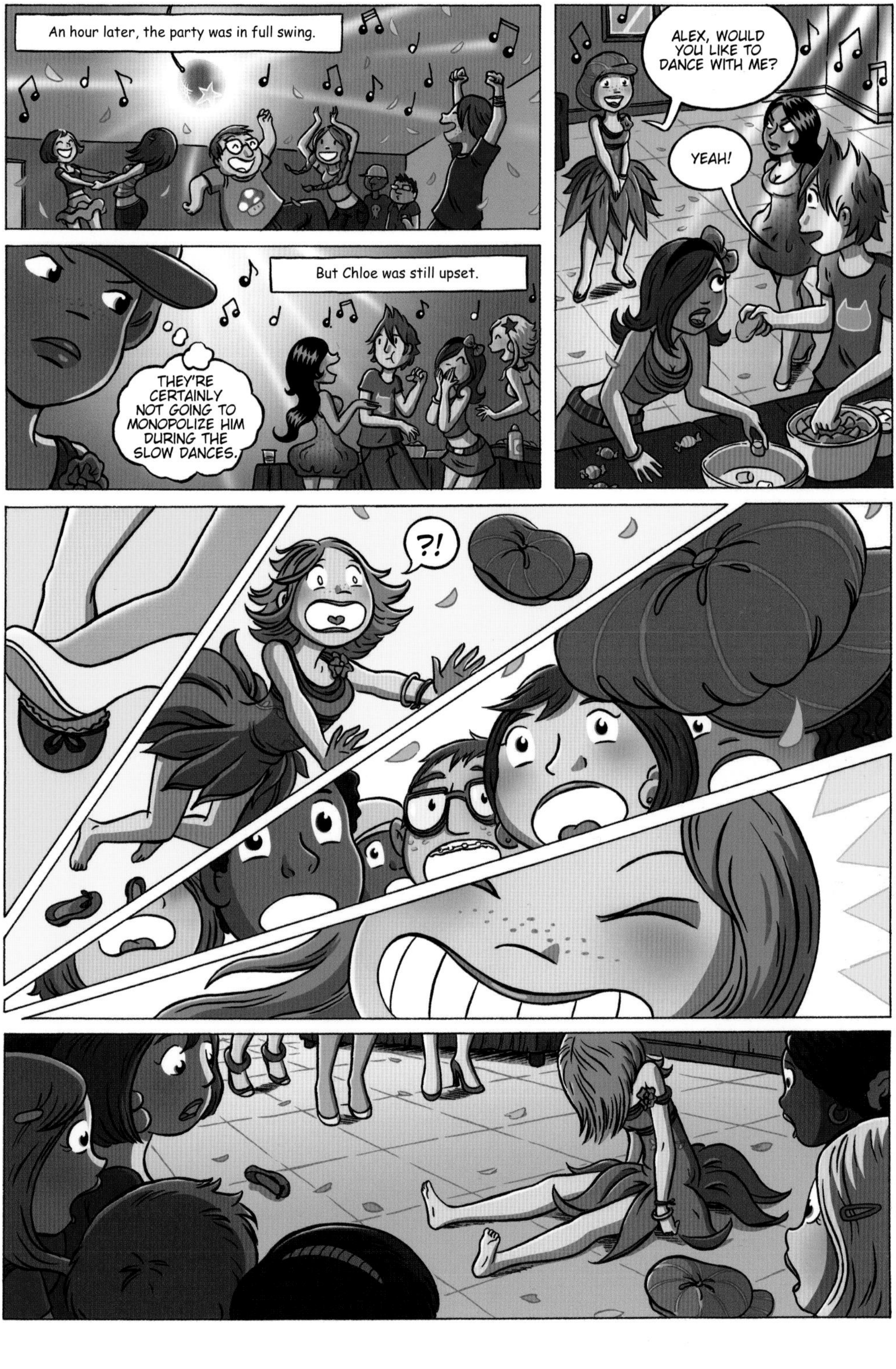
An hour later, the party was in full swing.
ALEX, WOULD YOU LIKE TO DANCE WITH ME?
YEAH!
But Chloe was still upset.
THEY'RE CERTAINLY NOT GOING TO MONOPOLIZE HIM DURING THE SLOW DANCES.
?!

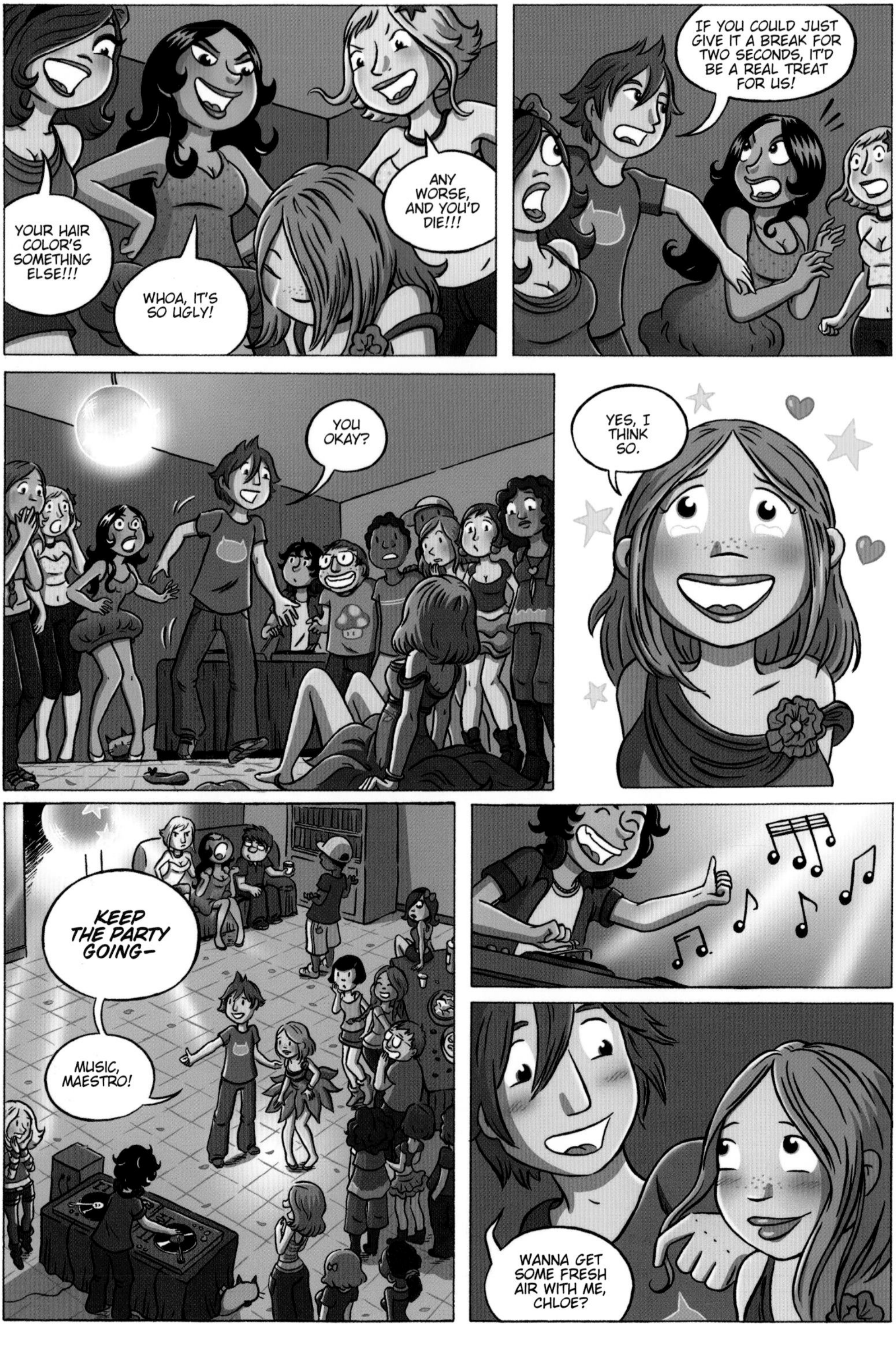
YOUR HAIR COLOR'S SOMETHING ELSE!!!
WHOA, IT'S SO UGLY!
ANY WORSE, AND YOU'D DIE!!!
IF YOU COULD JUST GIVE IT A BREAK FOR TWO SECONDS, IT'D BE A REAL TREAT FOR US!
YOU OKAY?
YES, I THINK SO.
KEEP THE PARTY GOING-
MUSIC, MAESTRO!
WANNA GET SOME FRESH AIR WITH ME, CHLOE?

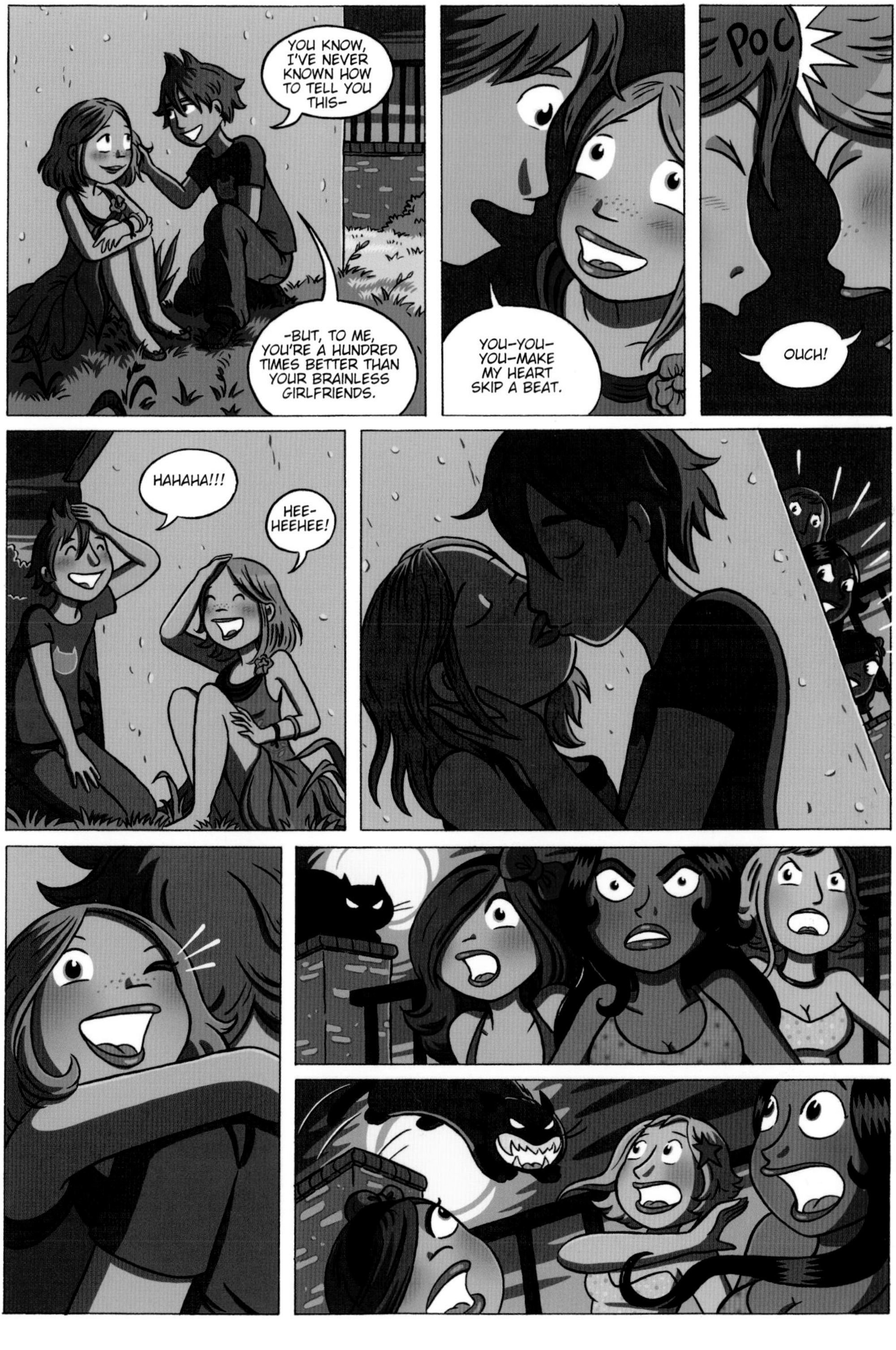
YOU KNOW, I'VE NEVER KNOWN HOW TO TELL YOU THIS-
-BUT, TO ME, YOU'RE A HUNDRED TIMES BETTER THAN YOUR BRAINLESS GIRLFRIENDS.
YOU-YOU-YOU-MAKE MY HEART SKIP A BEAT.
POC
OUCH!
HAHAHA!!!
HEE-HEEHEE!

Report Card

3rd Quarter

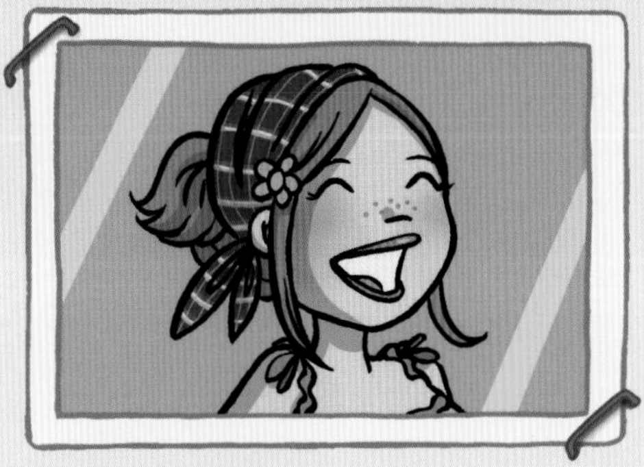

BLIN, Chloe, or "Misty,"
for those who love her.
- Eighth Grade, Group C -

Subjects	Student Grade Averages	Suggestions for Improvement
Appearance	A	You were finally able to silence your critics by creating your own style. Respect!
Self-confidence	A	Smart work. You succeeded in asserting your choices amid adversity.
Observation Skills	B	You didn't rest on your laurels. Good consistency. Bravo!
Attractiveness	B	Real involvement The whole package has become very satisfying.
Popularity	A	Congratulations. You finally understood that popularity wasn't very important if it doesn't come from the people you love.
Average for This Period	A	

General Comments:
All the readers would like to pay tribute to Chloe's tenacity. She was able to take charge of herself and adapt at her own rhythm without ever giving up. 9th grade holds a lot of promise.

Notification: this grade report is the original copy and must be preserved,

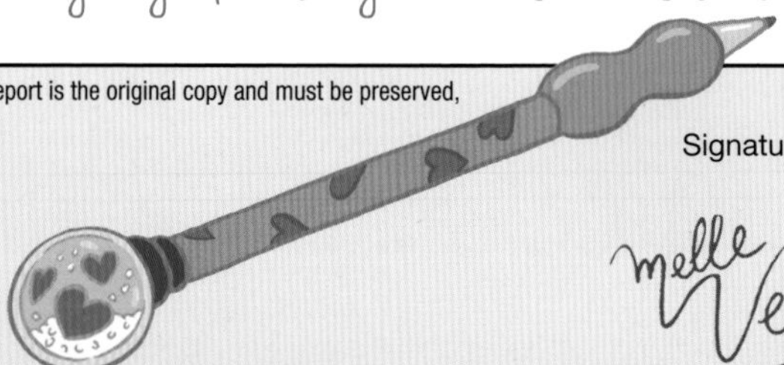

Signature of the home room teacher:

Melle Vernier

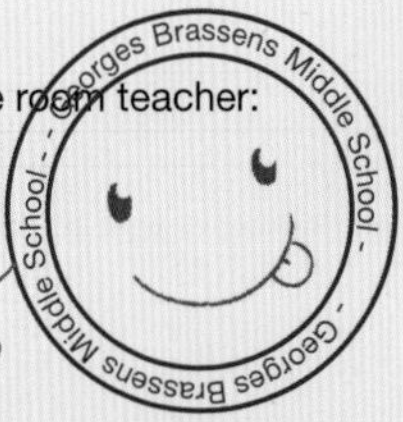
Georges Brassens Middle School - Georges Brassens Middle School -

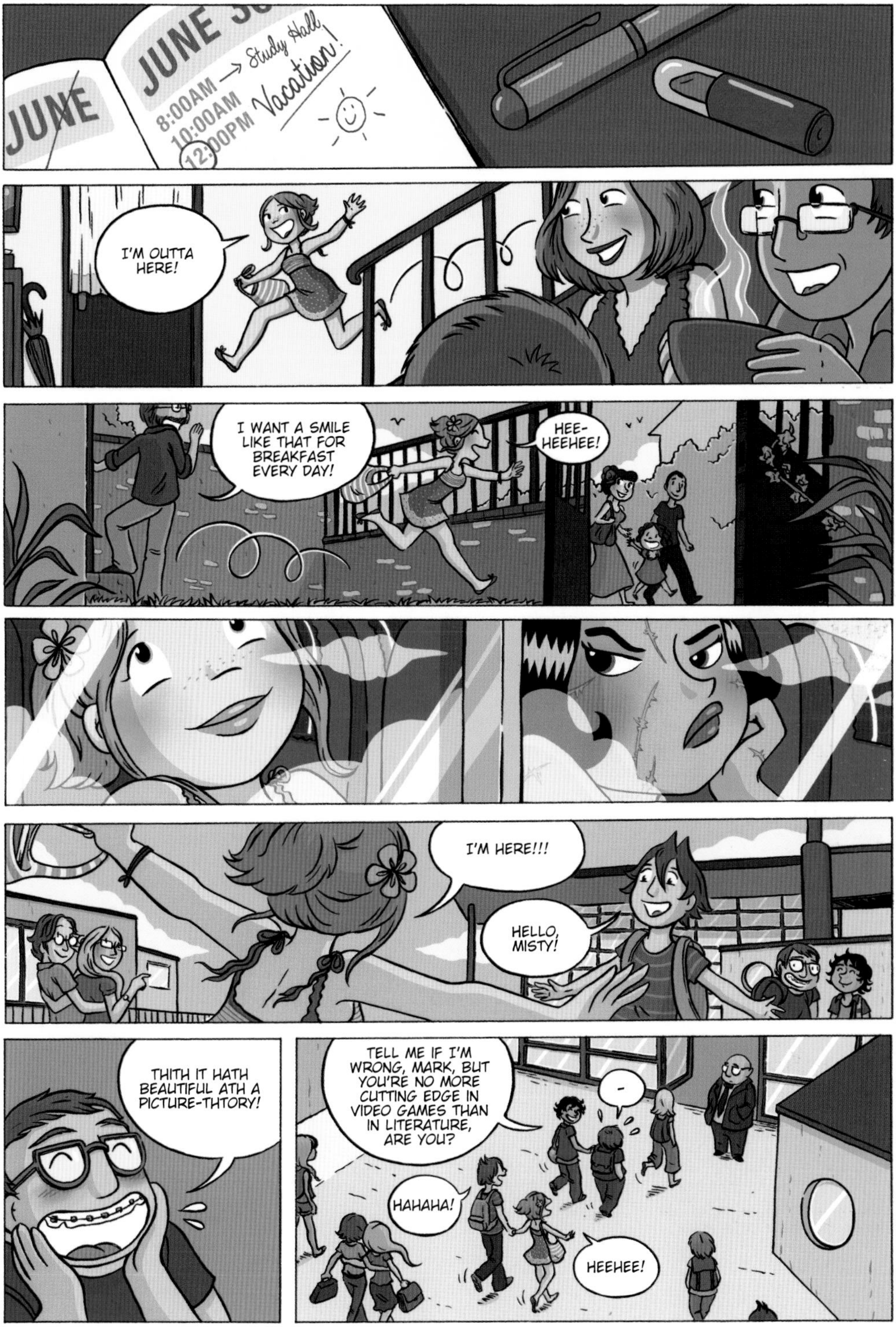
JUNE
JUNE 30
8:00AM → Study Hall
10:00AM
12:00PM Vacation!
I'M OUTTA HERE!
I WANT A SMILE LIKE THAT FOR BREAKFAST EVERY DAY!
HEE-HEEHEE!
I'M HERE!!!
HELLO, MISTY!
THITH IT HATH BEAUTIFUL ATH A PICTURE-THTORY!
TELL ME IF I'M WRONG, MARK, BUT YOU'RE NO MORE CUTTING EDGE IN VIDEO GAMES THAN IN LITERATURE, ARE YOU?
-
HAHAHA!
HEEHEE!

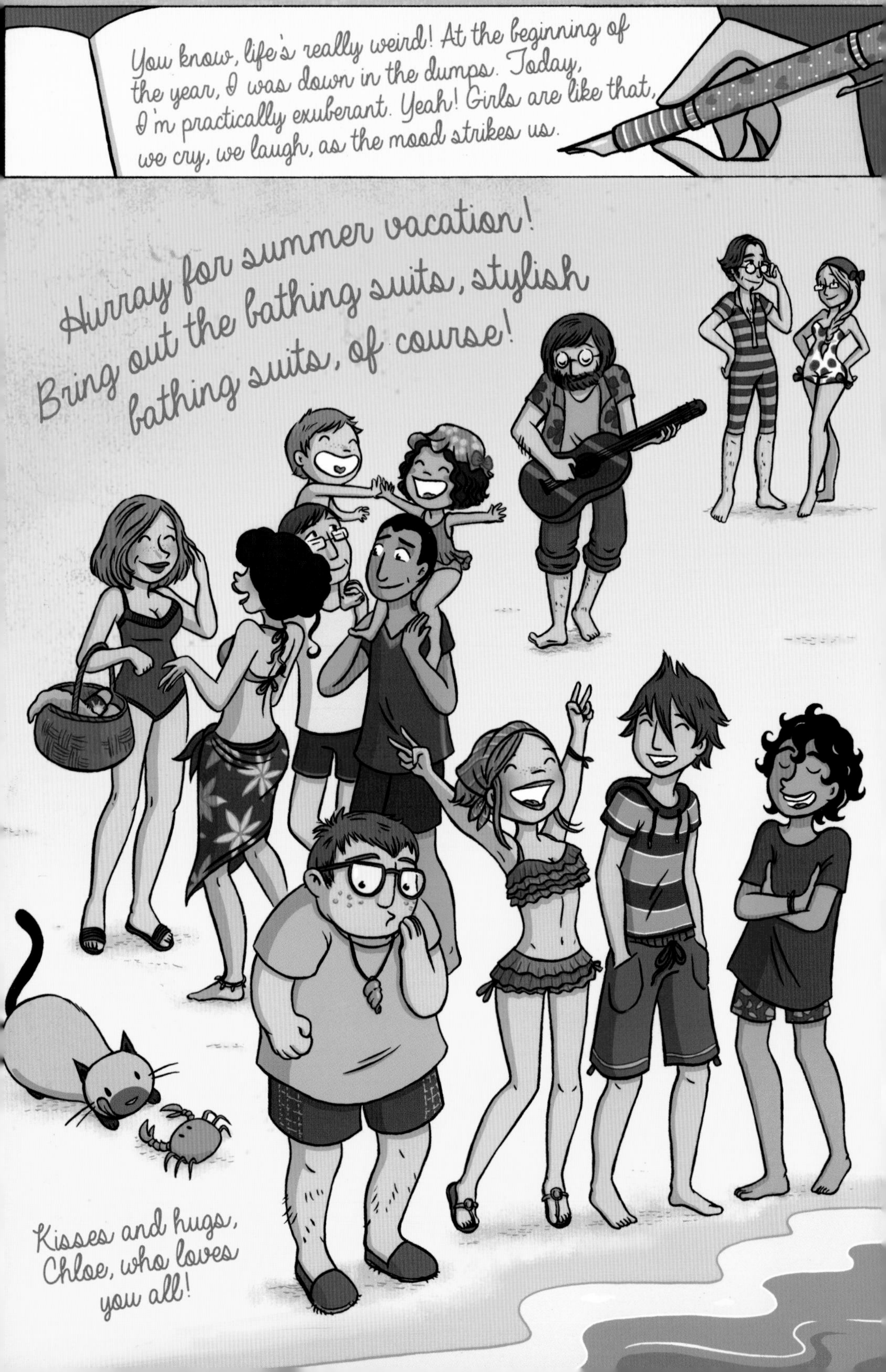
You know, life's really weird! At the beginning of the year, I was down in the dumps. Today, I'm practically exuberant. Yeah! Girls are like that, we cry, we laugh, as the mood strikes us.
Hurray for summer vacation!
Bring out the bathing suits, stylish bathing suits, of course!
Kisses and hugs, Chloe, who loves you all!

Kisses and Shells

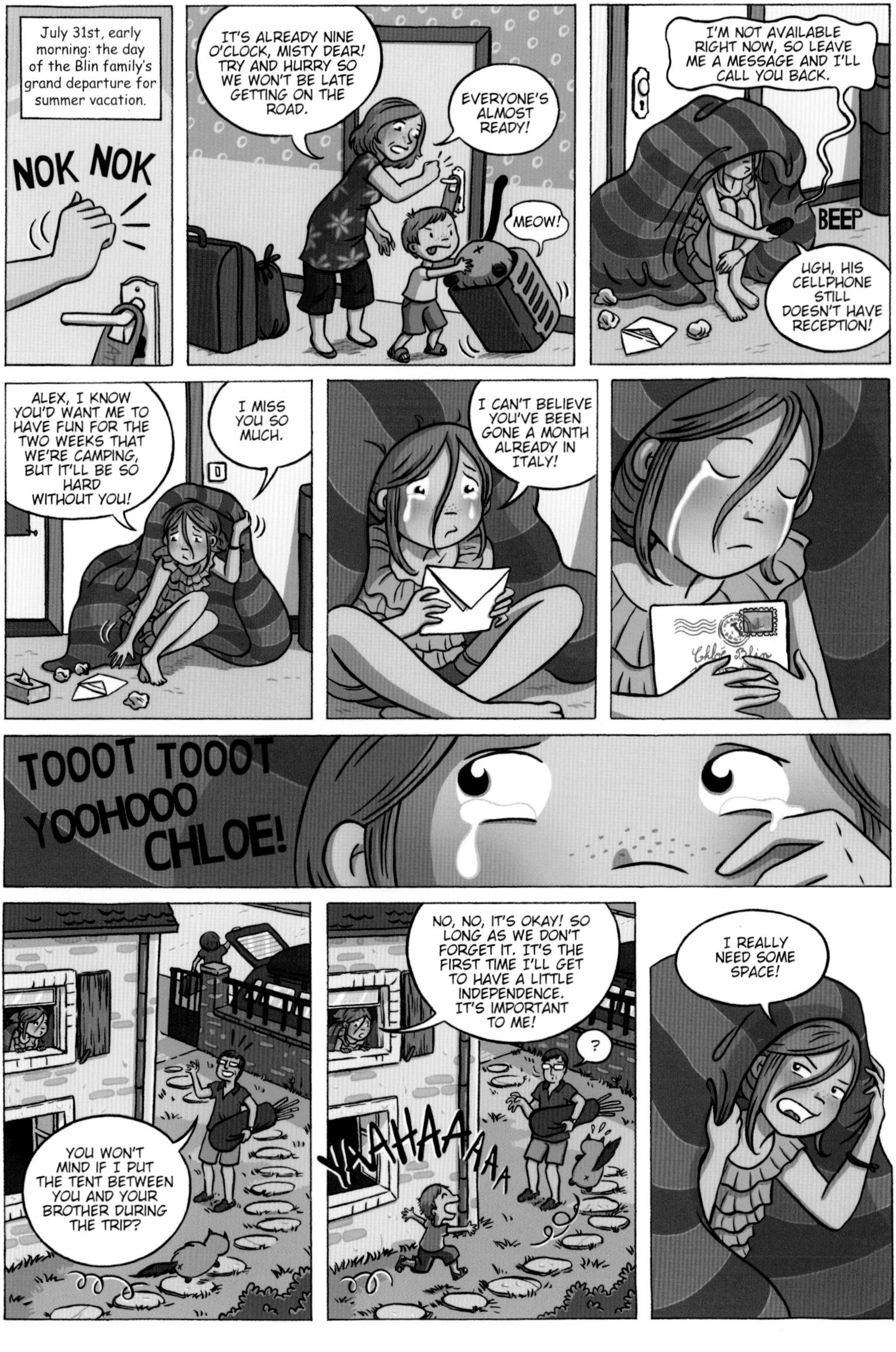

July 31st, early morning: the day of the Blin family's grand departure for summer vacation.
NOK NOK
IT'S ALREADY NINE O'CLOCK, MISTY DEAR! TRY AND HURRY SO WE WON'T BE LATE GETTING ON THE ROAD.
EVERYONE'S ALMOST READY!
MEOW!
I'M NOT AVAILABLE RIGHT NOW, SO LEAVE ME A MESSAGE AND I'LL CALL YOU BACK.
BEEP
UGH, HIS CELLPHONE STILL DOESN'T HAVE RECEPTION!
ALEX, I KNOW YOU'D WANT ME TO HAVE FUN FOR THE TWO WEEKS THAT WE'RE CAMPING, BUT IT'LL BE SO HARD WITHOUT YOU!
I MISS YOU SO MUCH.
I CAN'T BELIEVE YOU'VE BEEN GONE A MONTH ALREADY IN ITALY!
Chloé Blin
TOOOT TOOOT
YOOHOOO CHLOE!
YOU WON'T MIND IF I PUT THE TENT BETWEEN YOU AND YOUR BROTHER DURING THE TRIP?
NO, NO, IT'S OKAY! SO LONG AS WE DON'T FORGET IT. IT'S THE FIRST TIME I'LL GET TO HAVE A LITTLE INDEPENDENCE. IT'S IMPORTANT TO ME!
?
YAAHAAAAAA
I REALLY NEED SOME SPACE!

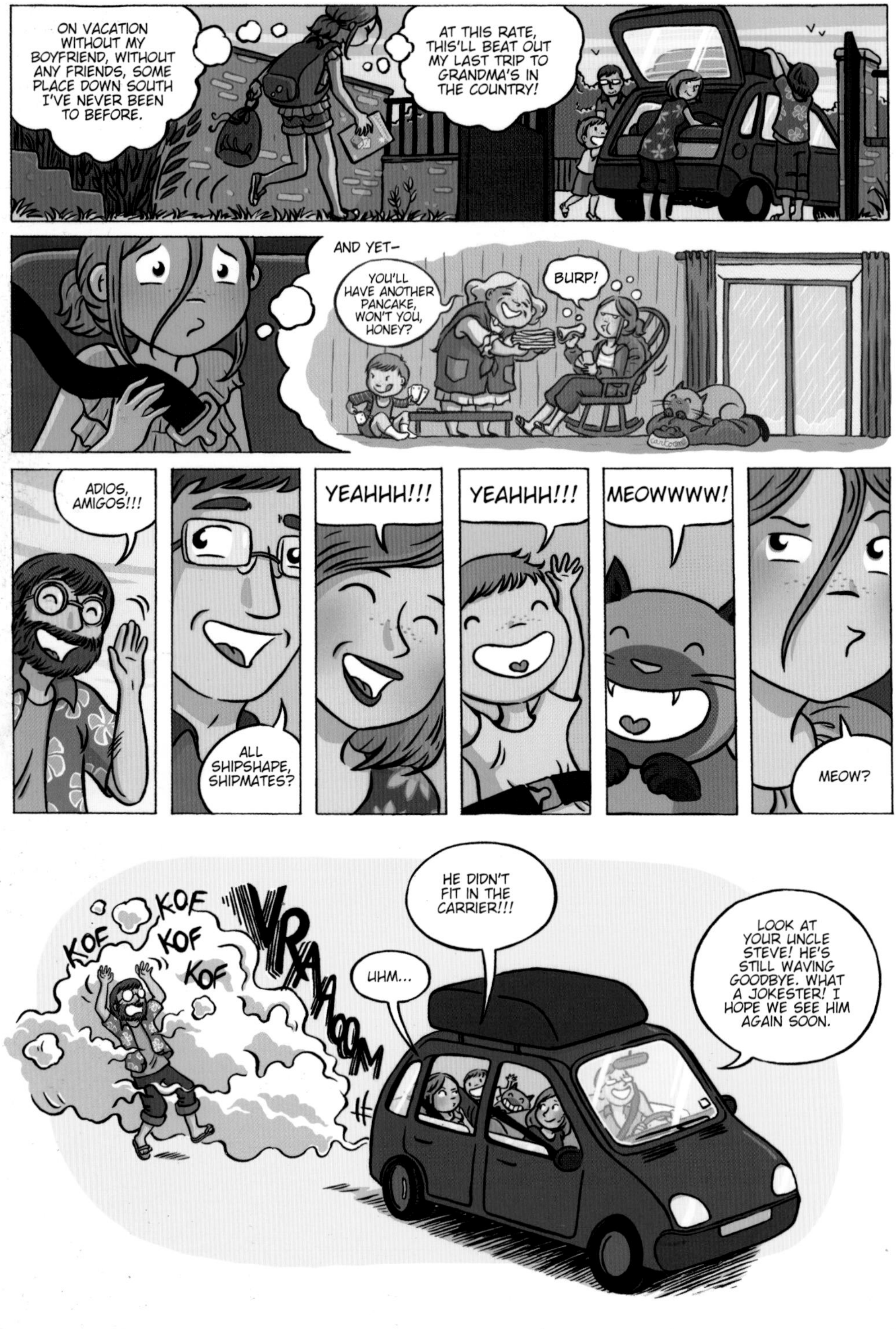
ON VACATION WITHOUT MY BOYFRIEND, WITHOUT ANY FRIENDS, SOME PLACE DOWN SOUTH I'VE NEVER BEEN TO BEFORE.
AT THIS RATE, THIS'LL BEAT OUT MY LAST TRIP TO GRANDMA'S IN THE COUNTRY!
AND YET–
YOU'LL HAVE ANOTHER PANCAKE, WON'T YOU, HONEY?
BURP!
ADIOS, AMIGOS!!!
ALL SHIPSHAPE, SHIPMATES?
YEAHHH!!!
YEAHHH!!!
MEOWWWW!
MEOW?
KOF KOF KOF KOF
VRAAOOOM
UHM...
HE DIDN'T FIT IN THE CARRIER!!!
LOOK AT YOUR UNCLE STEVE! HE'S STILL WAVING GOODBYE. WHAT A JOKESTER! I HOPE WE SEE HIM AGAIN SOON.

Wandering

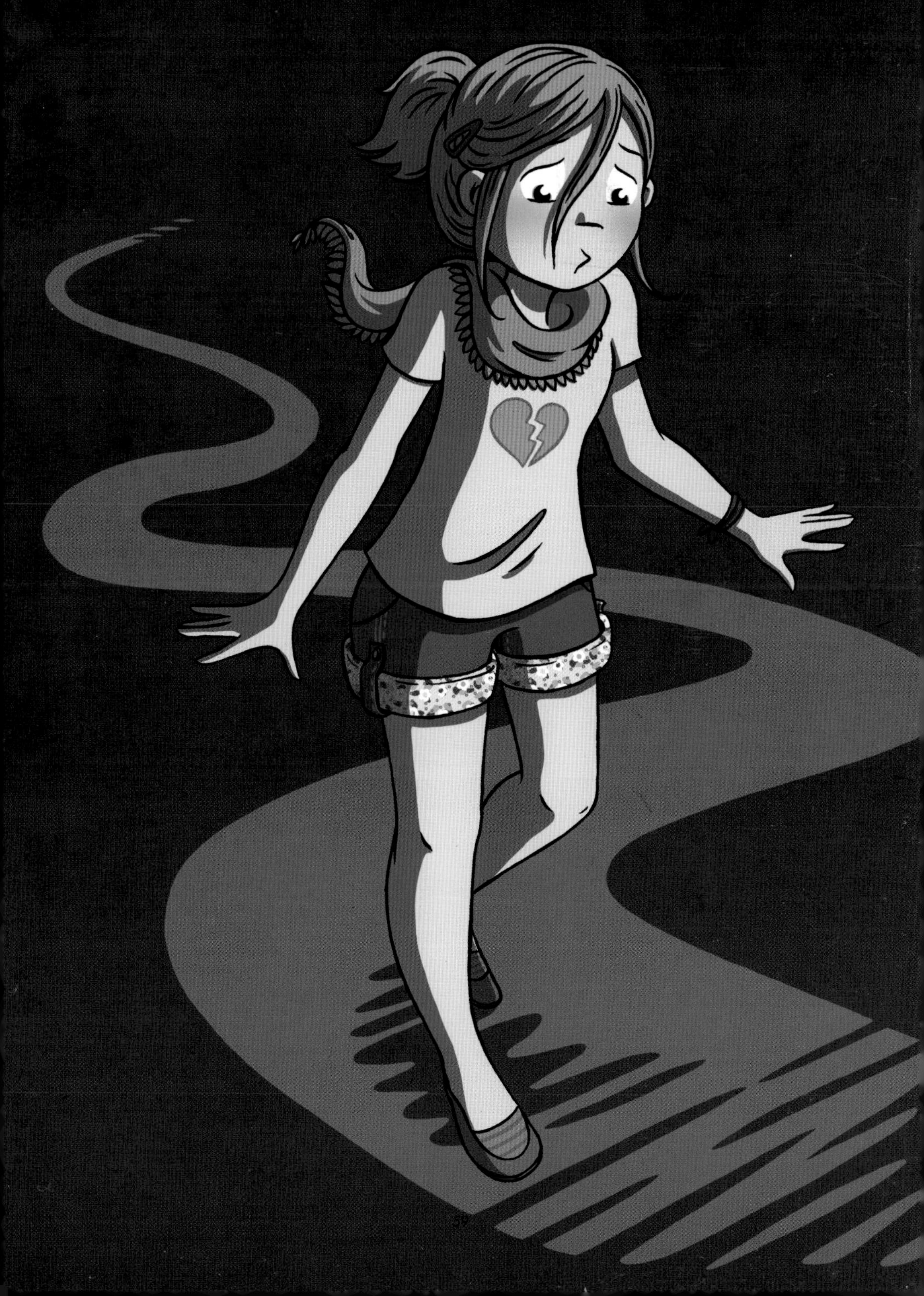

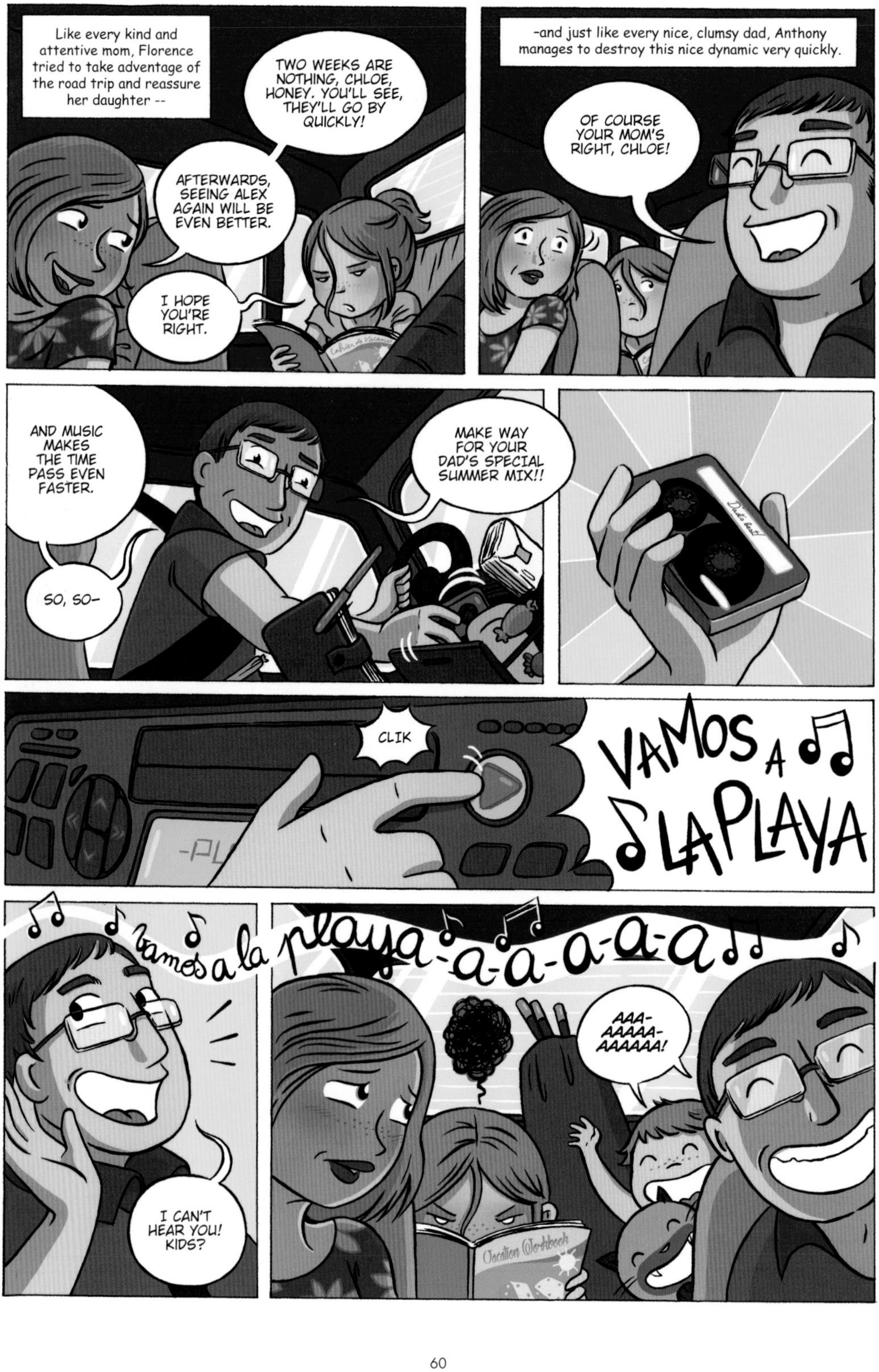

Like every kind and attentive mom, Florence tried to take adventage of the road trip and reassure her daughter --
TWO WEEKS ARE NOTHING, CHLOE, HONEY. YOU'LL SEE, THEY'LL GO BY QUICKLY!
AFTERWARDS, SEEING ALEX AGAIN WILL BE EVEN BETTER.
I HOPE YOU'RE RIGHT.
-and just like every nice, clumsy dad, Anthony manages to destroy this nice dynamic very quickly.
OF COURSE YOUR MOM'S RIGHT, CHLOE!
AND MUSIC MAKES THE TIME PASS EVEN FASTER.
SO, SO-
MAKE WAY FOR YOUR DAD'S SPECIAL SUMMER MIX!!
CLIK
VAMOS A LA PLAYA
vamos a la playa-a-a-a-a-a
I CAN'T HEAR YOU! KIDS?
AAA-AAAAA-AAAAAA!

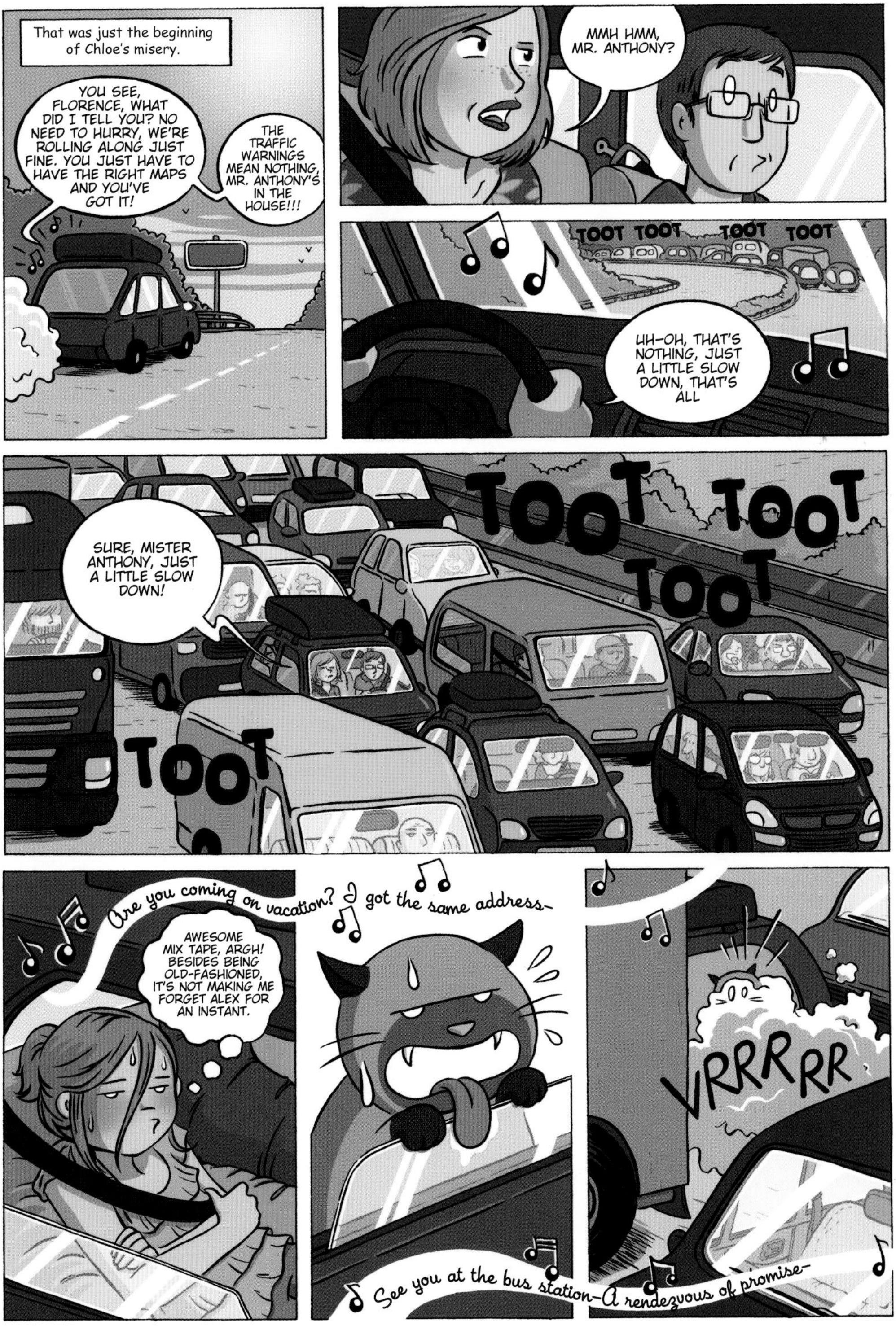
That was just the beginning of Chloe's misery.
YOU SEE, FLORENCE, WHAT DID I TELL YOU? NO NEED TO HURRY, WE'RE ROLLING ALONG JUST FINE. YOU JUST HAVE TO HAVE THE RIGHT MAPS AND YOU'VE GOT IT!
THE TRAFFIC WARNINGS MEAN NOTHING, MR. ANTHONY'S IN THE HOUSE!!!
MMH HMM, MR. ANTHONY?
TOOT TOOT TOOT TOOT
UH-OH, THAT'S NOTHING, JUST A LITTLE SLOW DOWN, THAT'S ALL
SURE, MISTER ANTHONY, JUST A LITTLE SLOW DOWN!
TOOT TOOT
TOOT
TOOT
Are you coming on vacation? I got the same address-
AWESOME MIX TAPE, ARGH! BESIDES BEING OLD-FASHIONED, IT'S NOT MAKING ME FORGET ALEX FOR AN INSTANT.
VRRRRR
See you at the bus station-A rendezvous of promise-

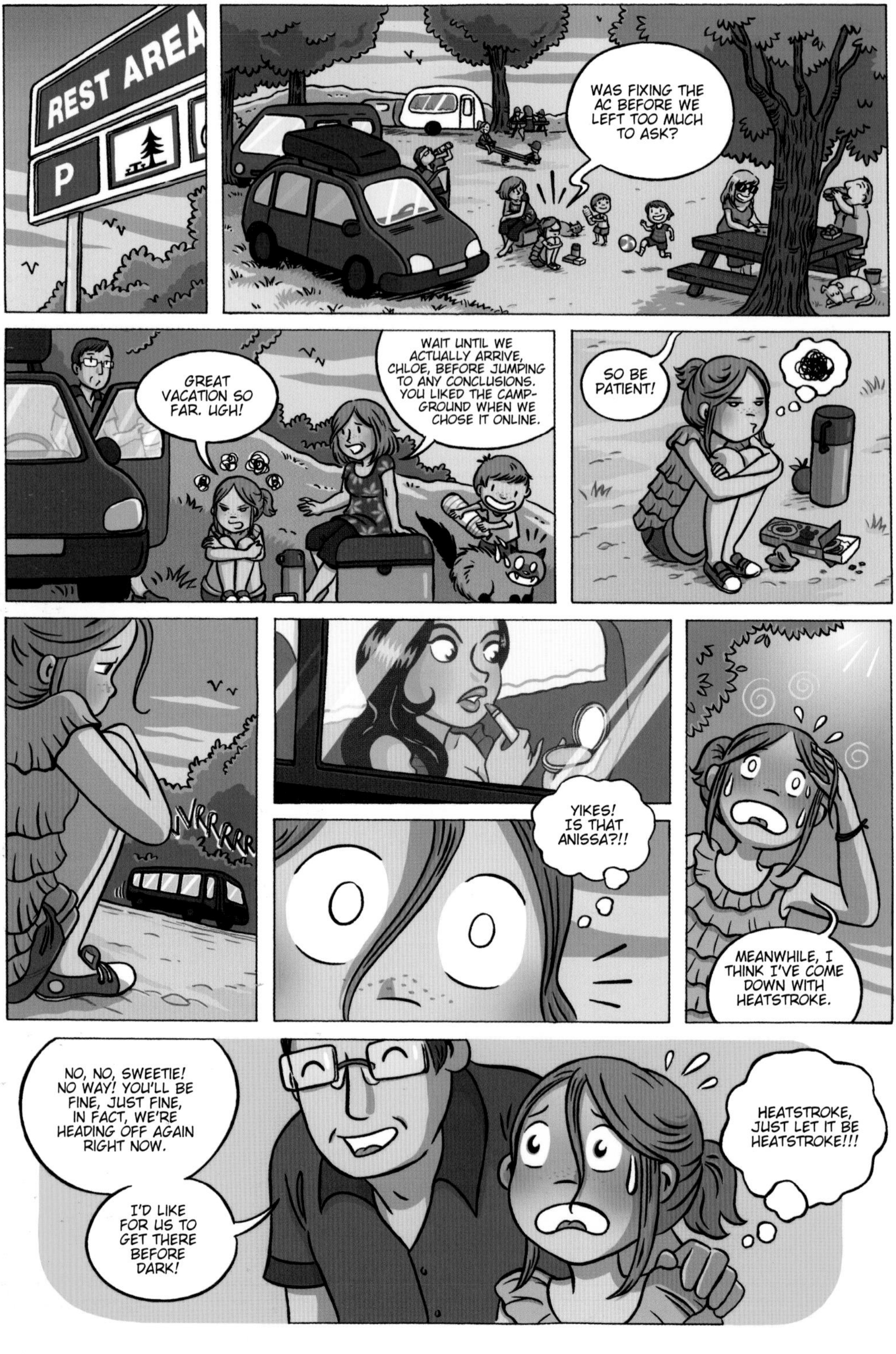
REST AREA
P
WAS FIXING THE AC BEFORE WE LEFT TOO MUCH TO ASK?
GREAT VACATION SO FAR. UGH!
WAIT UNTIL WE ACTUALLY ARRIVE, CHLOE, BEFORE JUMPING TO ANY CONCLUSIONS. YOU LIKED THE CAMP-GROUND WHEN WE CHOSE IT ONLINE.
SO BE PATIENT!
VRRRRRR
YIKES! IS THAT ANISSA?!!
MEANWHILE, I THINK I'VE COME DOWN WITH HEATSTROKE.
NO, NO, SWEETIE! NO WAY! YOU'LL BE FINE, JUST FINE, IN FACT, WE'RE HEADING OFF AGAIN RIGHT NOW.
I'D LIKE FOR US TO GET THERE BEFORE DARK!
HEATSTROKE, JUST LET IT BE HEATSTROKE!!!

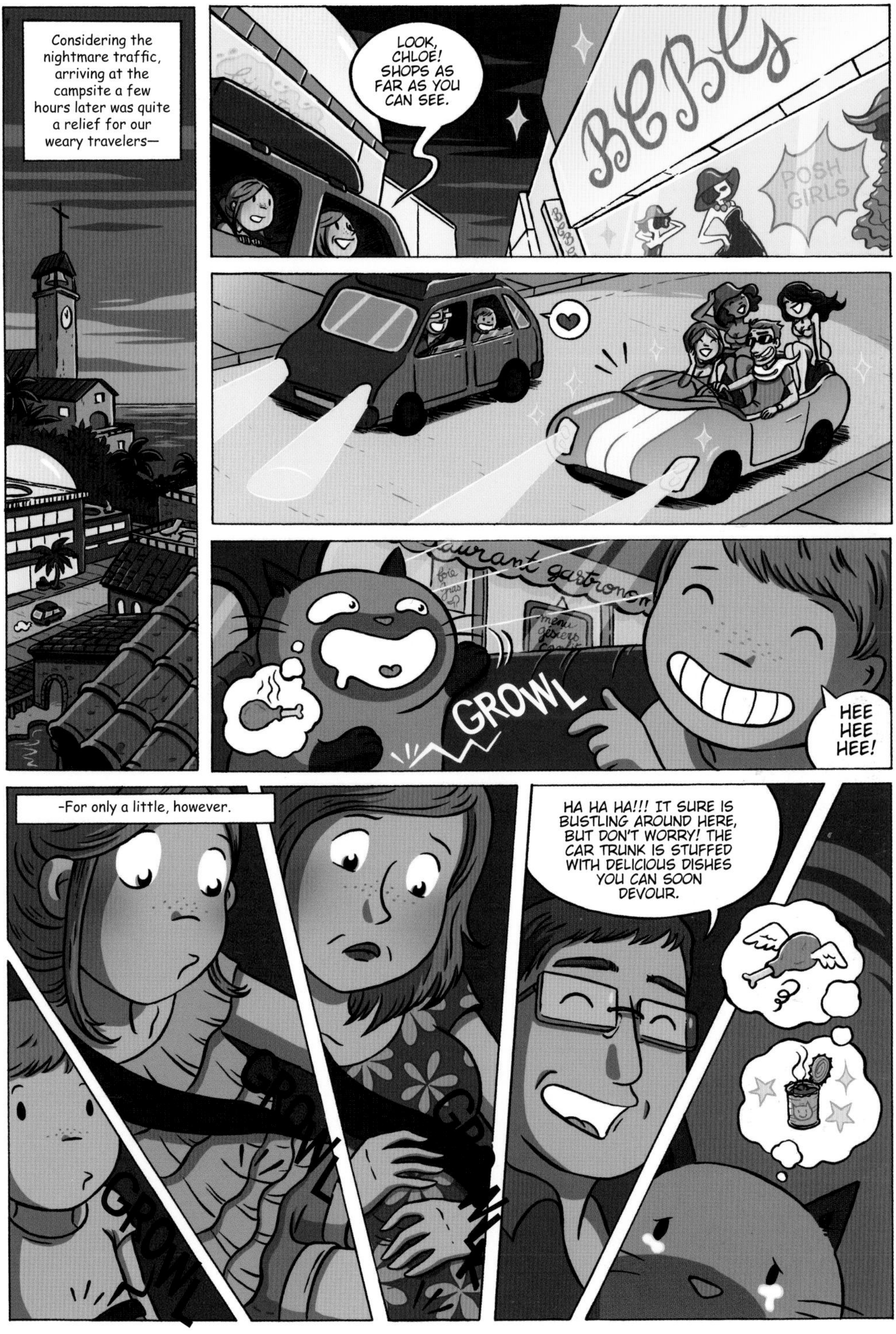

Considering the nightmare traffic, arriving at the campsite a few hours later was quite a relief for our weary travelers—
LOOK, CHLOE! SHOPS AS FAR AS YOU CAN SEE.
POSH GIRLS
GROWL
HEE HEE HEE!
–For only a little, however.
GROWL
GROWL
GROWL
HA HA HA!!! IT SURE IS BUSTLING AROUND HERE, BUT DON'T WORRY! THE CAR TRUNK IS STUFFED WITH DELICIOUS DISHES YOU CAN SOON DEVOUR.

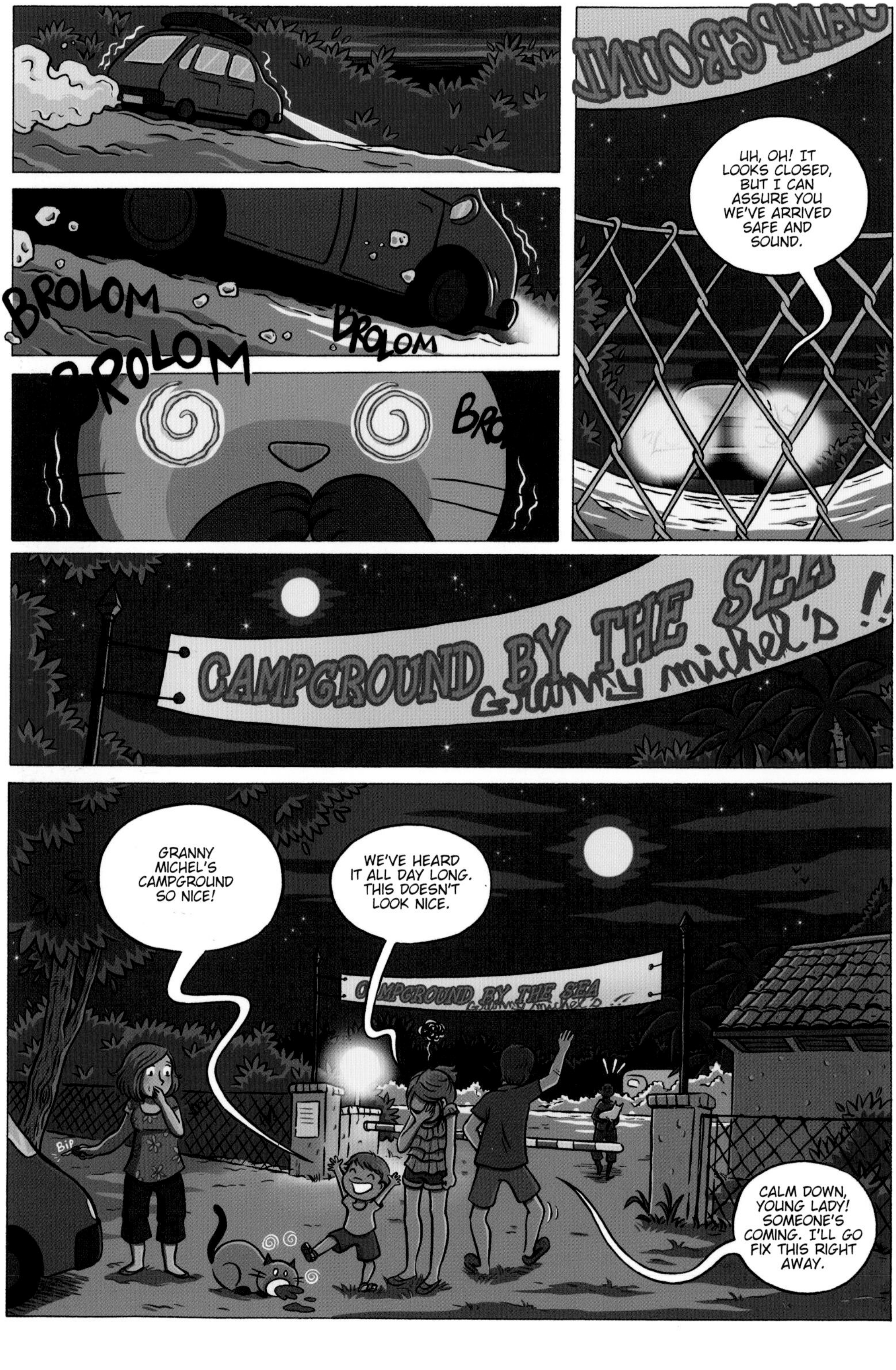

BROLOM
BROLOM
BROLOM
BRO
UH, OH! IT LOOKS CLOSED, BUT I CAN ASSURE YOU WE'VE ARRIVED SAFE AND SOUND.
CAMPGROUND BY THE SEA
GRANNY MICHEL'S
GRANNY MICHEL'S CAMPGROUND SO NICE!
WE'VE HEARD IT ALL DAY LONG. THIS DOESN'T LOOK NICE.
CALM DOWN, YOUNG LADY! SOMEONE'S COMING. I'LL GO FIX THIS RIGHT AWAY.

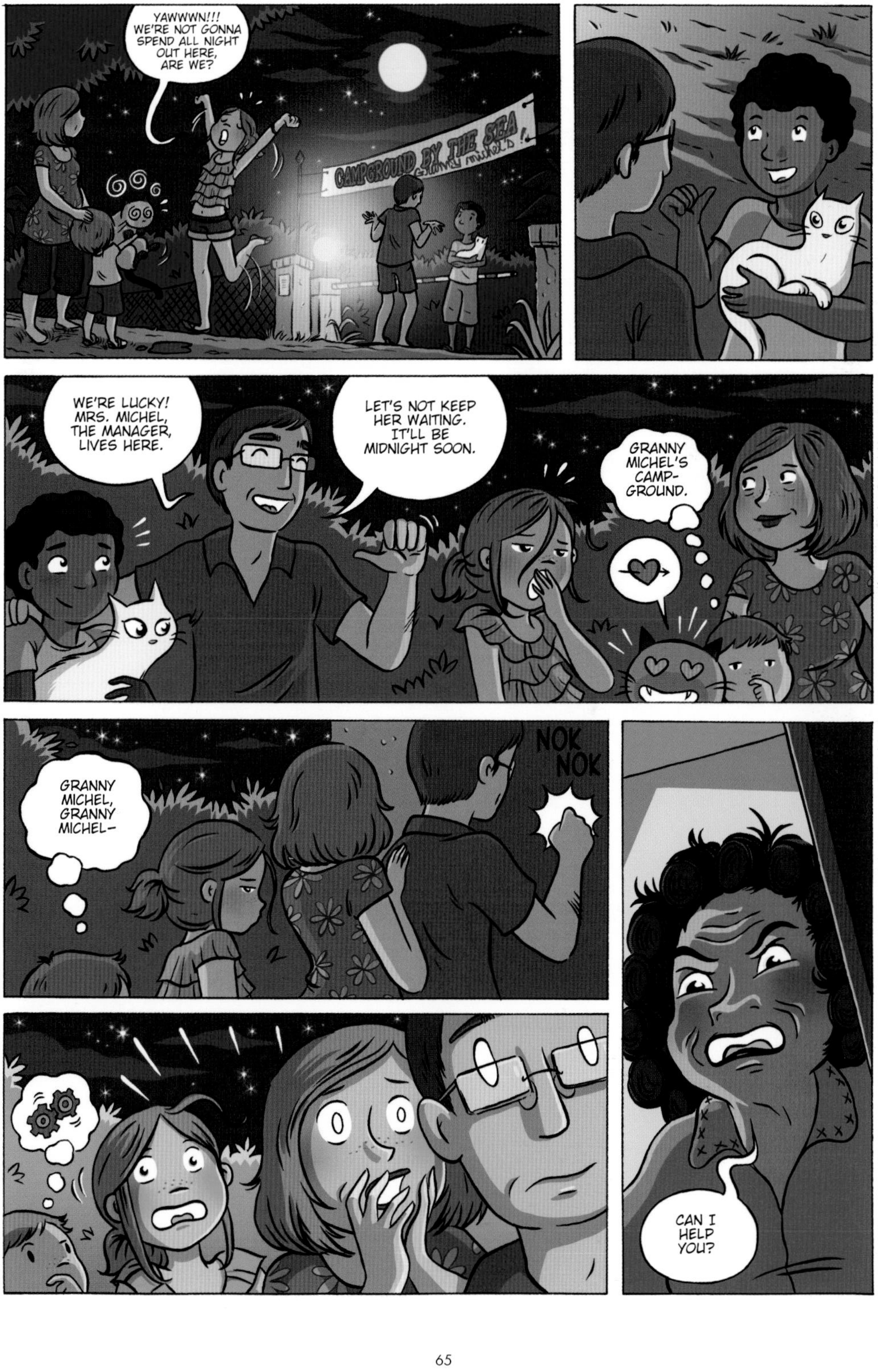
YAWWWN!!! WE'RE NOT GONNA SPEND ALL NIGHT OUT HERE, ARE WE?
CAMPGROUND BY THE SEA
WE'RE LUCKY! MRS. MICHEL, THE MANAGER, LIVES HERE.
LET'S NOT KEEP HER WAITING. IT'LL BE MIDNIGHT SOON.
GRANNY MICHEL'S CAMP-GROUND.
GRANNY MICHEL, GRANNY MICHEL–
NOK NOK
CAN I HELP YOU?

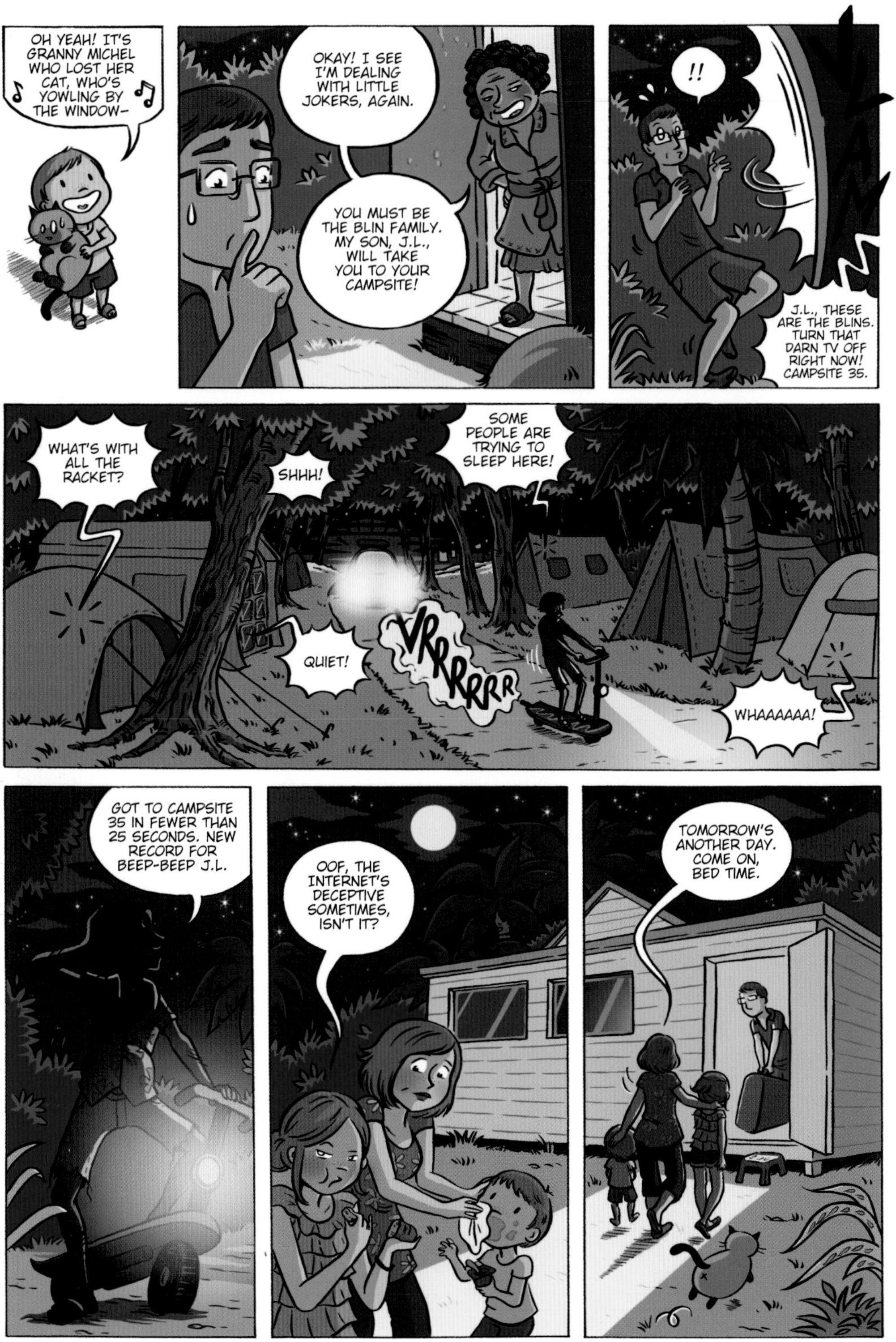
OH YEAH! IT'S GRANNY MICHEL WHO LOST HER CAT, WHO'S YOWLING BY THE WINDOW–
OKAY! I SEE I'M DEALING WITH LITTLE JOKERS, AGAIN.
YOU MUST BE THE BLIN FAMILY. MY SON, J.L., WILL TAKE YOU TO YOUR CAMPSITE!
!!
J.L., THESE ARE THE BLINS. TURN THAT DARN TV OFF RIGHT NOW! CAMPSITE 35.
WHAT'S WITH ALL THE RACKET?
SHHH!
SOME PEOPLE ARE TRYING TO SLEEP HERE!
QUIET!
VRRRRRR
WHAAAAAA!
GOT TO CAMPSITE 35 IN FEWER THAN 25 SECONDS. NEW RECORD FOR BEEP-BEEP J.L.
OOF, THE INTERNET'S DECEPTIVE SOMETIMES, ISN'T IT?
TOMORROW'S ANOTHER DAY. COME ON, BED TIME.

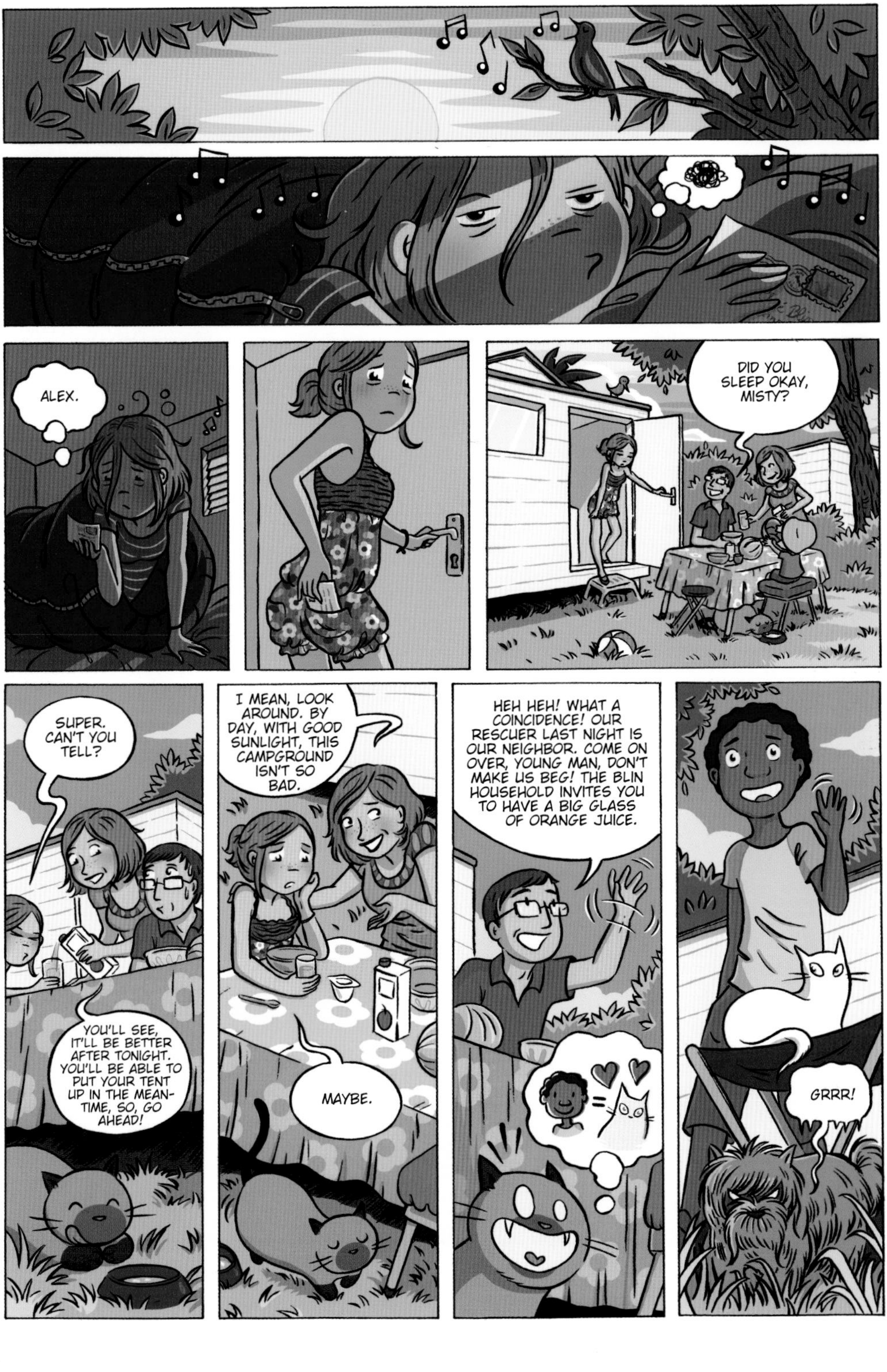
ALEX.
DID YOU SLEEP OKAY, MISTY?
SUPER. CAN'T YOU TELL?
YOU'LL SEE, IT'LL BE BETTER AFTER TONIGHT. YOU'LL BE ABLE TO PUT YOUR TENT UP IN THE MEAN-TIME, SO, GO AHEAD!
I MEAN, LOOK AROUND. BY DAY, WITH GOOD SUNLIGHT, THIS CAMPGROUND ISN'T SO BAD.
MAYBE.
HEH HEH! WHAT A COINCIDENCE! OUR RESCUER LAST NIGHT IS OUR NEIGHBOR. COME ON OVER, YOUNG MAN, DON'T MAKE US BEG! THE BLIN HOUSEHOLD INVITES YOU TO HAVE A BIG GLASS OF ORANGE JUICE.
GRRR!

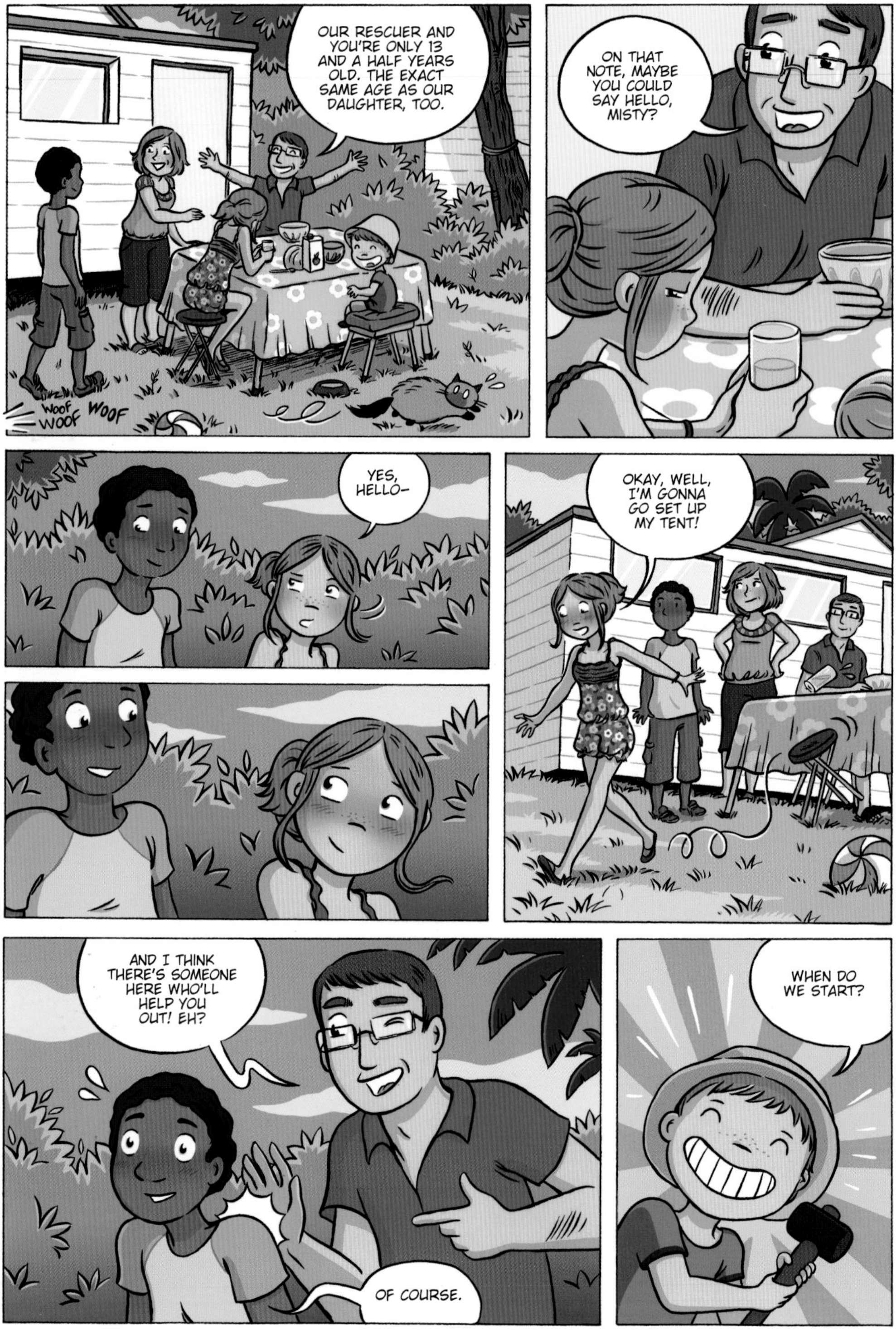
OUR RESCUER AND YOU'RE ONLY 13 AND A HALF YEARS OLD. THE EXACT SAME AGE AS OUR DAUGHTER, TOO.
WOOF WOOF WOOF
ON THAT NOTE, MAYBE YOU COULD SAY HELLO, MISTY?
YES, HELLO–
OKAY, WELL, I'M GONNA GO SET UP MY TENT!
AND I THINK THERE'S SOMEONE HERE WHO'LL HELP YOU OUT! EH?
OF COURSE.
WHEN DO WE START?

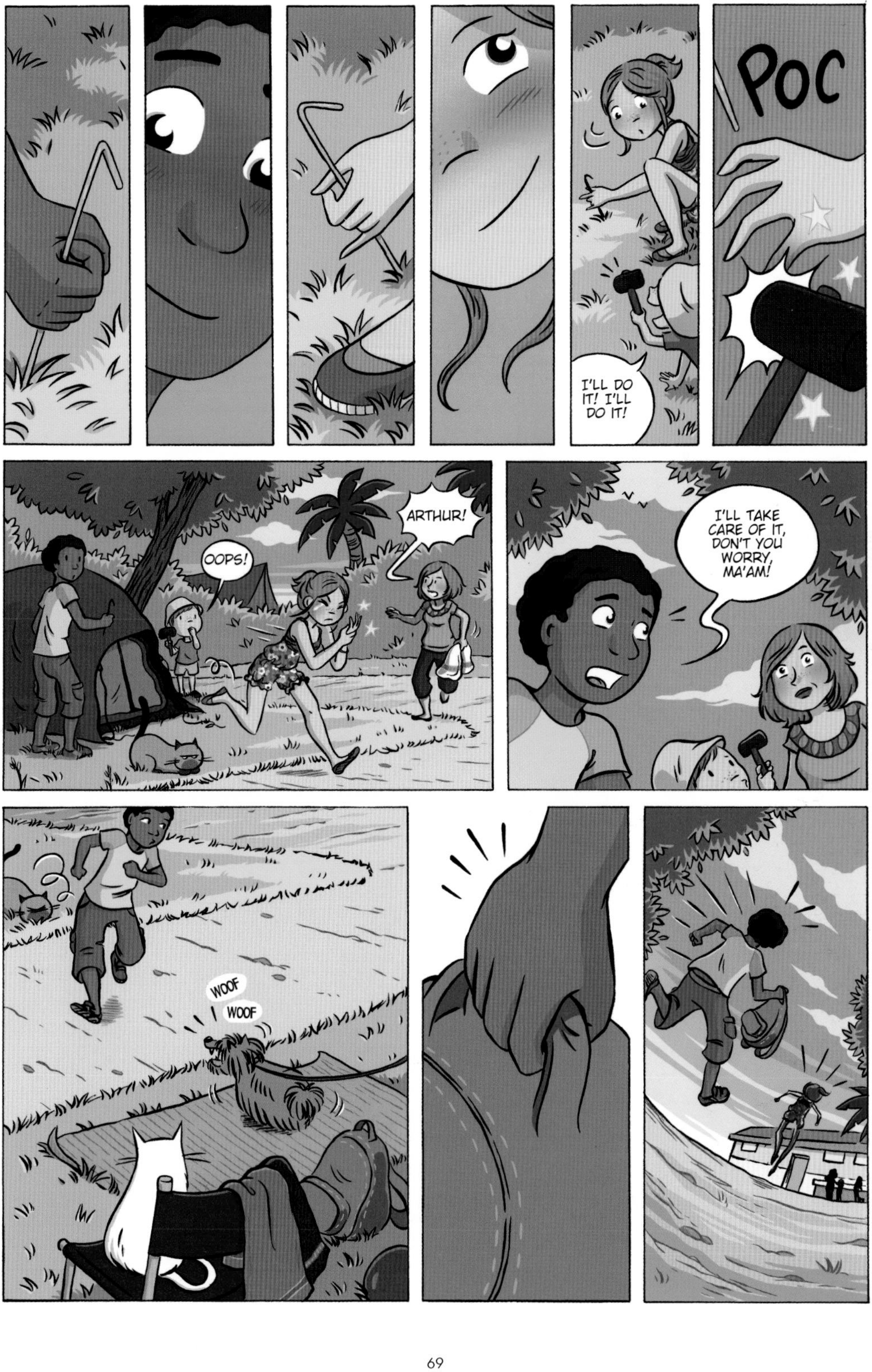
I'LL DO IT! I'LL DO IT!
POC
OOPS!
ARTHUR!
I'LL TAKE CARE OF IT, DON'T YOU WORRY, MA'AM!
WOOF
WOOF

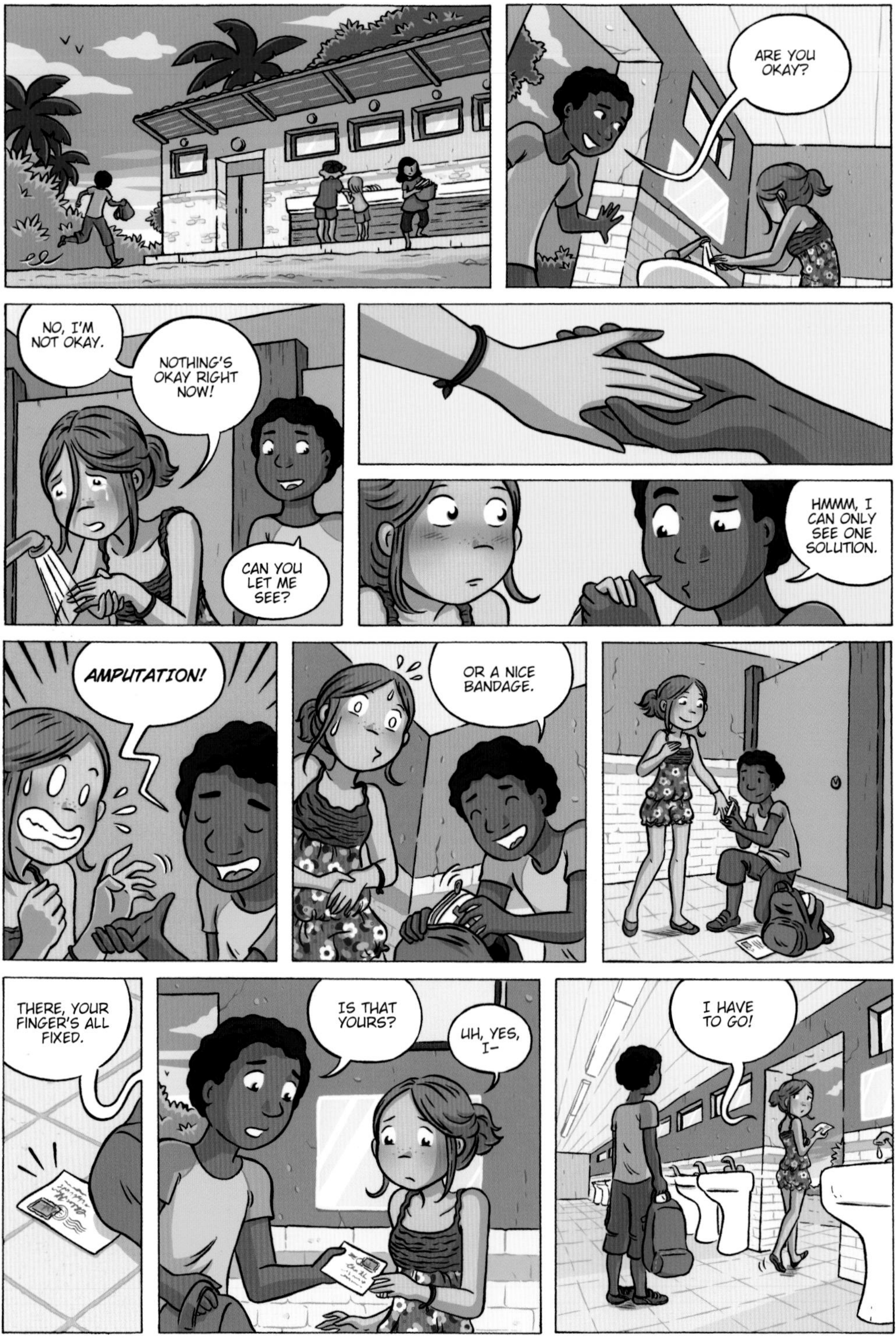

ARE YOU OKAY?
NO, I'M NOT OKAY.
NOTHING'S OKAY RIGHT NOW!
CAN YOU LET ME SEE?
HMMM, I CAN ONLY SEE ONE SOLUTION.
AMPUTATION!
OR A NICE BANDAGE.
THERE, YOUR FINGER'S ALL FIXED.
IS THAT YOURS?
UH, YES, I–
I HAVE TO GO!

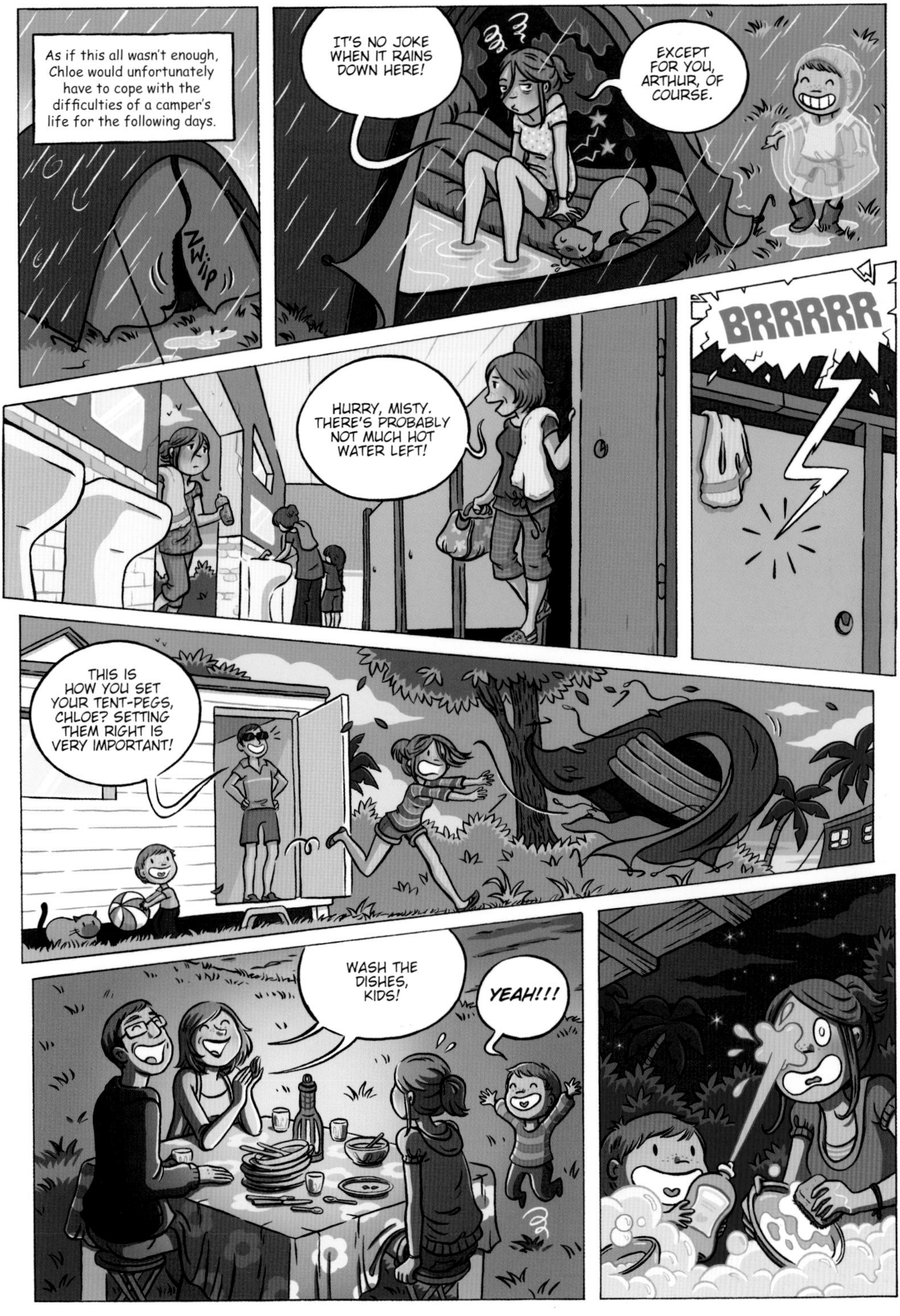
As if this all wasn't enough, Chloe would unfortunately have to cope with the difficulties of a camper's life for the following days.
IT'S NO JOKE WHEN IT RAINS DOWN HERE!
EXCEPT FOR YOU, ARTHUR, OF COURSE.
HURRY, MISTY. THERE'S PROBABLY NOT MUCH HOT WATER LEFT!
BRRRRR
THIS IS HOW YOU SET YOUR TENT-PEGS, CHLOE? SETTING THEM RIGHT IS VERY IMPORTANT!
WASH THE DISHES, KIDS!
YEAH!!!

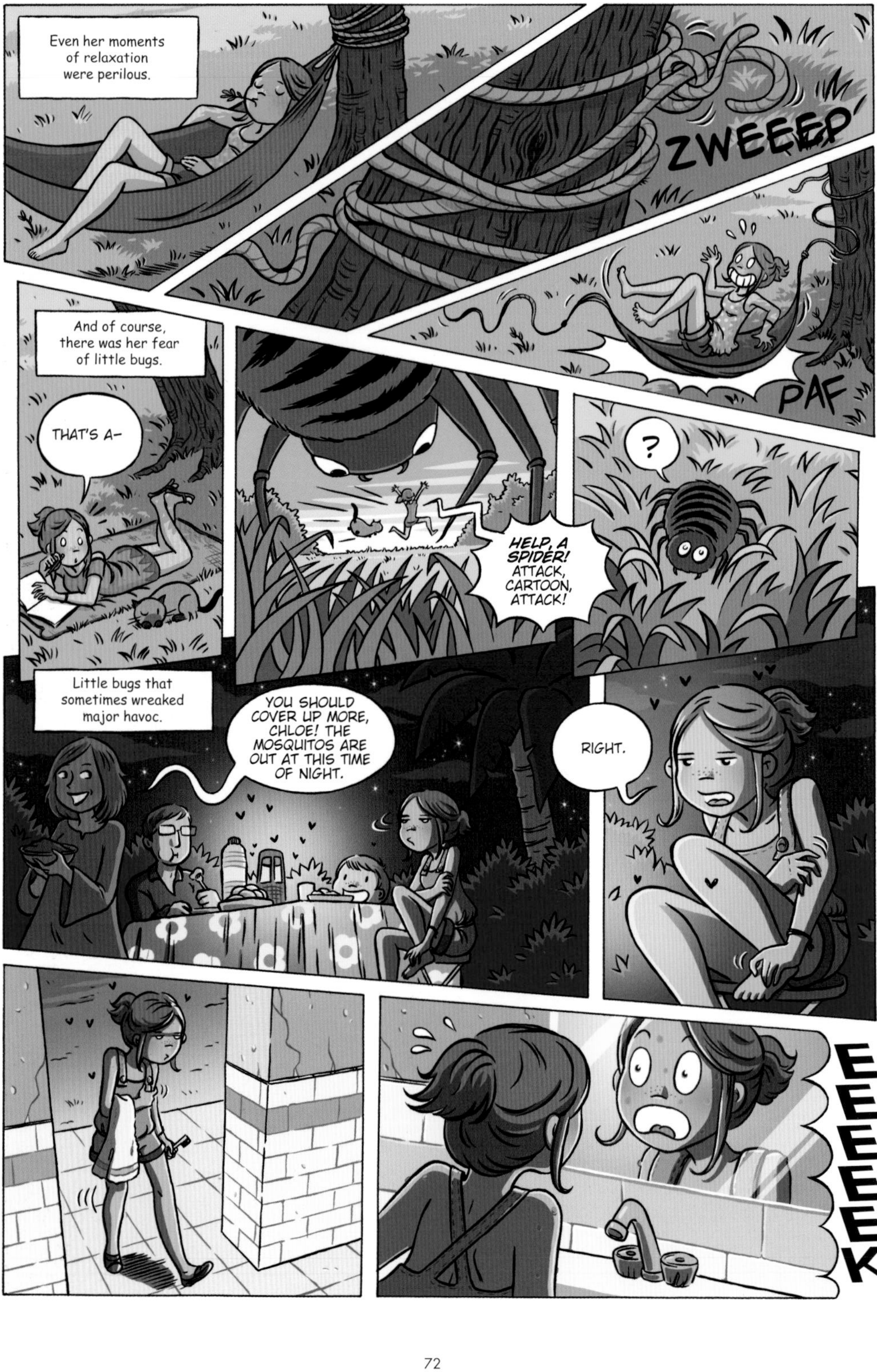
Even her moments of relaxation were perilous.
ZWEEEP
PAF
And of course, there was her fear of little bugs.
THAT'S A–
HELP, A SPIDER! ATTACK, CARTOON, ATTACK!
?
Little bugs that sometimes wreaked major havoc.
YOU SHOULD COVER UP MORE, CHLOE! THE MOSQUITOS ARE OUT AT THIS TIME OF NIGHT.
RIGHT.
EEEEEK

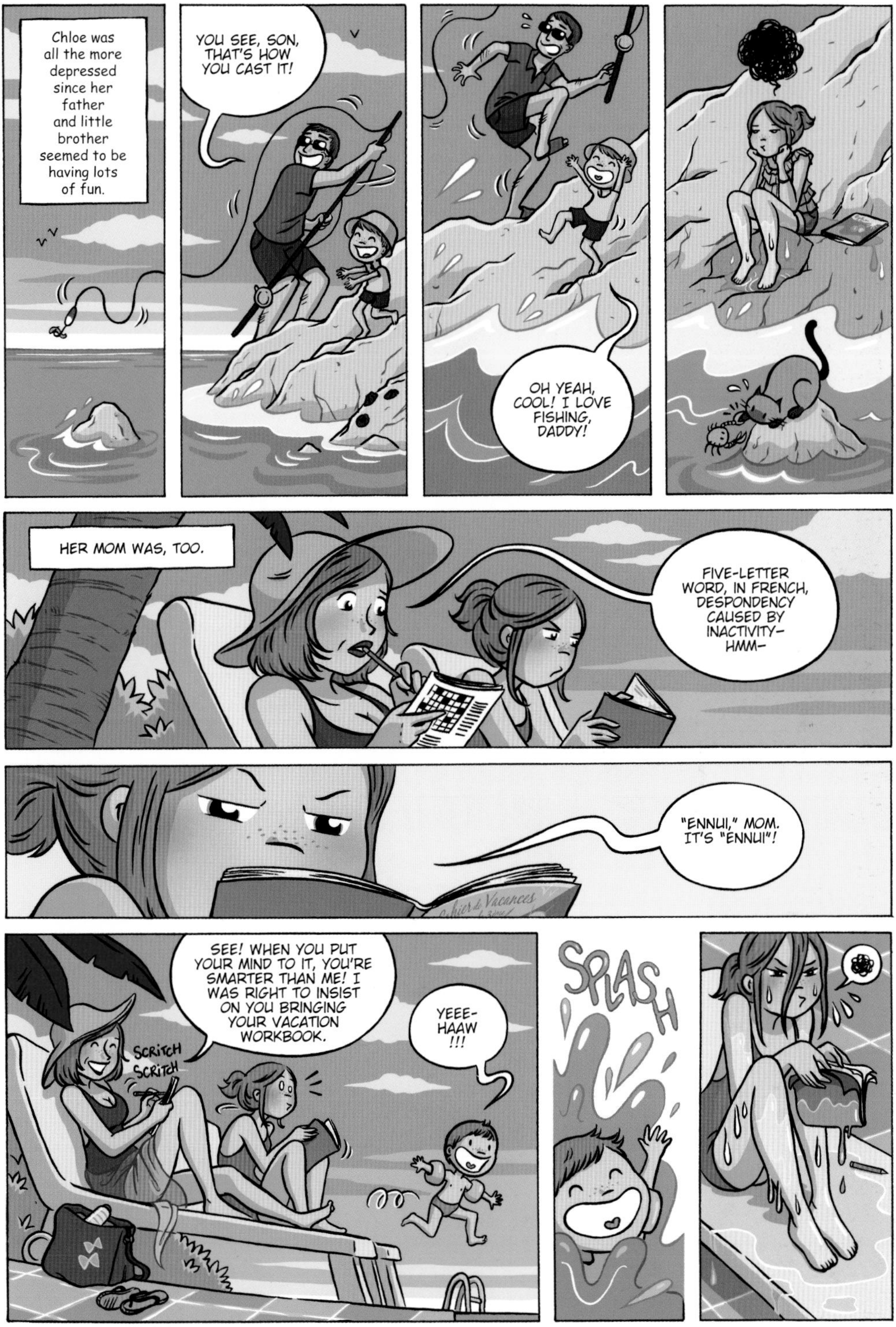

Chloe was all the more depressed since her father and little brother seemed to be having lots of fun.
YOU SEE, SON, THAT'S HOW YOU CAST IT!
OH YEAH, COOL! I LOVE FISHING, DADDY!
HER MOM WAS, TOO.
FIVE-LETTER WORD, IN FRENCH, DESPONDENCY CAUSED BY INACTIVITY— HMM—
"ENNUI," MOM. IT'S "ENNUI"!
Cahier de Vacances
SEE! WHEN YOU PUT YOUR MIND TO IT, YOU'RE SMARTER THAN ME! I WAS RIGHT TO INSIST ON YOU BRINGING YOUR VACATION WORKBOOK.
SCRITCH SCRITCH
YEEE-HAAW !!!
SPLASH

Perseverance

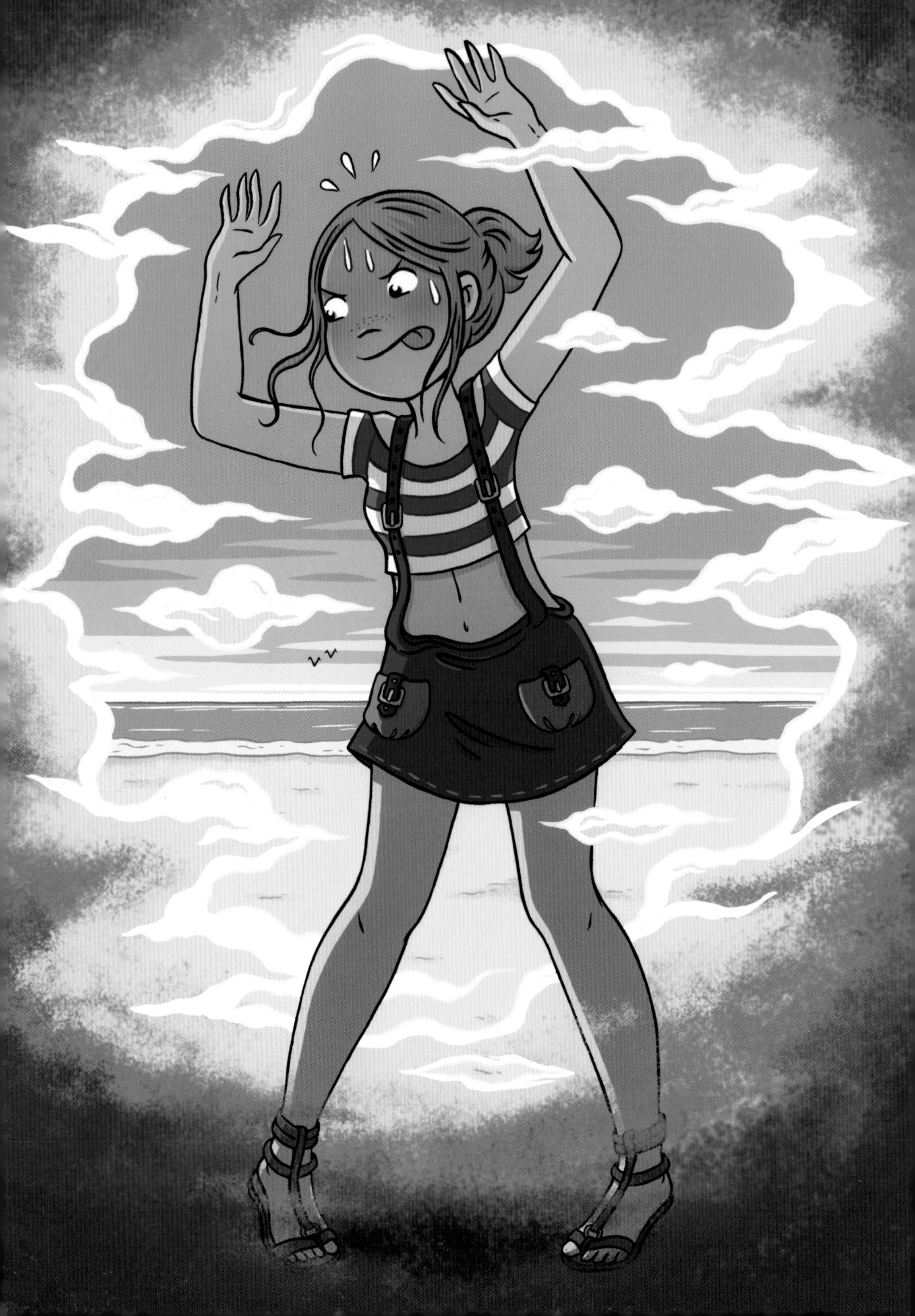

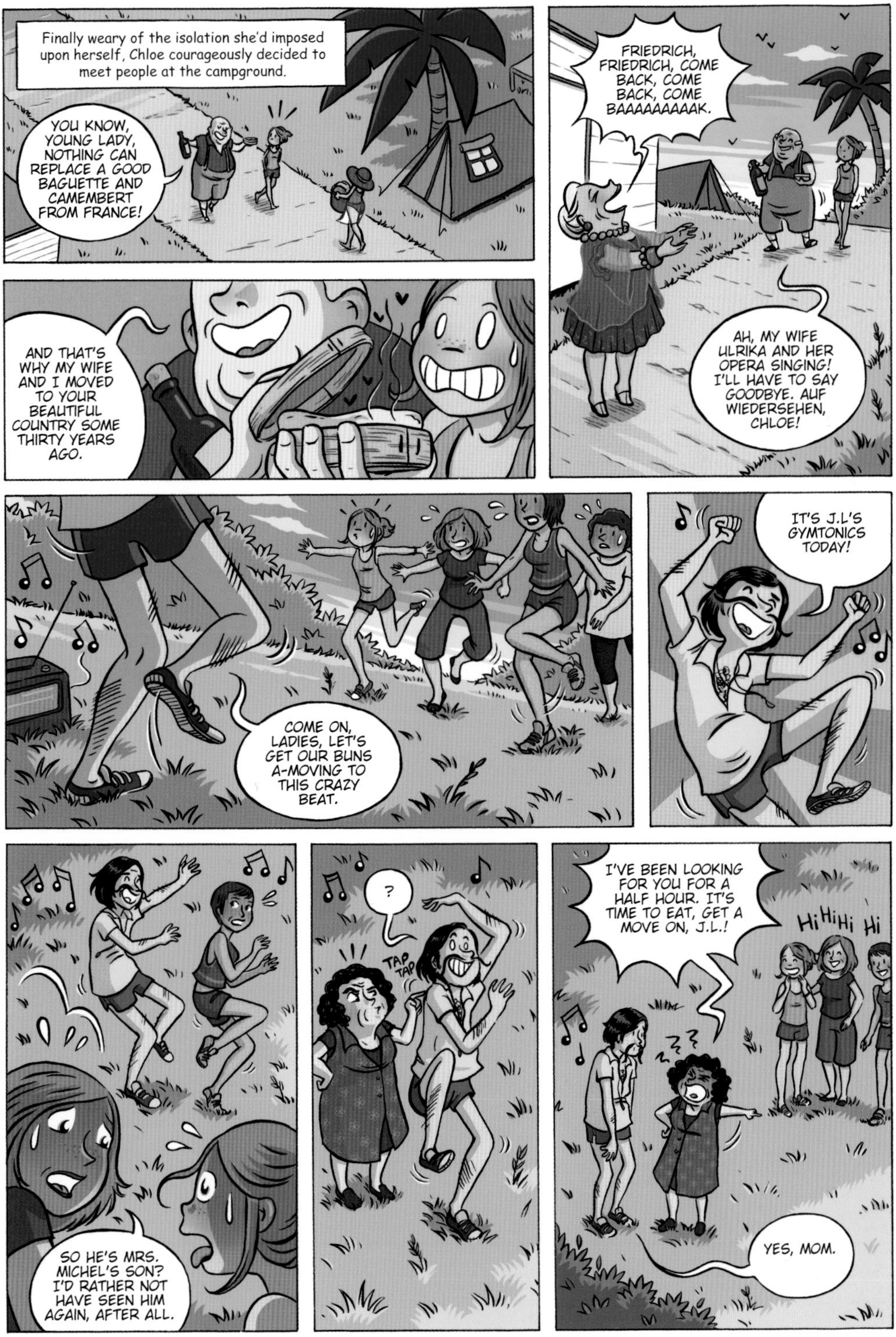

Finally weary of the isolation she'd imposed upon herself, Chloe courageously decided to meet people at the campground.
YOU KNOW, YOUNG LADY, NOTHING CAN REPLACE A GOOD BAGUETTE AND CAMEMBERT FROM FRANCE!
FRIEDRICH, FRIEDRICH, COME BACK, COME BACK, COME BAAAAAAAAAK.
AND THAT'S WHY MY WIFE AND I MOVED TO YOUR BEAUTIFUL COUNTRY SOME THIRTY YEARS AGO.
AH, MY WIFE ULRIKA AND HER OPERA SINGING! I'LL HAVE TO SAY GOODBYE. AUF WIEDERSEHEN, CHLOE!
COME ON, LADIES, LET'S GET OUR BUNS A-MOVING TO THIS CRAZY BEAT.
IT'S J.L'S GYMTONICS TODAY!
SO HE'S MRS. MICHEL'S SON? I'D RATHER NOT HAVE SEEN HIM AGAIN, AFTER ALL.
?
TAP TAP
I'VE BEEN LOOKING FOR YOU FOR A HALF HOUR. IT'S TIME TO EAT, GET A MOVE ON, J.L.!
HI HI HI HI
YES, MOM.

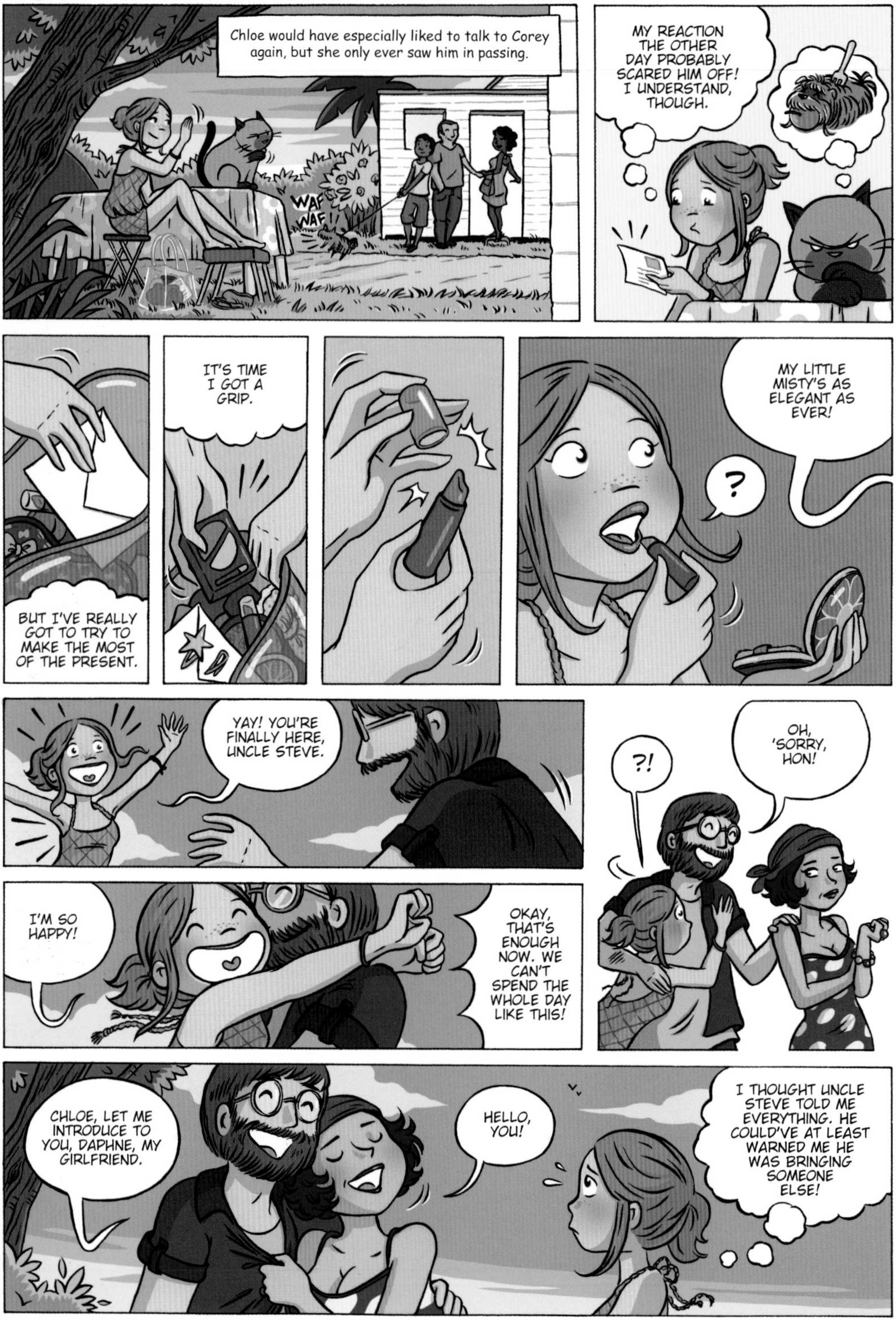
Chloe would have especially liked to talk to Corey again, but she only ever saw him in passing.
WAF WAF
MY REACTION THE OTHER DAY PROBABLY SCARED HIM OFF! I UNDERSTAND, THOUGH.
BUT I'VE REALLY GOT TO TRY TO MAKE THE MOST OF THE PRESENT.
IT'S TIME I GOT A GRIP.
?
MY LITTLE MISTY'S AS ELEGANT AS EVER!
YAY! YOU'RE FINALLY HERE, UNCLE STEVE.
I'M SO HAPPY!
OKAY, THAT'S ENOUGH NOW. WE CAN'T SPEND THE WHOLE DAY LIKE THIS!
?!
OH, 'SORRY, HON!
CHLOE, LET ME INTRODUCE TO YOU, DAPHNE, MY GIRLFRIEND.
HELLO, YOU!
I THOUGHT UNCLE STEVE TOLD ME EVERYTHING. HE COULD'VE AT LEAST WARNED ME HE WAS BRINGING SOMEONE ELSE!

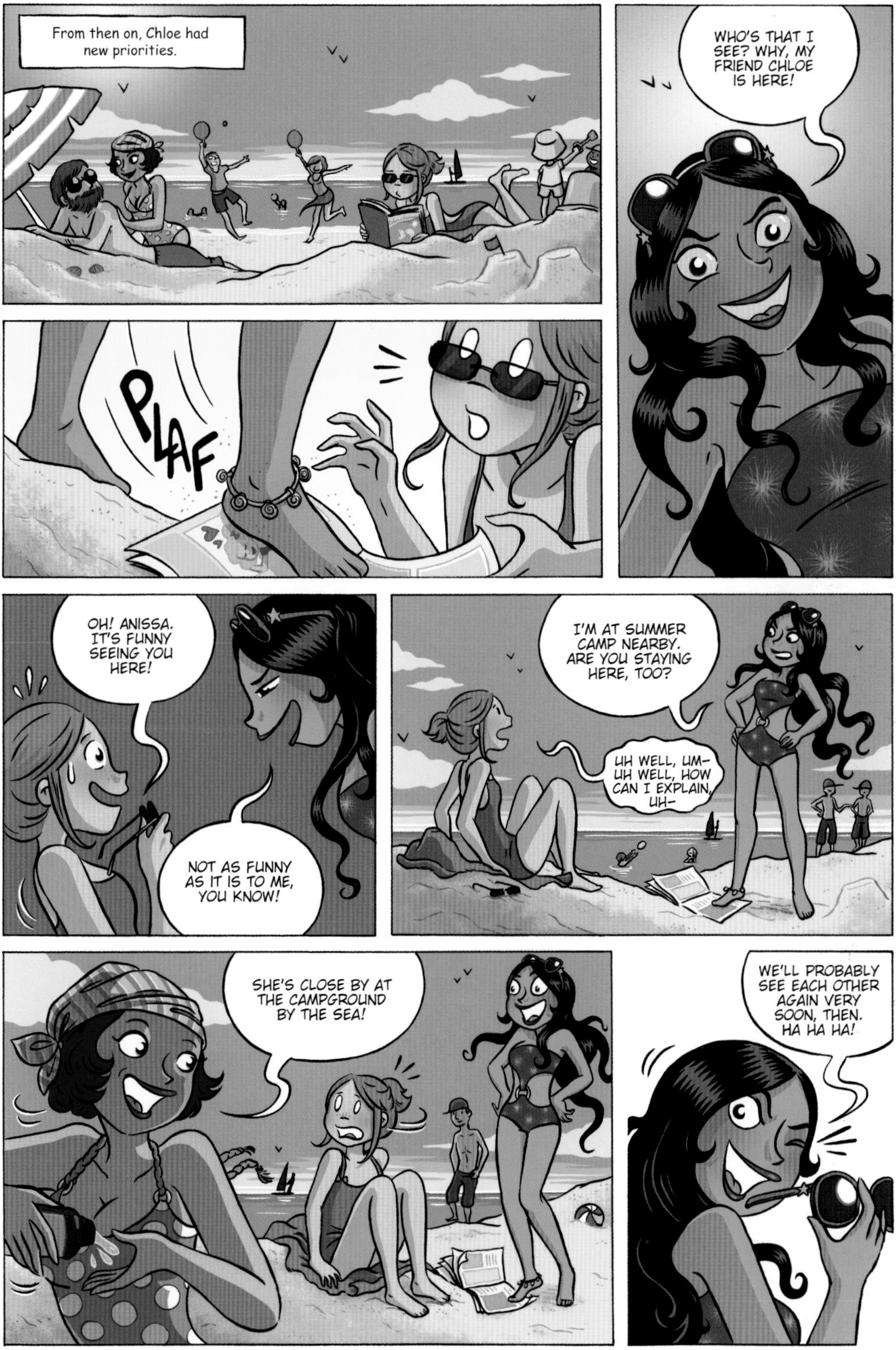
From then on, Chloe had new priorities.
WHO'S THAT I SEE? WHY, MY FRIEND CHLOE IS HERE!
PLAF
OH! ANISSA. IT'S FUNNY SEEING YOU HERE!
NOT AS FUNNY AS IT IS TO ME, YOU KNOW!
I'M AT SUMMER CAMP NEARBY. ARE YOU STAYING HERE, TOO?
UH WELL, UM– UH WELL, HOW CAN I EXPLAIN, UH–
SHE'S CLOSE BY AT THE CAMPGROUND BY THE SEA!
WE'LL PROBABLY SEE EACH OTHER AGAIN VERY SOON, THEN. HA HA HA!

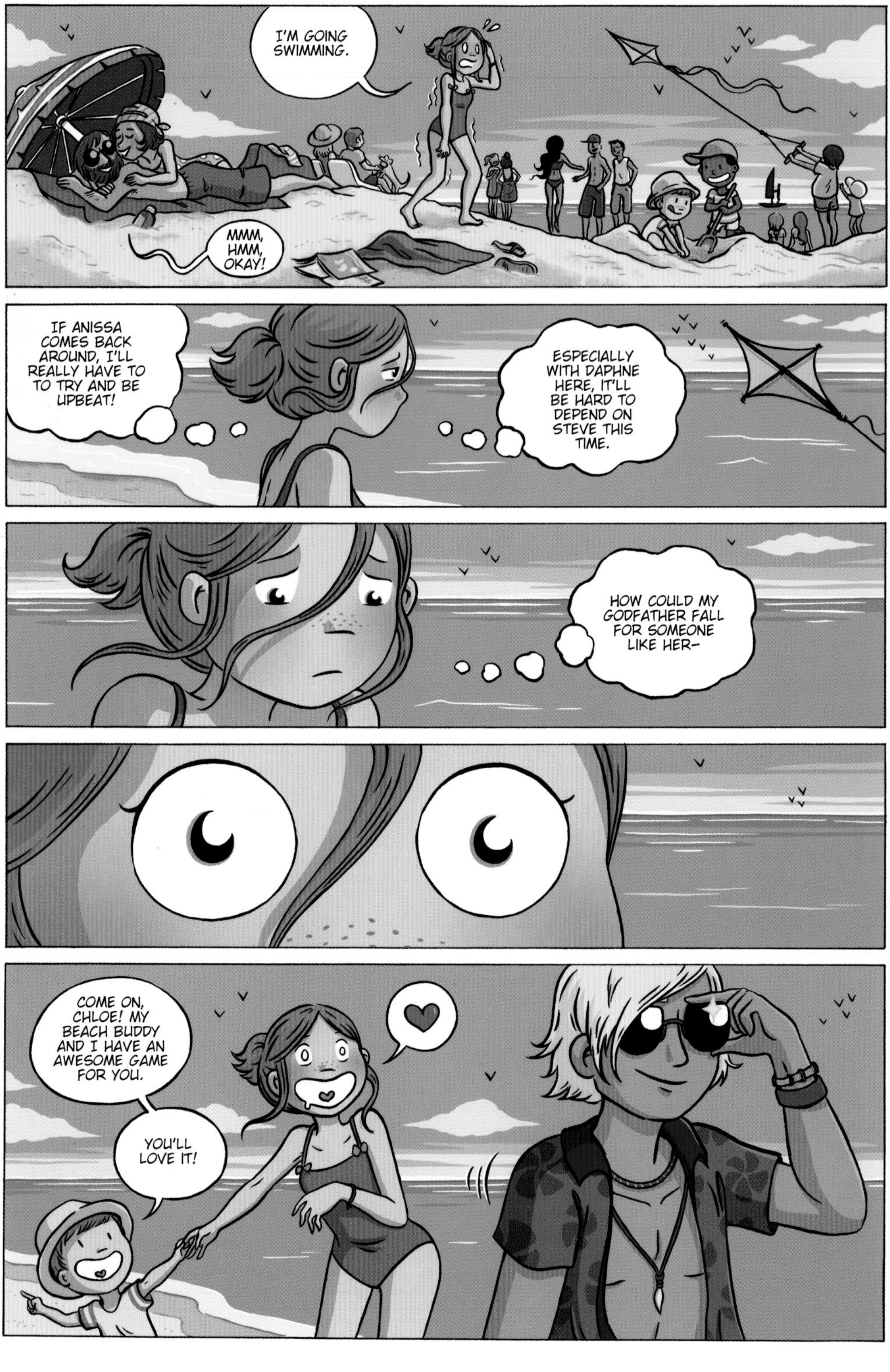
I'M GOING SWIMMING.
MMM, HMM, OKAY!
IF ANISSA COMES BACK AROUND, I'LL REALLY HAVE TO TO TRY AND BE UPBEAT!
ESPECIALLY WITH DAPHNE HERE, IT'LL BE HARD TO DEPEND ON STEVE THIS TIME.
HOW COULD MY GODFATHER FALL FOR SOMEONE LIKE HER-
COME ON, CHLOE! MY BEACH BUDDY AND I HAVE AN AWESOME GAME FOR YOU.
YOU'LL LOVE IT!

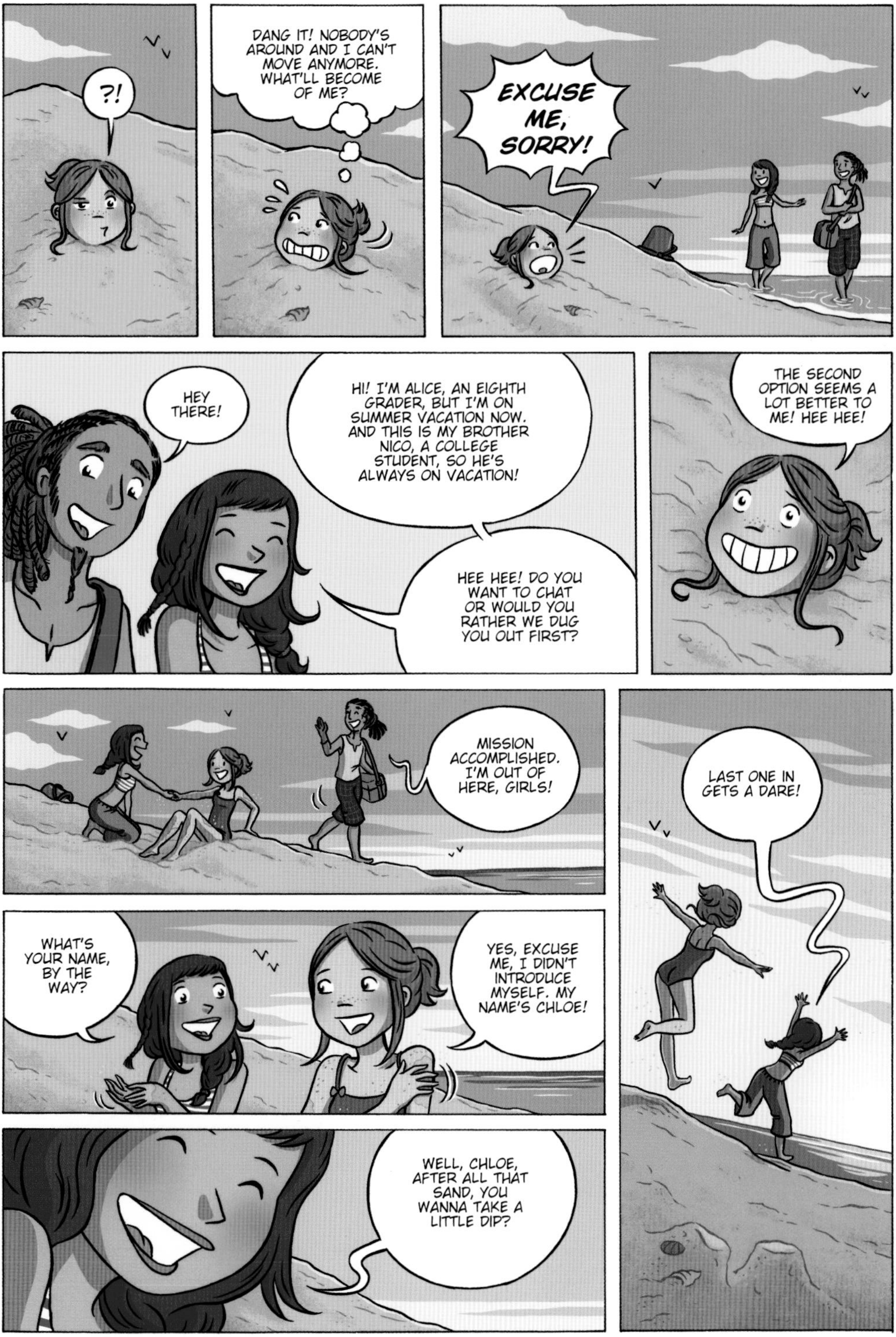
?!
DANG IT! NOBODY'S AROUND AND I CAN'T MOVE ANYMORE. WHAT'LL BECOME OF ME?
EXCUSE ME, SORRY!
HEY THERE!
HI! I'M ALICE, AN EIGHTH GRADER, BUT I'M ON SUMMER VACATION NOW. AND THIS IS MY BROTHER NICO, A COLLEGE STUDENT, SO HE'S ALWAYS ON VACATION!
HEE HEE! DO YOU WANT TO CHAT OR WOULD YOU RATHER WE DUG YOU OUT FIRST?
THE SECOND OPTION SEEMS A LOT BETTER TO ME! HEE HEE!
MISSION ACCOMPLISHED. I'M OUT OF HERE, GIRLS!
WHAT'S YOUR NAME, BY THE WAY?
YES, EXCUSE ME, I DIDN'T INTRODUCE MYSELF. MY NAME'S CHLOE!
WELL, CHLOE, AFTER ALL THAT SAND, YOU WANNA TAKE A LITTLE DIP?
LAST ONE IN GETS A DARE!

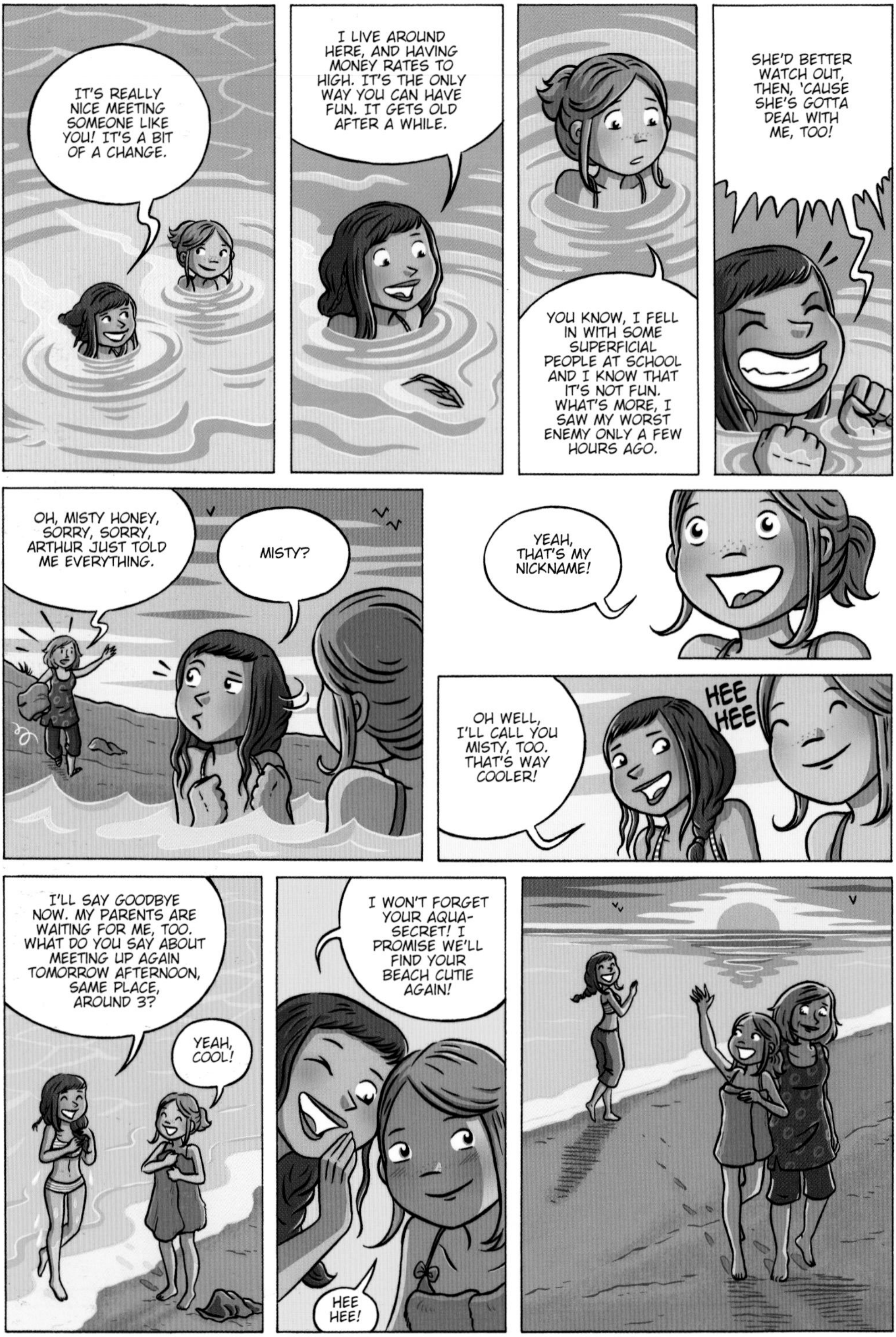
IT'S REALLY NICE MEETING SOMEONE LIKE YOU! IT'S A BIT OF A CHANGE.
I LIVE AROUND HERE, AND HAVING MONEY RATES TO HIGH. IT'S THE ONLY WAY YOU CAN HAVE FUN. IT GETS OLD AFTER A WHILE.
YOU KNOW, I FELL IN WITH SOME SUPERFICIAL PEOPLE AT SCHOOL AND I KNOW THAT IT'S NOT FUN. WHAT'S MORE, I SAW MY WORST ENEMY ONLY A FEW HOURS AGO.
SHE'D BETTER WATCH OUT, THEN, 'CAUSE SHE'S GOTTA DEAL WITH ME, TOO!
OH, MISTY HONEY, SORRY, SORRY, ARTHUR JUST TOLD ME EVERYTHING.
MISTY?
YEAH, THAT'S MY NICKNAME!
OH WELL, I'LL CALL YOU MISTY, TOO. THAT'S WAY COOLER!
HEE HEE
I'LL SAY GOODBYE NOW. MY PARENTS ARE WAITING FOR ME, TOO. WHAT DO YOU SAY ABOUT MEETING UP AGAIN TOMORROW AFTERNOON, SAME PLACE, AROUND 3?
YEAH, COOL!
I WON'T FORGET YOUR AQUA-SECRET! I PROMISE WE'LL FIND YOUR BEACH CUTIE AGAIN!
HEE HEE!

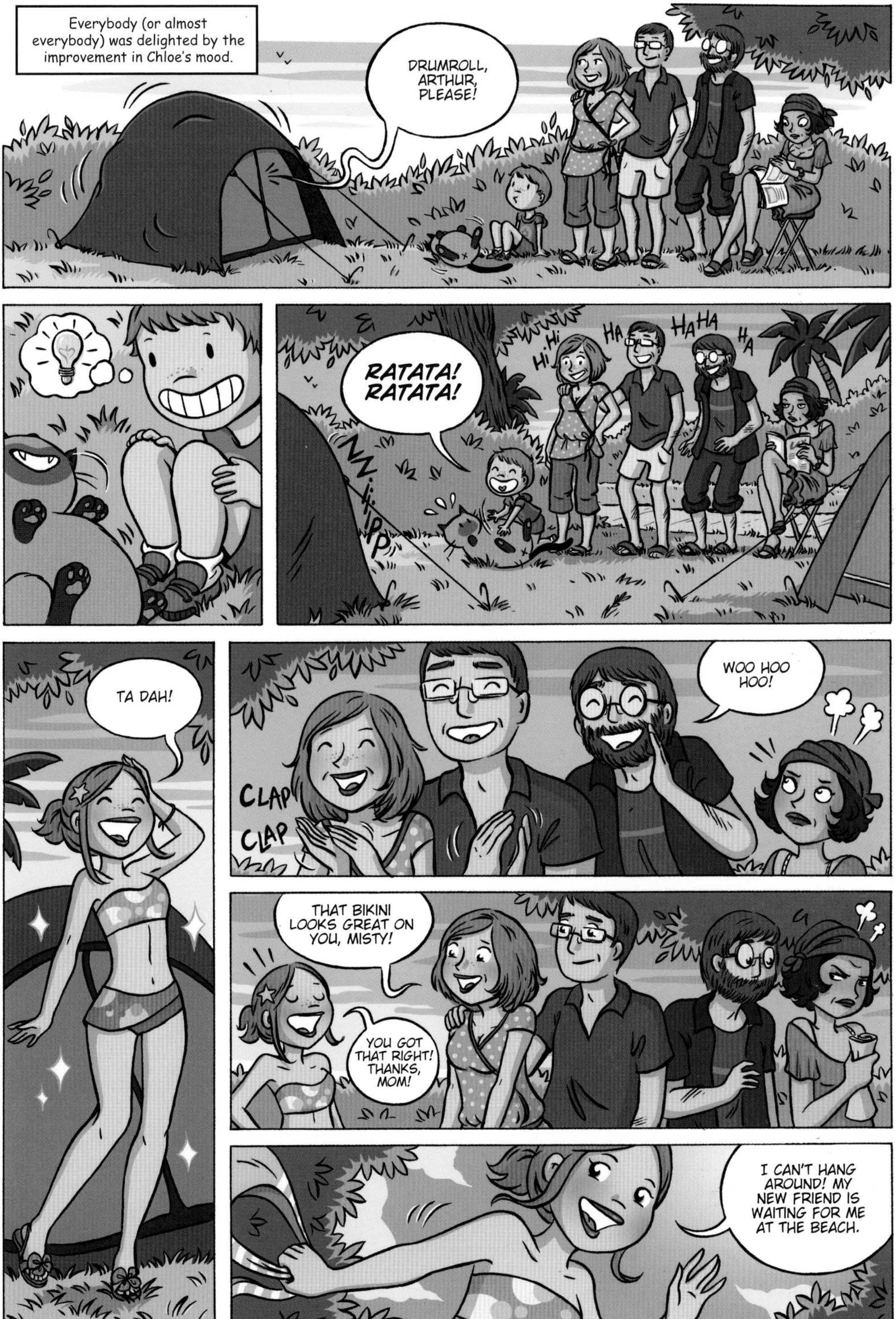

Everybody (or almost everybody) was delighted by the improvement in Chloe's mood.
DRUMROLL, ARTHUR, PLEASE!
RATATA! RATATA!
HI HI
HA HAHA HA
TA DAH!
CLAP CLAP
WOO HOO HOO!
THAT BIKINI LOOKS GREAT ON YOU, MISTY!
YOU GOT THAT RIGHT! THANKS, MOM!
I CAN'T HANG AROUND! MY NEW FRIEND IS WAITING FOR ME AT THE BEACH.

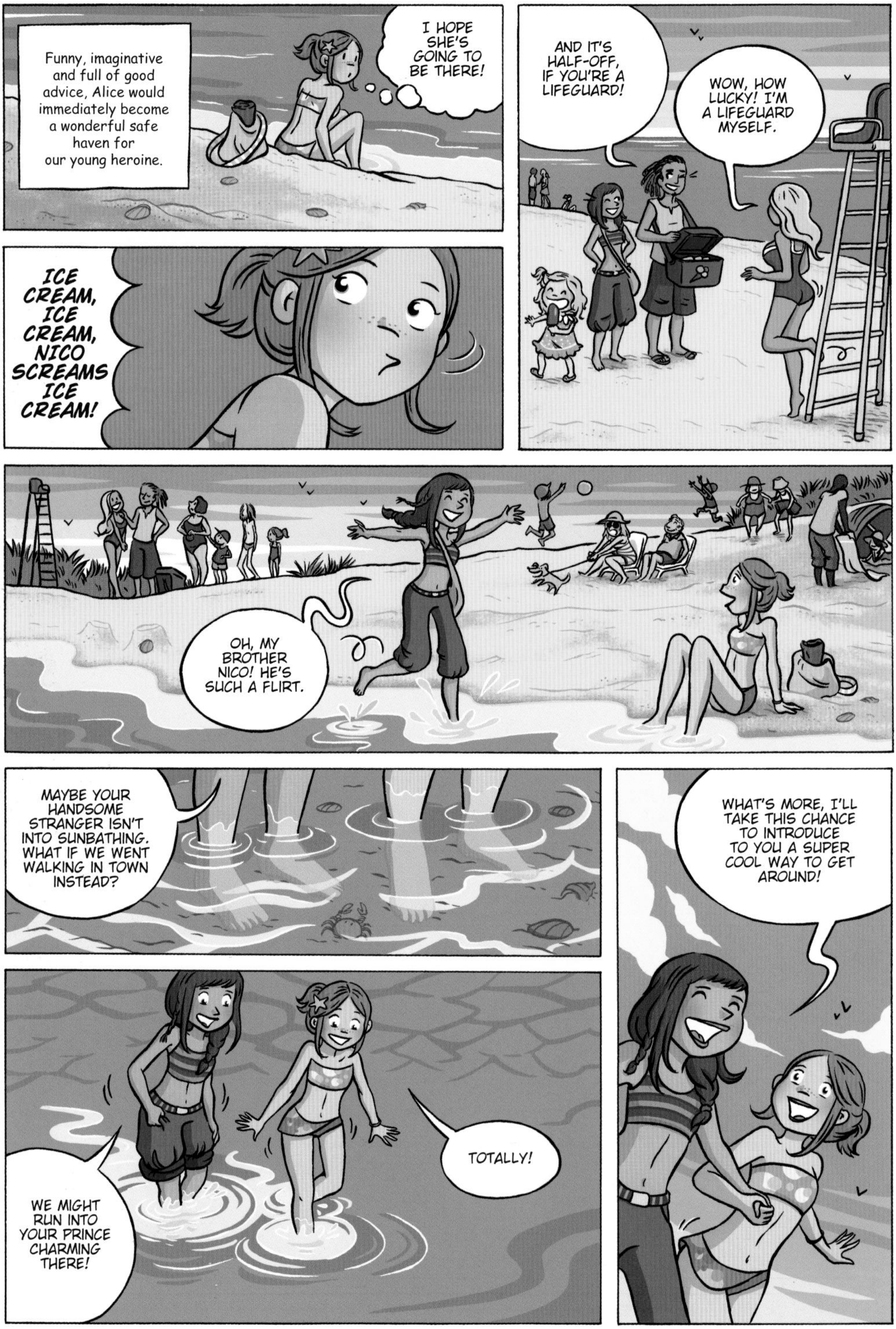

Funny, imaginative and full of good advice, Alice would immediately become a wonderful safe haven for our young heroine.
I HOPE SHE'S GOING TO BE THERE!
ICE CREAM, ICE CREAM, NICO SCREAMS ICE CREAM!
AND IT'S HALF-OFF, IF YOU'RE A LIFEGUARD!
WOW, HOW LUCKY! I'M A LIFEGUARD MYSELF.
OH, MY BROTHER NICO! HE'S SUCH A FLIRT.
MAYBE YOUR HANDSOME STRANGER ISN'T INTO SUNBATHING. WHAT IF WE WENT WALKING IN TOWN INSTEAD?
WE MIGHT RUN INTO YOUR PRINCE CHARMING THERE!
TOTALLY!
WHAT'S MORE, I'LL TAKE THIS CHANCE TO INTRODUCE TO YOU A SUPER COOL WAY TO GET AROUND!

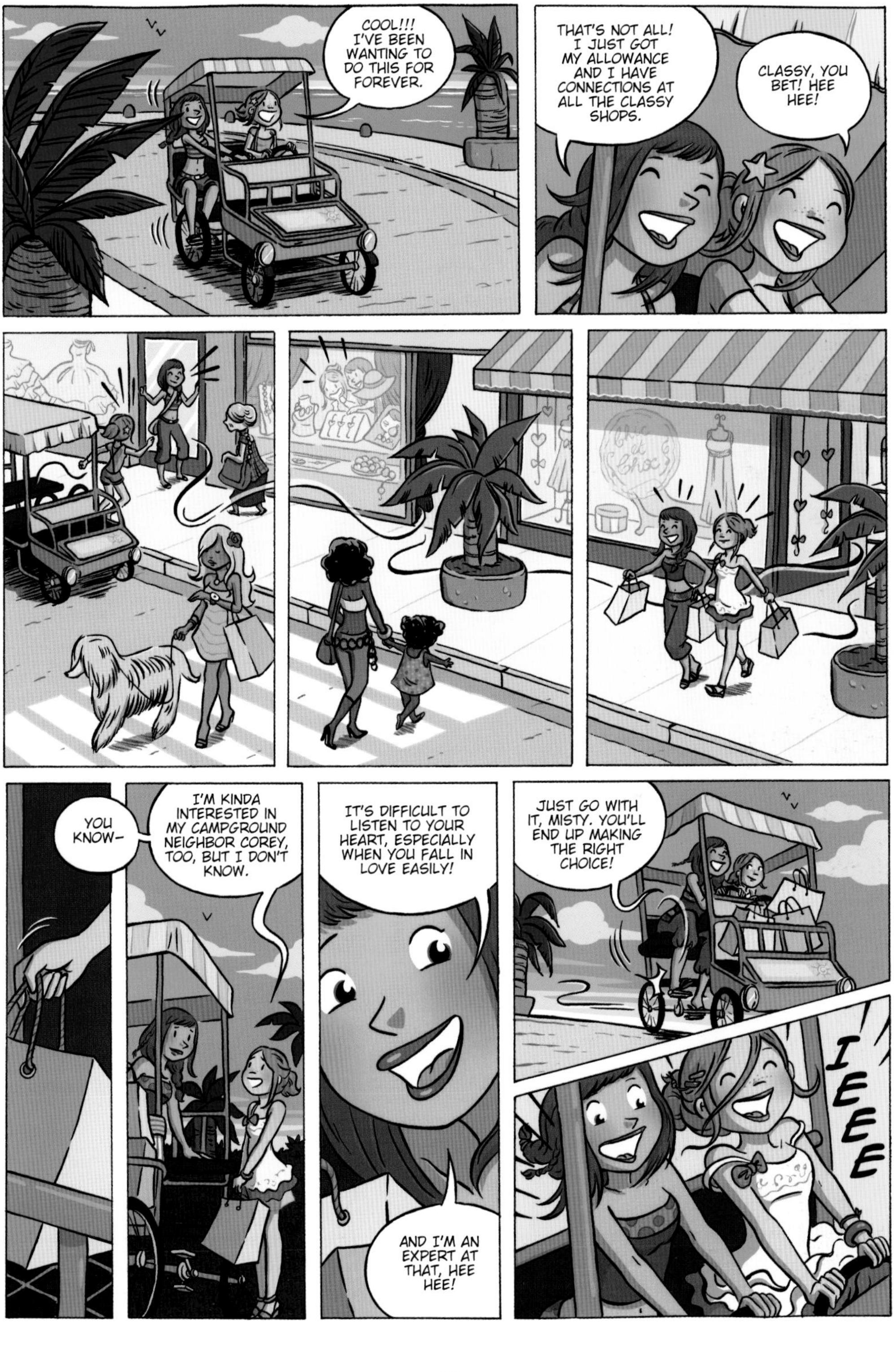
COOL!!! I'VE BEEN WANTING TO DO THIS FOR FOREVER.
THAT'S NOT ALL! I JUST GOT MY ALLOWANCE AND I HAVE CONNECTIONS AT ALL THE CLASSY SHOPS.
CLASSY, YOU BET! HEE HEE!
YOU KNOW–
I'M KINDA INTERESTED IN MY CAMPGROUND NEIGHBOR COREY, TOO, BUT I DON'T KNOW.
IT'S DIFFICULT TO LISTEN TO YOUR HEART, ESPECIALLY WHEN YOU FALL IN LOVE EASILY!
AND I'M AN EXPERT AT THAT, HEE HEE!
JUST GO WITH IT, MISTY. YOU'LL END UP MAKING THE RIGHT CHOICE!
IEEE

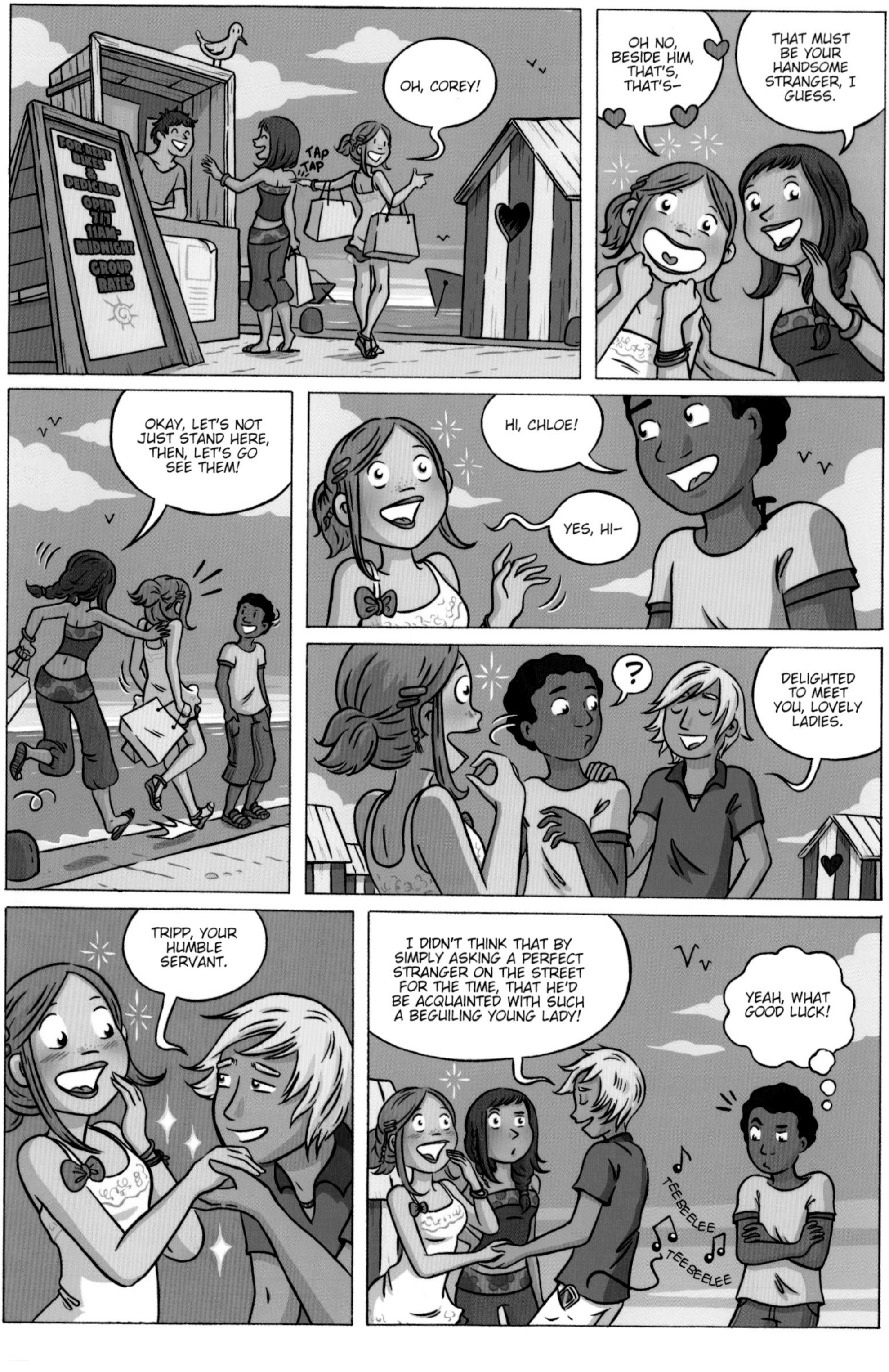
FOR RENT BIKES & PEDICABS OPEN 7/7 11AM-MIDNIGHT GROUP RATES
TAP TAP
OH, COREY!
OH NO, BESIDE HIM, THAT'S, THAT'S-
THAT MUST BE YOUR HANDSOME STRANGER, I GUESS.
OKAY, LET'S NOT JUST STAND HERE, THEN, LET'S GO SEE THEM!
HI, CHLOE!
YES, HI-
?
DELIGHTED TO MEET YOU, LOVELY LADIES.
TRIPP, YOUR HUMBLE SERVANT.
I DIDN'T THINK THAT BY SIMPLY ASKING A PERFECT STRANGER ON THE STREET FOR THE TIME, THAT HE'D BE ACQUAINTED WITH SUCH A BEGUILING YOUNG LADY!
YEAH, WHAT GOOD LUCK!
TEEBEELEE
TEEBEELEE

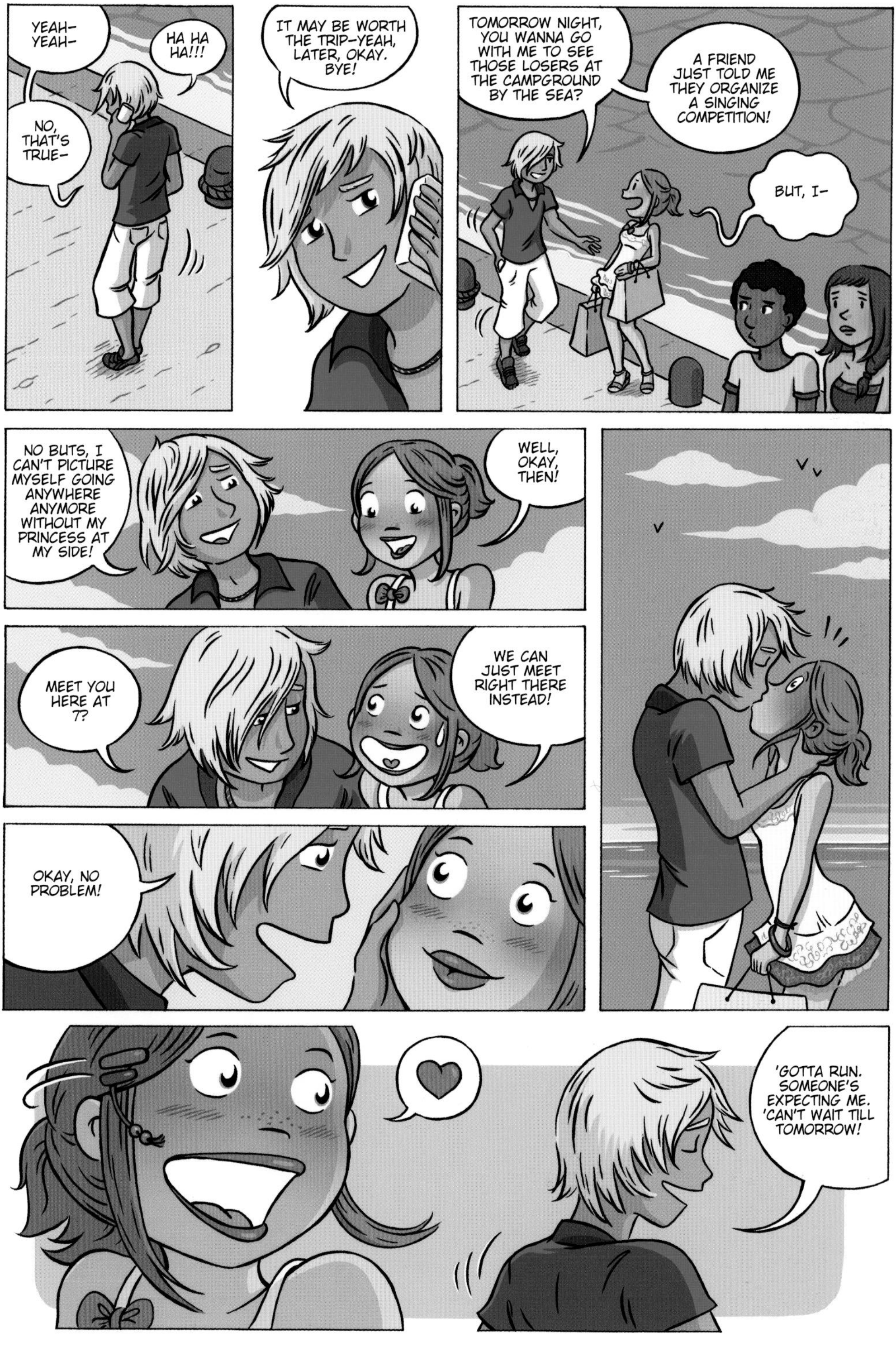
YEAH-YEAH-
HA HA HA!!!
NO, THAT'S TRUE-
IT MAY BE WORTH THE TRIP-YEAH, LATER, OKAY. BYE!
TOMORROW NIGHT, YOU WANNA GO WITH ME TO SEE THOSE LOSERS AT THE CAMPGROUND BY THE SEA?
A FRIEND JUST TOLD ME THEY ORGANIZE A SINGING COMPETITION!
BUT, I-
NO BUTS, I CAN'T PICTURE MYSELF GOING ANYWHERE ANYMORE WITHOUT MY PRINCESS AT MY SIDE!
WELL, OKAY, THEN!
MEET YOU HERE AT 7?
WE CAN JUST MEET RIGHT THERE INSTEAD!
OKAY, NO PROBLEM!
'GOTTA RUN. SOMEONE'S EXPECTING ME. 'CAN'T WAIT TILL TOMORROW!

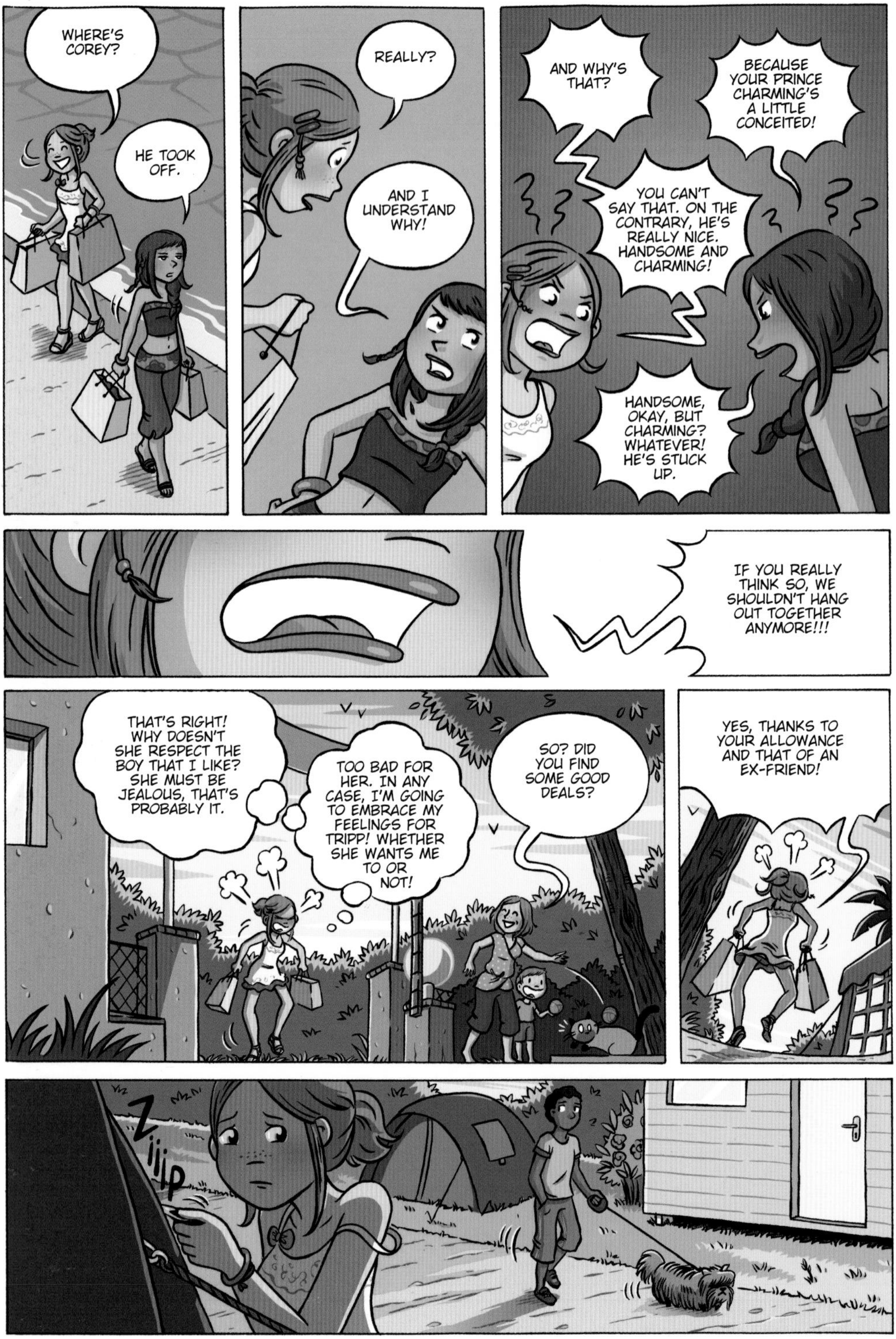
WHERE'S COREY?
HE TOOK OFF.
REALLY?
AND I UNDERSTAND WHY!
AND WHY'S THAT?
BECAUSE YOUR PRINCE CHARMING'S A LITTLE CONCEITED!
YOU CAN'T SAY THAT. ON THE CONTRARY, HE'S REALLY NICE. HANDSOME AND CHARMING!
HANDSOME, OKAY, BUT CHARMING? WHATEVER! HE'S STUCK UP.
IF YOU REALLY THINK SO, WE SHOULDN'T HANG OUT TOGETHER ANYMORE!!!
THAT'S RIGHT! WHY DOESN'T SHE RESPECT THE BOY THAT I LIKE? SHE MUST BE JEALOUS, THAT'S PROBABLY IT.
TOO BAD FOR HER. IN ANY CASE, I'M GOING TO EMBRACE MY FEELINGS FOR TRIPP! WHETHER SHE WANTS ME TO OR NOT!
SO? DID YOU FIND SOME GOOD DEALS?
YES, THANKS TO YOUR ALLOWANCE AND THAT OF AN EX-FRIEND!
ZIIIP

The Obvious

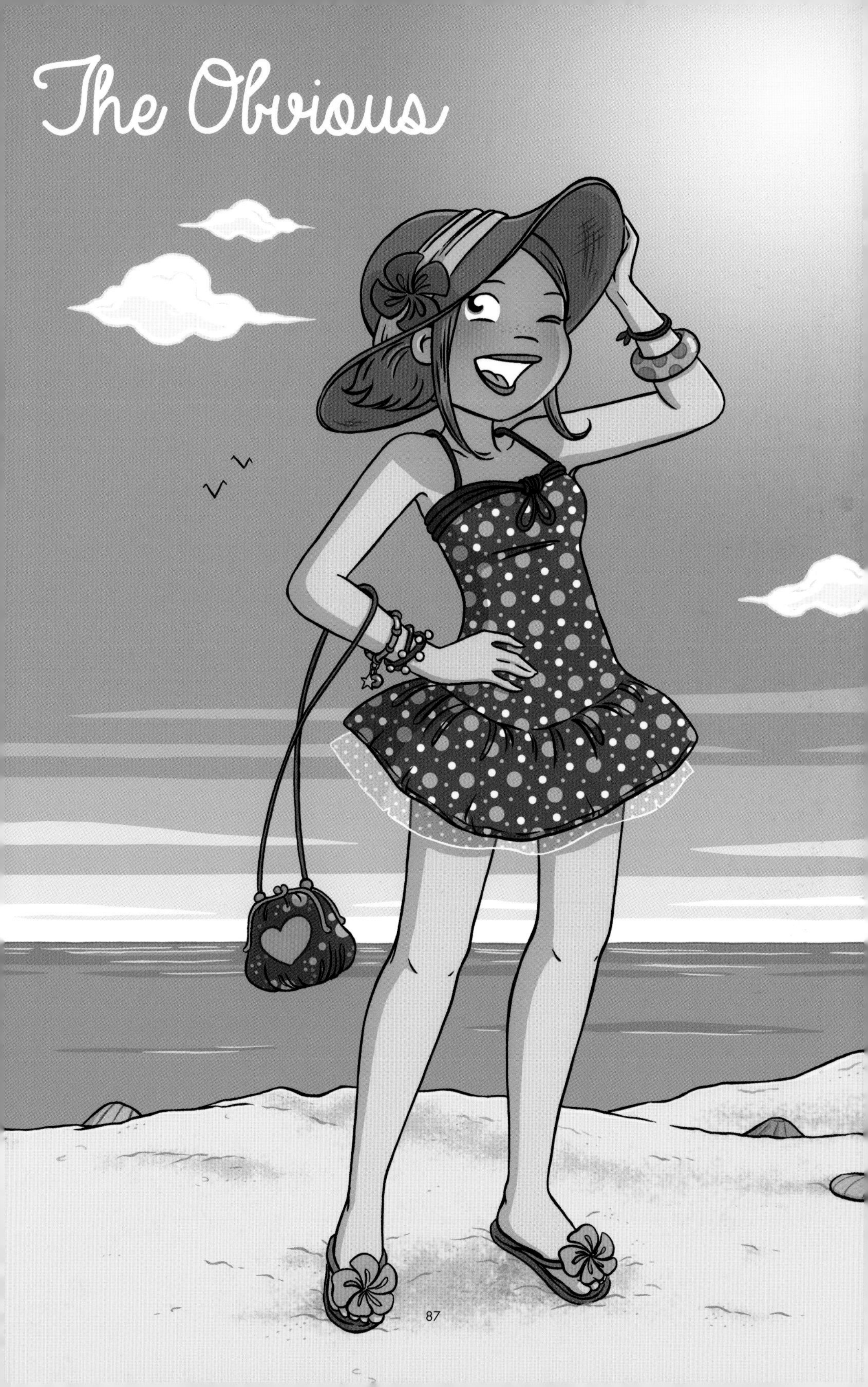

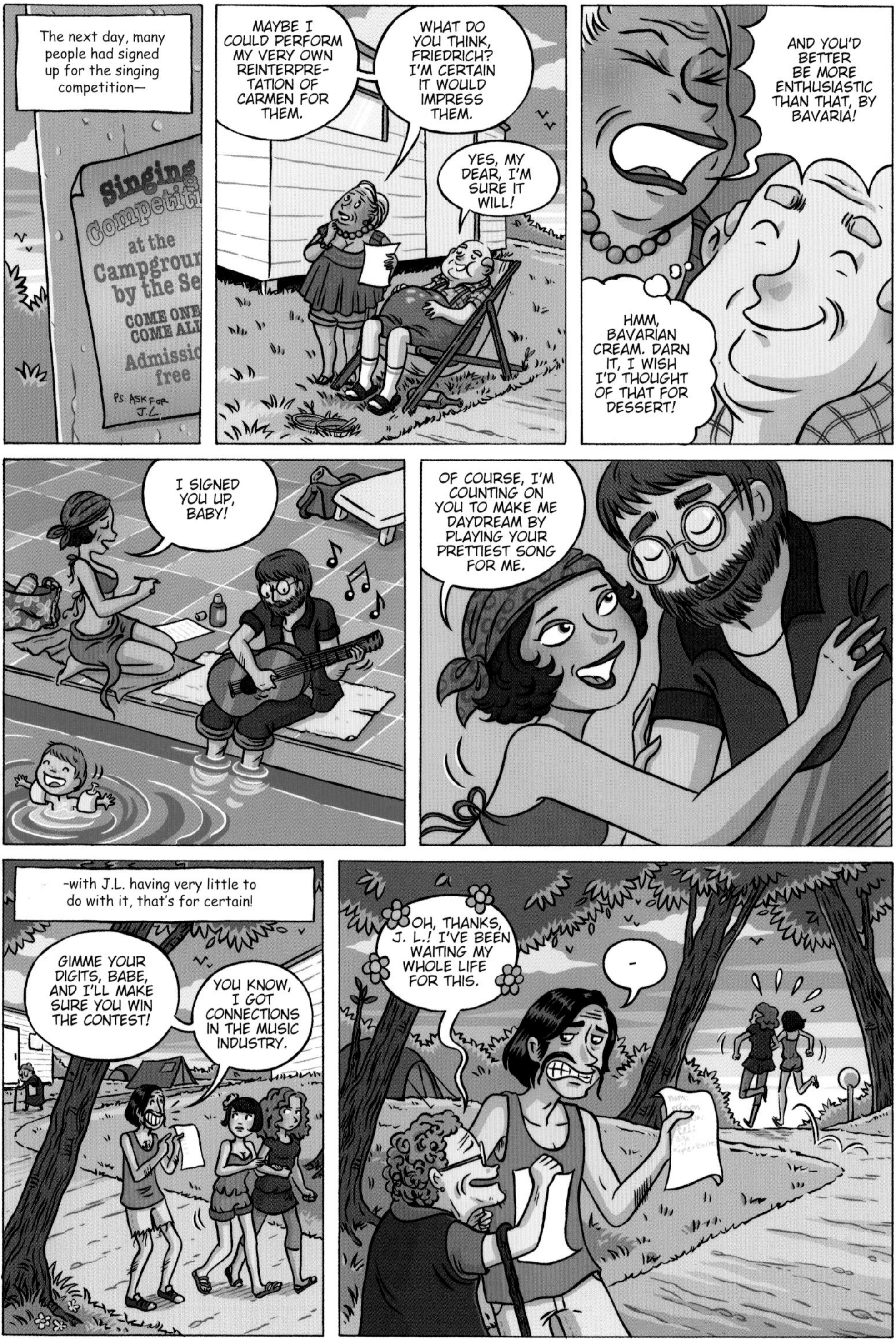

The next day, many people had signed up for the singing competition—
Singing
at the
free
PS: ASK FOR J.L.
MAYBE I COULD PERFORM MY VERY OWN REINTERPRETATION OF CARMEN FOR THEM.
WHAT DO YOU THINK, FRIEDRICH? I'M CERTAIN IT WOULD IMPRESS THEM.
YES, MY DEAR, I'M SURE IT WILL!
AND YOU'D BETTER BE MORE ENTHUSIASTIC THAN THAT, BY BAVARIA!
HMM, BAVARIAN CREAM. DARN IT, I WISH I'D THOUGHT OF THAT FOR DESSERT!
I SIGNED YOU UP, BABY!
OF COURSE, I'M COUNTING ON YOU TO MAKE ME DAYDREAM BY PLAYING YOUR PRETTIEST SONG FOR ME.
-with J.L. having very little to do with it, that's for certain!
GIMME YOUR DIGITS, BABE, AND I'LL MAKE SURE YOU WIN THE CONTEST!
YOU KNOW, I GOT CONNECTIONS IN THE MUSIC INDUSTRY.
OH, THANKS, J. L.! I'VE BEEN WAITING MY WHOLE LIFE FOR THIS.
-

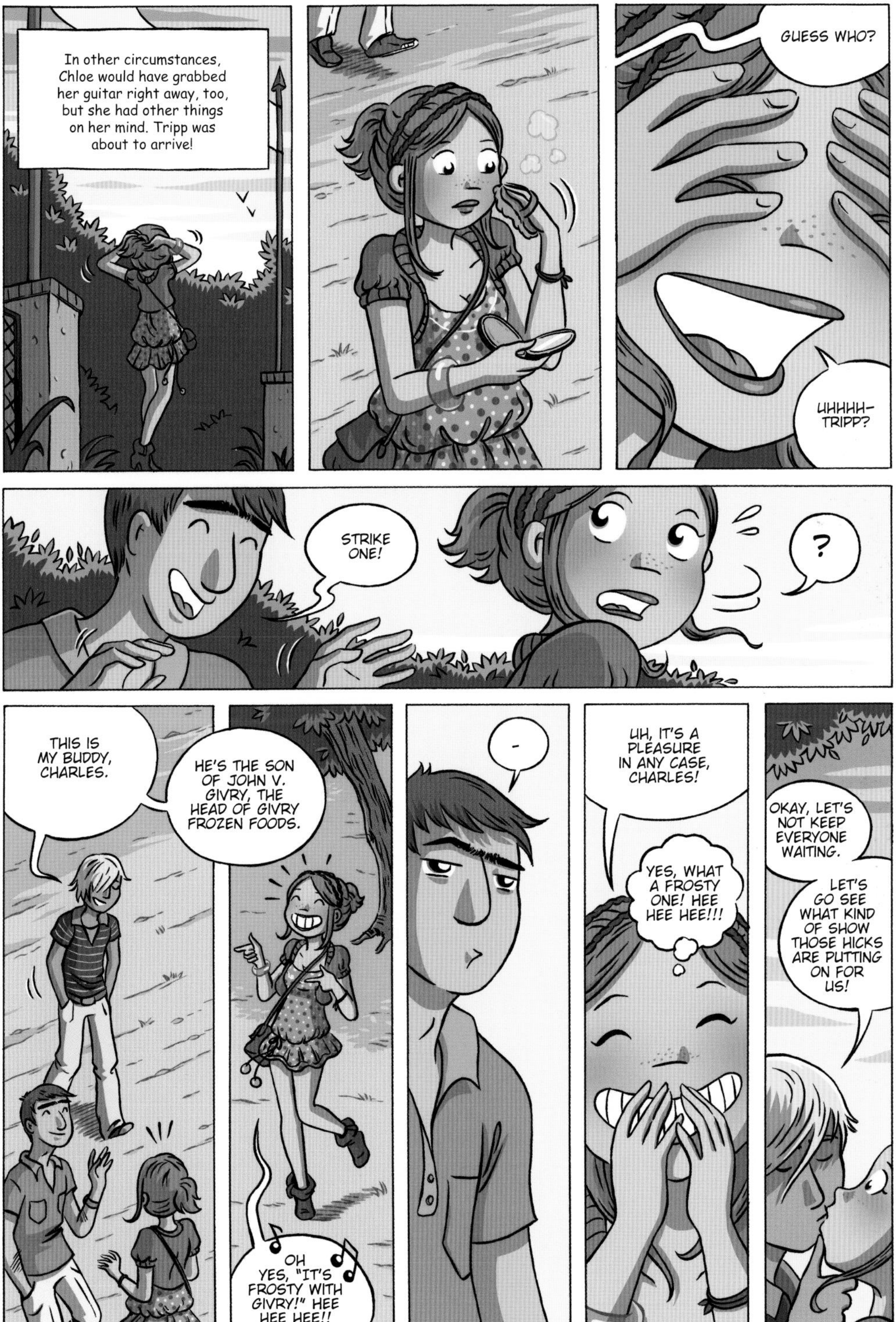
In other circumstances, Chloe would have grabbed her guitar right away, too, but she had other things on her mind. Tripp was about to arrive!
GUESS WHO?
UHHHH-TRIPP?
STRIKE ONE!
?
THIS IS MY BUDDY, CHARLES.
HE'S THE SON OF JOHN V. GIVRY, THE HEAD OF GIVRY FROZEN FOODS.
OH YES, "IT'S FROSTY WITH GIVRY!" HEE HEE HEE!!
-
UH, IT'S A PLEASURE IN ANY CASE, CHARLES!
YES, WHAT A FROSTY ONE! HEE HEE HEE!!!
OKAY, LET'S NOT KEEP EVERYONE WAITING.
LET'S GO SEE WHAT KIND OF SHOW THOSE HICKS ARE PUTTING ON FOR US!

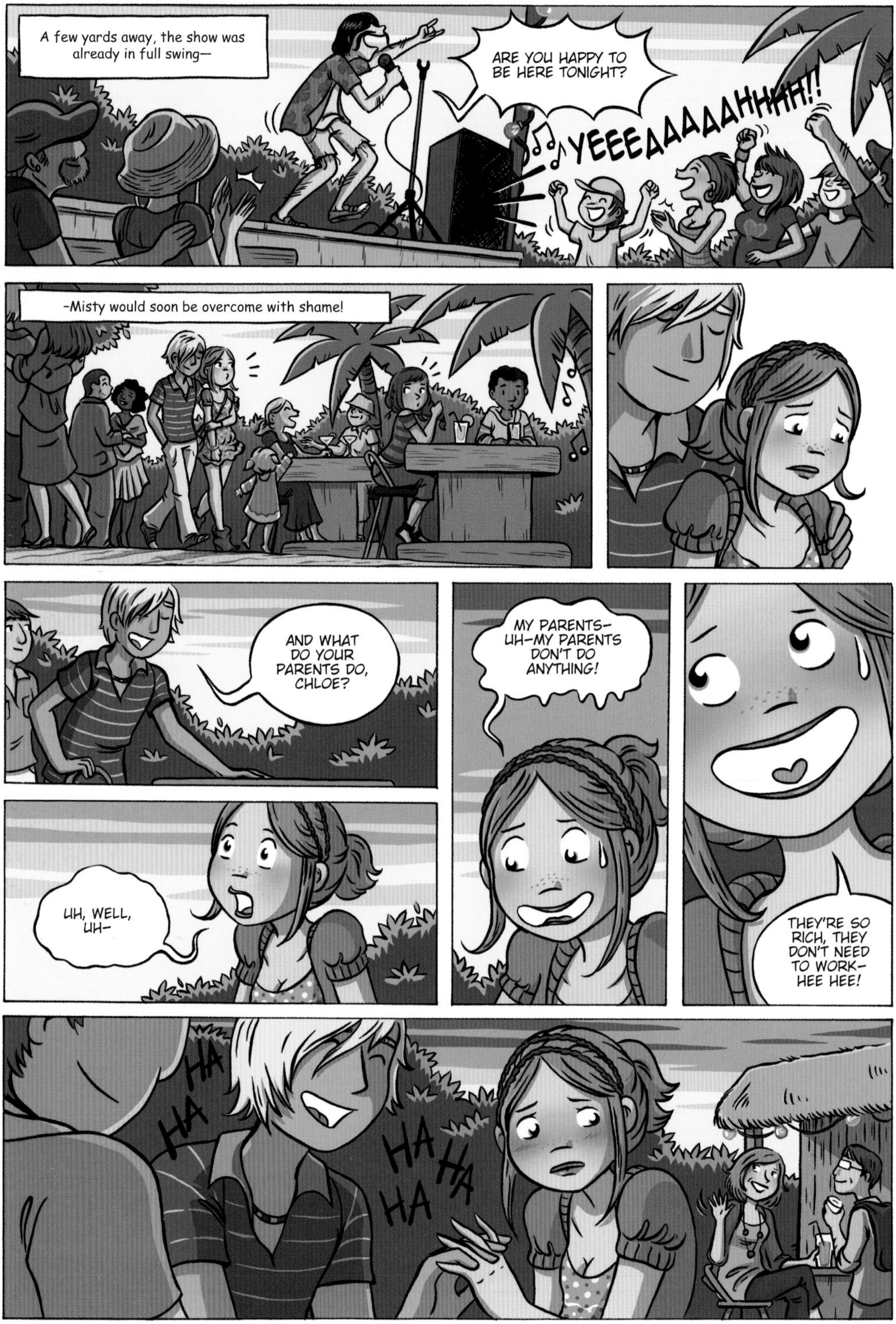
A few yards away, the show was already in full swing—
ARE YOU HAPPY TO BE HERE TONIGHT?
YEEEAAAAAHHHH!!
-Misty would soon be overcome with shame!
AND WHAT DO YOUR PARENTS DO, CHLOE?
UH, WELL, UH-
MY PARENTS- UH-MY PARENTS DON'T DO ANYTHING!
THEY'RE SO RICH, THEY DON'T NEED TO WORK- HEE HEE!
HA HA
HA HA HA HA

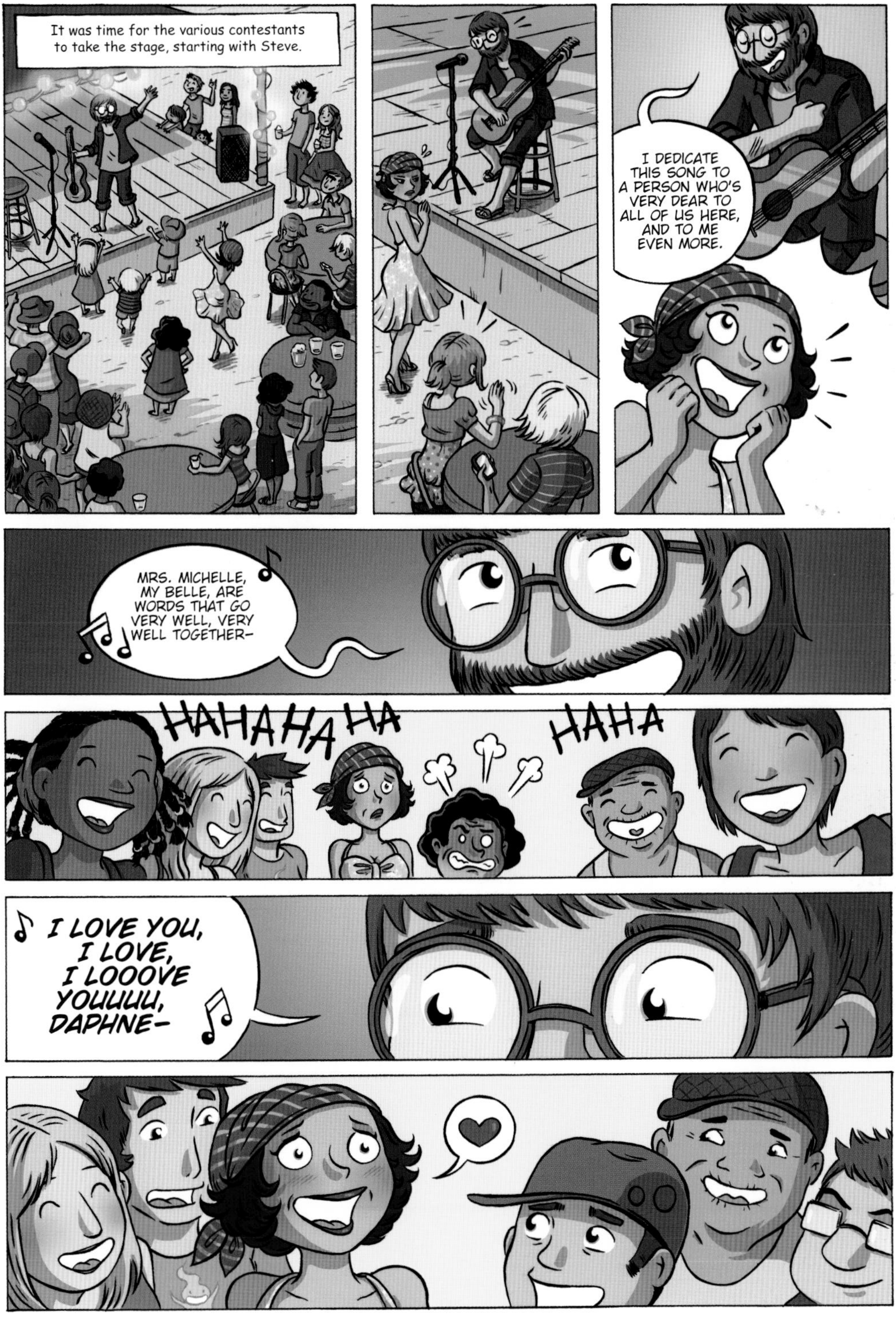
It was time for the various contestants to take the stage, starting with Steve.
I DEDICATE THIS SONG TO A PERSON WHO'S VERY DEAR TO ALL OF US HERE, AND TO ME EVEN MORE.
MRS. MICHELLE, MY BELLE, ARE WORDS THAT GO VERY WELL, VERY WELL TOGETHER–
HAHAHAHA
HAHA
I LOVE YOU, I LOVE, I LOOOVE YOUUUU, DAPHNE–

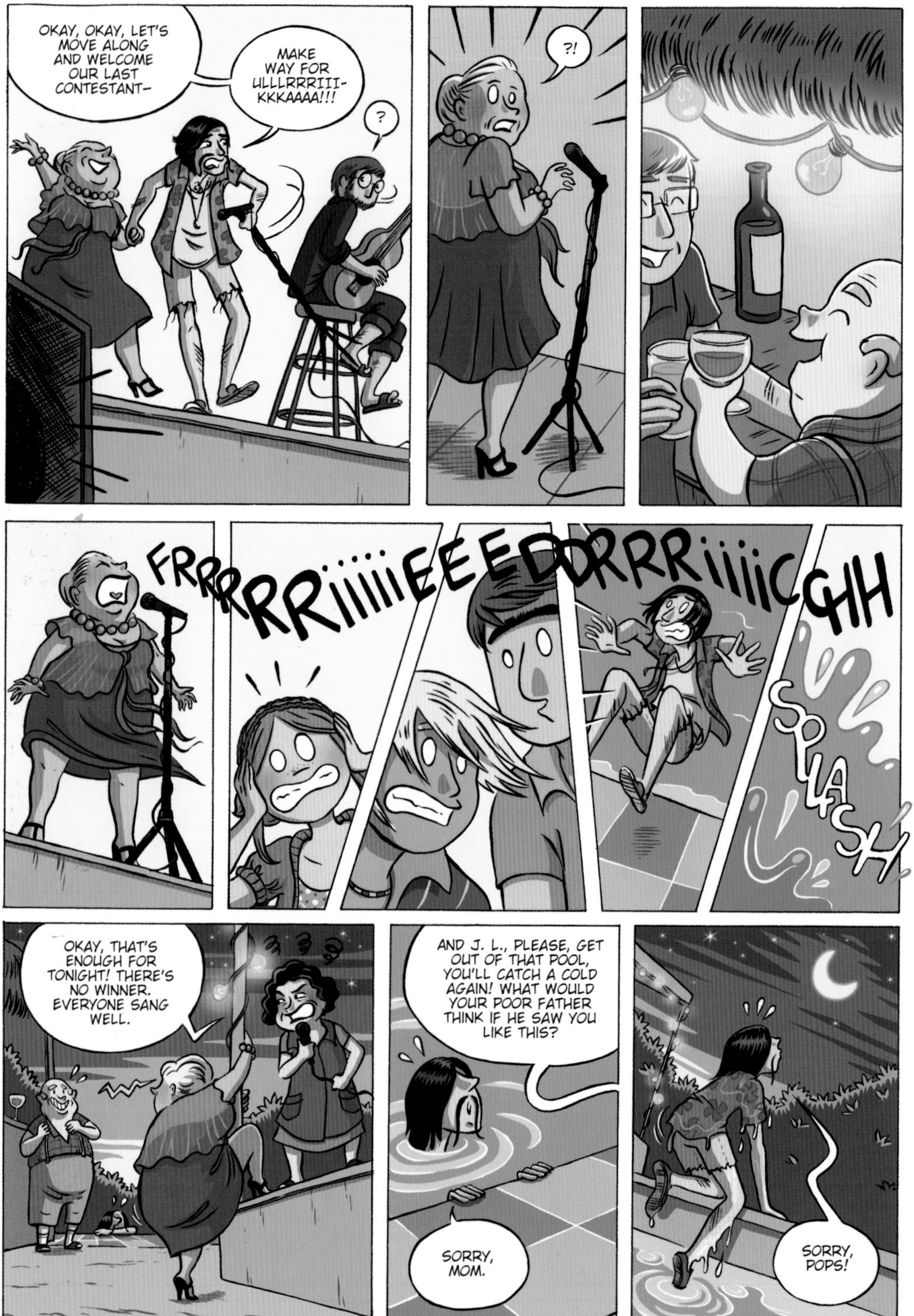
OKAY, OKAY, LET'S MOVE ALONG AND WELCOME OUR LAST CONTESTANT–
MAKE WAY FOR ULLLRRRIII-KKKAAAA!!!
?
?!
FRRRRRRiiiiiiEEEEDDRRRRiiiiiCCHH
SPLASH
OKAY, THAT'S ENOUGH FOR TONIGHT! THERE'S NO WINNER. EVERYONE SANG WELL.
AND J. L., PLEASE, GET OUT OF THAT POOL, YOU'LL CATCH A COLD AGAIN! WHAT WOULD YOUR POOR FATHER THINK IF HE SAW YOU LIKE THIS?
SORRY, MOM.
SORRY, POPS!

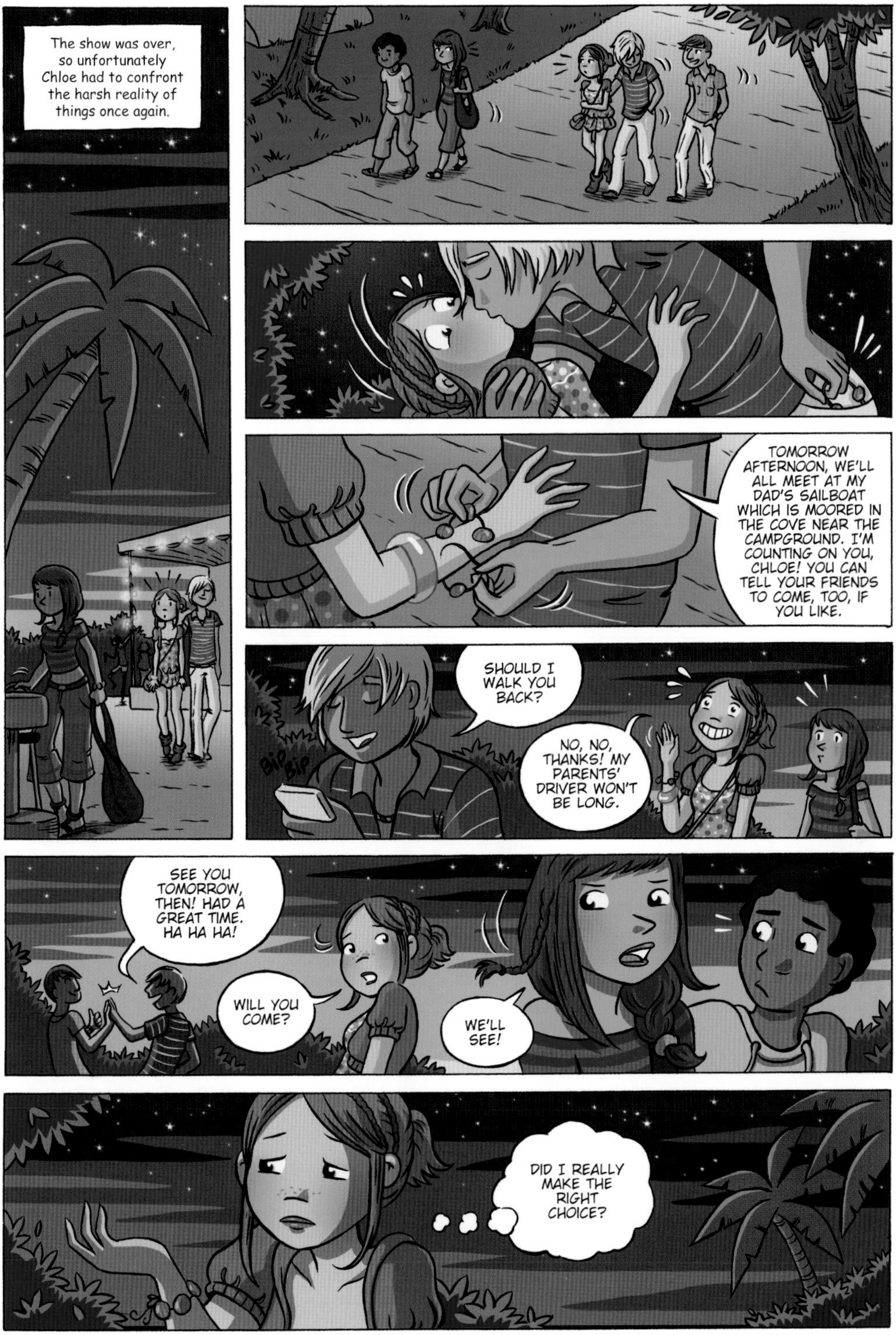
The show was over, so unfortunately Chloe had to confront the harsh reality of things once again.
TOMORROW AFTERNOON, WE'LL ALL MEET AT MY DAD'S SAILBOAT WHICH IS MOORED IN THE COVE NEAR THE CAMPGROUND. I'M COUNTING ON YOU, CHLOE! YOU CAN TELL YOUR FRIENDS TO COME, TOO, IF YOU LIKE.
SHOULD I WALK YOU BACK?
BIP BIP
NO, NO, THANKS! MY PARENTS' DRIVER WON'T BE LONG.
SEE YOU TOMORROW, THEN! HAD A GREAT TIME. HA HA HA!
WILL YOU COME?
WE'LL SEE!
DID I REALLY MAKE THE RIGHT CHOICE?

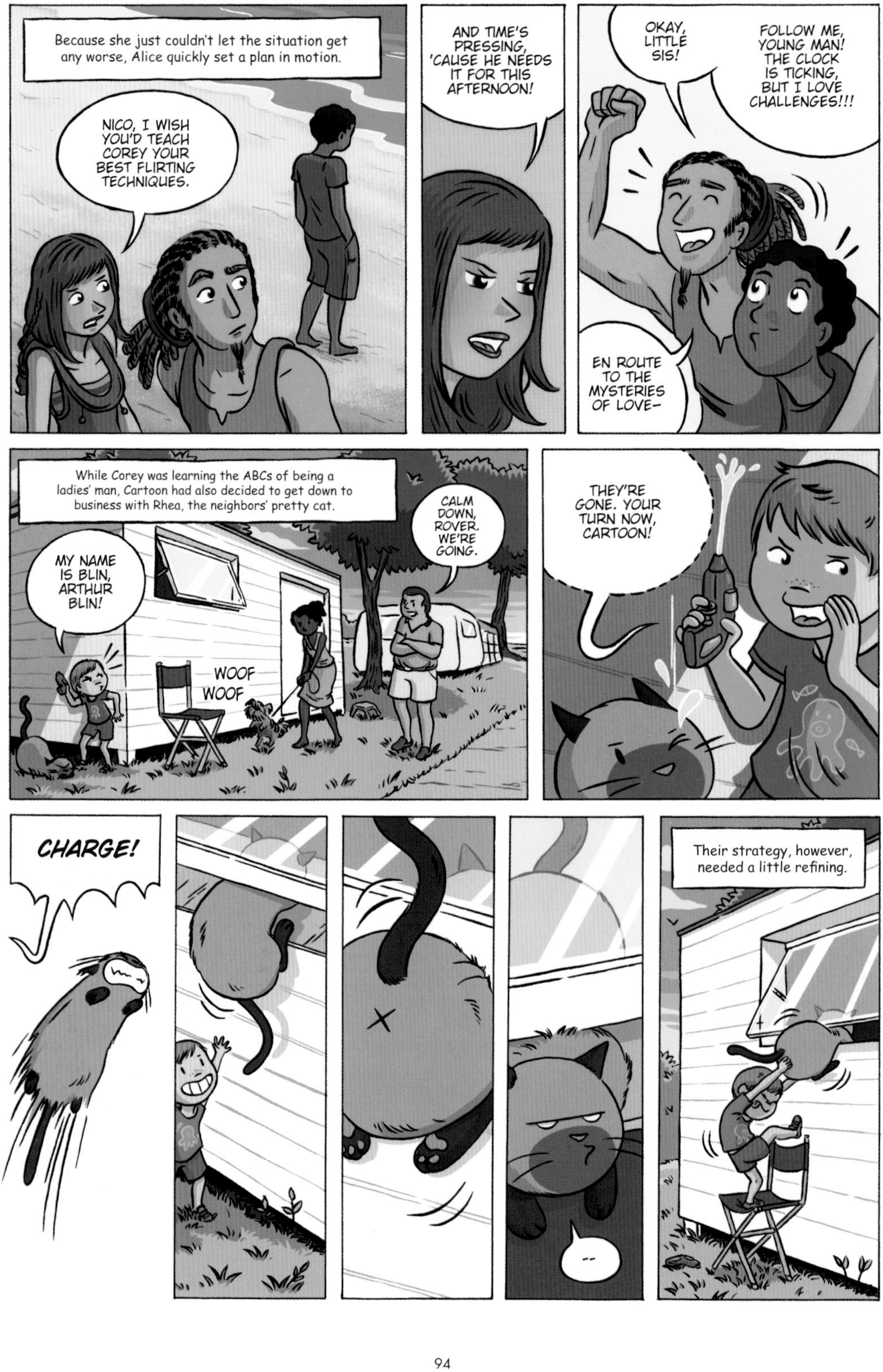
Because she just couldn't let the situation get any worse, Alice quickly set a plan in motion.
NICO, I WISH YOU'D TEACH COREY YOUR BEST FLIRTING TECHNIQUES.
AND TIME'S PRESSING, 'CAUSE HE NEEDS IT FOR THIS AFTERNOON!
OKAY, LITTLE SIS!
FOLLOW ME, YOUNG MAN! THE CLOCK IS TICKING, BUT I LOVE CHALLENGES!!!
EN ROUTE TO THE MYSTERIES OF LOVE—
While Corey was learning the ABCs of being a ladies' man, Cartoon had also decided to get down to business with Rhea, the neighbors' pretty cat.
MY NAME IS BLIN, ARTHUR BLIN!
WOOF WOOF
CALM DOWN, ROVER. WE'RE GOING.
THEY'RE GONE. YOUR TURN NOW, CARTOON!
CHARGE!
--
Their strategy, however, needed a little refining.

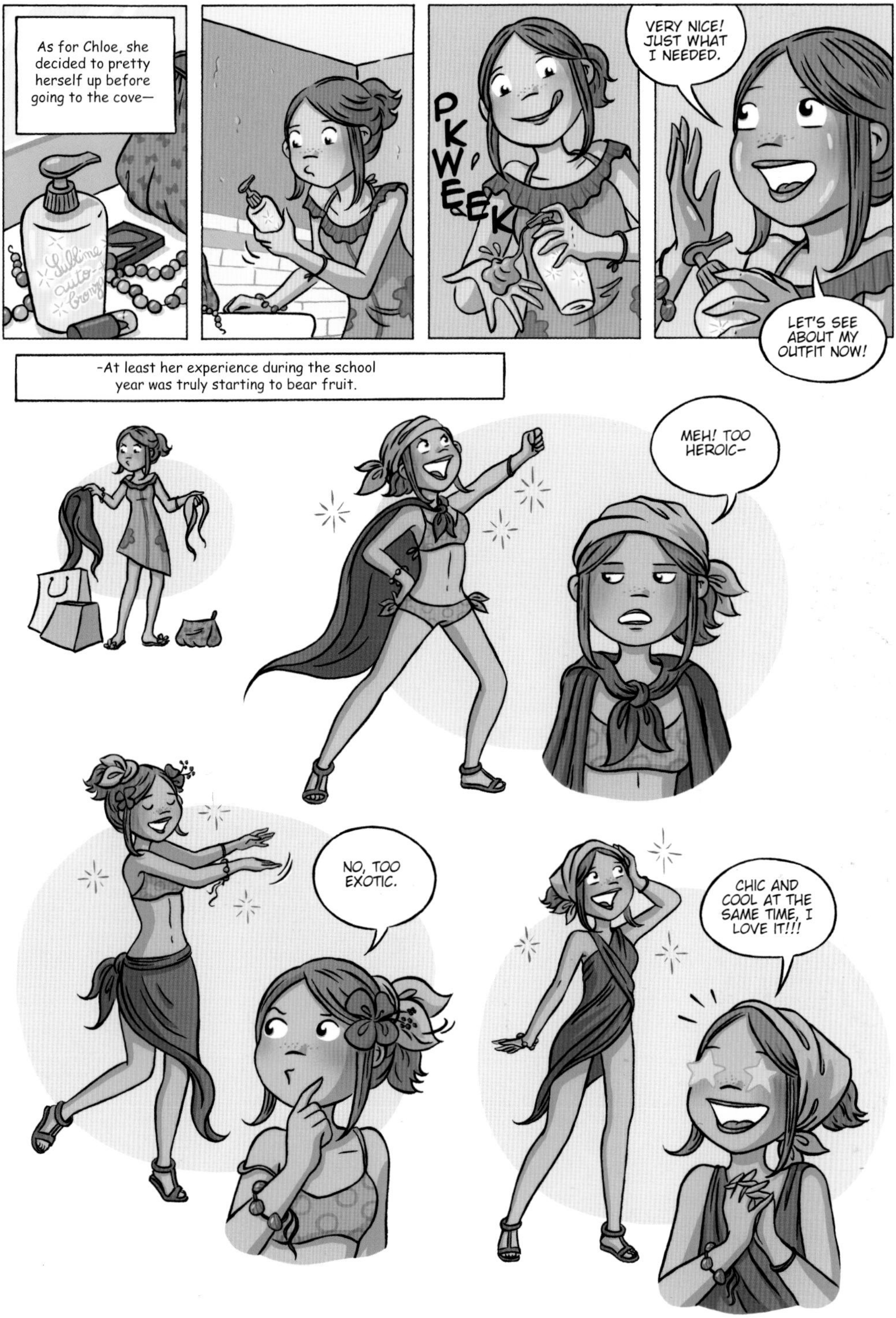
As for Chloe, she decided to pretty herself up before going to the cove—
PKWEEK
VERY NICE! JUST WHAT I NEEDED.
LET'S SEE ABOUT MY OUTFIT NOW!
-At least her experience during the school year was truly starting to bear fruit.
MEH! TOO HEROIC-
NO, TOO EXOTIC.
CHIC AND COOL AT THE SAME TIME, I LOVE IT!!!

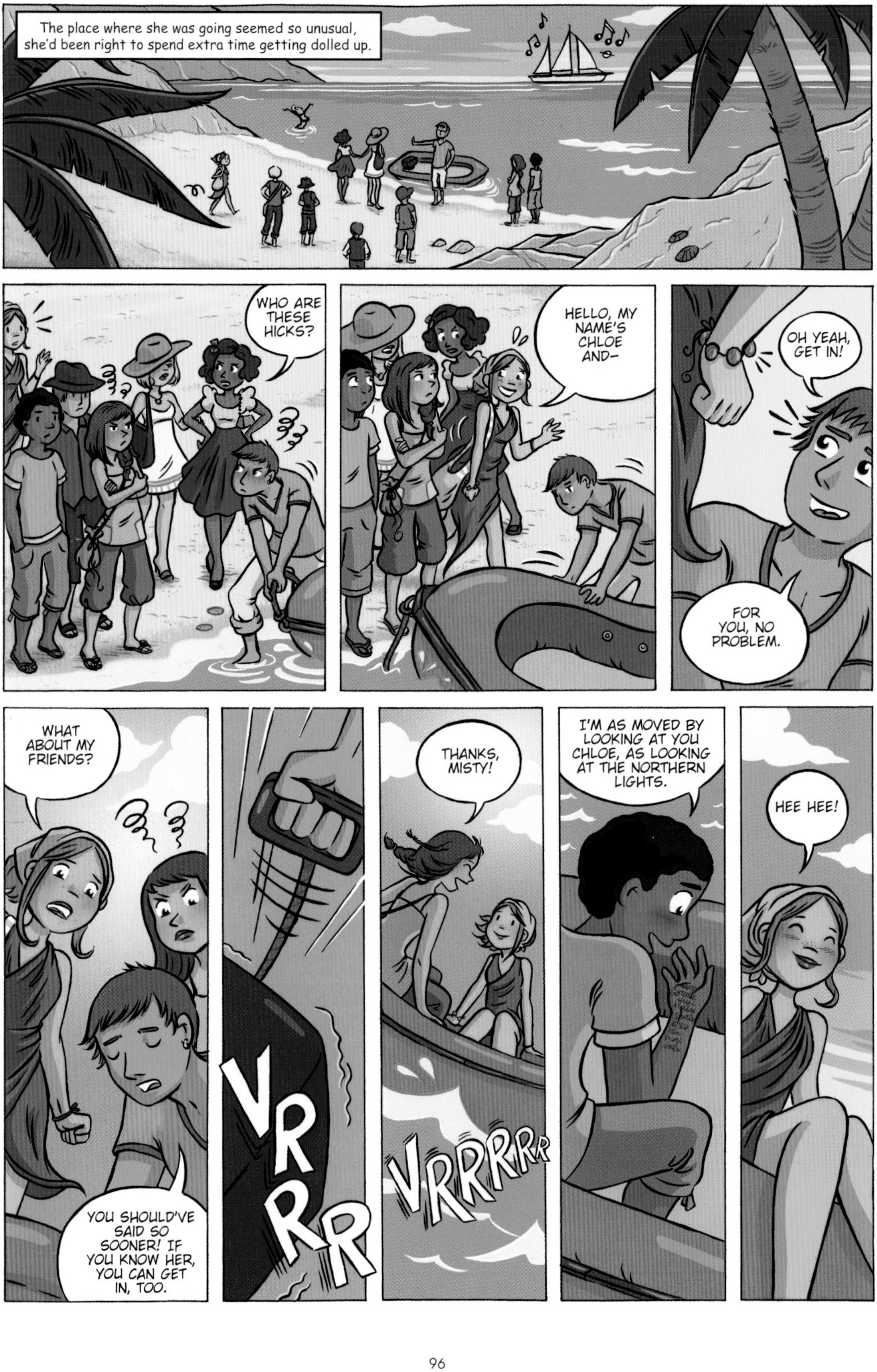
The place where she was going seemed so unusual, she'd been right to spend extra time getting dolled up.
WHO ARE THESE HICKS?
HELLO, MY NAME'S CHLOE AND–
OH YEAH, GET IN!
FOR YOU, NO PROBLEM.
WHAT ABOUT MY FRIENDS?
YOU SHOULD'VE SAID SO SOONER! IF YOU KNOW HER, YOU CAN GET IN, TOO.
VRRR
THANKS, MISTY!
VRRRRRR
I'M AS MOVED BY LOOKING AT YOU CHLOE, AS LOOKING AT THE NORTHERN LIGHTS.
HEE HEE!

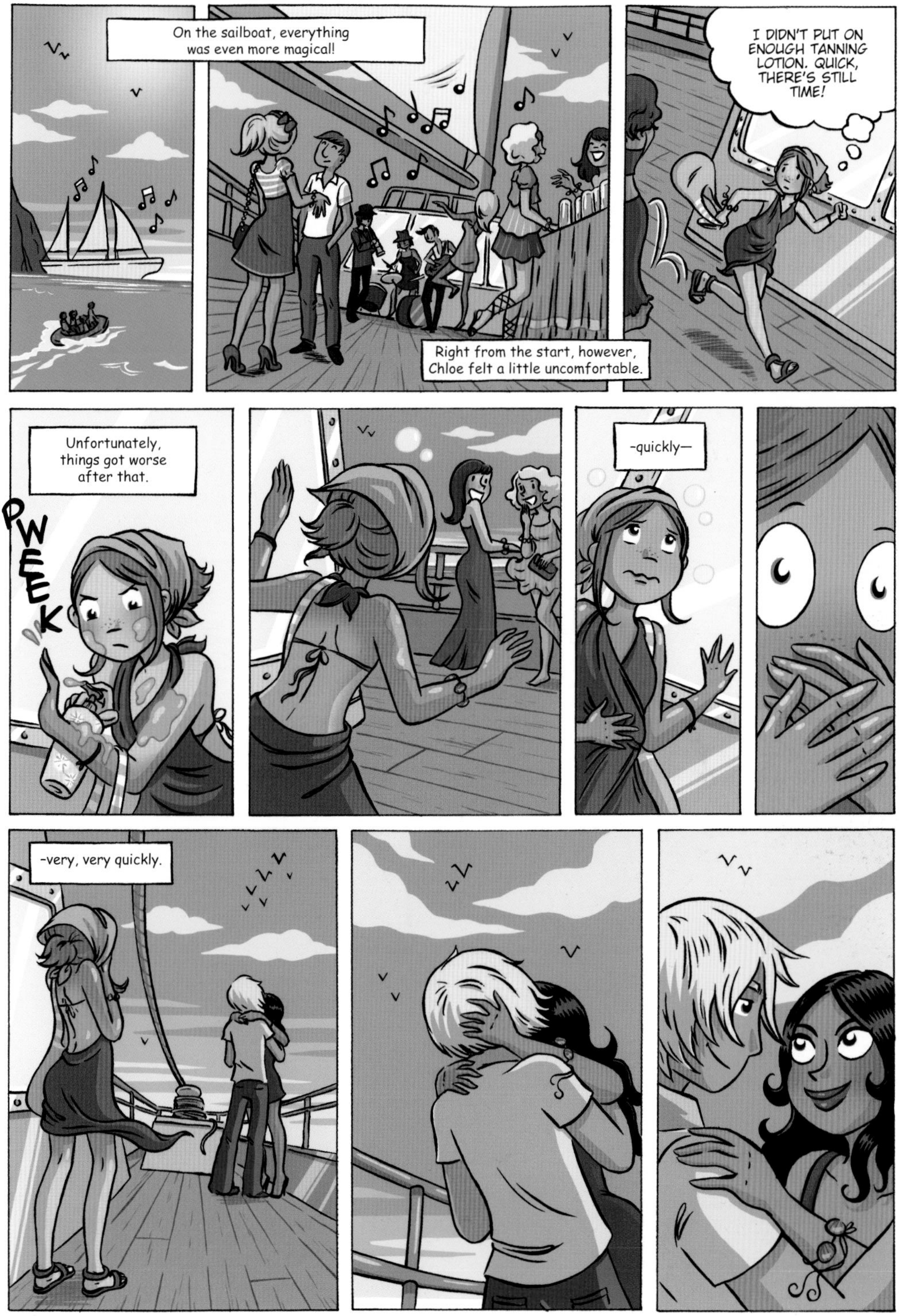
On the sailboat, everything was even more magical!
Right from the start, however, Chloe felt a little uncomfortable.
I DIDN'T PUT ON ENOUGH TANNING LOTION. QUICK, THERE'S STILL TIME!
Unfortunately, things got worse after that.
PWEEK
-quickly—
-very, very quickly.

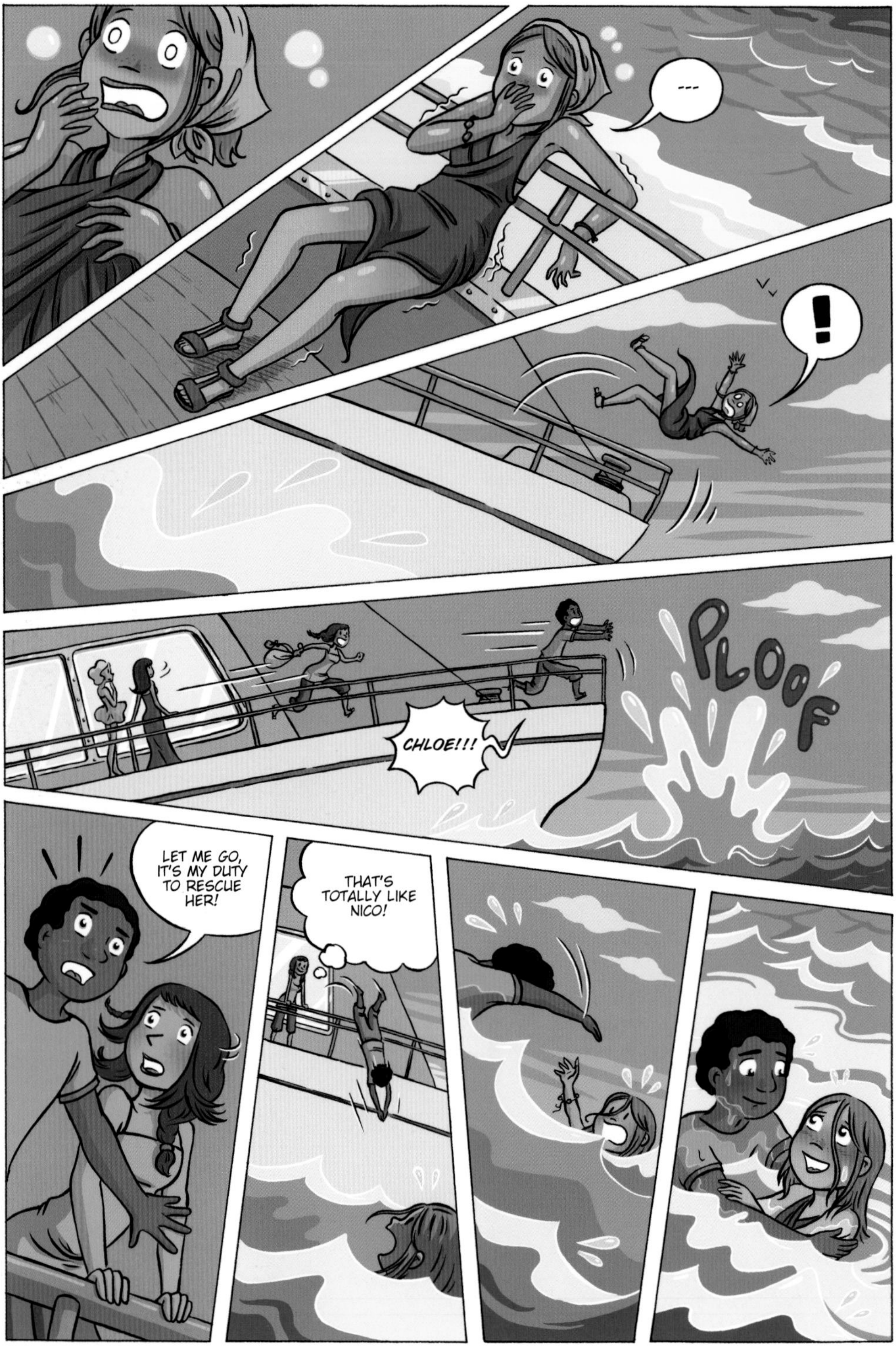
...
!
PLOOF
CHLOE!!!
LET ME GO, IT'S MY DUTY TO RESCUE HER!
THAT'S TOTALLY LIKE NICO!

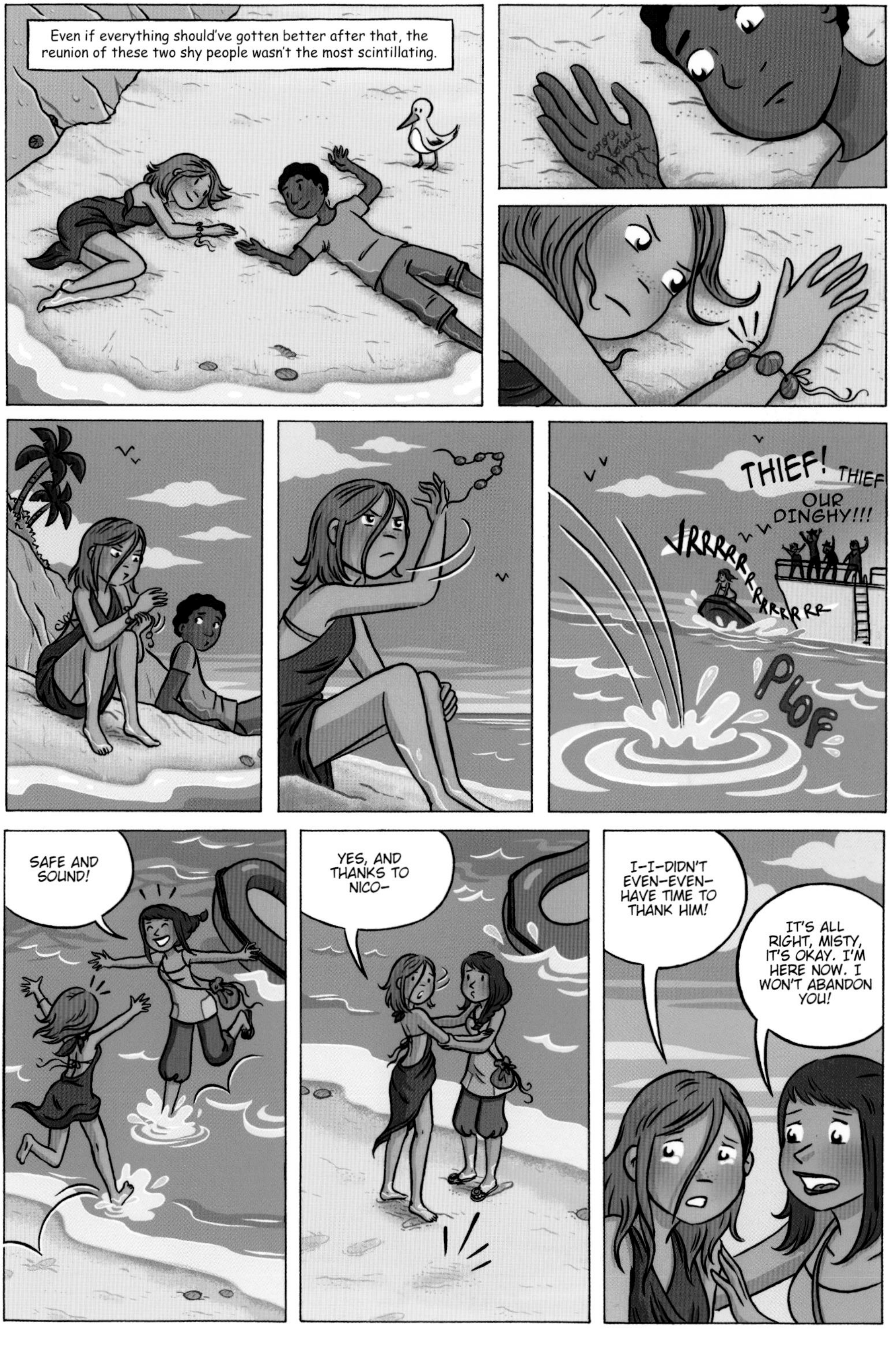
Even if everything should've gotten better after that, the reunion of these two shy people wasn't the most scintillating.
THIEF! THIEF
OUR DINGHY!!!
VRRRRRRRRRRRRRRRR
PLOF
SAFE AND SOUND!
YES, AND THANKS TO NICO–
I–I–DIDN'T EVEN–EVEN–HAVE TIME TO THANK HIM!
IT'S ALL RIGHT, MISTY, IT'S OKAY. I'M HERE NOW. I WON'T ABANDON YOU!

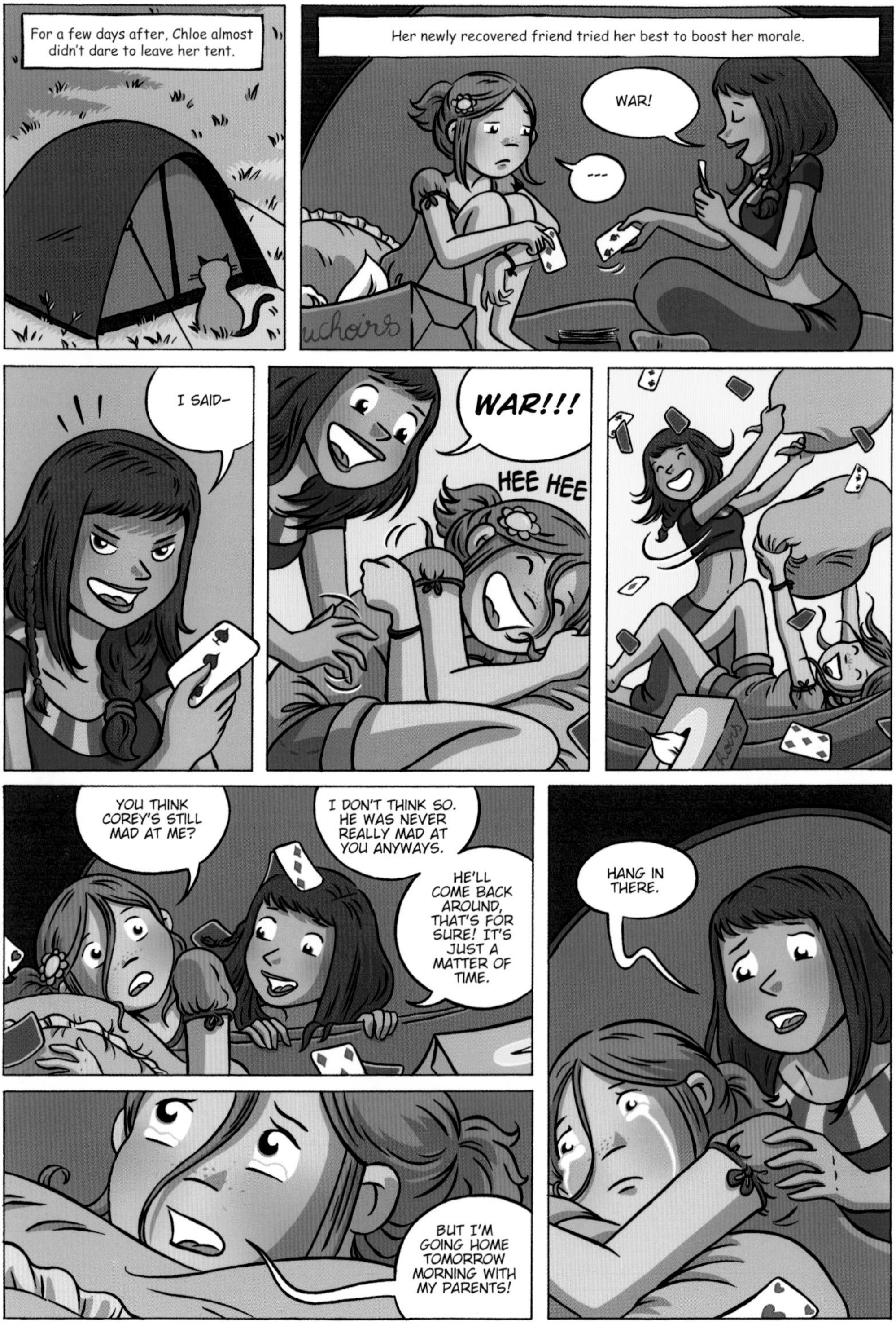
For a few days after, Chloe almost didn't dare to leave her tent.
Her newly recovered friend tried her best to boost her morale.
WAR!
...
I SAID–
WAR!!!
HEE HEE
YOU THINK COREY'S STILL MAD AT ME?
I DON'T THINK SO. HE WAS NEVER REALLY MAD AT YOU ANYWAYS.
HE'LL COME BACK AROUND, THAT'S FOR SURE! IT'S JUST A MATTER OF TIME.
BUT I'M GOING HOME TOMORROW MORNING WITH MY PARENTS!
HANG IN THERE.

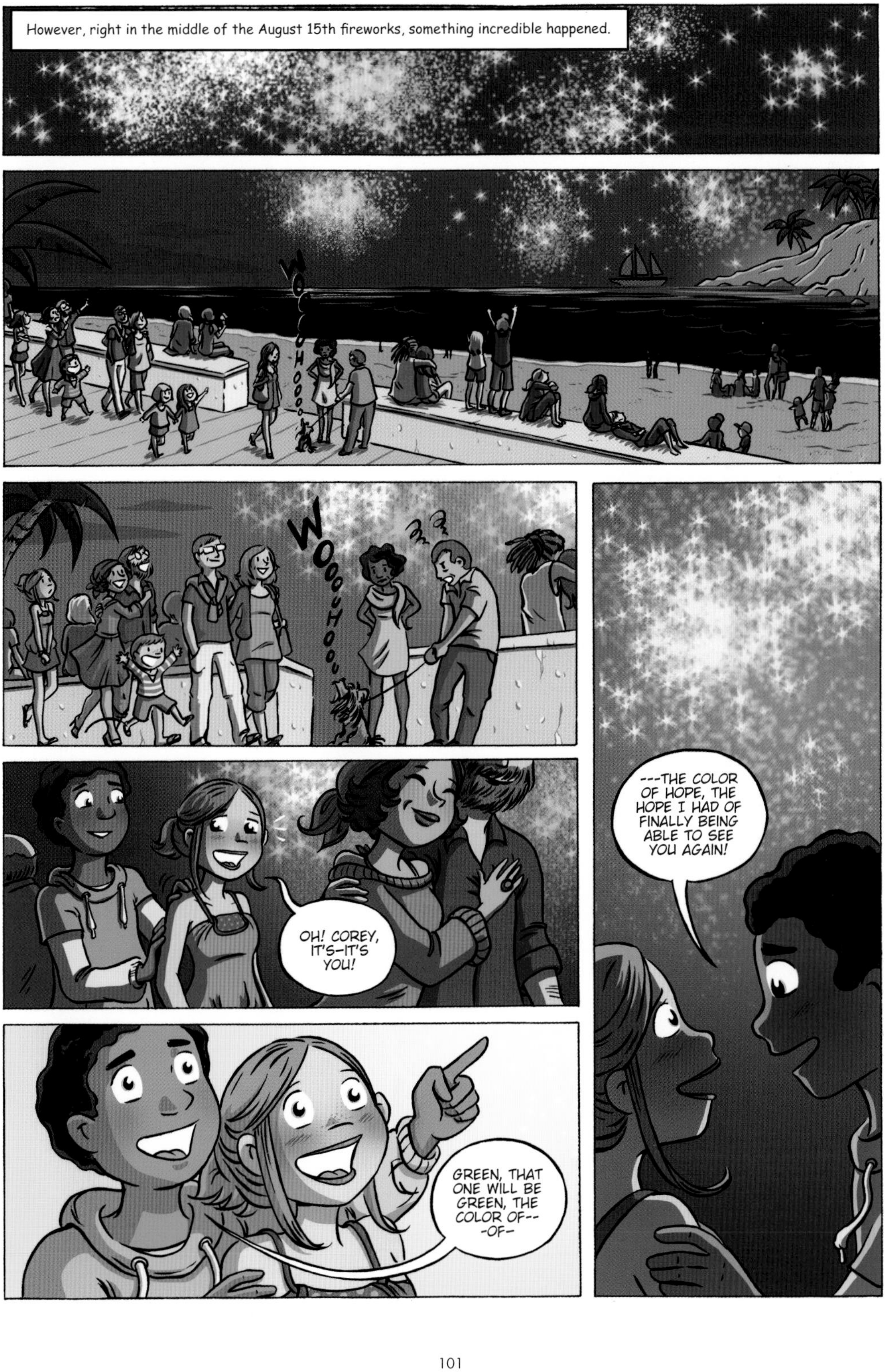
However, right in the middle of the August 15th fireworks, something incredible happened.
OH! COREY, IT'S—IT'S YOU!
GREEN, THAT ONE WILL BE GREEN, THE COLOR OF-- -OF-
---THE COLOR OF HOPE, THE HOPE I HAD OF FINALLY BEING ABLE TO SEE YOU AGAIN!

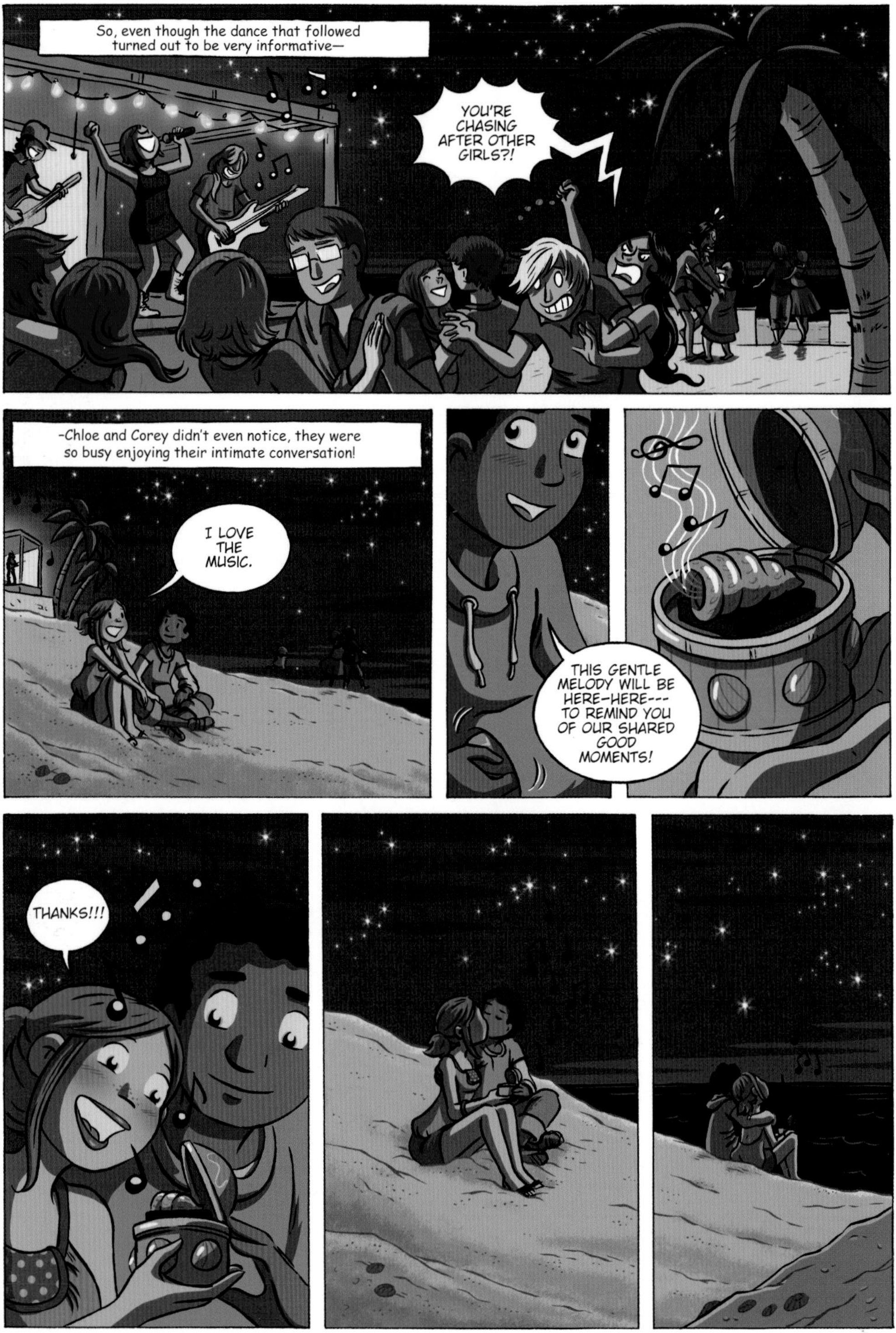
So, even though the dance that followed turned out to be very informative—
YOU'RE CHASING AFTER OTHER GIRLS?!
–Chloe and Corey didn't even notice, they were so busy enjoying their intimate conversation!
I LOVE THE MUSIC.
THIS GENTLE MELODY WILL BE HERE–HERE--- TO REMIND YOU OF OUR SHARED GOOD MOMENTS!
THANKS!!!

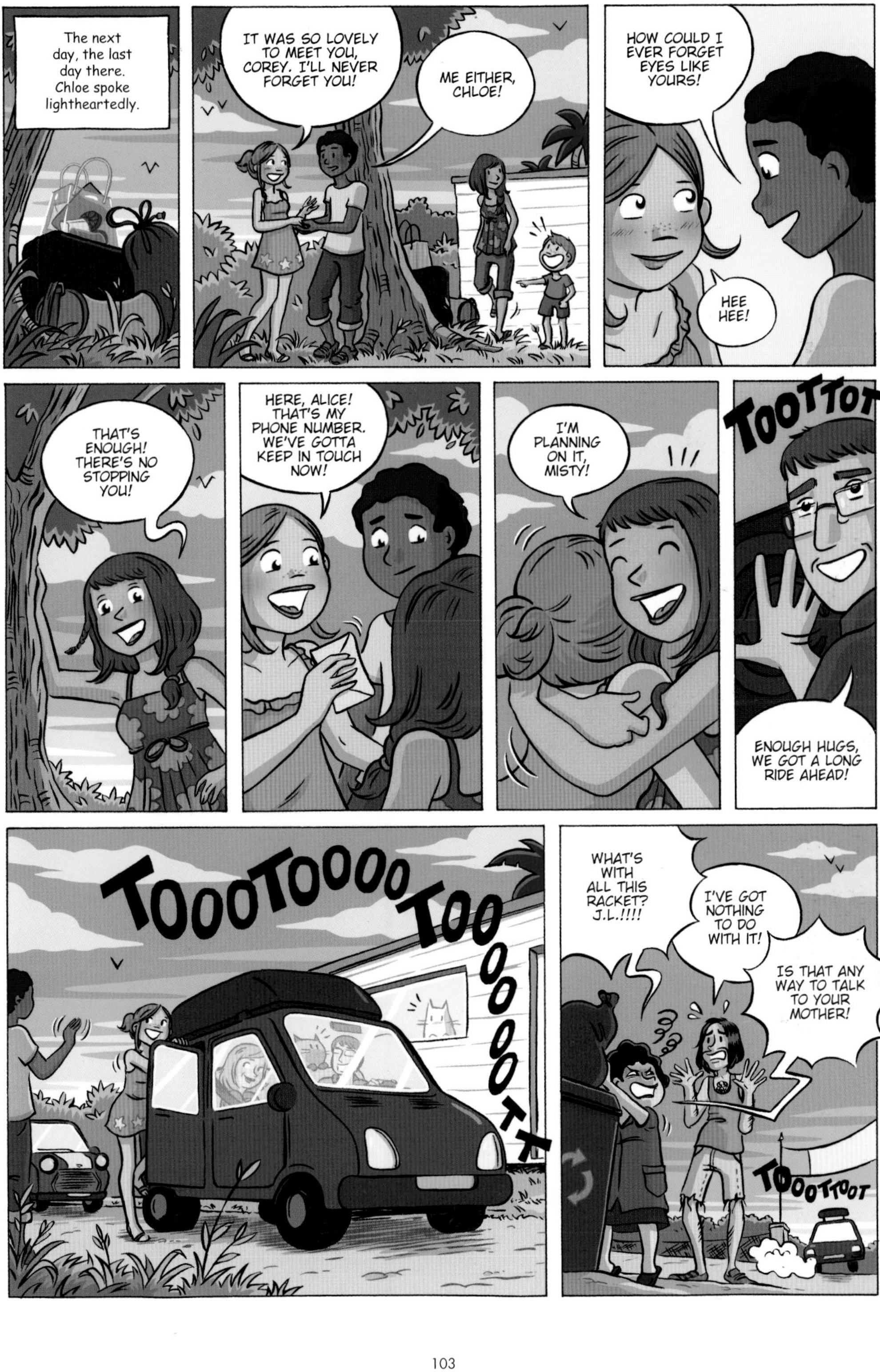
The next day, the last day there. Chloe spoke lightheartedly.
IT WAS SO LOVELY TO MEET YOU, COREY. I'LL NEVER FORGET YOU!
ME EITHER, CHLOE!
HOW COULD I EVER FORGET EYES LIKE YOURS!
HEE HEE!
THAT'S ENOUGH! THERE'S NO STOPPING YOU!
HERE, ALICE! THAT'S MY PHONE NUMBER. WE'VE GOTTA KEEP IN TOUCH NOW!
I'M PLANNING ON IT, MISTY!
TOOTTOT
ENOUGH HUGS, WE GOT A LONG RIDE AHEAD!
TOOOTOOOO TOOOOOOOOTT
WHAT'S WITH ALL THIS RACKET? J.L.!!!!
I'VE GOT NOTHING TO DO WITH IT!
IS THAT ANY WAY TO TALK TO YOUR MOTHER!
TOOOTTOOT

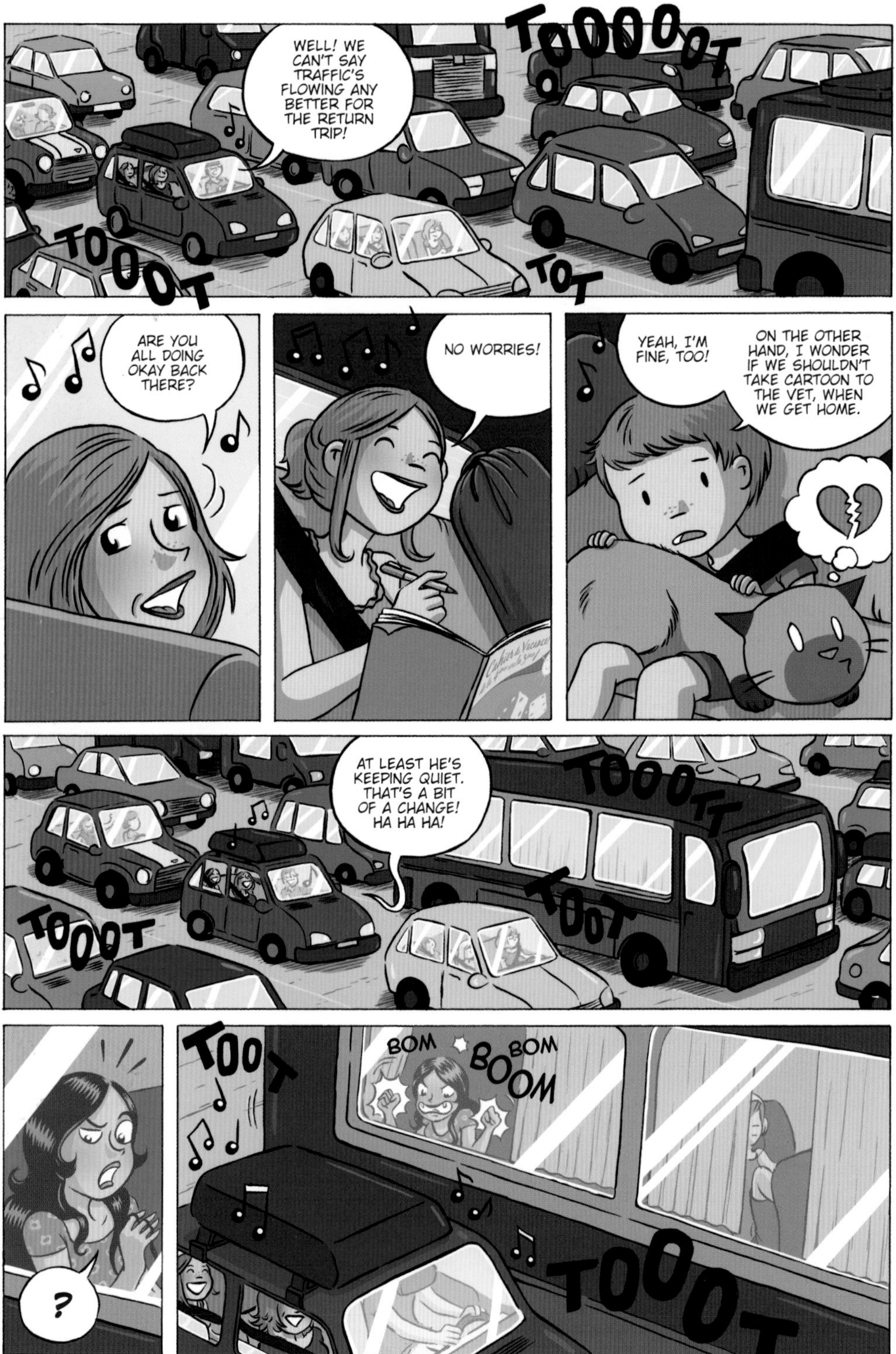
TOOOOOT
WELL! WE CAN'T SAY TRAFFIC'S FLOWING ANY BETTER FOR THE RETURN TRIP!
TOOOT
TOT
ARE YOU ALL DOING OKAY BACK THERE?
NO WORRIES!
YEAH, I'M FINE, TOO!
ON THE OTHER HAND, I WONDER IF WE SHOULDN'T TAKE CARTOON TO THE VET, WHEN WE GET HOME.
AT LEAST HE'S KEEPING QUIET. THAT'S A BIT OF A CHANGE! HA HA HA!
TOOOTT
TOOOT
TOOT
?
TOOT
BOM
BOOM
BOM
TOOOT

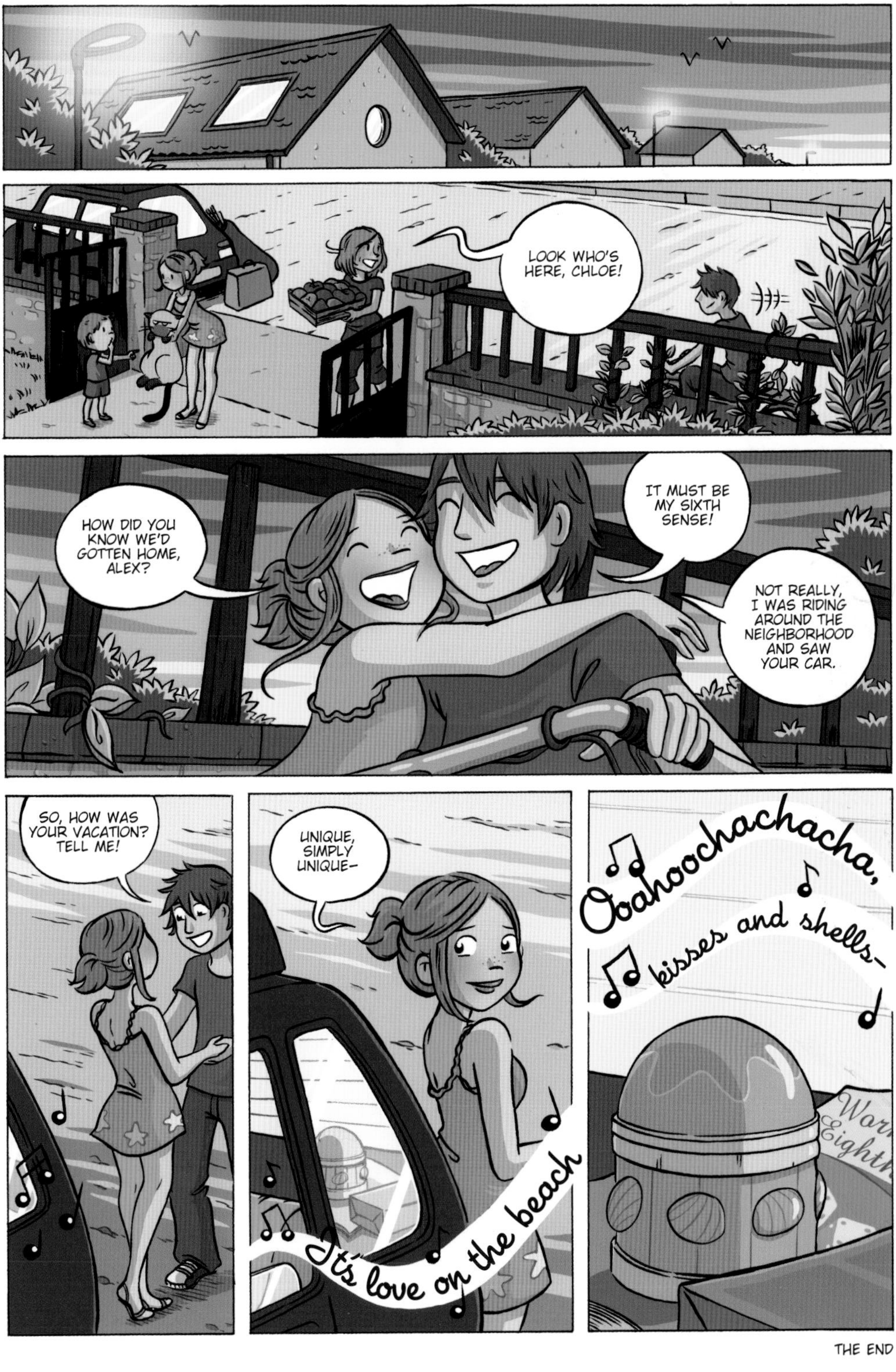
LOOK WHO'S HERE, CHLOE!
HOW DID YOU KNOW WE'D GOTTEN HOME, ALEX?
IT MUST BE MY SIXTH SENSE!
NOT REALLY, I WAS RIDING AROUND THE NEIGHBORHOOD AND SAW YOUR CAR.
SO, HOW WAS YOUR VACATION? TELL ME!
UNIQUE, SIMPLY UNIQUE-
It's love on the beach
Ooahoochachacha,
kisses and shells-

THE END

Preview of SWEETIES #1: A brand new family, a forbidden love, and all the sweets you can handle!

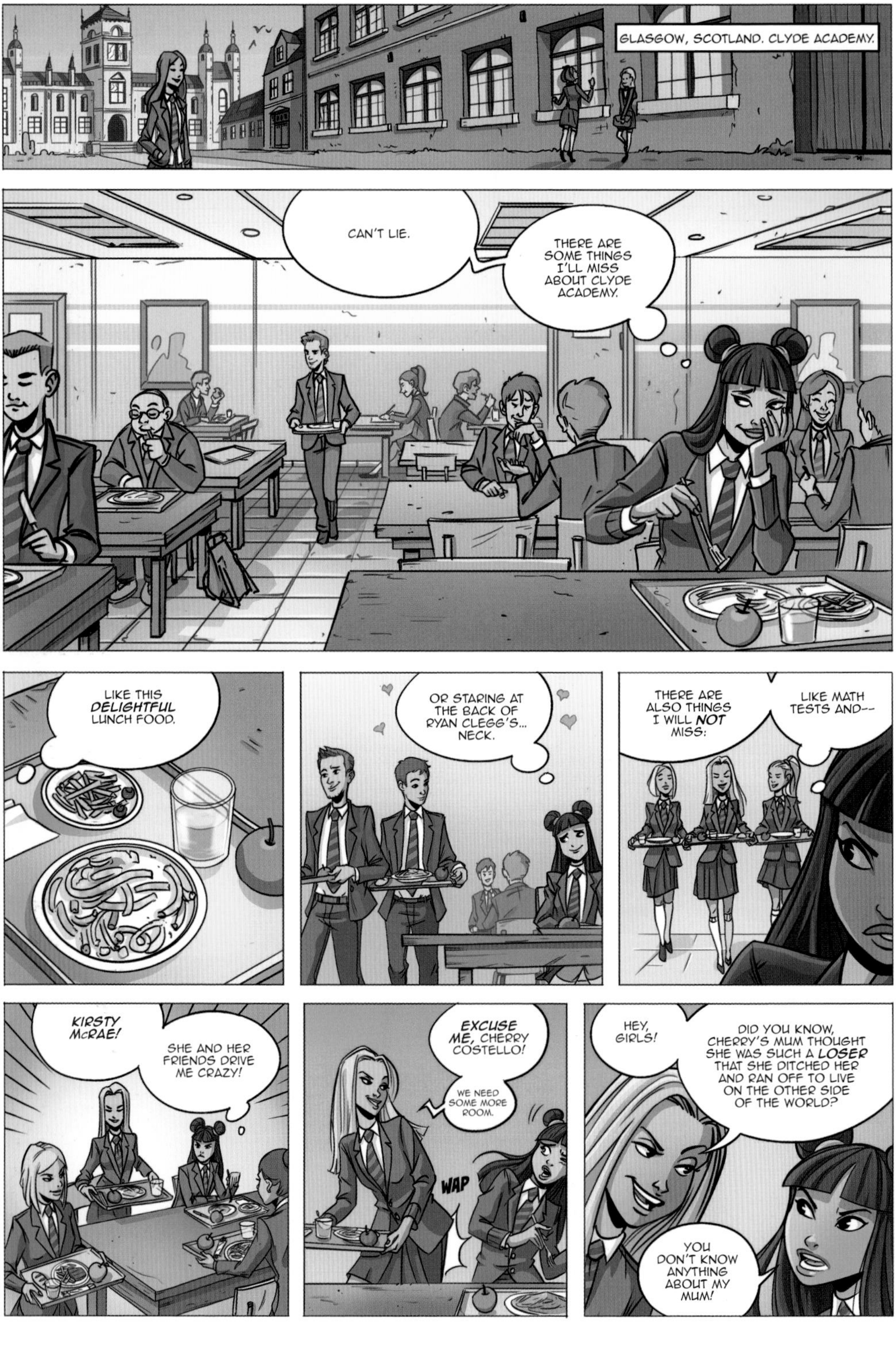
GLASGOW, SCOTLAND. CLYDE ACADEMY.
CAN'T LIE.
THERE ARE SOME THINGS I'LL MISS ABOUT CLYDE ACADEMY.
LIKE THIS DELIGHTFUL LUNCH FOOD.
OR STARING AT THE BACK OF RYAN CLEGG'S... NECK.
THERE ARE ALSO THINGS I WILL NOT MISS:
LIKE MATH TESTS AND--
KIRSTY McRAE!
SHE AND HER FRIENDS DRIVE ME CRAZY!
EXCUSE ME, CHERRY COSTELLO!
WE NEED SOME MORE ROOM.
WAP
HEY, GIRLS!
DID YOU KNOW, CHERRY'S MUM THOUGHT SHE WAS SUCH A LOSER THAT SHE DITCHED HER AND RAN OFF TO LIVE ON THE OTHER SIDE OF THE WORLD?
YOU DON'T KNOW ANYTHING ABOUT MY MUM!

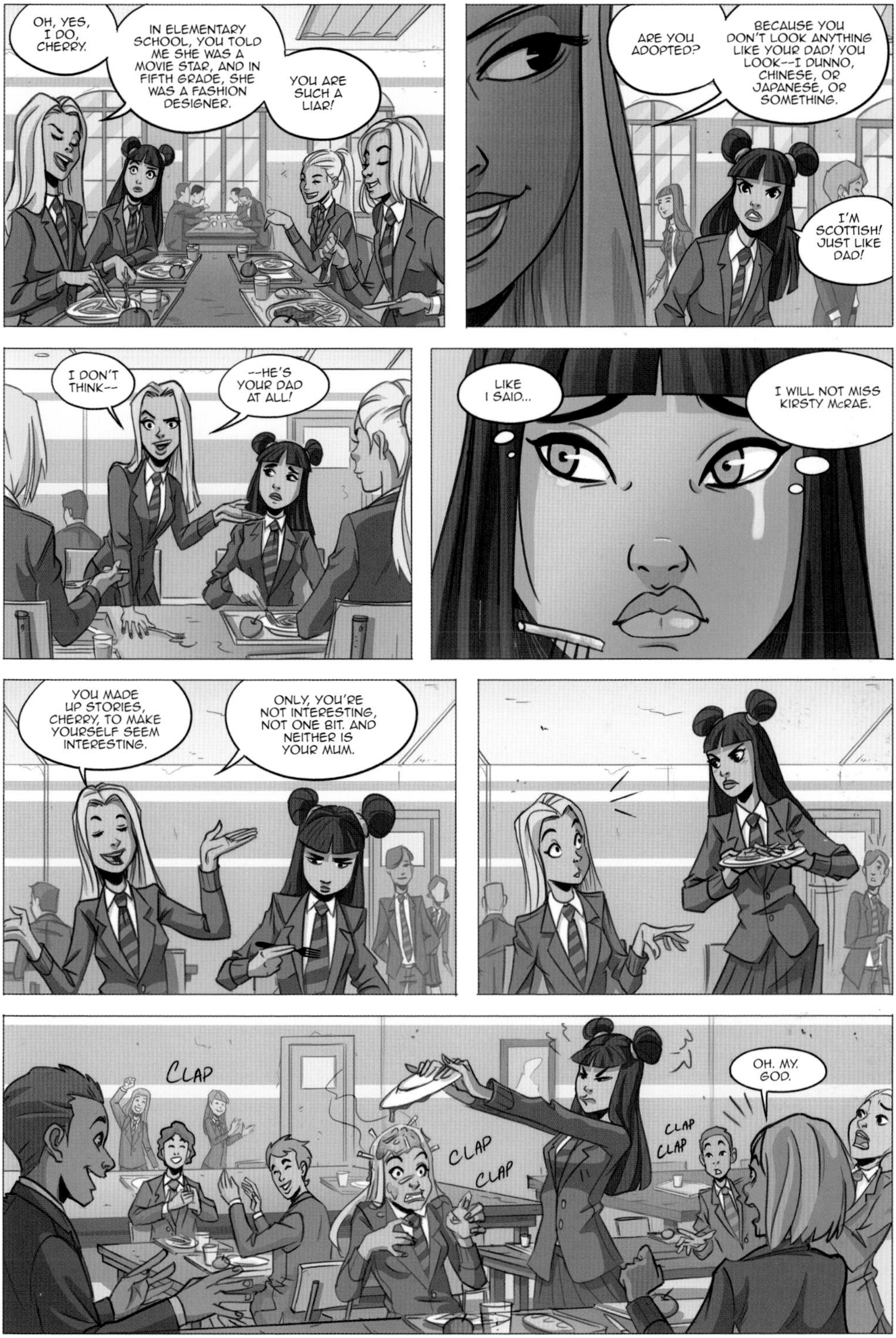
OH, YES, I DO, CHERRY.
IN ELEMENTARY SCHOOL, YOU TOLD ME SHE WAS A MOVIE STAR, AND IN FIFTH GRADE, SHE WAS A FASHION DESIGNER.
YOU ARE SUCH A LIAR!
ARE YOU ADOPTED?
BECAUSE YOU DON'T LOOK ANYTHING LIKE YOUR DAD! YOU LOOK--I DUNNO, CHINESE, OR JAPANESE, OR SOMETHING.
I'M SCOTTISH! JUST LIKE DAD!
I DON'T THINK--
--HE'S YOUR DAD AT ALL!
LIKE I SAID...
I WILL NOT MISS KIRSTY McRAE.
YOU MADE UP STORIES, CHERRY, TO MAKE YOURSELF SEEM INTERESTING.
ONLY, YOU'RE NOT INTERESTING, NOT ONE BIT. AND NEITHER IS YOUR MUM.
CLAP
CLAP
CLAP
CLAP
CLAP
OH. MY. GOD.

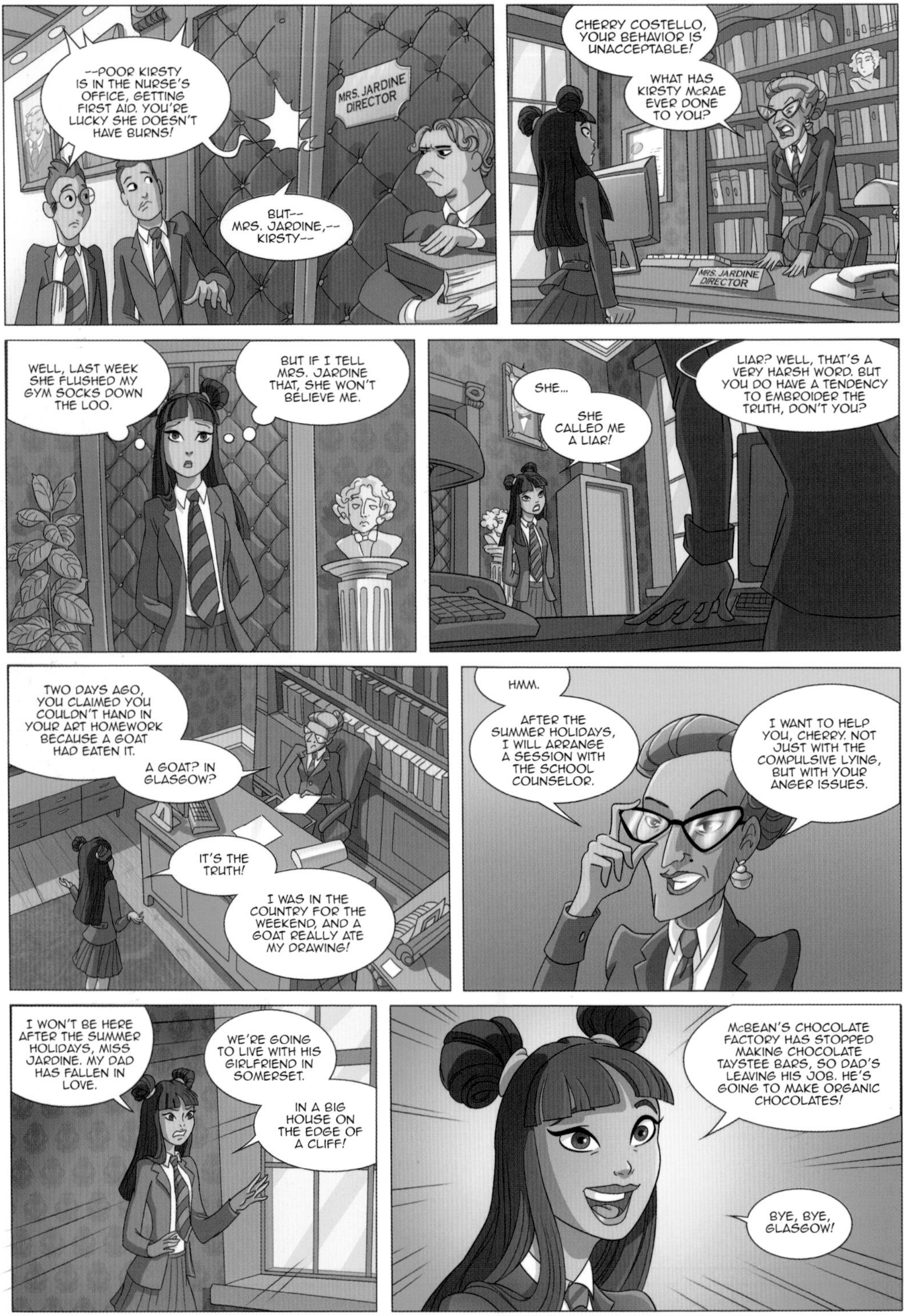
--POOR KIRSTY IS IN THE NURSE'S OFFICE, GETTING FIRST AID. YOU'RE LUCKY SHE DOESN'T HAVE BURNS!
MRS. JARDINE DIRECTOR
BUT-- MRS. JARDINE,-- KIRSTY--
CHERRY COSTELLO, YOUR BEHAVIOR IS UNACCEPTABLE!
WHAT HAS KIRSTY McRAE EVER DONE TO YOU?
MRS. JARDINE DIRECTOR
WELL, LAST WEEK SHE FLUSHED MY GYM SOCKS DOWN THE LOO.
BUT IF I TELL MRS. JARDINE THAT, SHE WON'T BELIEVE ME.
SHE...
SHE CALLED ME A LIAR!
LIAR? WELL, THAT'S A VERY HARSH WORD. BUT YOU DO HAVE A TENDENCY TO EMBROIDER THE TRUTH, DON'T YOU?
TWO DAYS AGO, YOU CLAIMED YOU COULDN'T HAND IN YOUR ART HOMEWORK BECAUSE A GOAT HAD EATEN IT.
A GOAT? IN GLASGOW?
IT'S THE TRUTH!
I WAS IN THE COUNTRY FOR THE WEEKEND, AND A GOAT REALLY ATE MY DRAWING!
HMM.
AFTER THE SUMMER HOLIDAYS, I WILL ARRANGE A SESSION WITH THE SCHOOL COUNSELOR.
I WANT TO HELP YOU, CHERRY. NOT JUST WITH THE COMPULSIVE LYING, BUT WITH YOUR ANGER ISSUES.
I WON'T BE HERE AFTER THE SUMMER HOLIDAYS, MISS JARDINE. MY DAD HAS FALLEN IN LOVE.
WE'RE GOING TO LIVE WITH HIS GIRLFRIEND IN SOMERSET.
IN A BIG HOUSE ON THE EDGE OF A CLIFF!
McBEAN'S CHOCOLATE FACTORY HAS STOPPED MAKING CHOCOLATE TAYSTEE BARS, SO DAD'S LEAVING HIS JOB. HE'S GOING TO MAKE ORGANIC CHOCOLATES!
BYE, BYE, GLASGOW!

Don't miss the full story in SWEETIES #1 "Cherry/Skye," available at booksellers everywhere!

PREVIEW OF STITCHED #1 "THE FIRST DAY OF THE REST OF HER LIFE," A SPOOKY LOVE STORY ABOUT PUTTING YOURSELF BACK TOGETHER!

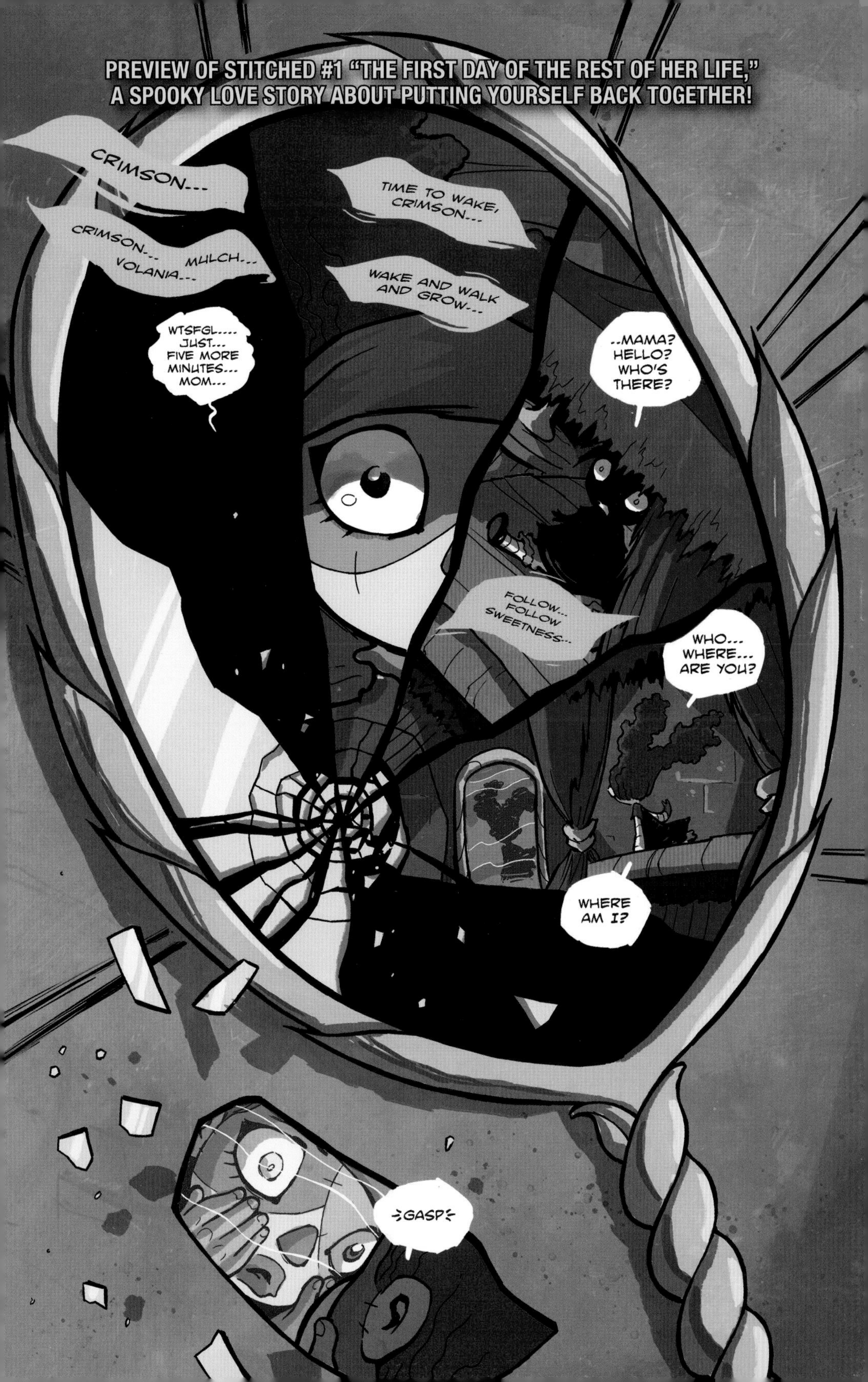
CRIMSON...
CRIMSON... MULCH... VOLANIA...
TIME TO WAKE, CRIMSON...
WAKE AND WALK AND GROW...
WTSFGL.... JUST... FIVE MORE MINUTES... MOM...
..MAMA? HELLO? WHO'S THERE?
FOLLOW... FOLLOW SWEETNESS...
WHO... WHERE... ARE YOU?
WHERE AM I?
GASP

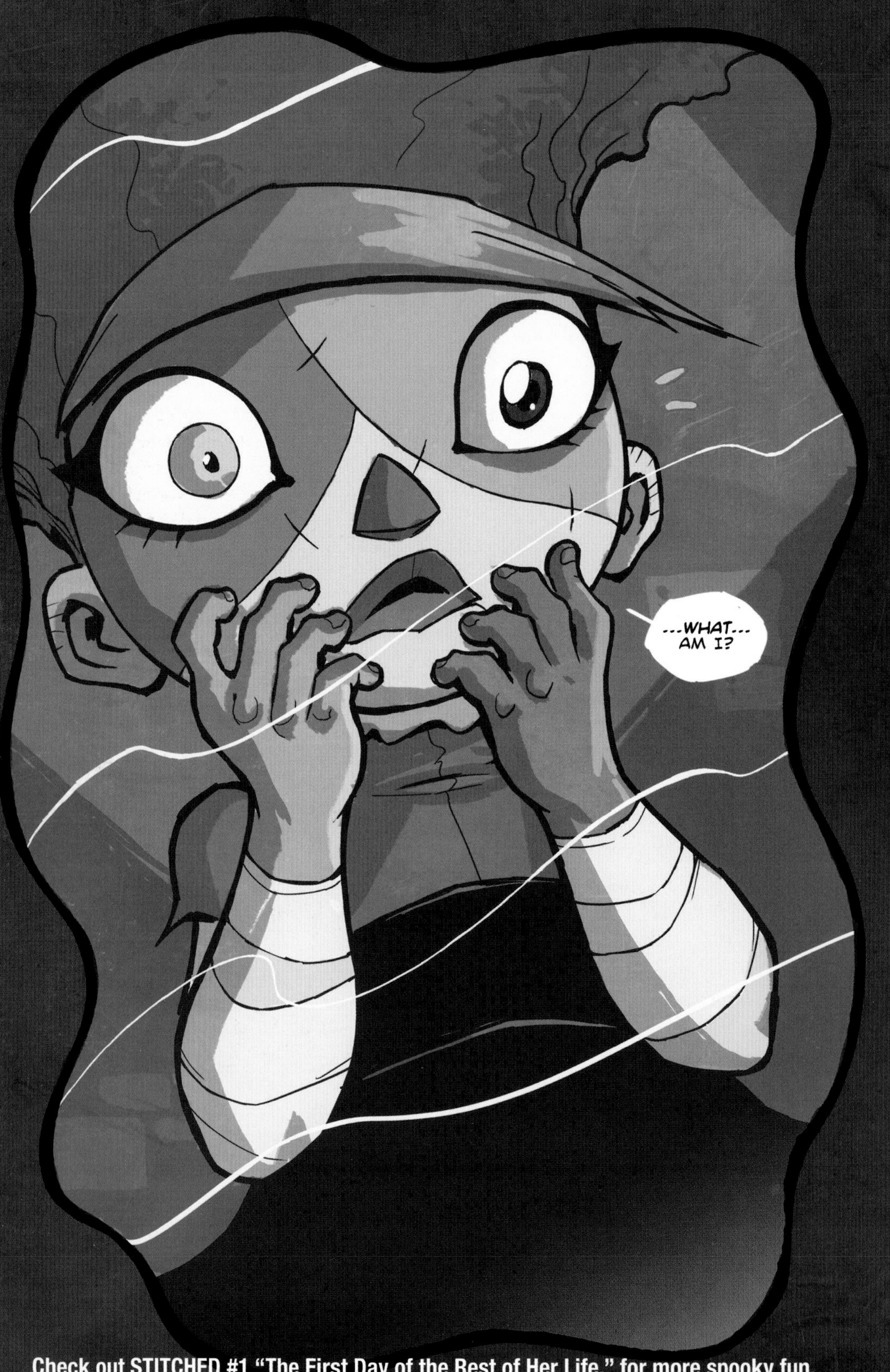
---WHAT--- AM I?

Check out STITCHED #1 "The First Day of the Rest of Her Life," for more spooky fun.

Welcome to Charmz

I am definitely obsessed with all things romance. It's fun, it's dramatic, and it's all about love. I think love is pretty amazing, don't you? When your heart beats faster at the sound of someone else's voice or the way they smile, you just feel more alive. And terrified! Or how about when just being around that special someone makes you feel like you're flying? Like you could do anything? Falling in love is one of the most incredible feelings, ever.

Of course, love is also complicated and painful sometimes. They don't call them "crushes" for nothing!

Yet, when I'm feeling kind of meh or sad, the first thing I want to do is read a romance. Maybe it's because everyone falls in love, has heartbreak and heartache. Maybe it's because there's really nothing like your first kiss. Whatever the reason, when I want to feel better, I pick up a romance and settle in. Usually with tea and chocolate, if I'm being totally honest.

Which brings us to Charmz, a new line of graphic novels just for you! With stories from all over the world, Charmz wants to celebrate love. Whether we're hanging out in Somerset, UK, the wilds of France, speeding through space, or waking up in a cemetery, love finds our characters and digs right in.

Whether you're in the mood for a (literally!) sweet tale about sisters, chocolate, and forbidden love, or exploring the mysterious darkness of Assumption Cemetery where vampires and swamp boys romance stitched girls, you'll find a lot to relate to.

My favorite kinds of romance are epic, sweeping, and probably just a little bit hilarious. As seriously as I take love, if you don't laugh a little at the things we'll do for it, well, you'll end up actually lovesick. Which is definitely something the girls in our books have to deal with from time to time. Not to mention fashion faux pas, weird chocolate recipes, ghosts, zombie sheep, and puzzles through time and space!

I've read a lot of romances and I definitely have my favorites. I think the one I would take on a desert island would have to be *Pride and Prejudice* by Jane Austen. I know, it's old, but it's so witty, and funny, and real. It's been adapted so many times but it always feels fresh and relevant. Anyone could be those characters. Me. You.

Aside from editing this line of graphic novels, I'm also writing one: STITCHED. This spooky little cemetery book with vampires, werewolves, swamp boys and stitched girls is very dear to me. It's the book I've always wanted to write, with spectacularly weird creatures, spooky adventures, and lots and lots of awkward, splendid, romance. Crimson Volania Mulch is my favorite kind of girl; complicated, smart, curious, kind...but a little bit preoccupied with her own problems. And way too judgmental. No one is perfect! And if I woke up only knowing my name in a strange place, I might be a little self-involved, too. I mean, just who is that pretty boy she meets on her first night "alive," and where is her mother? What does a badger/hedgehog actually eat? Do werewolves like cupcakes?

What I want Charmz to be for you is like the book equivalent of a hot chocolate; sweet, maybe a little dark sometimes, comforting, and made just for you. You can curl up with our tales, settle in, and enjoy falling in love with our characters just like they fall in love with each other.

Remember: stories matter, love is powerful, and there's nothing like a love story to make you feel alive.

–Mariah McCourt

Please write to me any time about Charmz! mariah@papercutz.com

I would love hear from you.

STAY IN TOUCH!

EMAIL:	charmz@papercutz
WEB:	www.papercutz.com
TWITTER:	@papercutzgn
FACEBOOK:	PAPERCUTZGRAPHICNOVELS
REGULAR MAIL:	Charmz, 160 Broadway, Suite 700, East Wing, New York, NY 10038

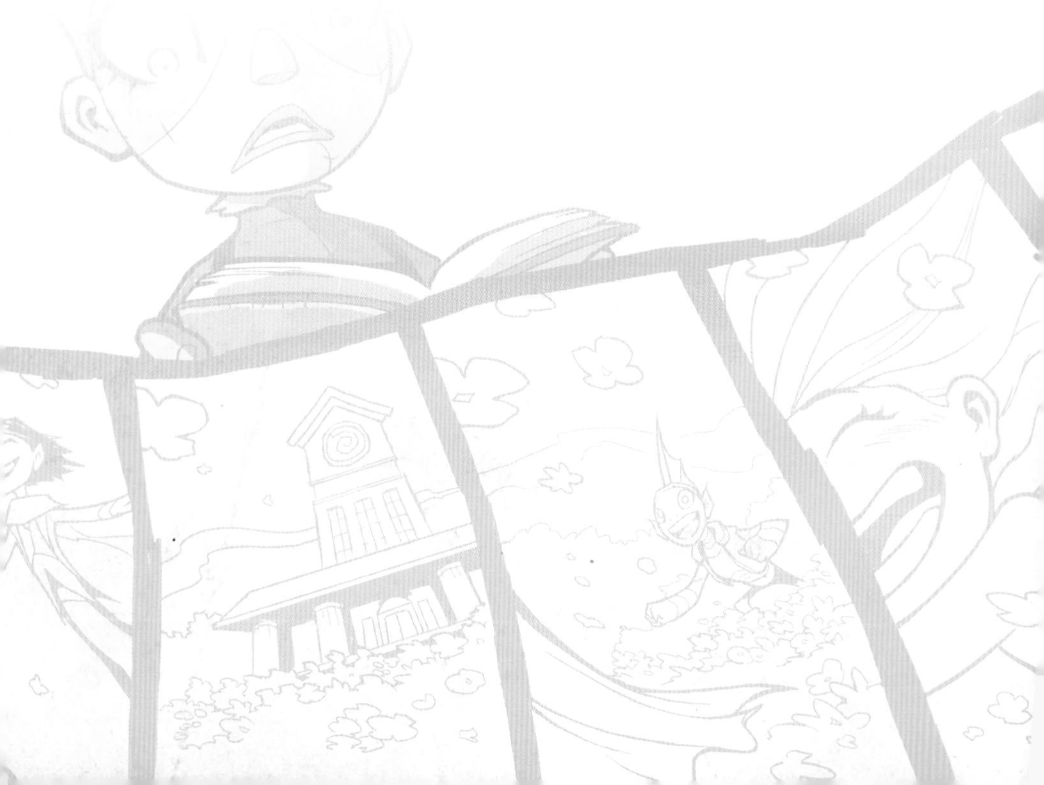